*To Bill & Sally McNew —
the best parents God
ever put on this earth.
I love you with all
my heart!*
  ♥ *Jennifer Sinclair*

## Jennifer Sinclair

# Angel Flight

# *ANGEL FLIGHT*
## A Novel By Jennifer Sinclair

Lorelei Publications
Gulf Shores, Alabama

*Also by Jennifer Sinclair*
**Fiery Dunes**
**Grant Denied**

This book is a novel.
Names, characters, places, and situations
are either products of the author's imagination or
used fictitiously. Any resemblance to actual events or
persons, living or dead, is purely coincidental.

**Copyright © 1997 by Jennifer Sinclair
First Printing 1998**

*All rights reserved.
No part of this book may be reproduced
in any form, except for the inclusion of brief
quotations in a review, without permission
in writing from the author or publisher.*

***Author Photo Credit: Glenn D. Appelt***

Library of Congress Catalog Card Number
98-090721

ISBN 1-57502-932-4

LORELEI PUBLICATIONS
P.O. BOX 3774
GULF SHORES, AL 36547-3774

Printed in the USA by

3212 East Highway 30 • Kearney, NE 68847 • 1-800-650-7888

# *Dedication*

For my friends on board NAS Pensacola and especially for the Blue Angel teams, 1992-1998, who fueled my imagination and fired my spirit. Thank you for brightening the skies over Fort Morgan, Alabama. Your bravery, skill, and dedication turned the clouds into sunshine every time you passed by.

# Chapter 1

"I love you, my darling, forever. I'll always be with you."

"Oh, Ben. Do you really mean that?"

"Yes, Desiree, you'll see."

Ben's sincere words of promise echoed in Desiree McAndrews' mind, but instead of bringing her comfort, their memory tore at her heart and brought tears to her eyes. Twelve years had passed since she'd been with Lieutenant Bennett "Cannon" Collier, yet it seemed like only yesterday when she'd last watched him board his aircraft. Deeply tanned and ruggedly handsome, he'd cavalierly waved to her and blown a kiss her way. She'd answered by patting her heart and then pointing toward him, her true love.

Desiree shuddered as she absentmindedly stroked the pen she held. She hadn't thought about Ben for a long, long time, but now she couldn't seem to get him out of her head.

"Of all people, why you, Ben? Why now?" she whispered. She shook her blonde curls as if to cast all images of him far away from her. She'd trusted him, loved him, idolized him. He'd been her world, her life. But those feelings were over, dead and gone, or were they?

She wondered whether she dared to find out as she studied her nameplate tacked to her office door made of recycled wood products. "Desiree McAndrews, Protector of Nature's Way, Boulder, Colorado."

\* \* \* \* \*

A thousand miles away in Pensacola, Ben Collier ran his hands through his thick dark brown hair and stared blankly out the window of his office overlooking the Sea Eagle complex he'd built with sheer grit and gutsy determination. Although he'd been ridiculed as a dreamer and foolish gambler, he'd taken his chances and beaten the odds by carving paradise out of a desolate swamp formerly home to water moccasins and hungry mosquitoes.

He paused as he surveyed his creation. Beneath him sprawled acres of natural beauty enhanced by Collier-designed structures that meshed into a collage of environmental harmony.

Success was his. Everyone knew his name and his work and believed he had it all. He was a self-made man. On the surface he appeared so complete, so together. But those closest to Ben knew that was a lie.

He opened a file drawer and searched for a well-worn manila folder he'd tried to discard many times but hadn't had the heart to destroy.

"Ah, here you are, my precious," he said as he tugged at a thick folder nestled between scrapbooks of his Navy glory days. He fondly touched the label faded by time and read the name he'd written in boyish script, "Desiree McAndrews."

"Should I?" he asked as he toyed with the rubber band he'd placed around the folder years ago to secure its contents from prying eyes.

Then he suddenly jammed the folder, unopened, back into the desk drawer and said, "Why look? I know what's there. Why torture myself?"

With eyes closed, he massaged his heart as though he felt an emptiness there. "Can't turn back time," he said, his voice filled with regret.

For a few minutes he sat quietly, lost in thought. He held his head in his hands that were weathered by work and the brisk sea air. Squaring his jaw, he breathed heavily. Suddenly, he turned lionlike toward his files and snatched up the folder. Within an instant, he tore through its seal. Love letters, a faded pink satin ribbon, and pictures of Desiree, beautiful and young, tumbled across his desk.

"My lost love, my only love," he sighed as he studied a photo he'd taken of Desiree the morning after they'd first made love. Delicately he traced over her kiss-swollen lips and then her blue eyes that still seemed to twinkle diamonds back at him. When he stroked the image of her sun-streaked hair held in place by the same satin ribbon he now caressed, he shuddered and cried, "Dear God, I still love Desiree."

\* \* \* \* \*

Desiree flipped on her laptop, blinked back the tears that clouded her vision, and entered two lines from her favorite poem by Robert Frost, "Two roads diverged in a wood, and I—I took the one less traveled by."

"Busy?" a young man asked.

Regaining her composure, Desiree shifted her attention to a junior associate who stood in the doorway. "What is it, Jeff?"

"We thought you might be interested in this fax. It just came in."

She took the raggedly torn sheet of paper, stared at the page, and turned it face down. Measuring her words, she barely whispered, "Thank you." Adding, "We'll talk about this later," she dismissed Jeff with a tight smile, all the while hoping the throbbing vein in her neck wouldn't give away the excitement she felt race through her. She couldn't believe what she'd just read.

Holding her breath, she waited until Jeff walked away. Once again alone, she leaned forward in her chair and allowed her eyes to devour the article someone had copied from that day's *Pensacola News Journal*. Slowly she studied each word; she had to be sure.

"Floridian proposes additional expansion over wetlands" declared the headline, but the name Bennett Collier placed lower in the text flashed in technicolor in front of her eyes.

As she stilled her heart, she listened to the office chatter in the outer suite and rolled her eyes at her staff's inquisition of Jeff.

"Was Ms. McAndrews surprised?"

"I don't know."

"You couldn't tell?"

"Not really," Jeff answered with a puzzled sigh.

"You can't be serious. She didn't go ballistic?"

"I know, it sounds odd, especially considering her usual reaction to any environmental threat."

"Surely she seemed interested."

"I couldn't tell."

"Do you think she has a plan of attack?"

Desiree glanced at the wall of awards her Nature's Way network had received for its outstanding protection of endangered areas. Much had been accomplished in a relatively short period of time, largely due to Desiree's determination and dedication to make the world a better place for future generations. She knew better, though, than to rest on past accomplishments. Her job was one that would never end. Hearing Jeff say, "Beats me what she has in mind, but I bet it's dynamite," Desiree turned her chair so she faced Boulder Canyon.

Gazing out the window, she said under her breath, "Now that's a thought, a dynamite plan of attack, my plan for Ben Collier. Goodness me, such an opportunity."

She let her mind concoct several reasonable options and she logged a few notes on her computer. "Plan A. Standard Operating Procedure. Notify the EPA and the Florida division, then follow up with an investigation by our fact team. Send Jeff, Gwen, and Elise; they're ready for the challenge. Remind them to go by the 'regs'."

She moved to key "Save" but then stopped, thinking, I know the rules and I know I should follow them, but then again, sometimes there are exceptions to the rules. Maybe this proposal fits that category.

Returning to her keyboard, she entered "Modify Initial Plan." She paused and pictured Ben Collier as she remembered him, young and daring, the man who'd broken her heart and crushed her dreams.

Haunted by the past, her mind kicked into overdrive and her fingers flew across the keys as she typed furiously: "Plan A. Business as Usual? Or Plan B? Explore uncharted territory? Does this case merit application of the hands-on exception rule? Should I become involved?"

A model of concentration, she studied the questions she'd posed on the computer screen, dwelling long and hard on the possible ramifications. "That's it. The best and only answer to a difficult situation," she said. Quickly deleting her lines of text, she entered "Final Decision: The Master Plan" and began a work session that would have shocked even the most hardened taskmaster.

When she finished her outline, goals and objectives, projected timetable, and cost analysis, she switched off the computer and sat a few inches taller in her chair. "Ready for a stroll down the road less traveled, Ben Collier?" she asked and then added, "I believe the exception rule definitely applies to your Heron Bay proposal, and since I've made the decision, I feel it's only fair that I deliver the news to you in person. You and your project deserve my undivided attention and that's exactly what you and it are going to receive."

Smile lines crinkled across her forehead as she congratulated herself for once again exhibiting her ability to assess problems and present solutions. She believed she was prepared and ready to meet any challenge Ben Collier might put in her pathway. Mere pebbles, perfect for kicking out of the way, she thought as she cleared her throat and spoke firmly into her intercom, "Jeff, call Beverly in the Tallahassee office and set things in motion on her end."

"Is this about the Collier Heron Bay deal?" he asked.

"Of course. I've assigned it top priority, so advise Beverly it's a go."

"You mean call her after I contact the EPA?"

"No, I think not."

"But they're the first agency we consult in these development matters."

"No buts, Jeff. I have a different plan. After you talk with Beverly, arrange a flight for tomorrow morning, early."

"I'm going to Florida?" he asked gleefully. "I've always wanted to see the Gulf Coast."

Exasperated, Desiree tapped her fingers on her desk and answered, "Sorry, Jeff, you're not going; I am. I want to see for myself what's happening down there. So stop whatever you're working on now and get our group focused on the Collier project."

"Okay, Ms. McAndrews," he answered and then added, "Tell me what you need and we'll find the data." Resigned disappointment sounded heavy in his voice.

Desiree blanched at Jeff's tone, but she rationalized that as head of Nature's Way, her duty line was clear and so she replied, "I need position statements from all our departments on this Perdido Key proposal. Also, I want a complete research package on the Heron Bay developer, Bennett Collier. Now."

Reacting to her orders, Jeff's assistants, Elise and Gwen, sighed collectively and exchanged glances.

"What's her deal?" Gwen asked.

"She's going solo, I guess," Jeff replied. "She doesn't usually take such a pit bull stance, at least not this early."

"Hmm," Elise said, raising her eyebrows and nodding her head. "Something's up, big time. I can feel sparks in the air."

"You may be right. She really tensed when I gave her the word," Jeff answered as he rubbed his forehead and culled the files for Property Transfers/Deeds in Escambia County.

A researcher scanning microfiche files for Bennett Collier entries turned and said, "You know what happens when Ms. McAndrews takes a personal interest in a case."

"Right, headaches all the way around," Elise replied. "I wonder if Bennett Collier senses an imminent attack is about to wreck his world. If so, I bet he's reaching for a bottle of aspirin right now."

"A fifth of Jack Daniels is probably more like it," Jeff added quietly, shaking his head as he placed Desiree's call to Florida. Catching her eye as she moved into the outer office, he covered the receiver and asked, "What should I call this project, Ms. McAndrews? Does it have a code name?"

Desiree didn't bat an eyelash as she answered without a smile, "*Angel Flight* will work fine."

"Angel Flight?" Jeff muttered.

Elise leaned toward Jeff and whispered, "Mr. Collier's Fortune 500 file lists a Navy connection with the Blue Angel Flight Demonstration Team. Do you think she already knew that?"

All speculation ended when Desiree walked into the staff area and announced, "Enough talk in here. Your reports are due on my desk before closing today. Does everyone understand?"

"Definitely snappish," Gwen mumbled as Desiree returned to her office, closed the door, and tried to still the pounding of her heart.

\* \* \* \* \*

Later than evening, Desiree, alone and still at her desk, skimmed through summaries of legislation aimed at protecting wetlands. More diligently, she studied the reports her staff had compiled on Bennett Collier. With a heavy heart, she rested her head in her hands and concluded, "Such blatant chicanery! He obviously has no regard for the public's interest. He's become an opportunistic land shark, a violator of the same earth he used to cherish." Saddened, she mentally shamed the Collier development team in general and Ben Collier in particular for their greedy, manipulative ways of conducting business in order to increase their personal fortunes.

Wondering how the man she'd once loved could've become the documented defiler of nature she now read about, Desiree turned away from the massive Collier Development files and asked, "How and when did this happen?"

She remembered when he'd been as starry-eyed as she, a champion of the universe, a steward of the earth. But that was her young Ben before. Before he'd kissed her good-bye, leaving behind a trail of smoke and a ribbon of broken promises. Quick and easy and with a surge of his jet's engines, he'd flown out of her sight and out of her life.

"Too bad, my sweet Ben," she said as she pictured his face, strong and smiling gallantly, her brave hero of days gone by.

Made uncomfortable by his image that she knew full well could set into motion a complete range of forbidden thoughts, she sat up primly and said, "It looks as though fate has drawn us together again, but the outcome this time will be different. You'll see, Ben Collier."

She let her mind fashion a variety of encounters with Ben, all with her placed in the starring role. Yes, she could see straight through to the final scene. She would hand Ben her screenplay and tell him to take his mark. Cameras would role and she would shine.

Faced off against Ben, her blue eyes would pierce his and accusations and denials would fly wildly as she zeroed in for the kill. She smiled at the thought. She would win and walk away the proud victor, her head held high.

Suddenly, though, the movie in her mind soared with purple passion as Ben turned the tables 360 degrees. Shuddering, she saw Ben rip her script into shreds and cast away its pages at Mach 1 speed.

"Oh, oh, oh!" she said and closed her eyes to shield herself from the image of Ben marching toward her, ready to even the score. She feared her iron will might crumble if she allowed him to take her in his arms, and oh my, what if he dared to tease her ears, her neck and lower with divine kisses? Could he still make her shiver in anticipation and delight?

Desiree's eyes flashed sapphire as she screamed, "Oh, good heavens! Whatever am I thinking? I should want to even the score with this man, not sleep with him!"

Shaking her head defiantly, she added, "Ooh, this must stop, right now." Desperately she wanted the desire she felt for Ben to disappear, but the harder she fought to dispel thoughts of him from her psyche, the more vivid he became in her mind's eye.

"This is not good, Desiree," she chided herself. "It's time for a reality check." Thinking about her job, her morning flight, and the clothes she needed to pack, she wondered if she should use the flight bag Ben'd left behind, the one he'd promised he would fill with treasures from his adventures on the other side of the world.

The memory of their last time together raced through Desiree like a live wire. He'd held her so closely and had reassured her he'd return to her soon, very soon. One more tour, the Indian Ocean this time, he'd said. The months would pass quickly, she'd see. He'd promised and she'd believed.

With heavy hearts, Ben and Desiree had parted, he deployed on another cruise and she left behind holding on to his flight bag and the remembrance of his loving words and his caring smile. Oh, how he could smile. She wondered into whose eyes he was smiling right now. She could feel his passion, his fire.

"That's it!" she shouted. "No more of this."

With renewed resolve, she jammed her file folders into a book bag she'd used during college when she'd lugged around biology textbooks and lab reports. Now she carried seismographic readouts and coastal surveys. And a faded newspaper clipping that announced "Pensacola welcomes home her heroes. Ceremony planned at Ferdinand Plaza."

Desiree completed a routine check of her office. Feeling all was secured, she flipped off the light switch and closed the door. She walked down the corridor but stopped halfway. The sun setting over the Flatirons cast a warm glow over all of Boulder, the city that'd saved her soul and her sanity when word of Ben's betrayal had reached her.

The sight of a sleek jet climbing above the mountains made her think of Ben and the bombshell he'd detonated by way

Southern Bell and a man who'd introduced himself as Ben's father-in-law.

For the zillionth time, she could hear that man drawl in slow Southernese, "Suga' plum, I sure do hate to be the one tellin' you this, but somebody's gotta do it. Ben's gone and taken up with another fine little lady. Sorry, darlin', but you've been replaced."

Another woman, a Miss Florida, he'd said.

Miss Susanna Delaney, a darked-haired viper and an heiress-in-waiting, Desiree had later learned.

Desiree often prayed the sneaky witch was still waiting. As for Ben, she wanted everyone to believe she had moved on in her personal life and cared nothing about their past relationship. But deep inside she did, maybe even more than anyone could ever imagine.

Thinking about Ben, Florida, and Susanna, Desiree left the building and walked to her car, a burgundy Volvo sedan that'd outlasted the marriages of most of her friends. She watched the sky begin to fill with stars and wondered what tomorrow would hold for her. Would Ben be surprised to see her? Excited, maybe? Would he think she'd changed?

Torn by thoughts of the past and regrets for what might've been, she headed her car down Arapahoe and toward Table Mesa Drive. All she wanted was to go home and sit by the fireplace where she felt safe and secure. No one, no Susannas and no Bens, could get to her there, at least as long as she kept the door to her heart slammed shut.

Peace washed over her as she pulled up the long, winding drive that led to her sprawling ranch-style home built of western cedar and stone. Floodlights along the driveway silhouetted the snowball lilacs, baby's breath, and mock oranges she'd planted and lavished her attention on every weekend during the short Colorado growing season.

Although her friends thought it impractical for a single woman to maintain such a demanding home, she found pleasure in the oasis she'd created in the middle of an older subdivision. Given the choice between the swanky condos that snaked along Boulder Creek and her neighborhood set high on a plateau, she'd willingly sunk her income and her heart into the place she called heaven on earth.

As it was, she saw enough brick, concrete, and tinted glass every day. In fact, her office building on Canyon reeked of the sterile materials. Still though, she didn't complain because the windows opened to a perfect view of the mountains and the sky.

She loved the snowcapped peaks, but the bright blue sky captured her fancy more. Watching cloud formations for hours at a time was nothing new to her; she'd spent what some might consider a lifetime doing it.

She paused before unlocking her front door and looked up at the clear, starlit sky. She closed her eyes to shut out any interference so she could better concentrate on the night sounds. Hearing only quiet she smiled, but then a roar that sounded like cracking thunder broke the silence of the night. "A Tomcat or maybe a Hornet," she said as she watched a fighter jet, shining like a jewel and trailing white smoke, snake its way over the top of the mountains.

Desiree thought about old habits dying hard. She couldn't deny she still looked up every time a military plane passed overhead, just as she'd done years before. Then though, the chances had been good she might catch a glimpse of Ben flying high. He'd commanded her air space a lot and she'd loved watching him work, so hard, so exciting, a thrill every time he'd flown her way.

"You can't go back, you can't go back," she repeated ten times. Thinking, Ben's not the same man I used to love, she flipped on the lights in the foyer and walked into the living room. She turned on the stereo, kicked off her shoes, and snuggled deep into the corner of a sofa she'd covered with heathered lavender throws.

"Baby, I love your way" floated out of the Bose speakers. The lyrics of her and Ben's special song touched her soul. She closed her eyes and allowed her mind to transport her back twelve years to the arms and love of Ben Collier, the only man she'd ever known.

Dreaming of love found and then love lost, she drifted off to sleep.

The next morning, she awakened with a smile on her face and a twinkle in her eyes. Buoyed by a feeling of excitement tempered by cool caution, she readied herself for her trip to Florida. Uncertain what awaited her there, she decided she would put her time on the Gulf Coast to good use. This was one trip she was determined Ben Collier would not soon forget.

Fortified by a cold shower and several cups of hot coffee, Desiree reviewed her flight schedule. Most people would've avoided the hassle of facing three airports and crossing two time zones, all within half a day, but Desiree wasn't like most travelers.

She believed an environmental disaster could possibly be averted and she was the catalyst in the dynamic equation. If only she could get to Tallahassee in time. Otherwise, coastal water quality and living marine sources along Perdido Key could become compromised, never to be recovered if the unscrupulous developer named Ben Collier had his way.

She rushed through her dressing room and shunned the mirror. She figured she'd have time during her layover in Atlanta to put on her best face and best attitude, both designed to give her the upper hand when she met Ben on his own turf. Stuffing her travel-safe clothes from her sensible mix and match wardrobe into Ben's flight bag, she grabbed another cup of coffee and made her way out the door.

She paced up and down the sidewalk in front of her house and waited for the Boulder Airporter to arrive. As daylight broke, she watched a large, white van careen around the corner.

Desiree signaled, but the bearded, droopy-eyed driver failed to stop. "Probably half-asleep," she said as she watched the man zoom past her and then back up half a block before he came to a lurching stop in front of her.

Swinging open the passenger door, she fumed, "You should be more observant, sir."

"Hey, ma'am, I do the best I can," the driver retorted. Rakishly adjusting a fisherman's cap over his braided hair that reached below his shoulder blades, he added, "This wasn't my first choice of a job, you know."

"Oh?"

"That's right. I've got a Ph.D. in economics from Berkeley and a certificate in applied music from the Cincinnati Conservatory. I'm a regular piano man."

Desiree didn't comment but studied the toes of her shoes instead.

Ignoring her nonresponse, the man continued, "I think it's a crying shame that driving this bus is the only work I could find in this sorry town. Tough place here, the good jobs bottomed out when all those high tech industry people moved in from California. Know what I'm saying?"

Not wanting to encourage conversation, Desiree coolly responded, "Hmm." She'd planned to put the transport time to better use, namely plotting the optimal way for her and Ben to address the issues at hand without allowing their personal baggage to muddy the waters.

"Now I commute from Nederland before I even start my day, every day, seven days a...," the driver droned on and on.

An hour and twenty-five minutes later, Desiree breathed a sigh of relief as she bolted from the shuttle and raced toward a flight schedule monitor posted beside the main entrance to Denver International Airport. She knew most of Delta's planes departed from the gates on the last DIA concourse, so not wanting to miss her flight, she kicked off her shoes and picked up her stride. She dashed across the polished marble floor and skirted around other passengers, cleaning carts, and vendor stands that clogged the narrow aisles. Time was of the essence and she had a flight to catch.

Clearing through security with her flight bag, briefcase, and shoes in hand, she breathed easier when she saw a sign listing her plane to Atlanta as the first flight out. Then she frowned deeply. Shaking her head in disbelief, she muttered, "Gate 3; it figures."

"Something wrong, ma'am?" a steward who'd overheard her asked politely.

"No, everything is fine," Desiree answered as she took a seat in the gate area and slipped on her dress pumps.

She tried not to fixate on the large "3" posted less than four feet from her chair. But even when she repositioned herself, she could only think about the #3 jet that had been Ben's plane and his position when he'd flown as a Blue Angel pilot. Thinking, left wing in the diamond formation, she felt perspiration form on her forehead and across the back of her neck.

"You must not be a runner," the steward said, handing her a tissue.

Puzzled, Desiree looked at him as if to say what are you talking about?

"I couldn't help but notice your ragged breathing and..."

"And?"

"And you're glowing," he added delicately. "You know what I mean." To illustrate, he mopped his brow with his handkerchief and said, "Whew? Who turned up the thermostat in here?"

Blushing and hating her reaction, Desiree folded the steward's tissue into a neat square and dried first her forehead and then her neck. Quietly she admitted, "I am a bit winded, that's all," but in actuality, she knew thoughts of Ben were the real cause of her discomfort.

For the next few minutes, she studied the lines of her shoes and willed her mind to regain control of her emotions. Strolling down memory lane isn't my mission, she reminded herself, preserving wetlands is.

When another attendant announced her flight, Desiree gathered her belongings and searched for her boarding passes she thought she'd stored in her briefcase. Hearing the call for her row, Desiree walked to the front of the line. "I know it's in here somewhere. I'm sure I didn't lose it," she said as she continued to search her briefcase. The gate attendant smiled tolerantly as Desiree fumbled through her papers and files.

Other travelers standing behind Desiree seemed less amused as one young woman sniped, "She must not get out of town very often."

"Obviously not," the woman's male companion agreed smugly.

Desiree colored at their words. She hated feeling incompetent because that was not her style. After all, she was a professional who prided herself on her work and her ability to produce positive results. She'd learned her lessons well and the hard way. From the grassroots up.

At that moment she felt sheer disgust for her flustered self. How could she have allowed her emotions to override her intellect? Why couldn't she keep her mind focused on her duties at hand and far away from the dashing aviator turned land developer?

Thinking she should probably give up the fight and retire to a club for lonely hearts, she heard a voice speak inside her head that changed her mind. "It's not your fault, Desiree. You're stronger and better than that. Somebody else is accountable for your psyche flip-flopping like a top that's spun out of control, and I believe you know who that man is."

To which, Desiree answered, "Thank you, Ben, for making me look and act like an idiot." Simmering with anger, she jammed her hand in her coat pocket and immediately connected with the boarding passes she'd tucked away deep inside. "Get a grip, Desiree," she muttered to herself as she muscled her way forward, seething heat and narrowing her eyes.

Those standing closest to Desiree backed away as she strode down the gateway, her back ramrod straight and her focus centered. Up and down the passenger line, clucks of sympathy rippled when the stunned travelers heard Desiree mumble eight words loaded with passion and desire, "Eyes right, Ben Collier. I'm headed your way."

# Chapter 2

From her vantage point high in the sky, Desiree studied the terrain below. Narrow roads twisted through patches of bright green pine forests that showed few signs of man's intrusion. Catching the eye of an elderly gentleman seated beside her, she said, "Beautiful, isn't it?"

"Oh yes," he replied with sadness in his voice. "Too bad it's about all that's left of vintage Florida since the developers decided to ravage the beaches and skin off the dunes."

"Are you saying the postcard scenes of seagulls, miles of open beaches, and clear emerald waters are a lie?"

"No, not really. There's some of that left," he replied, "but now high rises and planned developments have just about crowded out the few remaining spaces of unoccupied beachfront." He closed his eyes and shook his head.

"If you're talking about PUDs, I can identify with that problem. A lot of those communities stacked one on top of another blanket the Front Range of Colorado. It's heartbreaking to see a wall of vinyl siding where deer used to graze." Desiree noted the man's stony expression and interpreted his look as one of disapproval. She could sense she'd found a kindred spirit who shared her preservationist philosophy.

"I agree, ma'am. I've seen it time and again. Once developers set up shop, they stack houses, duplexes, and condos on every inch of the beach they can get their greedy hands on." Pointing to a row of condominiums with pastel faux stucco fronts, he added, "After those scoundrels max out their investments, off they go rich, and all that's left behind for the public to enjoy is an overbuilt sea of humanity."

"How unfortunate," Desiree said. "Surely one day someone in a position of authority will wake up and see what's happening to America's coastlines." She pursed her lips and pictured a group of developers sporting gold chains and Rolex watches, their hair carefully styled and their suntanned arms beautifully bronzed to perfection. Yes, she could see them as they strolled king-like along a fragile dune line. Sickened by the image, she frowned. "The alarm must be sounded and soon," she concluded with a determined toss of her head.

"I hope you're right," the man said wearily. "It angers me to watch bulldozers flatten the dunes and for what? Nothing but a mess of concrete and asphalt with maybe a pelican or two pictured on a sign out front."

"It sounds as though you have some firsthand experience with coastal development."

"You might say that," he acknowledged and then added, "I've seen paradise literally mowed down. Mark my words, ma'am, those back bays and bayous we're passing over now are next on the list of endangered places. When I think about the destruction of lands that should have been preserved, I get fighting mad. Believe me, this used to be God's country, but that was a long time ago."

"What was it like?" Desiree asked as she studied the man's face, chiseled by time and parched by the sun.

"Real peaceful, downright serene," he replied. "Miles of unspoiled beauty, you know what I mean. Fishing villages, gulls, herons, and a few old salts here and there."

"No tourists?"

"Oh, a few families from Alabama and Georgia might cross the border every now and then for a week of shelling and crabbing. That was about the extent of it."

Desiree listened as the man recalled his boyhood days along the Florida coast. She shared his sorrow for the loss of an era that'd been eroded more by man's greed than by nature's storms.

"The places I remember the best are memories now." He pointed to a narrow strip of sandy beach covered by thick grasses and stately rows of sea oats. "That's the way the whole coastline used to look."

"A natural seascape is a sight of beauty," Desiree said. "It's worth preserving, whatever the cost."

The man closed his eyes and frowned before saying, "I'm afraid there's not much left. That's why developers have turned their attention to other waterfront properties located away from the beaches."

Developers like Ben, Desiree thought darkly. Then she remembered the stories he'd told her about growing up along the Florida panhandle where he'd fished for reds during the day and for flounder at night. How could Ben have sold out the area he, too, had once called God's Country?

Desiree glanced away as Ben's image appeared in her mind. She wondered if he was one of the developers the man spoke of. She started to ask, but her words were cut off by a flight attendants' announcement that the plane had been cleared for landing into the Tallahassee Regional Airport.

As the jet touched down, Desiree unfastened her seat belt and reached underneath her seat for her briefcase. She wanted to find a Nature's Way brochure and a pledge card. "Here, sir," she said, "these are for you. I hope you find the brochure interesting."

He thanked her and said, "Well, ma'am, I guess we didn't save the world today, but I certainly enjoyed chatting with you. If you come up with a way to stop the developers, let me know. Here's my number." He gave Desiree his business card and nodded sagely before taking his place in the center aisle.

"Thank you," she said as she pocketed the man's card. She wished they'd had more time to talk. She might've had the chance to enlist him as an ally for her mission on the local front.

Gathering her belongings, she made a mental note to drop him a line when she returned to Boulder. Right now, though, she knew she needed to keep her focus on Ben's proposal for Perdido Key. With her resolve set and her commitment made, she readied herself for the Heron Bay challenge, development versus preservation. Convinced she was on the right side of the issue, she wasn't about to back down or compromise. Too much was at stake, too much could be lost forever, and she couldn't allow that to happen.

Entering the gate area, Desiree turned when a young woman with reddish brown hair and a deep tan touched her arm and asked, "Excuse me, are you Ms. McAndrews?"

"Yes, I'm Desiree," she replied, approving of the woman's environmentally correct attire of natural cottons and

Birkenstocks. Desiree extended her hand and added, "You must be with Nature's Way, Tallahassee."

"Hi, I'm Beverly Moran, and yes, I head up the marine biology division. Welcome to Tallahassee." Clearing her throat nervously, she added, "Was your flight okay?"

"Just a little turbulence and thankfully no delays," Desiree answered as she studied Beverly's face. Sensing the woman's shyness, she said, "It's very nice to meet you. I've been quite impressed with the work you've done on this end. Your reports have always been right on target."

"Oh, I'm relieved to hear you say that. I wasn't quite sure what you needed when Jeff asked for an aquatic update. And when he called back for more pH information and comparative data on the oyster beds in South Alabama and North Florida, I worried I was on the wrong track."

"Have you spoken with Jeff recently?"

"Yes, several times," Beverly said, blushing prettily. "Just this morning he said he needed the purity regulations for catfish farms in the Southeast, as well as the figures for last year's shrimp harvest in the Northern Gulf. That must be some aquatic safety protocol he's putting together."

Desiree smiled knowingly and decided Beverly was the reason for Jeff's keen disappointment about missing the trip to Florida. Raising an eyebrow, she said, "Jeff's dedicated to his work, almost a zealot at times. He's quite innovative and persistent when he sets his sights on a goal. If he ever applies his work ethic to his social life, the woman he goes after had better start shopping for a wedding trousseau."

"Really?" Beverly asked. Her cheeks flushed crimson and her eyes twinkled with joy. She motioned toward the baggage claim area and said, "Delta's carousels are over there. Do you want to check for your luggage?"

"What I have in my hands is all I brought. I don't plan to stay here very long. In fact, I hope we can stonewall the Heron Bay project before Ben Collier files any more permit requests."

Beverly lowered her voice to a whisper and said, "I don't know if that's possible. Mr. Collier stands firm on his plans, at least that was the word that came into the office this morning."

"Well then, we'll see about that," Desiree commented icily. More determined than ever, she looked into Beverly's big brown eyes and said, "Maybe this is one time Mr. Collier will have to change his mind."

"Now that's a thought," Beverly answered, seeming surprised by the intensity of Desiree's words. She hesitated for a moment, looked at her watch, and then said, "I know you're on a tight schedule, but would you like to freshen up at the hotel before I take you to the office?"

"No, I'll just step into the ladies room for a minute, then we can be on our way. I'll have all this evening to rest."

"But there's a reception and dinner tonight. I accepted an invitation on your behalf," Beverly said with a touch of panic in her voice.

Desiree frowned. She wondered who had wasted company funds on a hospitality function. Curtly, she said, "Nature's Way doesn't have discretionary money to throw away on party tickets."

Beverly bristled at Desiree's sharp tone and said, "No one in our office planned the event, if that's what you're implying. I guess Jeff didn't tell you about tonight."

"No, he didn't, so why don't you?" Desiree said coldly. She paused and instantly regretted that her words had come out so harshly. Unable to avoid the hurt look she knew she'd placed in Beverly's eyes, Desiree flashed a smile filled with apology and waited for Beverly's explanation about the social event.

"The Legislature's in session and tonight's function is sponsored by the Florida Building Council. It starts at 6 and it's semi-formal. I gave Jeff the details when he called about your trip. He must have forgotten."

"Oh, I see," Desiree said. Thinking, Ben's probably involved in this event, she said, "It never ceases to amaze me the lengths some people will go to in order to win influence at the Statehouse." To herself she thought, a pretentious soiree sounds precisely like something Ben and his precious Susanna would cook up to buy support for their development scheme.

"So, do you still want to go to the office or do you need to rest before the dinner?" Beverly asked.

Desiree sighed as she looked at Ben's flight bag and said, "I guess you should take me to a mall. I'm afraid my work wardrobe won't make much of a power statement at tonight's dinner. Where is it being held?"

"The Lands End Country Club," Beverly answered with a giggle. "The staff thought Lands End was a pretty amusing choice for a bunch of builders intent on destroying the environment with tacky PUDs and concrete towers."

"Maybe tonight we can turn the tables on the developers. You're going, too, aren't you?"

"No, the Building Council sent over only one ticket. You'll be seated at Table #3."

Hearing "3", Desiree winced and said, "Interesting, well then, you'd better fill me in on the legislative profiles as we shop." She shook her head and rolled her eyes in exasperation. She didn't like the idea of spending good money on a cocktail dress she'd probably never wear again, but given the circumstances, she decided to make the most of her evening out.

She followed Beverly to the parking lot and hoped she could find a suitable outfit on short notice. Spur of the moment actions were not her forte; the last time she'd acted spontaneously, she'd ended up in the arms of Ben Collier. An innocent, she'd given away her heart and her love. Now she knew that'd been a terrible mistake, one never to be repeated. Of that she was sure. Or was she?

* * * * *

"Did you say the Lands End Country Club, ma'am?"

"Yes, I'm attending a dinner there. Do you know where it is?" Desiree asked. She wondered if the cab driver planned to give her the "big city" run around in order to pad his fare.

The man hit the brakes of his aged lime green sedan that reeked of stale tobacco and pine-scented air freshener. Glancing over his shoulder, he grinned as though he'd read Desiree's mind. "Don't worry, ma'am. I know right where it is, out toward Cascade Lake." With a tip of his Seminoles baseball cap, he punched the accelerator and sped away from the Tallahassee Mall and headed down Monroe Street.

Desiree caught a glimpse of herself in the rearview mirror and muttered in disgust, "A raccoon in red."

"Did you say something?" the driver asked.

"No, not really," she answered. She smoothed the full skirt of her new dress over her knees and toyed with the band of crimson velvet that decorated its hemline. "I guess I'm a bit uncomfortable is all."

"Well, you don't look like a raccoon to me, if that's what you're sayin'."

"Oh, but I do," she replied. "The circles under my eyes and puffy lids pretty much say it all."

"You career types are all alike. Work, work, work. Too busy to have a real life or even a boyfriend. Am I right or what?"

Offended by the man's generalization, Desiree sat a bit taller and retorted, "For your information, sir, my life is actually quite full and very rewarding. And I have lots of friends, too."

"Whatever," the man replied as he flipped on his right turn signal and pulled the cab curbside.

"Why are we stopping?"

"Back in a flash, man on a mission," he said with a secretive wink as he put the car in neutral, set the emergency brake, and turned off the fare meter.

Desiree used the time alone to check the match of her make-up with her dress. "Worse than I thought," she moaned. "Whatever was I thinking to buy a dress this color when I'm as pale as a ghost and too old for a look like this." Dusting her cheeks with a light shadow of primrose blush, she chastised herself by saying, "I shouldn't have listened to Beverly and that clerk. Why didn't I follow my own instincts? I've been in Florida for only a few hours and I've already lost all measure of common sense. Why? Oh why now?"

Seeing Desiree balance a tube of lipstick in one hand and a mascara wand in the other, the cab driver stood aside and gave her the time, privacy, and space to fluff her hair and tug her dress first one way and then another. Then he heard her pray, "Dear God, please give me the strength and the courage to remember who I am and why I'm here, and please help me to do the right thing to keep our world safe and sound."

When she put away her compact, the driver tapped on the window and asked, "Is this my cab or is it a powder room?" When Desiree didn't reply, he added, "I bet a career lady like you knows how to use this stuff I found in the drugstore. Here, it's for you. Roll down the window and give it a shot."

Desiree lowered the window and took the cup of cracked ice and roll of paper towels he handed her. She smiled her gratitude as she fashioned a compress and placed it across her tired eyes. "Ooh, that helps. Thank you, I appreciate your kindness and I'll pay you for your trouble."

"No problem, missy. It's on the house. After all, me and ole José here, that's the name of my car, have a reputation to uphold."

"And what is that?"

"Getting the belle of the ball to the church on time."

Desiree laughed at the man's mixed metaphors and felt as though she'd just made another friend.

"See, I've got it all figured this way," the cabby said. "You've just gotten off the boat, so to speak, don't know anybody, and have a big doin's to go to. You're nervous, but who wouldn't be? So you go out and buy a fancy dress and new shoes, but you're not used to wearing such fine clothes so that's why you've been fidgetin' and twistin' ever since you got in José. It's true now, isn't it?"

Desiree blushed at the man's accuracy but she didn't say a word.

"I bet there's somethin' more to the story, though, than just a suit of new clothes. Like maybe you're worryin' 'bout who you're goin' see or who's goin' see you and... "

"And? And what?"

The man took off his baseball cap, scratched the top of his head, and answered, "And I bet a man's involved, a man you're not sure about."

"Why do you say that?"

"Let's just say I can sense it. Nothin' against your perfume, that's not it. It's just the scent, you know, the love sign some women give off, if you get where I'm headed."

"Sir," she fumed, "I hope you're headed only to the Lands End Country Club and in short order."

Whistling "Lady in Red," he straightened the bill of his cap and accelerated the cab so fast that Desiree lurched from side to side in the back seat.

"Hold on for the ride, ma'am; your wish is my command."

Desiree grimaced as he changed his tune to "Some Enchanted Evening" and broadly winked as he watched in the rearview mirror for her reaction.

She turned her face toward the window and tried to concentrate on the city scenes that spun by so fast she couldn't keep track of all she saw. After what seemed forever, she breathed a sigh of relief as the cab headed toward an elaborate entrance bordered by tall palm trees and lush tropical grasses.

The driver slowed the cab as he turned down a brick driveway that cut through banks of blooming oleanders and fragrant jasmines. "Nice digs for a princess," he said. As serious as a judge, he added, "And I mean that from the bottom of my heart, missy." Stopping at the front steps of a palatial plantation style building that looked as though it'd been transported from a Hollywood movie set, he added, "Pretty as a picture, that's you, ma'am. Whoever you set your eyes on tonight is a goner, of that I'm sure."

"I doubt that, sir," Desiree replied, "but I thank you for your kind words."

"I mean what I say. And that's God's truth," he said, pointing to the sky. Then nodding toward a doorman wearing a bright Hawaiian shirt, three hibiscus leis, and a straw hat, he whistled through his teeth and said with a booming laugh, "Some party this is gonna be. Your fun's about to begin, missy."

As the doorman walked toward the cab, Desiree opened her beaded evening bag and pulled out her invitation.

"May I see that, ma'am?" the doorman asked as he assisted Desiree from the cab. Glancing at the top of her invitation, he said, "Nature's Way. You must be Desiree McAndrews from Colorado."

"Why, yes, I am."

The doorman handed the driver a $50 bill and said, "Ms. McAndrews is a special guest. I trust this will cover her fare."

"Thanks, mister," the cabby said and with his eyes twinkling, he added, "I told you this is your night, Cinderella."

"Oh my goodness," she replied as she waved her thanks and allowed the doorman to usher her toward the receiving line positioned by a silver and gold door that gleamed its welcome to all who passed through.

Loudly, the doorman announced, "Ms. Desiree McAndrews of Boulder, Colorado." Then he bowed gallantly and passed her hand to her host, a handsome gentleman who looked as though he'd just died and gone to heaven.

# Chapter 3

Ben felt his heart go wild as he looked into Desiree's eyes and reached for her hands. "Desiree McAndrews, you look wonderful," he said. Unable to release her, he held her closer, an action that felt as natural to him as drawing his next breath.

Seeking first his eyes and then his smile, Desiree said, "Hello, Ben." She tucked her head into the curve of his neck and took in his scent that still carried a payload of fire power as strong as she remembered. Although tempted to succumb to the kiss he placed on her cheek, she heeded the advice of the warning voice in her mind that wouldn't allow her to give way to his tender embrace. She pulled back, but only slightly, as second thoughts flooded through her.

Ben brushed his lips against her wrist and so only she could hear, he whispered, "You're as pretty as ever, but I'm not surprised. I knew your beauty would never fade."

"Such flattery," she replied with a taunting smile that tore at Ben's heart.

With eyes downcast, he said, "We've got to talk, later." He turned his attention to a woman whose dark beauty stood in sharp contrast to Desiree's compelling softness.

"Well now, let me guess. From Ben's reaction, I assume you must be his lost love, Desiree," the woman said with ice in her eyes and hatred in her voice. She took Desiree's left hand and noting the absence of a wedding band, she released her clasp and sneered, "Still alone after all these years, such a pity." With cruel sarcasm, she added, "But then I guess it does get harder the older one becomes. At least that's what I've heard from other women who share your pathetic situation."

"I'm sorry, I don't understand," Desiree said, stepping away from the woman who seemed intent upon tearing her apart.

"You know exactly what I'm talkin' about, Ms. McAndrews, so save your naive act for somebody else. It doesn't carry beans with me."

Desiree almost uttered a sharp retort, but deciding to exercise the restraint she'd learned as a child, she studied the woman whose appearance was picture perfect except for an ugly scowl plastered across her painted face.

Upset, Ben stepped between the two women and protectively positioned himself in front of Desiree. "That's enough, Susanna. Remember your manners; after all, Desiree is a guest tonight. We wouldn't want to give her the wrong impression, now would we?"

"Oh please, Ben. You're as transparent as she is phony," Susanna huffed as she fixed her eyes on Desiree's bustline. "Are those real?" she asked snidely. Then she turned back to Ben and stiffly followed a butler toward a service entrance to the left of the ballroom.

"Stay put, right there," Ben instructed Desiree. "I'll find someone to take my place in this line so we can have a few minutes together, alone. I have so much to tell you."

Desiree put her hands on her hips and looked Ben straight in the eyes. "Sorry, Ben, you're twelve years too late. Besides, my schedule doesn't allow time for a social visit."

"Please, Desiree, we must talk." He motioned for a colleague to fill in for him, and then he guided Desiree to a secluded corner beside the foyer.

"I'm serious, Ben. Whatever we had is over. There's no point in traveling down memory lane. You should move on; I have."

"Have you? Really?" Ben asked. There was something about the look in her eyes that caused him to wonder if she spoke the truth.

Desiree paused and centered her thoughts. "Yes, I have and I can see that you have, too." She directed his attention to the ballroom where Susanna commanded a circle of waiters, who listened intently to her every order.

"No, Desiree, it's not like that. I don't know what you've heard and from whom, but... "

To silence him, she put her forefinger to his lips and said, "Ssh, Ben, no more, not now. Save your explanations for the next time we meet."

"Name when and where. I promise you I'll be there." Then he added, "I'll come even earlier if you want."

Bemused, Desiree smiled briefly, but then she reverted to her all-business self as she said, "You'll receive notice in the morning."

"Fine."

"Maybe not," she warned.

"Why?"

"It's probably only fair that you hear the news directly from me, so here goes. Simply said, I'm calling you to appear before the State Environmental Regs Board."

"Environmental Regulations Board? On what grounds?" Ben stood back stunned and looked as though he'd just been hit below the belt.

"Does Heron Bay mean anything to you?" she asked and waited for his reaction. What'll it be? she wondered. Anger? Or an apology for his destructive ways?

Much to her surprise, Ben's tone reflected neither response as he looked into her eyes and said, "Heron Bay means the world to me, Desiree. It's a concept I'm confident the board will find acceptable and environmentally sound. You'll see."

"Sure," she replied, totally convinced to the contrary but not wanting to prolong their discussion. "Time will tell."

"I'm sure of that," he said. He rested his hand across the small of her back and led her toward the reception area.

Comfortable with Ben's touch that erased time, Desiree faced the reality of the evening. She could hold on to only the good memories she'd shared with Ben or she could run from them. At that moment, flight seemed the better option; her dignity would remain intact and Ben would never know how closely he still held her heart.

Together, they approached the man who'd taken Ben's place in the receiving line. As Ben greeted his friend, Desiree nodded politely and excused herself.

Ben watched her walk away and swore under his breath. "Desiree McAndrews, you haven't changed a bit. You're still stubborn and as righteous as rain. I lost you once, but now that I've found you, I'll never let you go."

Unable to take his eyes off of her, he admired the way she moved from one group of people to another, sharing pleasantries and laughing lightly. When she tossed her golden curls just the way he remembered, he wanted to dash across the room, scoop her up in his arms, and carry her off into the tropical night. He reached for his handkerchief and mopped his forehead and his upper lip.

"Hot, hot, hot and no relief in sight," said a man to Ben's right. Nudging Ben's elbow, he whistled his approval and added, "Hmm, hmm, so she's the one, the pretty lady in red."

Ben nodded. "Yes, that's Desiree McAndrews."

"She's all you said and more, a knockout, pure TNT." He turned to watch Desiree out of the corner of his eye and added, "Lucky you, Ben, two beautiful women in your life, but remember, buddy, Susanna lives here."

"There are a thousand Susannas in the world but only one Desiree."

"Do you think you have a chance with her?"

Ben frowned and stared straight ahead. "Not if I don't take it, my friend. Wasn't that one of the lessons we learned during jet training?"

"Ah, what a time we had at Beeville. Cannon Collier and Maddog Mancini, two VT-26 Tigers on the prowl," Ben's companion said with a hearty laugh as he flicked the red carnation penned to the lapel of Ben's white dinner jacket. Then he wrapped his arm around Ben's shoulder and whispered something into his ear that made both men smile bigger and brighter.

Across the dance floor and far from the receiving line, Desiree concentrated on her surroundings and willed herself not to look back for another glimpse of Ben. She picked up a buffet plate and bypassed the roasted pig and glazed chicken wings, choosing instead papaya drops and kiwi kisses. When a waiter offered her a glass of champagne, she declined politely and requested sparkling water with a lemon twist.

Desiree found an open spot beneath a row of palm trees that'd been brought inside for the occasion. She wondered if they felt as out of place as she at that moment. Standing in the shadows, she watched the other guests who seemed at ease as they passed through the service lines. Balancing full plates and wine glasses posed no problems for this high society set. Desiree attributed their grace to years of practice at cocktail parties and other social events.

"More power to them. It takes all kinds," she said quietly. Given a choice, she knew she would always prefer the more relaxed lifestyle she associated with Boulder instead of an evening filled with glitz and glamour.

She smiled at those who glanced her way, but when a young lieutenant wearing dress whites decorated with wings of gold winked at her, she pretended she didn't see him. Male attention was not what she sought, and she wasn't about to share her haven underneath the tall palms, especially not with a handsome Navy aviator. She'd already been there and done that and if asked ever again to join in the dance of love, she knew she'd decline with no regrets.

Her resolve firm and her will steeled, she knew she must remain sharp and unwavering as she focused on the reason for her trip to Florida. Her mission was clear. Stop Collier Development and save Heron Bay.

Her reverie soon broke, though, when she sensed someone watching her from across the crowded room. She turned her head to the right of the receiving line. There her glance was met by Ben's dark eyes that offered her a prayer sent straight from his heart. She closed her eyes as tightly as she could, unable to confront his look of adoration and yearning that burned with intensity. Someway, she would have to extinguish that fire before it consumed her good intentions and compromised her goals.

Suddenly she felt a tug on the skirt of her dress. Surprised, she opened her eyes and gasped, "Oh!"

"I'm sorry. I didn't mean to scare you, but I thought you needed another one of these. Yours is on the floor," said a young girl whose beautiful eyes stole Desiree's breath.

Taking the satin napkin the girl offered, Desiree said, "Thank you, I didn't realize I'd lost mine." She figured the child couldn't be much older than twelve and she wondered why someone so young was working at the reception.

Desiree noticed the girl seemed uncomfortable in her debutante-style white leather shoes, so she said, "I used to cater banquets at a place called the Harvest House. When my feet hurt from standing too long in dress shoes, I'd back up against a wall and lose them as quickly as I could."

"Like this?" the girl asked. She kicked off her shoes and beamed joyously.

"Do you feel better now?" Desiree asked. She wondered if the child's parents knew the whereabouts of their daughter, and if they did, would they approve? Thinking, I'll check first with the Florida Department of Commerce before I notify social services, she decided she would find out if private parties were considered an exception to child labor laws. Then she asked, "What's your name?"

"Linnea," the girl answered. She blushed at Desiree's attention but didn't look away. Instead, she moved closer and said, "Your dress is very pretty. It's not like most others I've seen before. May I?"

Desiree wasn't sure what Linnea meant, but she nodded her head and waited to see what the girl would do.

Linnea hesitated a moment and then she touched the velvet trim of Desiree's dress and smiled. The lights from the blazing chandeliers cast a glow around Linnea who seemed mesmerized by Desiree's red taffeta dress.

Desiree studied Linnea's thoughtful expression and said, "I'm curious about something. Do you mind if I ask you a question?"

"I guess it's all right," Linnea replied.

"Are you working here tonight?"

Giggling, Linnea tossed her mane of heavy dark curls and answered, "No, of course not. I'm on a date."

"You? You have a date?" Desiree repeated, unable to keep the surprise out of her voice. She stared at Linnea and took double notice of her demure party dress tied with a pink sash. Then she noticed the girls' silk stockings and the pretty pumps with one inch heels she now held in her hands.

"Do you have a mirror in your purse?" Linnea asked. "I think I need more lipstick. Maybe I should check."

Desiree smiled. She remembered what it was like to be almost a teenager but not quite. "Sure," she answered, "my compact's right here, but ladies shouldn't fix their faces in public. Do you know where the ladies room is?"

"We say powder room in the South," Linnea corrected her as she put on her shoes and timidly reached for Desiree's hand. "Follow me," she added, "but before we go in, we should give your plate to one of the waiters. Ladies shouldn't carry dirty dishes either. Right?"

Desiree put her arms around Linnea and gave her a quick hug. Hand in hand they wove their way through the crowd, unaware they'd caught the attention of Ben who stood proudly by. Susanna, too, noticed and appeared less than amused by the scene.

"Isn't that just too cute? The nerve of that hussy!" Susanna hissed. "Who does she think she is? Wearin' that smug smile and tacky dress. Pure trash, plain and simple, just like I always thought. I think I'll have her thrown out, removed from my sight."

"Removed? You're talking nonsense," Ben said. He shook his head in disbelief at Susanna's words. "What's with you anyway?"

"You know the answer to that one, Ben."

"Oh, really?"

"Ben, darlin', come on, confess the truth. You and I both know she's the reason for our differences. Isn't that so?"

"I don't know what you're talking about, Susanna." Coldly, Ben turned his back to her and waited for Desiree to return to the ballroom.

Susanna motioned for a waiter to bring over a tray filled with glasses bubbling with fine California champagne. "Thanks, suga'," she said with a purr in her voice as she took two glasses. In rapid succession, she downed first one and then the other. Turning to Ben, she changed her tone to the roar of an angry lioness and shrilled, "Why I ever married you I'll never know. The cheaper a woman looks and acts, the more you want her. You think you're God's gift, Ben Collier, but I've got news for you. You don't have what it takes to score any more. Too bad you didn't stay in the Navy pipeline; that's when you were a real man."

"Susanna, stop it," Ben demanded. He looked nervously to his left and to his right.

"Oh, no, Ben, I've just started," Susanna replied as she reached for another drink.

"I think you'd better lay off the champagne," he warned. "You're causing a scene."

"You can bet your medals and your bank account on it, darlin'. But you'd better look out, big boy. I'm just revvin' up my engines for the real show that's about to start, so hold on 'cause here I go." She took a step toward Ben and stumbled on the front hem of her gown trimmed with pearls and silver sequins.

"Whoa, there, baby," called an older, deeply tanned and elegantly attired gentleman whose silver hair screamed distinction and sophistication. Rushing to Susanna's side, he untangled her footing from her dress and saved her in the nick of time from exposing her well-endowed and surgically enhanced front.

Ben watched the pair and muttered, "Senator Delaney, Big Jack to the rescue, just as always." He started to walk away, but remembering he was a gentleman, he stayed by Susanna's side. Taking her by the arm, he said, "Wait a minute, Senator. I'll help you get her to the table."

As discreetly as he could, Ben guided Susanna through the crowd. He nodded to some of his friends who knew the history of Ben and Susanna and he smiled politely at others who called out greetings of "Looking good, Ben" and "Evening, Senator."

"My poor darlin' Susanna," the older man said as he looked at her half-closed eyes and smeared lipstick that ran a staggery path from her mouth to her chin. "Whatever can we do?"

"We?" Ben asked. A look of incredulous disbelief flickered in his eyes.

"You heard me, son. You know what responsibility means."

"Yes, Senator, I do. As we all know, I've never shirked my duty."

Susanna, tipsy and somewhat subdued, ignored Ben, who held her left arm. She turned and moaned, "Oh, Daddy, thank goodness, you're here. Ben can be such a pill. What's a poor girl like me supposed to do?"

Ben's cheeks colored as he took charge of the situation and said, "Don't worry, sir. I'll handle Susanna."

Big Jack coolly studied Ben's expression, but then he relented when he saw Ben put his arm around Susanna's tightly cinched waist. "Okay, son, but if she needs me, I'll be right over there," he said as he nodded toward a party of four. "I need to talk to those folks about a campaign donation."

Ben shook his head disapprovingly. Seeming resigned to his fate for the evening, he sighed and held a chair for Susanna at the table marked with their reserved place cards.

"It's your fault, all your fault," Susanna wailed drunkenly. "You've done this to me." Then she rolled to her right and waved to a man with grey flecked hair who ambled toward her. "Trey, Trey LaBlanc, come here, darlin', and kiss my lips."

"My princess, my secret love," Trey replied as he seated himself beside Susanna and acknowledged Ben's presence with a sly grin. "Tell me what's wrong, Susanna," he said, his deep voice rich with concern.

"The same thing that's always been the problem; it's him, Ben Collier," she whined as she stared coldly first at Ben and then toward the powder room.

Trey produced a fat cigar, lit its tip, and leaned back in his chair. Puffing away, he looked down the front of Susanna's dress and proclaimed, "It's gonna be a good night. The scenery doesn't get much better than this."

Susanna coughed, fanned her face, and pointed to an ashtray. "Not if you don't put out that vile cigar, Trey LaBlanc."

Trey quickly extinguished his Juan Clemente and reached for Susanna's bejeweled left hand. He nibbled on her fingertips and said, "Is that better?"

"Hmm, gettin' there, but we'd oughtta stay on the lookout for that mean woman you call your wife," she answered with a pout as she positioned her body closer to Trey's and leaned forward.

Once again, he leered at Susanna's inviting decolletage, licked his lips, and said, "Oh yes." Then he glanced at Ben and sat back in his chair.

"Yes what, darlin'?" Susanna cooed. "If it's Ben you're bothered about, you should just forget he's here. He's nothin' to worry over," she added, nodding toward Ben, who now stood at attention as a woman dressed in pink and pearls walked toward their table. "Uh oh, here comes your ball and chain. She looks like a bee headed to the hive. Come on, quick, let's talk about you and me before she butts in."

"Bad timing, Susanna," Trey replied. "Pamela hasn't been very understanding as of late."

Susanna snorted her reply, "You're a fool, Trey, if you think for one moment she cares a feather about you. See how she's holdin' Ben's hand. Bet she's thinkin' about more than his glove size."

Trey frowned and relit his cigar.

"Oh phooey, Trey. Why do you fret so?" Susanna huffed. "Anyway, the more important issue is me, so tell me what you think I oughtta do about Ben."

Trey shifted his position and advised, "You and I both know everybody has bad days and nights. Why don't you give this one a rest and let Ben off the hook."

"That's easier said than done," Susanna said with a slur. She glanced about for a waiter and complained, "Where's a man with a bottle of champagne when I need him?"

Trey took her hand and adopted a brotherly tone as he said, "Please, Susanna, cut Ben some slack and watch the booze. Do it for me. And for yourself."

Susanna watched Trey through her eyes made red and hazy from smoke and alcohol. Smiling, she softened her voice and answered with honeyed charm, "Why, suga', you're such good medicine for me, but you'd better give me a real hug and a kiss. I've missed you so."

Trey shook his head and coughed nervously. "Better not, Susanna. After all, I am a married man," he said and then whispered, "but there's no denying I've always been in love with you." He stroked her hair and patted her hands.

Ben shielded Pamela's eyes from the sight of Trey with Susanna and reassured her, "Don't believe what you see. I'm sure Trey's intentions are pure. He only wants to help Susanna get through a bad night."

When Pamela shrugged her shoulders and looked away, Ben caught Senator Delaney's eye. Motioning for him to take his place at their table, Ben frowned as Big Jack, the consummate politician, continued to work those seated close by.

"Like father, like daughter, one in the same, all show," Ben mumbled as he studied a centerpiece made of magnolia blossoms and golden ribbons he knew Susanna had ordered special delivery from Mississippi. Even though he was well acquainted with her many faults, he still had to give her credit for her talents as a hostess. No one in all of Florida could top a Susanna Delaney affair. He knew that firsthand.

As the other guests began to find their designated dining tables, Ben toyed with his card that bore the #3. He wondered who else Susanna had chosen for dinner guests at their table. He counted the chairs, eight, and thought, well, there's Susanna and the Senator and his date, if she shows, myself, Trey and Pamela, and two more. I wonder who...hmm.

Ben's question of *who* soon turned into *why* when he heard a rustle of taffeta and saw a glimmer of ruby red headed his way.

Expecting to hear Desiree say, I hope you enjoy tonight, Ben, because tomorrow may not be as much fun, he smiled his brightest and braced himself. He could stand whatever she planned to deliver. In fact, he was looking forward to a match with Desiree, word for word and look for look. Too bad, though, he wasn't as equally well prepared for the quiet voice that stilled the night.

Instead of Desiree setting the time of a hearing, it was a pretty young girl who served notice as she strode forward and said, "Hi, Momma. Hi, Dad. I want you to meet somebody. This is my new friend and her name's Desiree."

Ben turned and the sight before his eyes caused his jaw to drop and his brow to sweat. In front of him stood Linnea, dark-haired and blue-eyed, the mirror image of her mother. Behind Linnea, Desiree waited, her eyes filled with questions Ben wanted to answer, but he didn't know where or how to begin.

# Chapter 4

Desiree stormed around Beverly's desk like a disoriented homing pigeon in territory that seemed familiar but still not quite right. After scanning the incoming data, she skimmed through the "Out" box files that held sediment reports from Bayou La Batre to Cedar Key.

"If you'd like some coffee, it's over there," Beverly said. "It's decaf with a kick, kind of like some of those high powered herbal teas Jeff said you're famous for." When Desiree didn't respond, she added, "Of course, I really don't know what he meant, but he said your recipes flew sky high from Pensacola to Miramar."

"Is that so?" Desiree replied. She wondered what other details about her Jeff had chosen to reveal. She'd always kept her personal and professional lives separate, but now she worried that her colleagues in Boulder had picked up on the one unresolved part of her background she thought she'd successfully concealed.

Brewmistress of teas she didn't worry about, but she feared knowledge of the love affair of her life blown out of proportion could carry disastrous results for Nature's Way's involvement in the Heron Bay project. Under no circumstances could she allow the authorities in power to believe her motives stemmed from bitterness and not from environmental responsibility.

Praying, please let the past be behind me now, she watched Beverly bustle around the office and wondered how fast the gossip mill worked in Tallahassee.

"Here's a taste of juniper java. Try it," Beverly said as she handed Desiree a cup filled with hot coffee.

"Thanks, I think," Desiree answered with a wary smile. She reached for a file of seismographic readings and maps of potential drilling sights in the Gulf and said, "I may need more than an infusion of faux caffeine to help me sift through this oil and gas company propaganda."

"That's the truth, for sure," Beverly said. "Exploration's a hot topic with the conflict going on between tourism and the energy industry along the Florida and Alabama coastlines. Which side do you think will win the contest?"

Angrily pacing around Beverly's desk, Desiree answered, "There won't be any winners as far as I'm concerned. Throughout the world, fragile and endangered areas of natural beauty are diminishing at an alarming rate."

Beverly pointed to an opened file cabinet whose drawers bulged with folders. "See that? Those are just a few of the impact studies we've compiled."

Running her hands through her hair, Desiree nodded and said, "I'm sure they substantiate what happens when companies come in with their drilling rigs, pipes, and paraphernalia. Time and again more of our natural landscape falls to the greed of those few who reap the rewards."

Beverly frowned and said, "It's tragic to see what's happened in Alabama to Mobile Bay and to the Gulf from Dauphin Island to Fort Morgan. Florida's probably the next frontier to go."

Desiree drained her coffee cup and looked out a window that faced Maclay Gardens, freshly bathed by a soft morning shower. Raindrops glistened on the borders of azaleas and camellias that shone like jewels in the sun. The sight struck a chord in Desiree.

She gestured toward the bright blue sky filled with puffy clouds and said, "Beverly, what we're dealing with here is more than an issue of aesthetics. It's a tragedy that's played out daily in the board rooms of huge corporations that are backed by foreign investors."

"I understand all you're saying, but what can be done?" Beverly asked. She pointed to another stack of data on environmental issues and shook her head. "Look at what's on the schedule for next week. More analysis and little action."

Desiree's eyes filled with tears of frustration. Waving her hands as though they were magic wands, she said, "I wish I had the answer, but I don't. One thing's a fact, though. We must do everything we can to save the beauty that's left because once it's gone, it's history. We've got to send a message to all developers and to all industrialists that America's wetlands and coastlines are off limits. What's happening isn't exploration; it's exploitation. A disaster that must be stopped before it's too late."

Energized by her thoughts, Desiree walked to the telephone on Beverly's desk, lifted the receiver, and dialed a number.

Beverly sat on the edge of her chair and asked, "Who are you calling?"

"We need to stop one entity at a time, so I'm starting with the current issue at hand."

"Heron Bay?"

"That's right. The Heron Bay project and its developer are at the top of my list," Desiree answered.

Under her breath, Beverly muttered, "The builders' reception must not have gone very well."

Desiree heard Beverly's comment but didn't have a chance to reply because someone came on the line. As she listened to the same voice she often still heard in her dreams on restless nights, she twisted the phone cord into a jumbled mess.

"Hello, Ben, this is Desiree." She waited and then she smiled, no longer playing with the cord. Instead, she picked up a pencil and rolled it between her thumb and forefinger.

"Yes, last night was an evening to remember, but that's not why I'm calling."

Leaning closer to the desk, Beverly inched her way toward the phone and reached for the speaker button. Mouthing, I need to hear this, she touched the phone's base, but that was as far as she got because Desiree placed her hand over the telephone and moved it far from Beverly's reach.

Into the receiver Desiree spoke firmly, "I agree we should talk." After a pause, she added, "Fine, I'm at the Nature's Way office. What's that? You don't know our location here?" She stopped and looked at Beverly for help.

Jumping to her feet, Beverly scribbled directions on a pad of recycled paper and held it in front of Desiree.

Squinting at Beverly's tiny handwriting, Desiree explained, "The office is in a renovated house off of US 319. It's close to the State Gardens." Tapping her pencil against her cheek, she added, "All right, if you really feel the need for neutral territory, I will meet you in town."

Beverly and Desiree rolled their eyes and sighed in sisterly camaraderie as Desiree listened to Ben's suggestion.

"Sure, a restaurant downtown is fine, but you're picking up my cab fare. Do you have a problem with that?" Desiree asked with a smile and then she said, "Yes, I'm still very health conscious." Unable to resist the opportunity, she added, "As well as environmentally aware." Then she rang off by saying, "Send the cab and I'll see you at Chez Pierre in about an hour. Oh, by the way, I'd like to review the aerial site photos you submitted to the federal permitting agency last week. Could you bring along a set?"

Hanging up the phone, she turned to Beverly and said, "Well now, we're set for the initial inquiry on the Heron Bay project. Is there any other information I need to know before I meet with Mr. Collier."

Beverly brushed her braided hair off of the back of her neck and studied the pattern of the floor.

"Well?" Desiree prodded.

Walking to the hanging files in the back of her office, Beverly sorted through the top level and pulled down a dozen folders.

"What are these?" Desiree asked as Beverly handed the files to her.

"Mr. Collier has lots of friends in high places. These documents tell the story of his connections from the Statehouse on down."

Desiree frowned and asked, "Why wasn't I informed about the deep pockets of his cronies? Someone in your department fouled up. I don't like going into a meeting unprepared."

Beverly recoiled from Desiree's insinuation and replied, "Look, I'm sorry we didn't get this to you sooner, but we usually respond through other channels. Had we known you were coming to Florida to conduct the review, we would've revised our protocol to fit your needs. I wish Jeff had advised me of your interest earlier."

Paging through a sheaf of reports as Beverly continued to explain her staff's position, Desiree stopped when she came to a section devoted to Senator Delaney and Susanna. Worrying once again she'd been too harsh in her criticism of Beverly's efforts and needing to study the papers she now held, she politely dismissed Beverly by saying, "You're right. I should've given both you and

Jeff some forewarning, but there's no harm, no foul since the data's here and my meeting's set with Ben, I mean, Mr. Collier."

"I hope you're a speed reader," Beverly said as she excused herself to allow Desiree time alone. Shutting the door behind her, Beverly shook her head and raced for the mapping office downstairs. There the staff maintained a pantry of real coffee and Little Debbie snack cakes, as well as a free fire zone for conversation that was too good to keep behind closed doors.

"Anyone ready for a break?" Beverly asked. She pushed open the door and made her way inside an area partitioned off by four plasterboard cubicles.

"Sure," "of course," and "always" came the answers rapid-fire as Beverly's colleagues turned away from their desks and headed to the break area.

As Beverly waited for the group to gather, she rinsed out her mug shaped like a fish and checked the coffeemaker. Catching the scent of Wings and seeing the youngest woman in the office come toward her, she said, "Hello, Celeste. I'll freshen the coffee if you'll send out for the donuts."

"I'm three steps ahead of you," Celeste replied as she tucked her long blonde hair behind her ears. "The work table's cleared, the sugar and cream are out, and the donuts arrived twenty minutes ago."

Beverly frowned and seeing her other friends, Deb and Elinor, head toward her, she called to them, "Okay, tell me why you let Celeste order so early? The donuts are probably cold by now."

Celeste laughed and said, "Maybe so, but Deb's news sure isn't."

"What's that?" Beverly asked. She reached for a can of Folger's and a measuring spoon.

Deb leaned against a counter, took off her gold-rimmed glasses, and rubbed her eyes. "It was a night and a half," she said. She stiffled a sleepy yawn and paused before she added, "You should've been there to see it."

"Well, I wasn't, so tell me what happened?"

"Are we alone?" Deb asked. She looked cautiously over her shoulder.

Beverly put one hand on her hip and answered, "Of course we are. Who'd you expect?"

Elinor, who wore a bright scarf wrapped gypsy-style around her waist, answered, "Her, you know, the boss. Ms. McAndrews. She isn't coming down here to check on our progress, is she?"

"No, I don't think so, at least not this morning."

Deb snickered and smiled devilishly. "I'm surprised she even came into the office at all, considering the big night she had at the reception."

"Tell all," Celeste said as Elinor and Beverly leaned forward so as not to miss one juicy detail.

Deb's eyes widened as she shook her frosted hair and took a deep breath. "Well, I was seated at the table directly behind Ms. McAndrews, so I had a clear view of everything that happened."

"How'd you get an invitation to the reception? The Builders' Council sent over only one guest ticket and that was for Ms. McAndrews," Beverly said.

Deb shrugged her shoulders and huffed, "She wasn't the only one invited to the party, you know. I guess you haven't heard, but I'm seeing Billy again, you know, Billy as in Bubba & Billy's Fine Home Construction. So last night I went to the party as his date."

"Well, well," Beverly said with a sigh and a shake of her head. "I hope you know what you're doing, Deb. Anyway, go on. Tell us what happened."

"I don't know where to begin; there's so much to tell."

"What did she wear?" Celeste asked.

"I can answer that," Beverly interrupted. "After all, I was the one who went shopping with her at the mall. In fact, I helped her pick out her outfit at Dillard's."

"Oh, I see," Deb replied. "Well anyway, I thought her red dress was pretty."

"Yeah, pretty short," Beverly interjected.

"That, too, but she looked really nice, kind of doll-like with her blonde hair, blue eyes, and fair complexion."

"She'd better stay out of the sun while she's here," Celeste commented. "We blondes have to watch, you know."

"Yeah, especially bottle blondes like you," Elinor teased. "Sorry," she quickly apologized when Celeste frowned.

"That's enough, you two," Beverly said. "Let's get back to Desiree."

"When did you get on a first name basis with her?" Deb asked.

"It's no big deal, really. She's friendly, down to earth, and actually approachable most of the time. I think I like her," Beverly replied.

Deb laughed loudly. "You're not alone. She's got another admirer, big time."

"Who's that?" Elinor asked.

"Ben Collier, that's who," Deb announced with a dramatic pause. "He proved that last night."

"What happened?" Celeste asked.

Deb motioned her friends to come closer as she whispered, "Even Billy, who's not easily surprised, was shocked to see what Mr. Collier did."

"Oh?" Beverly asked, putting down her coffee mug and tossing her half-finished donut into a trash can beside the table.

"Right there in front of everybody, and I mean everybody, including all his Navy buddies, his wife, and even Senator Delaney." She caught her breath and exclaimed, "I couldn't believe my eyes! Ben Collier got down on his knees and begged Ms. McAndrews for forgiveness. Then before she could say a word, he kissed her."

"With Susanna Delaney and the Senator watching? He actually kissed her? Oh my!" Elinor squealed with delight and then she lowered her eyes and her voice and asked, "What kind of a kiss was it? A peck on the cheek or more?"

Deb placed her hand on her heart and said solemnly, "As God is my witness, I saw Mr. Collier plant a big one on her to beat the band, if you know what I mean."

"Did she kiss him back?" Celeste asked. She toyed with a strand of her hair and licked her lips.

Her eyes bright with excitement, Deb answered, "Oh yes, with feeling. I'm talking major passion here. It was unbelievable!" She rubbed her hands together and leaned back on her heels.

"Something's wrong here," Beverly said and then explained, "Only thirty minutes ago I heard Desiree on the phone with Mr. Collier and she acted all business, not as though she had any sort of a relationship going on with him."

"That's not the way it looked to me and the entire Florida Building Council last night," Deb huffed.

"I know you're telling the truth, Deb," Beverly said. "I'm just surprised, that's all. But now that I think about it, Jeff, you know, my friend in the Boulder office... " She blushed and cleared her throat before continuing, "Jeff did mention that when Desiree first heard about Heron Bay, she ordered a standard inquiry into Mr. Collier's plans, but then for no apparent reason she changed it to a preliminary hearing she would personally oversee."

"Well, there you go, that's it," Elinor said.

"That's what?" Celeste asked as she looked from one woman to another.

"Desiree McAndrews has more than an environmental interest in Collier Development. She has an ax to grind, but what a way to sharpen it. Maybe she plans to love him to death," Deb concluded with a hearty laugh.

"Yeah, if Susanna Delaney doesn't finish him off first," Elinor commented.

"What a way to go," Beverly said. "A man held at the mercy of two women, one a brunette and the other a blonde, fire and ice on the stairway of love."

"That sounds like my Billy's greatest fantasy," Deb said as she rolled her eyes toward the ceiling.

"Excuse me," Celeste said, "but I have some questions."

"What is it?" Elinor asked as she adjusted her scarf over her skirt.

Celeste raised her eyebrows inquisitively and said, "I'm curious about his family life. I've seen his picture in all the papers, and I wonder why he's never photographed with a wife or kids in the background? And where's his wedding ring? Do you think maybe he's single?"

"Lots of married guys don't wear wedding bands these days. Mr. Collier may be one of those," Beverly replied, crinkling her nose in disdain.

While Elinor and Beverly debated the point, Deb finished her donut, waited a second or so, and then regained control of the conversation by saying, "Well, I don't know if he's still with Miss Delaney or not, but I am positive it was their daughter who broke into tears when Ms. McAndrews sat on Mr. Collier's lap."

"She did what?" Beverly asked.

Deb flashed a smile as wide as Kansas and said, "You heard me. Like a bird in a nest, she snuggled right into that handsome man's lap. That's when Miss Delaney passed out. The sight had to be too much for her to bear."

"Oh dear," Beverly said.

"Oh dear's right," Deb replied. "And when the Senator saw what'd happened, he screamed bloody murder at Mr. Collier and charged around the table to revive his daughter. All the while the little girl pulled on Mr. Collier's sleeve and cried buckets, wailing, 'No, Dad, no.' Any fool could see the poor child's heart was breaking."

Beverly winced at Deb's description and said, "That's terrible."

"I'm not finished. There's more," Deb said, lowering her voice. "After Mr. Collier and Ms. McAndrews kissed and kissed some more as though they were the only two people in the room, they snatched up the girl and stormed out of the reception without even so much as saying good-bye or boo. Poof, they were out the door, gone."

"No!" Celeste said. "The paper said Mr. Collier was supposed to be the featured speaker."

"Believe me, talking wasn't on his mind. Kissing Ms. McAndrews was," Deb said, clapping her hands in glee. "It was a show and a half; you should've seen it." When none of the women spoke, Deb turned to Beverly and asked, "So what do you think of Ms. McAndrews now?"

Beverly loosened her braid, fluffed out her hair, and replied, "I think there's more to Ms. McAndrews than Jeff knows and he's worked with her for five years or more. I wonder... "

"Wonder what?" Elinor asked.

"I probably should touch base with him, you know, just to see what Desiree told him about the reception. She said she called him when she got to the office this morning."

"Before you came in?" Deb asked.

"Yes, that's right. But now I'm wondering where she spent last night." Winking suggestively, Beverly added, "Desiree didn't say, but I think I may know."

"Where is she now?" Deb quizzed as her eyes darted nervously toward their office door that faced the hallway. "What was that sound?"

"I didn't hear anything," Elinor replied, but Beverly disagreed by saying, "I did; it came from outside. It's probably just a car door closing."

Celeste moved to a window that faced the street. She looked down and waved her arms frantically as she said, "Come here, quick! I think Ms. McAndrews is getting into a car. Look at that! What a taxi!"

Elinor, Beverly, and Deb jockeyed for positions at the window. Whistling, Elinor said, "That's not a taxi, but it doesn't look like a limo either. What kind of car is it anyway?"

Deb nudged her out of the way for a better look. "Goodness, me. That's a Rolls-Royce Silver Cloud and look who's behind the wheel."

"Who?" Celeste asked.

"Mr. Bennett Collier, all hunky 6'2" of him. My, my," Deb said, whistling even louder than Elinor.

Beverly put her hands on the window and squinted her eyes for a sharper view. "But they're not alone. There's somebody else in the backseat."

"*Somebodies* is more accurate," Deb observed. She stood on her tiptoes and balanced herself by placing her hands on Celeste's shoulders.

"Who is it, Deb?" Beverly asked.

Looking down in disbelief, Deb answered, "As I live and breathe, it's Susanna Delaney and the young girl who went to pieces last night. Oh to be a fly on that rearview mirror."

"I'm calling Jeff this very instant. He's got to know something about this," Beverly said as she left Elinor, Deb, and Celeste standing with their noses pressed to the window.

"My goodness," Deb said as she watched the shiny sedan pull away from the curb and blend into a long line of traffic.

"This sort of thing never happens at Nature's Way," Elinor said.

Wide-eyed, Celeste replied, "But maybe it's not such a bad thing. I think it's exciting. The mystery, the romance. I wonder what Ms. McAndrews and Mr. Collier are saying to each other right now?"

"Or doing?" Elinor asked. She smiled and turned away from the others. As she began to straighten up the break area, she added, "I guess we'll never know."

Reaching for a roll of paper towels, Deb dabbed at some coffee stains on the counter and replied, "The answer will be in what happens with Heron Bay. Does anyone care to place a small wager on the outcome?"

Shrugging their shoulders, the women who routinely mapped territories and studied surveys of fault lines along creek beds stood perplexed. They seemed at a loss as to the direction their office would follow with the Heron Bay controversy.

What they didn't know was that Desiree faced her own set of complex issues and for the first time in twelve years, she wasn't quite sure which road to follow. Thinking, the one less traveled, she stared out of the front window of Ben's car that raced toward the center of town.

As the chilly silence in the Rolls reduced to zero any possibility of conversation between the four passengers, Desiree stole a quick glance at Ben. Noting the tension in the set of his jaw, she wished she could read his mind, but then she decided it was probably just as well she couldn't. Before turning away, she dared another look. For only a split second, her eyes met his and she felt his sorrow and his pain cut through her like a knife. Unable to stop her hand, she reached over and touched him.

In response, he floored the gas pedal and the car charged forward, turbo engine roaring and bright chrome gleaming. Susanna shrieked, Linnea sulked, and Ben and Desiree tried to ignore the rhythm of their hearts that now beat as one.

# Chapter 5

Ben turned the corner and when he saw there were no empty parking spaces in front of the Courthouse, he pulled his car into a private lot across the street. He lowered the window on Desiree's side and greeted a guard seated inside a ticket booth that was cooled by a noisy fan and a hint of a breeze. When the man didn't look up from his newspaper, Ben repeated, "Hello, hello."

"Mornin' sir. Good to see you, Mr. Collier," the guard replied with a wave of his sweat-stained Gator's ballcap. "How can I help you and all those pretty ladies you've got with you?" he asked. He nodded to Susanna and Desiree and winked at Linnea.

"I need to stop by the Courthouse for a minute. I won't be inside long," Ben explained as he turned off his car's ignition.

The guard folded his *Tallahassee Democrat* in half and apologized, "Sorry, Mr. Collier, but this lot's already full. Something special must be going on downtown today."

Linnea leaned across the back of Desiree's seat and said, "Excuse me, sir. There's a spot over there. I think it's my Poppaw's place."

The guard scratched his neatly trimmed beard and said, "You're right, missy, but the Senator doesn't like me to park cars other than his in that space." Looking at Ben, he added, "Now you wouldn't want to get me in trouble with Big Jack Delaney, would you?"

Ben pointed to Susanna, who scowled as she fidgeted with her dark sunglasses, and answered, "If the Senator shows up while we're here, just tell him I brought his daughter to town. I'm sure he won't mind."

"Well then, I guess it's okay since you are with Miss Delaney and, and… " The guard stopped in midsentence and seemed at a loss for words. He quickly flipped open his newspaper and scanned the front page.

"And I'm with a friend. This is Ms. McAndrews; she's in town on business," Ben explained matter-of-factly as he started the car and raised Desiree's window. Saluting the guard, he headed his Rolls toward the space marked with a large 59.

"Some friend," the guard remarked and then under his breath he added, "So that's what they call it these days." Out of the corner of his eye, he watched Ben ease his car between two white lines and come to a full stop.

Ben looked in the rearview mirror and studied Susanna's puffed and pouty face. As he straightened his navy and gold striped tie, he ordered, "Best behavior, everyone, and especially you, Susanna. I mean it." Then he opened the door for Susanna, who accepted his helping hand.

She brushed a speck of lint from the sleeve of Ben's jacket and looked at him through her dark eyes that appeared red from crying. Ever the coquette, she blinked her eyelashes and spoke for the first time since Desiree had joined them that morning. With her voice filled with venom, she huffed, "The nerve of you to put me and my precious Linnea in the same car with that woman. Your friend, my foot!"

Linnea shut her eyes tightly and sighed as though she carried the weight of the world on her shoulders. She balled her hands into fists and rested them on her knees. When Ben told her it was time to go, she let herself out of the car and waited for him to come to her side. When he stepped in front of her to open Desiree's door, she grabbed his hand and whispered, "You can't do this to us. Momma needs you and so do I."

"You don't understand, Linnea," Ben answered as he gazed into the distance.

Thick tears welled in Linnea's eyes. Dutifully, she stood aside and allowed Ben to help Desiree from the car.

Unaware of the exchange between Linnea and Ben, Desiree looked at Linnea, motioned toward her, and said, "Come here, Linnea; walk with me."

Susanna bustled her way around the back of the Rolls, stopped inches from Desiree's face, and crowed hatefully, "You think you can have it all, don't you, Desiree McAndrews? Well, I've got news for you, you granola lovin' tree-hugger. You can forget your plans and get out of my town." Swinging her hips, she turned toward Linnea, grabbed her hands, and squeezed them tightly.

Linnea broke free of Susanna's clasp and whimpered, "I hate my life and I hate you."

"That's enough, Linnea," Ben cautioned. "Don't say things you'll regret later."

Susanna sneered and laughed as she added, "Or you'll have to live with the consequences. Isn't that right, Ben darlin'?"

Without answering, he stared straight ahead and marched toward the street. Traffic passing in both directions came to a standstill as he squared his shoulders.

"The evil eye works again," Susanna explained. "You've got it down pat, don't you, Ben?" When he didn't reply, she said, "Maybe you oughtta try it on Desiree. We'd all be better off if she'd go back to wherever the devil she came from."

Ben ran his hands through his hair and prayed for an amicable end to the morning that'd pitted him against the only three women he'd ever really cared about. Standing tall, he focused on what he knew had to be done if he hoped to save his reputation and that of his family. He took a deep breath, reached for Susanna's arm, and said, "Let's cross the street, now."

Desiree followed behind with Linnea, who struggled to keep up with Ben's long stride. Worried Linnea seemed so miserable, so terribly sad, she asked, "Are you okay?"

"I thought we were friends, but last night was all for show, wasn't it?" Linnea answered. She watched Ben and Susanna argue heatedly on the steps leading into the Courthouse, gestured toward them, and said, "See what you've done? I hope you're happy." As she brushed her hair away from her face, she shook a finger at Desiree and asked, "How would you feel if somebody tore up your home?"

Swallowing hard, Desiree denied she'd played any role in Ben and Susanna's marital discord, but Linnea wouldn't listen.

"I don't think you're here on business; you just want to take my dad away from us. That's it, isn't it?" Linnea asked as she tapped her foot against the sidewalk.

"No, Linnea, that's not it at all. I don't like having to disagree with you, but I can't stand here and let you think my motives are dishonest. I came to protect the wetlands your father plans to destroy and that's the truth."

"Oh, I get it. Since Dad wants to fill in some swampy old land, you think it's okay to tear apart our life."

Desiree's cheeks colored, but reasoning that Linnea was a confused and upset child who meant no malice, she calmed her emotions. Determined to ease the tension, Desiree decided to try another approach, so she said, "My job entails protecting the environment and when developers such as your dad file proposals that affect endangered areas, I work in an official capacity to see that Nature's rights are protected. Do you understand?"

"Blah, blah, blah," Linnea replied. She covered her ears with her hands and said, "I can't hear you; I can't hear you." Turning her attention away from Desiree, she watched Susanna repair her makeup with a Q-tip while Ben stood at attention by her side. "My poor, poor family," she cried as she swung around on pointe and faced a row of oak trees that lined a grassy commons area.

From across the street, Ben kept his focus on Linnea and Desiree. Miffed, Susanna tugged on his sleeve and launched into another tirade of his shortcomings, but he quieted her with a look. Then he waved to Desiree and Linnea to come forward. He pointed to the Courthouse door, opened it, and waited for the three women to file inside.

Desiree gasped in pleasure at her first glimpse of the stately foyer; it seemed an oasis from the real world. "An architect's dream," she said as she took in the twenty foot high ceilings and oak paneling along the walls.

"Probably built on top of wetlands," Linnea commented dryly before she stepped back to walk with Ben.

"Linnea," he warned, but he didn't hide his proud smile that stretched from ear to ear. Susanna, though, frowned and cackled loudly at Linnea's remark. Rudely, she offered one ugly comment after another and ordered those in the hallway who'd stopped to stare at her to move on or else.

When the corridor cleared, the Collier-Delaney-McAndrews party made its way across the slate flooring, their footsteps sounding a staccato beat. Without speaking to one another, they passed a row of office areas filled with people who waited in lines to register cars, file deeds, or get fishing licenses.

"Wait a second, I'm saved," Linnea said, breaking the silence as she broke away and ran toward a man standing beside a water fountain. "Poppaw," she cried and then exclaimed, "Am I ever glad to see you!"

"Darlin', darlin'," he replied, hugging Linnea and motioning to Susanna. "Come on over here, Susanna, and give your daddy a kiss." When he saw Ben turn away from the scene, he waved the morning paper at him and bellowed, "Hey, Ben. The least you can do is thank me for not having that whale of a car of yours towed. You oughtta know better than to pull into old 59, that number's mine and mine, alone, son."

"What's he talking about?" Desiree asked Ben, who shook his head and answered, "The Senator takes great pride in the fact that the Seminoles retired his football jersey, #59. Ever since then, he's claimed the number as his own."

"Oh, I see," Desiree said as she watched the Senator charm smiles out of Linnea and polite manners from Susanna. "Love's a true miracle worker," she observed. She tried to keep envy out of her voice. Even so, she couldn't hide the look of longing that haunted her eyes.

"Shoeshine, shoeshine, sir?" called a man wearing tatoos of an anchor on one arm and a woman on the other.

"Excuse me, Desiree," Ben said. "I think my shoes could use my friend Marco's magic touch. How about yours?"

Marco waved his chamois cloth like a flag and called out, "Step right up here, missy. Since you're with Mr. Collier, this shine's on the house. Us Navy guys help each other out whenever we can."

Ben winked his thanks and helped Desiree climb up the stand that held two wooden chairs. "May I?" he asked, nodding toward the empty seat next to Desiree.

"Sure," she replied as she admired Marco's kindly smile. Then she grimaced when Marco frowned at the dry cracks in her shoes and added, "I may be here awhile."

"Awe, I've seen much worse," Marco reassured her as he launched into a spirited rendition of "Anchors Aweigh." Delighted, Ben and Desiree sat knee to knee and hummed along while Marco sang, all three seeming oblivious to the daggers Susanna glared their way.

Marco opened two cans of polish, one oxblood and one brown. "These should work," he said as he matched the oxblood hue to Ben's Italian loafers and then the other color to Desiree's shoes. When Ben gave him the thumbs up sign, he smiled and asked, "So, tell me, sir, what's new? How's life treating you?"

"I can't complain," Ben answered. "The twists and turns keep coming, though, and when least expected." Then he nodded toward Desiree and said, "She's my latest."

"Latest?" Marco asked, raising an eyebrow.

Desiree frowned and asked, "Latest what? Do you care to explain yourself?"

Ben picked up a newspaper from a side table on the stand and fanned his face before replying, "How does challenge sound?"

Thinking, challenge sounds a lot better than conquest, Desiree bit her lower lip and kept quiet. Then she glanced at a picture on the front page of the paper and gasped, "Oh no!"

Marco dropped his polishing cloth, looked at the newspaper, and whistled through his porcelain-crowned teeth. "Well now, missy, that's you, isn't it, in that party picture? But what's wrong with your dress? It looks kind of twisted or something."

Ben grinned at the photo and said simply, "Nice picture." But when Desiree didn't respond, he added, "When I opened the paper this morning, I thought to myself, now that's a photo that'll cause a big stir."

Just then Susanna and the Senator swarmed around the shoeshine stand like carpenter bees on the attack. As Susanna slapped a copy of the paper against her open palm, Big Jack nudged his way in front of her.

"What do you intend to do about this?" the Senator barked. "And what about her?" he added as he pointed toward Desiree and frowned.

"Yes, Ben, tell me about your plan to fix this mess," Susanna shouted and then she whined, "You've really gone and done it this time. How could you pull such a stunt at my country club and in front of all my friends? How could you?"

Linnea stood close by and watched Desiree's face. When she saw tears brim in Desiree's eyes as she studied her photograph in the paper, Linnea reached out for Desiree's hand. Linnea's action didn't go unnoticed by Ben, who leaned forward to stroke her cheek.

Snapping her fingers, Susanna swung around wildly and shouted, "Is there a photographer in the house?" And seeing one approach, she ordered, "Mr. Photographer, get yourself on over here. I'm gonna make a scene that needs to be recorded." Swelling up like a puffer fish, she glared at Desiree and challenged her to a fight. "Come on, you knobby-kneed floozy. Show me what you've got."

"Hush, darlin', I'll handle this," the Senator said as he pulled Susanna to his side. To Ben, he sniped, "See what you've done to my Susanna. You've just about driven her out of her head, you and that woman." Then, lowering his voice and changing his tone to one of pure venom, he added, "I don't give a continental damn about you, but I won't allow you to make a laughing stock out of my Susanna, you hear me, boy?"

Ben ignored Big Jack's comments and returned his attention to Marco. "Thanks for the shines, buddy." He then helped Desiree from the stand and shook hands with Marco, tucking a large bill into the man's shirt pocket as he waved and walked away. To Desiree, he said, "Marco's a good man and he was a brave sailor. He served with me aboard the *Enterprise*. That was the year my life changed."

"Mine, too. How could I forget?" Desiree whispered.

"I never will," Ben answered.

Off to the side, Susanna fumed and said to the Senator, "Watchin' Ben flirt with that hussy turns my stomach." When Big Jack offered her a cup of iced lemonade, she said, "This'll make good ammunition if he dares to kiss that two bit Ms. Wetlands one more time in front of me. I swear I'll, I'll, I'll... "

"You'll no such thing, Susanna," the Senator said, cutting off her threat. "Remember your child's standin' over there with them," he said sternly. "She's already had enough hurt to deal with for one day."

"Of course, you're right, Daddy," Susanna replied and added, "You know how I love my darlin' baby." Pouting, she took a sip of her lemonade, made a sour face, and then begged, "Please, Daddy, let's spike this stuff. I gotta have a little somethin' to take off the edge. You know what I'm sayin'?"

The Senator shook his head and answered, "I'm afraid so, darlin'. We'll get on out of here, but before we go, I need to straighten somethin' out with Ben."

"Good luck," Susanna said with a smile as she patted her hair and smoothed the jacket of her flowered suit. As the Senator walked toward Ben, she called out, "Daddy, tell him you think I'm still pretty as a picture."

"Uh oh, here comes Poppaw," Linnea warned Ben, tugging on his sleeve. "And he looks upset, actually pretty mad."

"So what else is new?" Ben muttered. He turned to Desiree and said, "Stay with Linnea. This won't take long, I promise." When the Senator approached him, Ben jammed the morning paper into his coat pocket and asked, "What is it, Jack?"

The Senator pursed his lips together and made a fist. "Look, Ben. I know Susanna can be a handful, but Tallahassee is her town and she has an image that means the world to her. You're wrong to roll in here from Pensacola and create a nasty ol' fuss. It looks bad, especially when another woman's involved." He stared at Desiree and swore a foul oath under his breath.

Ben took the Senator by the shoulders and replied, "Sir, if you want to help Susanna, you'll quit coddling her. She's a grown woman and quite capable of taking care of herself. As for you, you're a fine one to comment about impropriety." He gave the Senator a knowing look and backed away.

"I'm a respected man who acts responsibly," the Senator huffed as he glanced toward Linnea. "So I think Linnea should go with me and her mother. Susanna needs somethin' to settle her stomach, so we'll sit a spell at Chez Pierre. Are you comin'?"

Ben smiled in Desiree's direction and answered, "Yes, but first I'd like to show Desiree the zoning board offices upstairs."

"Oh? For damage control purposes?"

"Possibly. At least, she'll have a better understanding of our plans for Heron Bay," Ben answered. "So we'll meet you at the restaurant later."

The Senator studied the toes of his wingtip shoes and replied, "All right, then, but don't be long. I have my own agenda today." Chuckling, he faked a punch at Ben's cheek and motioned for Linnea to follow him as he sauntered away.

Desiree waved good-bye to Linnea and although she felt like giving her a hug, she stopped short when Susanna opened the newspaper to the front page and cackled cruelly.

"Such a woman, Ben," Desiree said.

"I thought you forgave me last night," he reminded her.

"Forgiving is easy; forgetting's the hard part," she commented as she walked with Ben.

"Maybe that's something we can work on," he replied. Hope filled his eyes.

"Maybe so," she answered. She turned for a last look at the Senator, who shuffled along with Susanna and Linnea by his side. Linnea dropped behind a few steps, turned around, and called out, "I love you, Dad. Don't forget about helping me with my project. It's due tomorrow."

"Don't fret, Linnea; we'll finish it this afternoon," Ben replied. "Otherwise, your teachers will get after me for keeping you out of school today. I don't need that kind of trouble, now do I?"

"No, sir," Linnea said with a giggle and a parting wave.

Ben watched Linnea for a moment and smiled proudly. He reached for Desiree's hand and said, "Linnea's one fine girl, and in a way I'm glad you two finally met. She needs a strong woman in her life. What do you think?"

Desiree sighed and weighed her thoughts before answering, "Just as I told Linnea a little while ago, I'm here because of the Heron Bay wetlands you've placed at risk. That's the only reason, and when that situation is resolved, I'll catch the first plane back to Colorado. That's where my heart is and where I know I belong." She set her chin firmly and looked straight ahead.

Ben shook his head in denial and said, "I don't think that's true."

"Are you calling me a liar?"

"No, Desiree, but I, too, have a long memory."

"What's that supposed to mean?" she asked as she pulled her hand away from Ben's.

"Only that your cute little nose crinkles right there whenever you fib," he answered. Smiling, he reclaimed her hand and said, "So, like it or not, I can tell you're not telling me the truth." When she uttered a sigh of disbelief, Ben bent down and kissed the tip of her nose and said, "Thank you, nose, for being a trustworthy barometer of emotion and desire."

Desiree laughed and asked, "Do males come equipped with such instrumentation?"

"Want to check me out?" Ben asked huskily and then he caressed her curls that felt like silken threads to his touch.

"No, Ben," she said, brushing his hand away. "We can't go back to the way we were."

Ben frowned and replied, "But we can move forward, together." He searched into the depths of her eyes and hoped he'd find a sign that she, too, believed they had a chance to start anew.

"Ben, Ben," she answered as she looked away, unable to meet his gaze that penetrated the center of her soul. "It's not going to happen; surely you can see that. We're two different people now, and besides, our priorities, our philosophies, make any type of personal relationship between us a total impossibility."

Frustrated, Ben stormed ahead of her and called back, "If you'd forget your philosophy, Desiree, you might actually get a life."

"Like you did, Ben?" she retorted.

He stopped in his tracks and quickly spun around.

Desiree felt her heart flutter when she saw the look on Ben's face. Gone was his handsome smile that reminded her of sunny days and hot, sultry nights. Missing, too, was the diamond-like sparkle in his eyes she'd always loved and still dreamed about.

Suddenly, she wished she could recall her catty words. Wanting to erase the pain she saw reflected through Ben's eyes, she reached out for his hand, but he ignored her gesture and said, "I'm sorry that's the way you feel, Desiree, but I can't blame you."

"Ben, Ben, I... "

Cutting her off, he continued, "You have every right to hate me for the way I treated you. I was wrong and I used poor judgment. For that I apologize, but as long as I draw breath, I'll always thank God Linnea came into my life. Maybe one day you'll understand."

"Listen to me, Ben. It's not about Linnea," Desiree said. She wanted desperately to explain and to close the distance she felt growing between them. Now awakened to the joy of his teasing, his fun, she realized how much she'd missed being with him.

"Look, Desiree, I'm human and human's make mistakes."

"I know that, Ben. I've made my own share."

"Well then, you tell me what we're going to do about it."

She reached again for his hand, but this time he didn't turn away. Instead, he held her hand in his and walked slowly with her toward an elevator at the end of the hallway.

Desiree knew Ben waited for her reply, but she couldn't answer his question right away. Torn by the debate she felt being hashed out inside her soul, she prayed for the courage to make the right decision.

Although her heart whispered, "Go ahead, do it, fall in love again, float to the heavens," her head warned, "Watch out, girl. He'll only break your heart again and leave you behind when the choices get tough."

"Well?" Ben asked as he held the elevator door for Desiree. "What about us?"

When the door closed behind them, Desiree held her breath and surveyed the empty elevator. "We're the only passengers," she commented. "Do you think that's a sign?" She wondered if she should act on the feelings of her heart.

"Yes, Desiree," he answered. "It's a go, a go for us."

She wet her lips and looked into his eyes. Her eyes softened as did his when she placed her arms around his neck and kissed him.

"Desiree, Desiree," he whispered. He held her closely and allowed her to feel his desire.

Just then, the elevator stopped on the second floor and the door creaked open.

Much to Desiree and Ben's chagrin, lights flashed all around them as bright bulbs popped three rows deep and a camera crew from "Eye Witness News" charged forward.

"What the devil do you want?" Ben shouted to an eager reporter, who juggled a microphone in one hand and a pad and pencil in the other.

"Mr. Collier, is it true that you're cancelling the Heron Bay project and forfeiting your investment?"

A writer from the *State Journal* tapped Desiree on the arm and asked, "What is your role in Mr. Collier's decision?" But before she could answer his question, he added another one that caused her cheeks to flame. "Do you realize the impact your interference will have on Florida's development initiative?"

Ben hastily leaned on the "Close" button and cursed as the elevator door shut.

Safely away from the media that seemed more intent on making news instead of reporting it, Ben, red-faced with anger, and Desiree, flushed with surprise, looked at each other and shook their heads. He pushed the "3" button and listened to the elevator's motor hum and then groan. Feeling the car begin its climb toward the top floor, he rested against the back wall and said, "That's a relief."

Desiree smiled and asked, "Whatever on earth was that all about?"

"Beats me," Ben answered and then he said, "I'm beginning to think you're a press magnet. Do you always attract cameras and crowds everywhere you go?"

"No, never."

"Too bad," he replied.

"Why's that?" she asked.

"Because I have something in mind that I think should be recorded for posterity." He drew her beside him and watched her eyes widen.

"Oh?" She shuddered in anticipation as she felt her spirit soar along with her heart rate.

He leaned forward and teased her eyelids with the tip of his tongue. "Tell me, Desiree," he said, "isn't this where we were before that interruption?"

She answered him with a kiss, angel-soft but spiked with fire.

"Desiree, Desiree, how you continue to surprise me," Ben said. Although he was trained to respond to the unexpected in a fraction of a second, he now found himself virtually immobilized by his good fate and even better fortune. Did he dare explore the option his present position provided?

He knew any rash action on his part could carry dire consequences, but even so, he decided the benefit to risk factor warranted his throwing caution to the wind. He reached for the elevator's "Stop" button and pushed it so hard that a bell sounded. As the elevator lurched to a halt, he held Desiree at arm's length, took a deep breath, and asked, "Do you have any idea what you do to me? The thoughts you've put into my head?"

She snuggled against Ben's chest and loosened his tie. Then she unfastened the top button of his shirt.

Drowning in the passion of her eyes, Ben nuzzled her neck and whispered, "Does this mean you've forgiven me? That you still care for me?" When she didn't answer, he said, "Please, Desiree, tell me you believe we have a chance. It's what I've prayed for and dreamed about for a long, long time."

"Oh, Ben," she answered, "I don't think it's possible. You have Linnea and Susanna to consider. They both need you; there's no denying that."

Ben frowned and not caring that he wore his heart on his sleeve, he replied, "Desiree, I beg you. Let me try to win your love again. I promise you won't regret it. You've got to give us another chance."

Desiree felt her body yield and then tense in response to Ben's plea. Torn by the reality of their past and tempted by the dream of a future, she stammered, "Give me one good reason, Ben, just one."

Caressing first her fingertips and then the curve of her neck, he confessed, "Because I love you, Desiree. I always have and I always will."

# Chapter 6

"Now, Susanna, darlin', don't you fret," Big Jack consoled. "Ben'll come to his senses; trust me." Reaching across the table set with bone china and Gorham silver, he handed her a handkerchief to dry her tears.

Weeping softly and hiccupping delicately, she replied, "Oh, Daddy, if only that were so."

Linnea folded her arms across her chest and warned, "I'll make him, Momma. Just you wait."

Susanna dabbed at her eyelashes and checked her appearance in a mirrored wall that ran the width of Chez Pierre. The restaurant was filled with a mix of well-heeled patrons and a few tourists whose attire of open-collared shirts, flowered bermudas, and strappy sandals made them stand out in less than a positive way.

"Plebians," Susanna commented smugly as a handsome waiter approached the table. Staring first at his dark hair he'd slicked back into a ponytail, she then focused on his deep green eyes. "Hmm," she purred and nudged Linnea.

The waiter bowed only to Linnea and then said, "Welcome to Chez Pierre. My name is Etienne and I'll be your waiter." He handed over the day's menu, nodded toward the empty chairs to the right of Susanna, and asked, "Should I remove the extra place settings?"

"No, Mr. Etienne, we're expecting two others any time now," Big Jack replied.

Linnea tugged on the Senator's sleeve and quietly corrected him by whispering, "Monsieur Etienne, not Mister, Poppaw."

Hearing her soft voice, Etienne winked at Linnea and removed the rose boutonniere he wore on the lapel of his heavily starched white waistcoat. "Something special for mon petite mademoiselle," he said as he presented the flower to Linnea.

With her dark eyes dancing, Linnea blushed and said, "Oh, thank you." She held her breath as Etienne took her hand and kissed her fingertips.

"Ahem, ahem," Big Jack coughed and sputtered. "What were you saying about today's specials, boy?"

"Oh, yes, the specials," Etienne stammered. His every look indicated he'd become captivated by Linnea. Spontaneously, he leaned over Linnea and said, "To have a heart-shaped face is rare, but your dimpled cheeks beg for the kiss I would like permission to give you."

"Excuse me, son," resounded a deep voice from across the room. "That's my daughter you're standing way too close to, and I'll thank you to unhand her, now. She's only a child or haven't you noticed?"

Frowning, Linnea fumed, "Oh, Dad, how could you?"

With a quick about-face, Etienne turned and faced a pair of eyes that burned with fatherly intensity. "The beauty belle's papa, I presume," Etienne said as he nodded to Ben and to Desiree, who stood by his side. Etienne took two steps back and allowed Ben and Desiree access to the table.

"Come here, Ben. I saved this spot just for you," Susanna cooed as she patted the seat of the chair beside hers.

Big Jack beamed his approval at Susanna, stood up and grinned at Desiree, and then shook hands with Ben. Out of the side of his mouth, he said, "Tell me, Desiree, don't you think my Susanna's a firecracker?"

Under her breath, Desiree muttered, "She's definitely hot stuff all right, a real crowd pleaser I'm sure."

Susanna pouted and leaned across Ben to get to Desiree. Writhing in her chair, she said, "I heard that! Just who the jim dandy do you think you are comin' to my party last night and snakin' away my Ben? It burns me red hot seein' as how he and I were doin' just fine 'til you showed up and spoiled all the fun."

Ben rolled his eyes toward the ceiling fan that circled above their heads. After counting ten rotations of the oak blades trimmed with gold, he looked at Susanna and said, "Can you please try for a little civility, at least through lunch."

"Yes, let's put last night behind us and make a good show for these fine folks sittin' all around," Big Jack agreed. "It'd never do to have the whole town talkin' unkindly about us, especially not with Heron Bay and election day comin' in the same year. The last thing this family needs is more bad press."

Linnea smoothed the front of her skirt and tilted her head toward the Senator. Lowering her voice, she said, "But, Poppaw, Momma's right. We were doing fine until she came here and stirred everything up." For emphasis, she pointed at Desiree, who glared darkly at Susanna.

Smirking back at Desiree, Susanna seethed, "See, Ben, just like my baby says, this trouble is all that woman's fault; she's done nothin' but make a mess of our plans." Then she added with a bitter sneer directed toward Desiree, "You say you're here on business, but I say your motive is shameful monkey business and Ben's the banana you wanna peel."

"You puffed up bag of big hair," Desiree replied. She tossed her linen napkin on her plate and stood to leave.

Ben took Desiree by the elbow and gently pulled her back to her chair. "Ladies, ladies," he implored, "this is neither the time nor the place for this discussion."

Once again counting to ten, he allowed Desiree and Susanna time to regain their composure and then he snapped his fingers for Etienne to come forward. "Waiter, we're ready to order," he called a bit more loudly than he'd intended.

Etienne warily approached the table and appeared confused as his eyes darted from Desiree to Susanna. "Uh, uh," he started and then seeming uncertain as to which woman ranked highest at the table, he glanced at Big Jack and asked, "Which one is the lady of your house?"

"Susanna, princess, go ahead and tell the lad here what you want for lunch."

"Thank you, Daddy," she said, "but I'm not sure. I have that pageant to emcee next month at Panama City, so I really should count my calories. One of the swimsuit photo sessions is set for the beach, and I know they'll want me in the picture." She sat regally in her chair, wrapped her hands around her waist, and puffed her lips in a kiss blown toward Ben. "I wonder if I should wear my Gottex swimsuit or the gold bikini you brought me from Maui. What do you think, Ben darlin?"

"I think you should order lunch, Susanna," he replied as he opened a menu for Desiree.

"Well, I never," Susanna huffed. "That'll be the last time I ask for your opinion, Ben Collier."

While Linnea and Etienne exchanged embarrassed glances and Ben and Desiree stirred uncomfortably in their chairs, Big Jack patted Susanna's hand and consoled, "There, there, sweetheart, I'll help you. Lunch now, wardrobe later." He studied the menu written in French with English translations printed in parentheses and then turning to Etienne, he said, "My daughter will have the baked salmon." He shifted his glance to Desiree and nodded for her to give her order next.

Still flushed and envisioning Susanna roasted and served up on a platter, Desiree calmed her anger and requested a watercress and almond salad.

"It figures Ms. Seeds and Weeds would pick that," Susanna said with a raucous giggle that caused Linnea to look away and Ben to cast Susanna another warning look.

"Linnea? Are you ready?" Ben asked.

"Yes, baby, go ahead," Susanna said. Taking a closer look at Etienne, she blurted, "You never want to keep a good lookin' man waitin', at least not too long 'cause he might lose interest."

Averting his eyes so as not to stare at Linnea, who blushed crimson, Etienne assumed a look of cool indifference and waited patiently by Linnea's side.

Linnea focused on the menu and then peeked up at Etienne, who busied himself refilling Susanna's and the Senator's water glasses. Linnea nudged Susanna's foot under the table and whispered, "Thanks, Momma, for making me look like a fool. Now what should I do?"

When Susanna shrugged her shoulders, Desiree, who'd overheard Linnea's question, answered softly, "Ask his opinion."

Linnea nodded her head and followed Desiree's instructions by asking sweetly, "Etienne? What would you recommend?"

Seeming pleased with the way Linnea said his name, he smiled and answered, "The tenderloin medallions bourguignon and poularde en brioche are Chez Pierre's specialties."

"Oh, I see," Linnea responded. She frowned as she quickly scanned the menu descriptions that were enhanced with sketches of fat hens, scaly fish, and baby snails.

With his voice neither condescending nor rushed, Etienne added, "I think the mademoiselle would enjoy the beef more than the chicken."

"Sounds good, Linnea," Big Jack said impatiently. "In fact, I think I'll have some of that myself."

As Etienne waited by Linnea's side, he scribbled something on a sheet at the back of his order pad and slipped the message to Linnea. "So?" he asked Linnea. "May I bring you the tenderloin medallions?"

"Thanks, but I don't think so. I'd rather have a watercress salad," Linnea replied as she watched Desiree react to her order. When Desiree's eyes sparkled, Linnea avoided Susanna's frowns and looked away and quickly tucked Etienne's note into her skirt pocket.

"Very well," Etienne said and then he turned toward Ben and asked, "And for you, sir?" When Ben reeled back in his chair and made eye contact with Linnea, Etienne cautiously stepped a foot back from Ben's reach.

Without looking at Etienne, Ben handed him the menu and said, "I'll have the same as the Senator, but prepare mine rare."

Desiree shook her head in disapproval and warned, "You really should watch what you eat. Surely you're aware that red meat poses a major health hazard."

Susanna flipped her hair and leaned across Ben to poke one of her brightly polished fingernails into Desiree's arm. Tossing her head, she said, "I'll have you know that Ben loves my steak tartare." When Desiree remained silent, she added, "In fact, he craves it the most right after we've… "

"Susanna," Ben said, cutting her off.

Desiree frowned, her mind filled with questions and her heart robbed of joy.

"And for your drinks?" Etienne interrupted.

"Iced tea is fine," Ben answered for the party.

"Make mine extra sweet, suga'," Susanna said with a purr and a wink. When Etienne passed through the kitchen door, she smiled at Linnea and said, "He's darlin', Linnea. You should ask him to escort you to your Cotillion Ball this weekend."

"I don't think so, Susanna," Ben interjected. "She's way too young to date. Besides, that guy's probably twice her age."

"Pooh on you, Ben. I make the rules in our house, not you."

Desiree looked puzzled and glanced at Ben. "You and Susanna? In the same house? I thought last night you told me you live in Pensacola and were only in Tallahassee for the builders' meeting."

Laughing and smirking with sheer abandon, Susanna yelped, "Uh oh, I guess I've let the cat out of Ben's bag of dirty tricks and now the mouse wants to run off, but without any cheese. I think that's somethin' I want to drink to. Care to join me, Desiree?" She motioned toward a bartender, who acknowledged her signal with two hastily shaken dry martinis he personally delivered to Susanna in record time.

Taking the martinis, she said, "Put these on Mr. Collier's tab." To Desiree, she chimed, "Ben pays all my bills."

Desiree tried to hide her feelings, but she couldn't stop the pain she felt. As for Ben, he closed his eyes and tried to project himself out of the danger zone he'd entered without an eject button to save his perfectly tanned hide.

"Here, Desiree, you look like you need this more than I do," Susanna said as she slid one of the martinis down the table. Then she downed her drink in one rude gulp and said, "So, granola girl, let me tell you how it is. Ben and I share a house and lots more."

Desiree gasped and studied the martini. Picking up the glass, she rolled it in her hands and stared at Ben who couldn't meet her gaze.

Without skipping a beat, Susanna continued, "I don't know what other lines Ben's fed you, but you'd better watch out if you know what I mean." As she watched Desiree put the martini down and push it aside, she said, "My advice to you, dearie, is to drink up and then move your act to some other place and time. We don't need you here. Our house is full and there's no room in my inn for the likes of you."

"Susanna! Your mother taught you better," Big Jack chided as he glanced nervously over his shoulder.

"Maybe so, Daddy, but I watched her lose you to every blonde, brunette, or redhead who looked your way. That's not going to happen to me. I simply won't have it."

Ben pounded his fist on the table, jarring the silverware and causing tea to spill over the tops of the glasses Etienne had just set on the table. Not caring who heard and filled with rage, Ben shouted, "Tell me, Susanna. How the hell can you lose something you don't have?"

"What?" Susanna sputtered.

"Tell Desiree the truth," he commanded as he reached for Desiree's hands that'd turned to ice.

"Now, Susanna! I mean it!"

"I don't think she'd find the details of our little relationship very interesting," Susanna whined. She grabbed for the martini Desiree obviously had no intention of consuming.

Linnea shook her head in dismay and declared, "The truth will win out." As she watched Etienne send her a wink of encouragement, she took a deep breath and confided to Desiree, "Momma and Dad aren't really married. She just likes to act like they are."

"No, Linnea, that's not quite right," Susanna whimpered.

Ignoring the warning wave of Susanna's open hand, Linnea continued, "But my dad stays with me whenever he's in town and he does pay our bills 'cause Momma says work's for peasants, not queens."

"I don't understand," Desiree said. She searched the depths of Ben's eyes for the truth she desperately needed to hear.

"Last night meant the world to me, Desiree," Ben said.

When he put his arm around the back of Desiree's chair, Susanna cackled, "I've heard that!"

Desiree moved out of Ben's reach and replied, "I've been such a fool. Will I never learn?" Memories of the night before flooded her mind. She shuddered when she relived the sensation of falling headfirst into Ben's arms and heart first into his kisses. Although she'd called on each neuron and every cell of her body to stop her from making the same mistake twice, she'd given up the fight, and instead, she'd teased, tempted, and nearly seduced the man she'd sworn she'd never love again. "Oh no," she said, "Oh no, oh no."

Watching Desiree's discomfort and seeming to enjoy the scene, Susanna sniped, "Twice burned by the same man has got to be hard to take." She reached into a silver breadbasket, selected a croissant, and picked at its flaky crust. "You know what, Desiree?" she said. "This roll reminds me of you. See how it kind of falls apart when it's touched in its soft spots. I guess that's how you feel right about now." She smiled into Desiree's face and shook her head in mock sympathy.

Ben silenced Susanna with one harsh word and tried to make Desiree understand that all he'd told her had come straight from his heart. "You've got to hear me out, please, Desiree," he said, but she wouldn't allow herself to have any part of it.

Willing herself to remain strong, she tried to cast her present situation into its proper perspective. "Help me maintain my dignity; oh, please, dear God, please make me strong," she prayed. Perhaps as an answer, she heard a tiny voice in her head tell her to think about Heron Bay, think about osprey nests, think of anything or anyone except Ben Collier.

With her eyes shut, she pictured Colorado 72, the Peak-to-Peak Highway above Nederland. The image of snowbanks and evergreens soothed her psyche, and she began to feel stronger and very much in control. Supported by her mental images, she soon believed she could carry through with the Delaney-Collier luncheon, get a hearing date scheduled for Heron Bay, resolve the issues, and then head straight for home.

Ben, determined to right the wrongs of his past, nudged Desiree and asked, "Are you all right? Please say something." He inched toward her and stroked her hair that glistened like gold.

Smiling serenely as her new found peace comforted her soul, Desiree knew what she had to do. Compromise was out of the question, so she opened her eyes and leaned forward to kiss Ben good-bye. But when her lips touched his, she felt her heartstrings tighten and the rational voice in her head succumb to silence. She froze on the spot, unable to follow through on her honorable intentions. She couldn't kiss Ben farewell. Instead, hello became the message of the moment.

It was only Linnea's pitiful squeak of "Dad, not here, not now!" that stopped Ben and Desiree from excusing themselves from the table and hailing the first taxi to heaven's door. With reluctance, Desiree and Ben parted although their hearts drummed a primitive beat neither could ignore.

"Later, Desiree," Ben whispered into her ear. "I promise I will make you understand."

Still filled with fear for her heart and torn by Linnea's tear-stained face and the terror she saw in her eyes, Desiree shook her head. She knew she and Ben couldn't roll back time. It was too late for them, in fact, twelve years too late.

Ben, on the other hand, tossed caution to the winds of fate. He'd lost Desiree once before, and now with her by his side, he, unlike Desiree, didn't worry about his heart or much else for that matter. He loved Desiree and that was all that counted. Unaware of Desiree's divided emotional state and protected from prying eyes by the tablecloth, he rested his hand between her knees and went for broke.

His touch, his look, his sheer bravado sent chills through Desiree. "No, Ben, you're making this too hard on me; you must stop," she demanded as she reached for his hand to still his soul-shaking march along her inner thigh.

In response, Ben's eyes spoke the loaded question: Who's doing what to whom? And then with uncharacteristic abandon, he moved Desiree's hand across her lap to his.

Taken by surprise at his brashness and his marvelous masculinity, Desiree felt her eyes widen and her mouth form strong words of protest, but none came out.

Ben put his head next to hers and said, "You still carry the power of a ten alarm fire, Desiree McAndrews. Let me flame it higher."

She couldn't bring herself to face the others at the table, so she shielded her eyes with her free hand and repeated a silent mantra, No way, not now, not ever; no way, not now, not ever. She knew she shouldn't risk loving Ben again, but the feelings he'd awakened in her were a powerful force to combat.

How she wished she could forget the closeness they'd shared the night before, the glory of the stars and the way they'd twinkled bright and beautiful when Ben had carried her to his balcony that overlooked a valley rich with night sounds and thousands of fireflies. Deep inside, she felt her body quake with the memory; it was so real and so alive that she could still taste his kisses that'd transported her to a happier time.

"Desiree, Desiree," he said, smoothing her brow with his hand. "Let's find somewhere private, somewhere... "

Before Desiree had a chance to reply, Linnea broke the magical moment. She pitched her napkin in her plate, stood on her tiptoes, and asked, "Dad? What are you doing?"

Susanna, wild-eyed and well-oiled, lifted the tablecloth for a peek at the show going on underneath the linen and lace. "Oh my goodness!" she yelped and then she fumed, "Ben Collier, you'd better stop that right now!" She swatted at the table and promptly ordered another martini.

The Senator raised his eyes prayerfully to the textured ceiling and said, "Bless my soul and don't let these insane people cost me the election!"

Acquiescing to the family's protests, Ben folded his hands on the table like an altar boy and confessed to Desiree, "I haven't been completely truthful, I... "

"Hush, Ben, hush. No explanation's needed," she answered. She knew now for certain that the road less traveled was the only one she must follow. She could not, no, she would not, allow her feelings for Ben to take precedence over her common sense. That way no one could get hurt, especially not Linnea, an innocent child.

"Desiree, listen to me. I didn't tell you everything last night. There's more."

"Hush, Ben! Some things are best left unsaid," Susanna fumed.

Deciding that she'd heard enough, Desiree centered herself and let her mind digest the events that'd transpired. She hated that their luncheon had taken such an unpleasant turn. Ben versus Linnea and then Susanna versus herself, the bottle, and more. How sad, she thought. She wondered if she meditated doubly hard on only good deeds and positive outcomes, would her efforts bring a sense of stability to all of Chez Pierre? Go for it, her mind called, and so she did.

Her plan seemed to work because within minutes silence settled around Desiree's table and the other diners soon returned their attention to roasted lamb, puffed potatoes, and creamy desserts.

Relishing in the peace of the moment, Desiree breathed a sigh of relief, but the quiet abruptly broke. From inside the kitchen, she heard Etienne call out, "Coming through, coming through."

The door that separated the kitchen from the main dining area swung open as Etienne cleared the way for Chef Pierre, who proudly led a parade of waiters carrying silver trays laden with haute cuisine.

Big Jack ambled to his feet, saluted the chef, and then slapped the man on the back, saying "Viva la France! Viva la France! And God Bless America!"

"Sit down, Daddy. You're creatin' a scene," Susanna said, bleary-eyed and speech impaired. "That's their specialty, not yours," she added, pointing dramatically at Desiree and Ben.

Ben frowned at the accusation, but not wanting to inflame the situation, he reverted to a considerate gentleman mode and helped Susanna with her plate of salmon decorated with cauliflower hearts and mushrooms stuffed with garlic and parsley butter. "Taste this; food always helps."

Thinking, *food calms the starving beast*, Desiree wondered what on earth Ben had ever found so attractive about Susanna.

"I can't eat this bad food," Susanna wailed as Ben fed her first a bite of salmon and then a mushroom cap. "Egad, Ben! What are you tryin' to do? Poison me?"

He frowned and muttered, "Oh Susanna, don't be ridiculous. You know better than that." When she remained quiet for a minute, he helped her with a sip of water and then suggested she try the cauliflower.

While Desiree toyed with her salad and Linnea followed suit, Big Jack wolfed down his lunch and leaned back in his chair, a picture of contentment. "They make a nice couple, now don't they?" he asked Desiree.

"Excuse me," she replied.

"My Susanna and Ben, that's who, of course," he replied. "Surely you can see the way he takes care of her and how much she relies on him. Then, of course, there's Linnea. She loves her momma and respects her dad more than any child I've ever seen."

Ben's frown deepened at the Senator's words. He knew their negative impact on Desiree would sound bells on any sailor's scale of sinking ships, especially his.

As if on cue, Desiree excused herself from the table and turned toward the powder room.

Linnea watched Desiree weave her way through the crowded restaurant. When she was out of sight, she clapped her hands and declared, "Well, Dad, it looks like it's just you and me again. Maybe you should move here. We could have so much fun."

"Now, Linnea, you know that isn't our arrangement."

"It could be if you'd let it."

"Linnea has a point, son," Big Jack agreed.

Susanna perked up at the thought and whined, "But what about me? Where do I fit in this picture of family bliss?"

Ben shook his head and lowered his voice as he said, "No, Susanna, no."

"Why not?" she whimpered.

"You know the answer to that," Ben replied.

"You ol' stick of stone," she muttered.

"What did you call me?"

"You heard me, Ben, and I'm not sorry because I'm right. You're rigid and you're rotten, as well."

"Look here, Susanna, you're the mistress of extortion and the destroyer of dreams and you know exactly how you ruined my life. Someday maybe you'll tell me why, but for now, just please butt out," Ben concluded as he searched the restaurant for any sign of Desiree.

Susanna cried and hiccupped and cried some more. So many tears flowed like rain that she took on the appearance of a waterfall. "Ben, Ben, you don't mean that. I need you, and Linnea, our darlin' Linnea, she does, too."

Linnea covered her ears and closed her eyes. Then without saying a word, she slipped away and dashed for the powder room. Finding Desiree talking on the telephone, she sat beside her on a Victorian bench covered in burgundy velvet.

As natural as the sunshine on a clear day, Desiree reached out and took Linnea's hand. She hung up the phone and studied Linnea's sweet face that looked pinched and tired. "Do you want to talk?" she asked.

"Yes, Desiree, yes," she replied. "I've lots to say and I hope you'll listen."

# Chapter 7

Surprised and flattered that Linnea had turned to her, Desiree said, "I'll be more than glad to help you, but you should clear it with your parents first."

Linnea frowned and replied, "I would, but this isn't a good time to ask them. They're not in much of a talking mood."

Thinking quickly, Desiree nodded toward the telephone on the cherry credenza and said, "You could always call them at their table. They could probably use a break about now." She pictured the scene going on inside the restaurant and shook her head at the thought of Susanna waving a fork in one hand and a martini glass in the other while Ben stared off into space.

"Okay, I'll do it," Linnea said as she walked toward the phone. Taking a deep breath, she picked up the handset and pushed the number for the maitre d' stand. On the third ring, she heard, "Thank you for calling Chez Pierre. This is Etienne; may I help you?"

Linnea held her hand over the receiver and whispered to Desiree, "It's him, Etienne, the cute waiter. What should I do now?" Nervously, she twisted the phone cord and waited for guidance.

"I'll handle the call if you want me to," Desiree answered.

"Oh, thank you," Linnea replied as she handed Desiree the phone.

Thinking, nothing's sweeter than puppy love, Desiree gave Linnea an encouraging wink and asked if Etienne would deliver a message to Ben.

"What's he saying? Will he do it?" Linnea asked. She danced toward the phone but stayed far enough away so her voice didn't carry.

"Yes, Etienne, that's right. I was with that party earlier, but something, uh, uh… , what I mean to say is that I have a business matter to attend to, so I won't be returning to the table. Please give Mr. Collier my regrets."

Flushed, Linnea motioned to herself and said, "Me, me. What about me?"

"Oh, just one moment, Etienne," Desiree added. "Miss Delaney's daughter, Linnea... yes, that's right; Linnea's the pretty mademoiselle with dark hair."

Linnea's eyes opened wide and then wider still as a gleam of ecstasy flickered across her face. "He's talking about me?" she whispered as she held her heart and collapsed in a mock swoon against a chintz covered wall.

Distracted by Linnea's antics, Desiree laughed and then added, "Anyway, Etienne, please tell Miss Delaney that her daughter asked me to help her with a school project, so she plans to work with me this afternoon in the Estuary Office. She'll call from the Courthouse when we're finished. Did you get all that?" Desiree tapped her fingernails against the phone base as she listened to Etienne repeat her message.

"Thank you very much," she said and started to ring off, but then she paused and added, "Excuse me, Etienne. Did you say something else?" She listened and then replied, "Okay, I'll ask her." Covering the handset, Desiree motioned for Linnea to come closer.

Linnea waved her hands frantically, shook her head, and said, "No, no, I can't come to the phone."

"He only wants to know if you read his note," Desiree explained. Then she covered the mouthpiece and asked, "Did you?"

Desiree didn't have to wait long for an answer as Linnea's deep blush gave her away. Adopting a serious tone, Desiree said, "Etienne, I believe Linnea read your every word." After Etienne spoke awhile longer, Desiree smiled at Linnea and said, "Sure, I'll be glad to give her the rest of your message."

Before Desiree could straighten the phone on the credenza that also held notepads embossed with Chez Pierre in golden script, she felt Linnea's hands on her shoulders. Turning around, she asked, "Yes?"

"You've got to tell me everything he said, now," Linnea commanded, suddenly looking not nearly as distressed as she'd appeared to Desiree only moments before.

Desiree reached for Linnea's hands and pulled her closer. Looking straight into her eyes, she said, "Your dad and your mother may not approve of me telling you this, but Etienne said he thinks you're prettier than any model he's seen in France or in Florida. He also said the number he gave you is his and he wants you to call him if you'd like to meet one of his friends who's a fashion photographer for *Elle*. He believes you have a future modeling and he wants you to consider a photo shoot."

"No way! You're making this up!" Linnea said as she backed away from Desiree and took a closer look at herself in the dressing table mirror. Disdainfully, she turned up her nose at her school uniform of a plain cotton skirt and a simple blouse with a Peter Pan collar. "Models don't dress like three-year-olds. I've got to get some new clothes. Will you go with me? Please, Desiree, please say you will."

Desiree massaged her temples, considered her options, and then said, "You should discuss this with your mother. After all, isn't she the fashion consultant in your house?"

"Well, yes, but Momma doesn't understand much beyond bathing suits and evening gowns for competitions. You know what I mean? But there is my dad. Maybe he can help."

Shuddering at what she thought Ben would say about Linnea's needs for a trendier, more adult wardrobe, Desiree asked, "How long do you think your dad would last at a mall?"

Linnea put her hands on her hips and answered, "Half a second. That's why he has personal shoppers at both Saks and Steinmart."

"No wonder he dresses so well," Desiree replied.

Linnea nodded her head and said, "I think he's handsome. Do you?"

Desiree felt her cheeks color and she looked away. Sensing, though, that Linnea wouldn't let the matter rest without an answer, she replied, "Yes, your dad is very good looking, quite handsome, in fact."

"Do you think I look like him?" Linnea asked. She stood at arm's length from Desiree and struck a stern military pose.

Giggling, Desiree hugged Linnea. She looked so precious and fragile, a young girl about to blossom into a beautiful teenager.

"Well? Do I?" Linnea persisted.

Desiree studied Linnea's profile, her dark hair and eyes that now twinkled with mischief and charm. She considered hedging her answer, but then she decided Linnea deserved the truth, so she replied, "Yes, I see a definite resemblance to your dad, but actually, I think you look more like your mother."

"Oh, I see," Linnea said as she sat back down on the velvet bench and emulating Desiree, she crossed her legs primly and folded her hands in her lap. "That's what everyone says. I was hoping, though, that since you're close to my dad you might see him in me."

"Oh, I do," Desiree replied and explained, "I only meant I see your mother's beauty in you. That should make you happy, not sad."

Linnea turned toward Desiree and took her time framing her words. "It's this way, Desiree. Pretty is as pretty does and beauty's only skin deep."

"Yes," Desiree agreed as she gave Linnea a nod of encouragement to express her feelings.

Pointing to her head, Linnea continued, "Believe it or not, Momma's got a brain. She's really smart and great at judging situations and acting the way she's expected to. She's also pretty when she wants to be and our house is full of proof. I bet we've got a thousand or more photos of her wearing her Miss Florida crown."

"That's a lot of pictures," Desiree said, thinking she'd be hard pressed to produce even a snapshot of herself other than the one on her driver's license.

"Momma loves cameras, but I want to be like my dad, strong, silent, and good inside and out, all the time, not just when photographers show up."

Listening and realizing that although she was probably reading her own interpretation of Linnea's household into the girl's words, Desiree felt she understood Linnea's needs, fears, and dreams. She took a risk and asked, "Are you worried that if you agree to the model shoot, you'll become just like your mother?"

Linnea nodded and answered, "I think so, and if I do, then I'm afraid Dad won't love me anymore because I'll be more like her and less like him."

"Oh, Linnea, Ben would never turn from you. I've seen how much he adores you."

"Really?"

Desiree reached out to Linnea and answered, "Yes, really. In fact, after we took you home last night, your dad told me about the morning you were born when he was overseas on an aircraft carrier. He said he'd never been prouder to know he had a beautiful little girl waiting for him to come home."

"Dad told you that?"

"Yes," Desiree replied as she reached for a tissue to dry Linnea's eyes that'd filled with tears. What she didn't tell her, though, was the rest of the story Ben had shared with her in the middle of the night.

She could still hear him say, "When Susanna asked me to name the child, I chose Linnea in honor of you, Desiree, the incredibly beautiful woman who taught me about Linnaeus, botany, and the world of wildflowers. It was my way of making Linnea our baby, yours and mine." The memory of Ben's sweet confession caused tears to brim over from Desiree's eyes.

"What's wrong? Why are you crying?" Linnea asked as she tried to wipe away Desiree's tears.

"Oh, nothing, really," Desiree answered. "I was just thinking about how much your dad loves you, a fact that will never change."

"Even if I become a model and not a Navy pilot?"

"I'm sure your dad wants you to choose a career that makes you happy."

Linnea leaned forward and said shyly, "That's what I think he wants for you, too. I can tell he cares about you."

"Hmm, that's interesting, all things considered," Desiree replied as her eyes flashed sparks and then softened.

Linnea picked up a notepad and a pen, handed them to Desiree, and said, "Write down your address and I'll send you proof."

"Proof of what?" Desiree asked.

Linnea sighed impatiently and nodded toward the notepad. "Go ahead and give me your address, that is, if you're not afraid."

"What are you talking about?" Desiree asked, becoming quite curious.

"I said I have lots to tell you, but maybe you should see for yourself."

"I already have," Desiree answered. Her face clouded when she thought about Susanna's big house on the hill, her beauty queen photos plastered on every wall, and her bedroom with mirrors all around.

Linnea shook her head and said, "Never mind then. I guess we'd better leave."

"Yes," Desiree agreed and added, "otherwise, we'll be working on your project until daybreak. Why did you wait so long to get started?"

"It wasn't my fault. Dad was supposed to help me this week since Momma was busy working on the reception he didn't want to have anything to do with. He didn't even plan to go, but then all of a sudden, he changed his schedule and got involved in the party. That's when he said my project would have to wait until today."

"And now the day's half gone and you still don't have anything to turn in tomorrow."

"My teacher's going to be real mad since I missed class today to work on it, and if I get a bad grade, which I probably will, then Momma will flip out when she's called from school."

"What about your dad?"

Linnea huffed her reply, "He's so preoccupied right now I doubt he'd even notice."

"I think you're mistaken, Linnea. You're first in his life; he told me that," Desiree said, remembering the way Ben's voice softened whenever he spoke of Linnea.

"When did he say that? 2 a.m.?" Linnea asked. Her voice sounded weary and worried. "You were still with him then, weren't you?"

Desiree blushed and confessed, "Yes, I was."

Watching Desiree closely, Linnea said, "I knew you were going to stay with him," and then she huffed, "I may be only twelve, but I know my dad and he wasn't acting like my dad last night. He couldn't wait to drop me off at the house. That was because he wanted to be alone with you, right?"

"Linnea!" Desiree protested.

"Where'd he take you?"

Desiree thought, almost to heaven, but she answered shamefully, "To a suite at the Killearn Inn."

Linnea's eyes widened and her mouth opened in horrified surprise. "My dad took you there? To his company's suite?" She stepped back from Desiree and stared at the floor.

"Yes, Linnea, but nothing happened. That's the truth."

"Oh sure," Linnea answered, shaking her head and sighing heavily. "You can say what you want, but now I know why Dad looks so tired today and acts worse."

"It was a late night; we talked for hours," Desiree explained.

With a touch of anger in her voice, Linnea asked, "On his bed? You slept with the man whose career you plan to ruin? And if you do that, who's going to pay for my college education?"

Desiree avoided Linnea's eyes as she thought, I can't believe I'm being called on the carpet by a twelve-year-old. She paused and struggled with her dilemma. Should she reveal the entire truth to Linnea or should she offer a partial fabrication? She decided honesty was the best policy, so she answered, "My relationship with your dad goes back to before you were born. You may not believe this, but last night we had lots of catching up to do. We just talked, that's all."

"Where'd you sleep then? And what about your clothes? What happened to your red dress?" Linnea asked rapid-fire.

Feeling her temper flare but then considering the special bond between Linnea and Ben, Desiree counted to twenty and answered, "I slept in his bed, alone; he stayed on the sofa. As for my clothes, I changed them early this morning at the Nature's Way office."

"Why are they so wrinkled?"

Almost losing her patience, Desiree retorted, "Because I only brought a few changes with me from Colorado. Believe me, if you'd been stuffed in a bag with file folders for a trip cross country, you wouldn't be all pressed and perky, now would you?"

"Oh, I see," Linnea replied thoughtfully and then she added, "I guess you'd better shop for some clothes, too, when we go to the mall. You're still going with me, aren't you?"

"A promise is a promise, Linnea," Desiree said, wishing Ben had kept his promise to her long ago. "But I don't think I'll need many new outfits since I'll be leaving Florida soon."

"Really?"

"Yes, as soon as I testify at the Heron Bay hearing, my job here will be finished and I'll return home," she explained. She tried to still the emotional pull she felt on her heart.

"I see," Linnea replied. "Well then, we'd better go on over to the Courthouse. I'd hate for you to change your plans like my dad did."

"Oh, Linnea," Desiree huffed.

"Oh, Desiree," Linnea mocked in reply.

Giggling like kindred spirits, Desiree and Linnea linked arms and slipped out the front of Chez Pierre without being detected by either Ben or Etienne, who'd stationed themselves as lookouts on either side of the coatroom door.

\* \* \* \* \*

Linnea led the way through the Courthouse door and up a flight of stairs. Desiree followed behind and took note of the various commissioners' offices and storage rooms filled with maps, charts, and boxes stacked to the ceilings.

"Over here," Linnea called as she pointed to a closed door.

Admiring the handpainted Division of Fish and Wildlife sign Linnea indicated, Desiree started to open the door but hesitated. She thought she recognized the voice she heard on the other side. "Wait a second, Linnea," she said, leaning against the door to listen. After a few minutes passed, she said, "I think I've met that man."

"Who?" Linnea asked, seeming about out of patience. "We don't have all day, you know," she reminded Desiree. "Let's go on in."

Desiree quieted Linnea by putting her finger to her lips. She dug into her purse for a particular business card and finding it, she said, "Listen to this," and then she read, "Tip Carlisle, Commander, U.S. Navy, Retired. Geographic Information Specialist, Department of Conservation, State of Florida."

Just then, she felt the door swing open and she looked up. In front of her, Linnea walked toward the receptionist's desk.

Beaming a look loaded with confidence, Linnea said, "Hello, ma'am, I'm Linnea Delaney, a student at the Foxcroft School. You may know my grandfather, Senator Jack Delaney. He spends lots of time here at the Courthouse." She smiled at the woman and upon receiving a kindly nod, she pointed to Desiree and explained, "And that woman over there is Desiree McAndrews from Colorado. She's working against a project my dad, Ben Collier, is planning, but we're all friends anyhow and she's helping me with a science project. That's why we're here." Out of breath, Linnea glanced at a watercooler in the corner and said, "Excuse me while I get a drink. She can tell you what I need."

Desiree started to explain but was interrupted when an older man dressed in a tan and green uniform stepped forward and said, "So we meet again, Ms. McAndrews. This is a pleasure."

"Aren't you the gentleman who sat beside me on the plane from Atlanta?" she asked. "You're Mr. Carlisle, right?"

Linnea shouted at Desiree from across the room, "Poppaw calls him Commander, being military and all that, you see."

Raising her eyebrows, Desiree apologized, "Excuse me, sir, I mean, Commander."

"I don't stand on formality, Ms. McAndrews," he answered gently. "These days I answer to Tip."

"Then Tip it is, and please call me Desiree."

"With pleasure, Desiree. Now with the introductions out of the way, tell me how I can help you and this fine young woman," he said as he opened the door to an inner office and waved Desiree and Linnea inside.

"Wow!" Linnea exclaimed as she viewed his collection of photographs that captured the beauty of maritime forests, salt marshes, and sandy beaches. "These are neat, so natural, so… "

"So endangered," Tip completed her sentence and shook his head sadly. "Remember our talk on the plane, Desiree?"

Nodding her head, Desiree walked to a seascape collage and answered, "Of course, I remember, that and your offer to help me target unprotected areas. But the deadline for action is nearing and I'm afraid we may already be too late."

Off to one side of Tip's office, Linnea tapped her foot impatiently and picked up a push-pin that'd fallen to the floor. She walked to a map tacked on the wall and studied it for a second. "Here's my target area, Desiree." Taking aim at the Florida panhandle, she stuck the pin into a large circle marked "Endangered" and said, "Give me all the information you've got on this place so we can get out of here."

"Excuse me for a minute," Desiree said to Tip. Quickly she signaled Linnea a look that screamed, Mind your manners, young lady.

Defensively, Linnea whined, "But my time's running out." Her tone became almost livid with brashness as she added, "You're not the only person around here with a deadline." Pausing dramatically, she eyed first Desiree and then Tip before asking, "So, what is it? Are you two going to help me or not?"

Tip whistled and commented, "Little missy, I can tell you're a true Delaney, through and through."

"Genetics don't lie, do they?" Desiree commented as she walked toward Linnea, who'd picked up a colorful brochure she'd found on Tip's desk.

Linnea flipped it open and said, "This looks like you, Desiree. But why's your picture here?"

"Because she's the fire behind the Nature's Way storm," Tip answered. He handed Linnea a Sierra Club magazine and said, "Sometime you should read in here about Ms. McAndrews. She's a very important person on the environmental battlefront."

"That's what my dad said," Linnea replied, flipping open the magazine. "But he didn't tell me she had a title and all that."

"All that what?" Desiree asked.

Linnea skimmed through the article and said with a smile, "Well, now, if this stuff is true about you and your work, then I guess you're sure to help me get an A on my project." But then her expression changed to a frown when she added, "That is, if I don't lose points for lateness."

"All right, Linnea, let's get to work," Desiree said with an exasperated shrug. She tried to remember her mindset at age twelve and wondered if she'd been as demanding then as Linnea was now.

"So, Miss Delaney, tell me what sort of information you need for your project," Tip said as he opened a metal filing cabinet stuffed with brochures and pamphlets that described hiking trails and camp sites.

Linnea sifted through the materials and turned up her nose. "I don't think these are what I'm looking for. I want my project to be original, not just a collection of outdoor places people should visit on their vacations."

"I have an idea," Desiree said as she pointed to the spot Linnea had marked on the map. "You've included the Maritime Bay Estuary in your target zone, so you could study the ecological impact of the estuary system on the Northern Florida community."

"I can do that?" Linnea asked. "In half a day?"

"Sure, if we get busy," Desiree answered. "And if you're willing to work hard."

"Maybe I can get an extension for my project," Linnea replied as a deep frown creased her brow.

"I don't think so," Desiree replied. She sorted through a box of leaflets and said, "Deadlines are given for a reason, you know."

"I bet if Dad called my teacher, he could get things changed for me."

"But Dad's not going to do that, not this time" came a stern reply from the outer office.

"Dad!" Linnea called as she spun around and greeted Ben with a bright smile. "Am I ever glad to see you."

"Why's that, princess?" he asked, striding forward to shake hands with Tip. He tried to catch Desiree's eye, but she remained engrossed in the message of a memorandum Tip had just handed her.

Linnea stamped her foot impatiently and said, "Dad, I'm talking to you." When she regained his full attention, she said, "I'm in a mess because Desiree came up with a project for me that'll take days, maybe years, to complete, and I only have until tomorrow to get it done." Linnea raised her hands heavenward and said, "I need a miracle."

"That's not quite right, Linnea," Desiree said as she looked up to find Ben staring at her. She wondered why now he seemed so relaxed and unburdened when only a short time before he'd appeared tortured by guilt and chained by shame.

"Tell me about it," Ben said, walking toward Desiree. "What do you have in mind for Linnea?"

"Wait a minute, people," Linnea interjected. "It's my project, so I think I'm the one who should talk about it."

"She's right; it's her call," Tip agreed. He sat down behind his desk, opened a book of detailed drawings and folded his arms in anticipation. "I bet she can read these sediment maps better than our soil scientists out in the field."

Ben moved closer to Desiree and winked at Linnea. Proudly, he said, "My Linnea's something, isn't she?"

"Yes, she's very special," Desiree answered.

Ben smiled and now standing beside Desiree, he added, "She's one of a kind. Much like you."

Feeling Ben's nearness and the touch of his thigh against hers, Desiree breathed more rapidly. She shifted her position to the right, but her progress was stilled by Ben, who first glanced at Tip and then at Linnea to see if either was watching.

Thinking, thank God for relief maps and water levels, he listened while Linnea quizzed Tip about storm runoff and drainage patterns. Then, he leaned forward and whispered, "Don't move, and please, don't push me away. This feels too right."

Desiree closed her eyes and rested against Ben. She wasn't about to admit the truth to him, but at that moment, she knew she didn't have the power to walk away. As though her body had entered into a conspiracy with her heart, she felt perfectly content to stand still and let Ben have his way with her.

As Ben nodded his encouragement to Linnea, who continued her inquiry into the issue of saving natural resources through environmental awareness, he massaged Desiree's back and dropped his hand lower.

"Ben, oh my," Desiree said in a hushed tone that she wondered if Ben would interpret as either, "Yes, yes, don't stop" or "No, no, not here, not now."

As if in answer to her thoughts and no longer caring about who might see what, he continued his loving exploration of Desiree's curves.

Desiree felt her body respond to his touches. Lost in the moment, she drew a complete blank when Linnea looked up from Tip's sea of maps and asked her to define wetlands.

"Wet, wet," Desiree started, her mind reeling with agonizingly incredible thoughts of Ben caressing her au naturale and au so wildly. "Wildlands, oh, no, I don't mean wildlands. I mean wetlands, that's it, wetlands," she corrected herself. Valiantly, she fought the sensations Ben continued to send through her that were so vibrant she felt her head swim and her resolve soften.

"Yes, Desiree, tell us about wetlands. How wet are they?" Ben teased, but only Desiree got his message.

She willed herself to step clear of Ben's reach, but as she moved forward, he wrapped his hands around her waist and pulled her against him.

"Oh, Ben!" she exclaimed. She spun around quickly and locked her eyes with his. At that moment she felt herself fall under his spell.

He held her glance but didn't speak. Discussion was unnecessary for he'd made his point perfectly clear. His need for Desiree matched hers for him, and before long, he knew they would dance to the rhythm of love.

Out of the corner of her eye, Linnea watched Ben hold Desiree and then she glanced away as she said to Tip, "I think I have enough information, sir. If my teacher likes my project, will you come to my class to help me explain the biology parts?"

"Sure, but I don't think you'll need me since Ms. McAndrews is an authority on the subject."

Linnea cut her eyes toward Desiree and said, "Well if that's so, then tell me why someone as smart as she's supposed to be can't tell a wetland from a wilderness?"

Ben laughed and releasing Desiree, he said, "Believe me, Linnea, Desiree knows the difference." Lowering his eyes to take in Desiree's tempting figure that was heaven sent and designed for pleasure, he added, "Desiree's just a bit confused right now; jet lag's caught up with her. All she needs is some quality time in bed."

Desiree felt her cheeks color as an image filled with Ben's raw passion and her heated desire flashed through her mind. Struggling to control her racing heart, she retorted, "I'll thank you not to make excuses for me, Ben." She smoothed her hands against her skirt and added, "Besides, I don't require much sleep."

Ben raised an eyebrow as if to say that's good news and then he laughed shamelessly.

"What's so funny, Dad?" Linnea asked. "Are you feeling okay? Maybe you need some water. Your face is red. And so is hers."

Tip looked baffled, Linnea showed deep concern, and as for Ben and Desiree? They kissed once lightly and then as deeply as they dared.

"Oh, no," Linnea moaned and then she wailed pitifully, "This is just what I need, my dad in love with a woman who's not my mother. I know I'm about to become a statistic and that's not good."

Unable to ignore Linnea's whimpers, Ben came up for air only long enough to cast her a reassuring grin and to salute Tip. Then he returned to the job at hand with a joyous heart. Lovingly, he embraced Desiree, the woman of his dreams, once lost but now found, alive and well and ready to soar with him like a missile on a course labeled *Eternity* and a mission called *Desire*.

# Chapter 8

"Can somebody down there get that blasted phone? It's hurtin' my head and I'm havin' a hard enough time thinkin' straight," Susanna bellowed to her maid staff. The longer the telephone rang, the angrier she became. "What's wrong with your hearin'? Don't you understand English?" she asked, raising her voice to the level of a howling fish wife. When no one answered either her questions or the caller, she rolled over on her side and snatched at an antique Mediterranean telephone.

She stretched forward and feeling only the wooden top of the nightstand, she muttered, "Phooey," and then called out, "Who moved the stupid phone out of my reach?" When no one replied, she growled sleepily, "It was probably that new maid the cleaning service sent over. She obviously can't hear worth beans and, of course, she 'speaka no English' either."

For a while Susanna listened to the phone's shrill ring and after counting to twenty, she sang in a childlike soprano at the top of her lungs, "Ring on, ring on, I don't give a fig. Whoever's callin' is a fat, ugly pig." Her message must have failed to carry any weight with the caller because the phone continued to ring.

"Hush up, phone!" she shouted into a pillow. "I'm not movin' so quit ringin' in my ears." Abruptly, the ringing ceased. Susanna sighed and said, "Good, they gave up, 'bout time." She snuggled deeper into her pillows and drifted off to sleep.

Five minutes later, the phone rang again. Susanna raised up on one elbow and groaned, "I'm not believin' this." She struggled to sit up in her brass bed, but then she fell flat on her back. As her head sank into her nest of fluffy pillows, she moaned, "Everybody knows my naptime's sacred, so who could be callin' and spoilin' my beauty rest? Maybe if I pretend I can't hear it, that awful ringin' will stop."

She covered her head with another pillow and shut her eyes tightly, but when the phone continued its persistent ring, she roared, "This'd better be good or I'll really pitch one."

Lurching sideways, she pulled the nightstand toward her and grabbed for the phone, but her aim was off, so she only succeeded in overturning a hurricane lamp and a crystal carafe filled with lemon-flavored water. She gasped and watched in horror as a yellow stream splashed and then dripped to the floor.

"So much for Ben's Persian rug," she wailed as she reeled in the phone cord and wrapped her hand around the receiver. Before speaking into the phone, she pressed the handset against her cheek and surveyed the mess she'd made.

"Well now, that's one fine howdy do; look at that big ol' puddle. Too bad for the person who put all that stuff in my way; that's gonna cost somebody a week's pay," she fumed as she raised the handset to her ear and slurred into the receiver, "Who's this?"

"Susanna? You don't sound like yourself. Did I wake you?"

"Who's callin' me?" Susanna demanded as she toyed with the edge of her flowered bedspread trimmed with ribbons and lace. She glanced at her fuzzy image in a mirror, made a face, and then finger-teased her hair into place while she listened to the caller's answer. Licking her lips, she said, "I don't recognize your voice, darlin', but I kinda like the way you sound, all male, sexy, too."

"Susanna, it's me, Trey. Surely you couldn't have forgotten me after all we did last night."

"Trey LaBlanc, sweetie pie, why if I'd known it was you on the other end of this line, why I'd have raced to answer your call. You're just the best boy in town." She pinched her cheeks and studied her image in the mirror. Admiring the color of her pink negligee against her skin, she smiled and listened to Trey's reply.

"Ooh, Trey, I do love it so when you talk like that. Say it again, pretty please?" she begged as she reached for a tube of icy pearl lipstick. While she renewed her lip color, she giggled and said with a laugh, "The way you do go on. You're one amazin' man, Mr. Trey LaBlanc." Fanning her face, she added, "Oh, yes, we will have to do it again, soon."

Then she asked, "What's that you just said, suga'? You know I remember every little and big thing we did. Why are you askin'? Was I bad or somethin'?"

She laughed again at his reply and said, "Maybe I wasn't wild enough, but I know for sure I'm better on a bad night than that cold stone Pamela is on a good one. That's why you're callin', isn't it? You wanna see me again, don't you?"

Half-listening while she studied her ankles, she suddenly frowned and then howled into the phone, "Why that little McAndrews witch? I can't believe she pulled it off. Oh, mercy me, Ben'll have a cow when he hears this! Promise me, Trey, that you'll let me give him the news." No longer taking time to preen in front of her mirror, Susanna made plans to meet Trey for dinner the next evening and rang off.

She lunged around her bedroom and dug under a pile of evening clothes she'd tried on and then tossed haphazardly across the floor. Muttering, "Where'd I put that phone number Daddy gave me? It's gotta be somewhere in all this mess," she flung a yellow chiffon strapless gown over her right shoulder and hurled an emerald green one toward a fainting couch Ben had given her as a parting gift years before. Digging through frilly lingerie and dozens of pairs of pantyhose turned inside out, she cursed a blue streak when she snagged a nail on a camisole decorated with purple sequins.

With a sigh of defeat, she made a mat out of her rejected silks and satins, fell into it, and held her head in her hands. "If I could only think. If only I didn't feel as though I have two heads." Raising her eyes to the ceiling, she prayed, "Please, please quit the poundin'. I promise I'll never drink again, at least not as much, if only you'll make my head stop hurtin'."

She closed her eyes, curled into a ball, and tried to rest, but after tossing and turning for about half an hour, she gave up and willed herself to concentrate. Suddenly, she shouted, "My shoes, my dancin' shoes! Of course, that's where I hide all my secret numbers. How silly of me to forget?"

She reached under a chair for the beaded pumps she'd worn to the builders' reception and dug into the toe box of the right shoe. Laughing, she jumped up and waved a scrap of paper high above her head. She danced a shaky jig around her bed and screamed, "Ah ha! Too bad for nature girl. She's in for a surprise, and I'm not even gonna bother gift-wrappin' her present."

Eyeing the now empty carafe that'd come to rest by the side of her bed, Susanna said, "I dub thee, Desiree," and then she kicked the carafe with great disdain. When she heard it shatter against a baseboard, she smiled and gracefully sidestepped the soaked center of the rug as she made her way to a huge closet.

She maneuvered around stacks of discarded clothes and said, "Thank goodness for maids! This room is one sorry mess!" Her eyes followed the path of soiled clothes she'd strewn from her dressing room to her bath. Focusing on her jewelry chest, she headed for its deepest drawer where she stashed bags of Hershey kisses, boxes of caramel corn, and a carton of Salems, along with a diamond tiara from Tiffany's.

"Umm, chocolate, yummy," she said as she unwrapped one of the candies and popped it into her mouth. Then she fished in another drawer for an ashtray, a book of matches, and an opened pack of cigarettes. Saying, "A puff or two of menthol won't hurt," she lit a cigarette, inhaled deeply, and stared at a newspaper she'd tossed on the floor.

She picked it up for a closer look and said, "Well now, that's some picture of the two of them." She held her cigarette mere inches from the paper and said, "I wonder how Ms. McAndrews would like to have a little hot ash dropped on her face. I bet Ben wouldn't think she looked like such a doll with a big ol' smudge right between her eyes." She flicked an ash on the photo and smeared it with a vengeance. "That's much better," she said as she admired the ruined picture. Then she snuffed out her cigarette and yawned lazily.

Turning her attention to the photo's caption, she read aloud, "Who's the new woman in Ben Collier's life? Word has it that the mystery lady from Colorado was the belle of the ball at the Builders' Gala held last night at the Lands End Country Club. How interesting, though, that the event was planned and hosted by Tallahassee's own beauty, Miss Susanna Delaney, a woman who never settles for runner-up. Hmm, more later."

In a rage, Susanna ripped the photo from the paper and tore the party picture in half as she walked to her dressing table. She reached for a pin cushion and selected a hatpin the size of a knife. Positioning the pin in the middle of Desiree's head, she drove it home and shrieked, "Talk about brain pain, you swamp kissin' bag of bad memories. You'll pay for stickin' your ugly puss back in my Ben's face."

She smiled at her handiwork and reached for the other half of the photo. Studying Ben's face, she said with a deep purr, "Tiger man, you're about to become my lover again. Just you wait. You'll see what fun we're gonna have. Linnea, too, she'll be oh, so happy." Tracing his lips with her forefinger, she added, "It's for the best, darlin'. You'll feel no pain, only pleasure, the kinda pleasure I give best."

She lowered the front of her filmy negligee and placed Ben's photo next to her heart. "That feels better already," she said with a sigh as she stood and took another look at herself in the mirror. Smiling at her image, she said, "Radiant as a rose" and turned to pick up the telephone. As she placed her call, she laughed loudly and cruelly and then she waited, but not for long.

"Thank you for calling Nature's Way. This is Celeste Kulhaney. How may I direct your call?"

"Suga', this is Susanna Delaney. I'd like to have a word with Ms. McAndrews."

Celeste's eyes widened as she glanced at the morning newspaper and gushed, "Oh, I'm sorry, Miss Delaney, but Ms. McAndrews is out of the office. Is there anything I can help you with? I'm one of your biggest fans."

"Why you sweet thing, you," Susanna said. She smiled and patted her hair into place.

"It's true. I've followed your career ever since we met a few years ago at the Santa Rosa Community Center."

"Is that so, darlin'?" Susanna cradled the phone under her chin and reached for an emery board to smooth her one rough fingernail.

"Yes, Miss Delaney, I'm sure you don't remember me, but we talked for a while backstage in a dressing room." As she talked, Celeste reached for a notepad and scribbled "Susanna Delaney, pretty woman, well connected."

"Dressing room, you say?" Susanna asked as she cocked an eyebrow and nodded her head approvingly. "That must've been when I judged either the Miss Seaside pageant or was it Miss Sailboat Bay?"

Celeste flipped her blonde hair and answered proudly, "I was a finalist in the Miss Seaside competition my freshman year at Pensacola Junior College. I'd only made it to the Florida Junior Miss semifinals before, so I was thrilled."

Susanna bobbed her head and said, "Well, now, that's a fine accomplishment. So many people don't realize how tough pageant work is. They think it's all makeup and lights, but you and I know differently." Then she hesitated for a second before asking, "How'd you finish?"

"First runner-up," Celeste answered. When Susanna didn't reply right away, she quickly added with a frown, "My swimsuit was a bad fit."

Susanna clucked sympathetically and consoled, "That's somethin' I worried about when I first started competin', but the more pageants I entered, the better I got at fixin' those nasty little problems that can cost points. When I went to Atlantic City as Miss Florida, I made sure Daddy packed my beauty bag with Vaseline and a spool of wire, just in case."

"Wire?"

"Underwire support, baby, for fuller cups. Any beauty queen worth her crown knows an uplifted figure's gonna score more than a flat front! I can still remember the heads I turned when I strolled down that runway." Susanna turned sideways and studied her image in the mirror. Frowning, she said, "Hold on, suga'" and put the phone down. She made a slight upwards adjustment, smiled, and mumbled, "That's better," but when she let go, gravity kicked in. "Humph," she muttered as she reached for the phone and asked, "What were we talkin' about, darlin'?"

"Oh," Celeste answered, "I was just going to say something about my talent. I was thrilled when you told me how much you enjoyed my performance."

"Well, I'm sure I did, but what was it?"

"An oral interpretation of 'The Ancient Mariner' and a song about boating safety," Celeste answered as she added to her notes: "NAS Pensacola, Ben Collier, hunky husband or hunky ex?" Then she asked, "Do you remember me, now?"

Susanna's eyes widened as she replied, "Why, darlin', I think I do. Our last names sound almost the same, right?"

"Yes, Miss Delaney, but I don't think we're related."

"Oh, but we are," Susanna disagreed. "We're sisters in beauty and grace and that means a lot to me."

Celeste sat up straighter and threw her shoulders back. "That's very sweet of you to say, Miss Delaney."

"You may call me Susanna, suga'."

"Oh, thank you," Celeste said with a secretive tone in her voice.

Susanna's eyes glimmered as she smiled and then asked, "But tell me somethin'. Why are you workin' with that Nature's Way bunch?"

Celeste seemed torn by what to answer. "That almost sounds like a finalist's question," she stammered and then added, "To tell you the truth, I became involved in environmental issues through beauty pageants."

"Oh?"

"When I transferred to Florida State, I needed scholarship money, so beauty contests seemed the answer. Since I had to declare a platform as part of the program, I chose environmental awareness."

"How enterprisin' of you!" Susanna said and added, "Girls like us know how to max out the moment better than most CEOs I've met. Don't you think so?"

"Why, yes, Miss Delaney, I mean Susanna."

"Which reminds me why I'm callin'." Pausing, she tapped her emery board against the tip of her nose and said, "I need some information about Ms. McAndrews, but since she's not there, maybe you can be so kind and help me."

"Sure," Celeste said. "Ask away."

"You're a doll," Susanna replied and as she smirked smugly, she said, "First, I was wonderin' if you know where she is now."

"She called from a restaurant a few hours ago and said we could reach her this afternoon at the Fish and Wildlife office in the Courthouse. Evidently, she promised to help a student with a project or something like that."

Susanna sneered and said, "Helpful, isn't she?"

"I really don't know her personally. We've never actually met since she deals more with Beverly Moran in the administrative office upstairs. I work in mapping and I answer the phones."

"Oh, I see," Susanna commented. "Well, then I guess I should speak with Ms. Moran. Maybe she can give me more details."

Celeste's eyes darted to the Tallahassee newspaper. Picking it up and unfolding it quickly, she said, "Actually I do have an opinion about Ms. McAndrews, and although I probably shouldn't say this about my superior, I personally found that picture of her in this morning's paper to be highly unprofessional, as well as just plain wrong."

"Wrong?" Susanna asked.

"Yes, terribly so, I mean her there with Mr. Collier, your, your, your... " Celeste bit her tongue and then spit out the question, "Your husband?"

"Well, he is, yes and no," Susanna replied and looked at her unadorned ring finger. "We don't live in the same house anymore, but we do have a daughter who keeps us together as a family. Her name's Linnea and she looks like Ben, at least that's what everyone says." She reached for another cigarette and lit it.

"Oh, so then you're divorced?" Celeste asked and held her breath.

"It's complicated," Susanna answered. "Let's just say Ben and I untied the knot, but we're still close, very close."

Moving to the door of her office, Celeste closed it and said, "Oh, I hadn't heard that, but maybe you and Mr. Collier will get back together." She held her breath and waited for Susanna's reply.

"Well now, that's a thought, but I'm afraid my darlin' Ben seems to have other business on his mind right now," Susanna answered. Blowing a smoke ring, she watched it float like a crown above her head and then added, "Thinkin' of Ben makes me wonder somethin', Celeste."

"What's that?"

"Well, suga', since you work at Nature's Way, has anything about Ben's Heron Bay project come across your desk?" She took a long draw on her Salem and smiled cagily. Then she explained, "I heard you people want to have it investigated or somethin' mean like than."

Celeste studied her notepad and drew a heart by Ben's name as she answered, "I believe that's Ms. McAndrews' plan."

"Well, darlin', what's she done?"

Lowering her voice to a whisper, Celeste answered, "A lot. After she learned of the Heron Bay application, she flew here from Colorado to convince the State Environmental

Management Department to set a hearing about a list of concerns she's raised about the whole proposal."

Impatiently, Susanna prodded, "Tell me quick. When and where is the hearin' and what are her concerns?" She extinguished her cigarette and reached for pen and paper.

Celeste drew a deep breath and replied, "The State's set a hearing for the day after tomorrow at 1 p.m. in Commander Carlisle's office in the Courthouse." She picked up a copy of a confidential memorandum and explained, "Now as for the issues the State plans to address, they look pretty much routine, the usual."

"Tell me more," Susanna said. "I'm a taxpayer, so I do believe I have a right to know."

"Okay, let me read them," Celeste said as she flipped through the document. "Irreversible damage to the wetlands, loss of wildlife, disruption of nesting habitats, density of planned projects, infrastructure concerns... "

"Yeah, yeah, yeah, I get the picture, beach mouse, beach moose; what's the difference and who cares?" Susanna interrupted as she jotted some notes furiously. "The things people drum up to stop progress. Sometimes I wonder how Destin ever got built. Where'd tourism be today without all those fine condos?" When Celeste didn't reply, Susanna answered, "Well, I tell you, there'd be nothin' but a fishin' village with a few huts and bait shacks. That's all we'd have and what a shame!"

"That's not the Destin I know," Celeste commented.

Susanna huffed and bragged, "Thank goodness for the brave souls who aren't afraid to bet on the future, men like my daddy and my former husband who know how to build things right and make some money, too. By the way, you may not know this, but it was my daddy, Senator Delaney, who got Ben started in the buildin' business. That was right after he'd separated from the Navy."

"Oh really?" Celeste said. She added a row of dollar signs beside Ben's name on her notepad.

"Yes, but that was awhile ago, past history, I guess," Susanna said as she paused to wipe a tear from her eye. Sniffing, she said, "Is there anything else you think I should know since I am an investor in Ben and Daddy's projects."

Celeste's eyes widened in horror as she gasped, "Oh my! I didn't realize you had a personal stake in Heron Bay. Please don't let anyone know I tipped the State's hand." She nervously twisted a strand of her hair and reached for her notepad where she placed a large X through Susanna's name.

"You didn't give away much, sweetie," Susanna reassured her. "If anything, you just helped even the odds, and fair play's always important in real estate matters. So don't fret. I won't breathe a word of our little talk to anyone, except of course to Ben, just so he'll be prepared."

Celeste sighed and said, "Oh, thank you. I really admire Ben, I mean, Mr. Collier, and I think his projects are neat. In fact, I don't really understand why Ms. McAndrews seems so determined to stop Heron Bay."

"I could write a book on that one," Susanna confided. "Maybe one day I will and if I do, I think I'll call it *The Way the War Was Won*."

"I believe some other author has already used that title," Celeste replied.

"Whatever," Susanna huffed and then added, "You know, Celeste, I just had another thought. Since we have so much we can talk about and if you're not busy tomorrow night, why don't you plan to have dinner with me and a friend here at the house? We could share war stories about humidity hair and maybe develop some environmental platforms of our own. Would you like to come over?"

Celeste fell back in her chair and stammered, "My goodness, oh, yes, of course, I'll come. Thank you, thank you so much. I can't wait; what time?"

"Now as a Southern lady, you know the protocol. Cocktails at six and dinner at seven and, of course, we do dress for dinner," Susanna said. She ran her tongue over her front teeth and sniped, "Although you work for that bunch of forest friends, surely you dress better than your leader."

Celeste laughed uncomfortably and replied, "I think I have something appropriate."

"Well then, dearie, I'll see you tomorrow night," Susanna replied as she rang off and reached for a Hershey kiss and another Salem.

Gently replacing the receiver in its cradle, Celeste clapped her hands and said, "Thank you, Susanna Delaney. This is the stuff dreams are made of and you're about to make mine come true."

Hearing shouts of joy reverberate from Celeste's office, her colleagues in the outer office exchanged mystified glances. Deb said, "I wonder what that 'yes, Miss Delaney, and no, Miss Delaney' stuff was all about," to which Elinor replied, "Probably nothing Ms. McAndrews would approve of."

"Maybe I should advise her since she's so concerned about the Heron Bay project," Deb suggested as Celeste opened her door wide and broke into a dance of joy.

Cutting her eyes toward Celeste, Elinor watched her freshen her makeup and smile at her reflection in a window. Picking up the phone and handing it to Deb, she said, "If I were you, I'd start first with Beverly. She'll know what to do."

"You're right, but I think I'd rather tell her in person," Deb replied as she rolled up a map. "That way I can watch her reaction and be there if she calls Ms. McAndrews right away."

"Keep me posted, okay?"

Deb nodded her head and slipped a rubber band around the map. As she turned her back to Celeste's office, she lowered her voice, winked at Elinor, and said, "Thank goodness we just finished this watershed drawing Beverly needed on the Collier development. It'll give me a reason to bring up the Delaney name since the Senator's engineering firm submitted the original design." Tucking the map under her arm, she called out on her way to the corridor, "Beverly's expecting this information, so I guess I'd better get it to her before she calls. I shouldn't be gone long."

Deb took the steps two at a time as she bustled her way into the main office. Almost breathless, she pushed open the door and announced, "Stop what you're doing. I have some news I think you should know. It's about Celeste and Susanna Delaney; they've... " But before she could complete her story, she suddenly stopped in her tracks when she saw Beverly engaged in a highly animated telephone conversation. Deb plopped her map on the front counter, tapped her fingers against the formica top, and waited for Beverly to acknowledge her presence.

When signaled to wait outside, Deb frowned and started to leave, but then she glanced at a stack of letters piled in the "In" box. Mouthing, Okay if I read these? she busied herself by leafing through the supportive comments Nature's Way had received from citizens concerned about wetlands preservation and butterfly migrations.

As she skimmed through the correspondence, she nodded her head every now and then although she seemed much more interested in Beverly's reaction to whatever she was hearing on the other end of the telephone line. Deb listened for a while and then suddenly snapped to full attention when she heard Beverly apologize, "I'm sorry, Desiree, I may've jumped the gun and tipped our hand, but I didn't know Mr. Collier would be with you in the Commander's office. How'd he take the news? Was he furious?"

After several minutes of silence on Beverly's end, she finally said, "Look, I think we can regroup when you come back to the office this afternoon. You are returning, aren't you?" Then she frowned and replied coolly, "Well, all right, fine. I'll do what I can by myself. I'll check with the Boulder office for any updates Jeff may have on the project. He's probably been waiting all afternoon for your call, you know." Sighing, she added, "I hope you know what you're doing, Desiree, especially since we've invested so much time working on our position." With an exasperated "See you in the morning," she hung up and waved Deb into her office.

"Trouble?" Deb asked.

"Maybe so, maybe not," Beverly replied. "Our work had better stand on its own merits because I'm afraid Desiree's vision has become blurred."

"How so?"

"Does the phrase sleeping with the enemy mean anything to you?" Beverly asked as she drew a large heart on a Nature's Way notepad. When Deb didn't answer, she explained, "Desiree just announced she will be out of the office for the rest of the day because she and Mr. 'Heron Bay' Collier plan to work on a school project."

"So?" Deb replied.

"Oh, it gets better," Beverly said. "The contact phone number she left matches the one where she spent last night."

With her eyes burning bright with curiosity, Deb asked, "Where's she staying?"

Beverly leaned forward in her chair and answered in a slow drawl, "The Collier Development suite at the Killearn Inn."

"Oh my!" Deb said.

"Oh no is more appropriate, considering she's scheduled to lead the attack on Mr. Collier's project."

Deb whistled, shook her head, and said, "Boy, I'd sure like to be a fly on that wall tonight."

"Better than a bedbug, I think," Beverly answered as she closed the Heron Bay folder with a snap. Reaching for the phone, she said, "For the sake of the public's interest, we'd better all pray Desiree will show more restraint than we've seen out of her since she came to town."

"That's for sure," Deb agreed and added, "but I don't think she could top her performance at the builders' reception."

"Evidently she got rave reviews because Mr. Collier's called her back for an encore," Beverly remarked snidely as she placed her call to Boulder.

Deb put her hands on her hips and said, "I wonder what the real story is about her and Mr. Collier. Something big's brewing and I'd like to know what it is."

"Me, too, but not through the morning news!" Beverly replied and looked off into space.

"Better stay tuned," Deb called out as she left the office.

Watching the door close, Beverly shrugged her shoulders and muttered under her breath, "Sure, Deb, I'll watch, but I wonder which show's playing? 'Collision Course' or 'Entertainment Tonight'?"

# Chapter 9

The afternoon sun cast a shadow across Desiree's face as she watched Ben eye the notice Tip held out for him to see.

"Before you leave, Ben, you ought to look at this Environmental Board agenda that came across the wire," Tip said, moving aside to make room for Desiree, who inched forward for a quick peek at the document.

Reading Collier Development at the top of the page, she stepped back and bit her lower lip in anticipation of an explosive response from Ben. She felt her forehead bead with perspiration and worried that guilt now spread like wildfire across her face.

Tip studied Desiree as her appearance shifted from sexy siren to shamed sinner. Narrowing his eyes, he asked, "Is this why you're in town, Ms. McAndrews? To stop Ben's Heron Bay project?"

She shook her head and answered, "I wouldn't put it quite that way, sir. My visit stems from the public's need for scientific representation in the planning phase of developments that may impact fragile natural areas."

When Tip smiled and winked at Ben, Desiree threw back her shoulders and walked toward Tip's desk. "May I?" she asked as she reached for a folder labeled Heron Bay.

"Be my guest," Tip replied.

Linnea sighed, "Oh, brother" and stood a bit closer to Ben, reaching for his hand. Then she motioned toward Desiree and warned, "You'd better watch her, Dad. In fact, I think you'd better not kiss her anymore; she could be dangerous or worse."

"What?" Ben and Desiree asked in unison.

"Duh," Linnea replied. "Does the phrase 'loose lips sink ships' mean anything to you?"

Ben exchanged a bemused glance with Desiree and then said, "Linnea, here's a lesson I think you should learn."

Linnea stared at Ben as Desiree retreated out of the way. "Well?" she asked, her face upturned and her eyes filled with curiosity.

Having joined Desiree by the window, Ben leaned against the sill. Casually, he slipped his arm around her waist and waited for Linnea to close her mouth that'd opened at the sight. "It's this way, Linnea," he explained as he drew Desiree toward him so they represented a united front. "Adults may not always agree on all issues, but the wise ones remain open to fair discussion. And that's how compromises come about. You see, when disagreeing parties establish common ground, they have a better chance of working together from there. That's why public hearings are held so everyone concerned can have some input and, hopefully, reach a point of agreement along the way."

"Nice, Ben," Tip said. "No wonder your mediation skills on the flight deck always worked like a charm." He smiled proudly at Ben and to Desiree he quipped, "That's probably how he's survived the Delaneys all these years."

Desiree frowned at the mention of the name and broke free from Ben's grasp. "I'm not Susanna Delaney, Ben Collier, so don't try to patronize me with your silver tongued mumbo jumbo," she retorted. Her eyes dancing with life, she said, "The issues on that hearing agenda fall into the catastrophe about to happen category, so I think compromise is mere wishful thinking on your part."

Linnea rushed to Ben's side and said, "So much for common ground."

Ben studied the stern expression on Desiree's face and then replied, "Some disagreeing parties can be more quarrelsome than others, and when that happens, all the peacemaker can do is go for broke." He fell to one knee, and as he reached for Desiree's hand, he said, "Marry me, Desiree. I've always loved you, and if dropping the Heron Bay project will make you happy, it's a done deal."

"Dad?" Linnea shrieked. "Are you crazy? You can't do that. Poppaw will shoot you, and if he doesn't, there's no telling what Momma will do. Besides, you said Heron Bay would put us on the map and make the world a better place." She flipped open an atlas and whined, "Don't you remember promising me you would build a Linnealand Waterpark right here."

Tip surveyed the situation, rubbed his hand across his forehead, and advised, "I think you had better consider the consequences of your actions, Ben. I've never known you to yield to pressure before, so do you think you should start now?" He took the Heron Bay folder from Desiree's hand and watched Ben out of the corner of his eye.

Ignoring the commotion around him, Ben kissed the top of Desiree's hand and pleaded with his eyes. "It's your call, Desiree. What'll it be?"

"You're impossible, Ben. How dare you trivialize this situation. Can't you see that Heron Bay must be stopped, otherwise..."

"Otherwise what?"

She breathed deeply and gathered her thoughts before answering, "Otherwise, another Heron Bay will spring up and I'll have the same fight somewhere else on another day."

"So then, are you saying you want us to go head to head at a public hearing?"

"That's exactly my position," she replied, running her hand through her hair that suddenly felt out of control.

Still on bended knee, Ben held Desiree's eyes with a look that spoke volumes. When she didn't blink or look away, he sighed a curse and said, "So be it, Ms. McAndrews. You're one tough foe." He studied the angelic glow that radiated from her face, shrugged his shoulders, and stood up. Stroking her hair, he said, "You and your idealized principles versus me and my project. My, my." Then he asked, "How did this happen? The two of us feuding about the land we both love?"

Linnea broke between Ben and Desiree and waving her finger accusingly at Desiree, she said, "Can we maybe put Dad's project aside and work on mine? You promised to help me or have you forgotten?" When Desiree didn't answer, she turned her attention to Ben and added, "If I'm not ready for class tomorrow, you get to tell Momma and my teacher why. There's only so much I can do, and if you don't help me finish this project, I may have to drop out of school and become a..., a..., a French model," she blurted and looked to Desiree for help. When Desiree rolled her eyes and shook her head in disbelief at Linnea's threat, Linnea quickly explained, "Come on, Dad, surely you can tell I'm desperate and almost beside myself with worry about my future and yours."

Frowning, Ben saluted Linnea and replied, "Yes ma'am, I hear you loud and clear, but please consider my position." He pointed first at Desiree and said, "Let me start with you, Ms. McAndrews. By refusing to acknowledge my marriage proposal, you're breaking my heart. Shame, shame, shame on you for being too rigid to recognize true love when it's staring you in the face."

When Desiree looked away, Ben shifted his focus and his accusatory finger to Linnea and asked, "What is this nonsense about quitting school and your new career choice? A French model? Why, Linnea, why?" His eyes glistened with emotion as he shifted his stare from Linnea back to Desiree and then over to Tip.

Linnea made a beeline for Desiree, who placed her hands protectively on top of Linnea's shoulders. "Do you think he's really mad?" she asked.

Desiree whispered so only Linnea could hear, "No, he's just grandstanding. It's a guy thing."

"Oh," Linnea replied. "He never acts this way around Momma."

Desiree smiled and caught Ben's eye. She winked at him, but he only frowned and motioned for Tip to hand him the Heron Bay file folder.

Flipping it open to the hearing notice, he commented dryly, "Let the record show that I received this summons from Commander Tip Carlisle, my Navy pal turned conservationist." He scanned the information and chuckled as he read the list of concerns Nature's Way had raised about Heron Bay. He continued his perusal and laughed with confidence. "Piece of cake, Desiree. Twenty items, twenty minutes, max. That's all the time I'll need to address these issues and allay the board's fears."

Desiree's eyes widened as she replied, "Twenty minutes? Get real, Ben. You can't possibly be serious."

Ben slapped Tip on the back and crowed, "File this, Commander. I don't need a copy."

Beaming with pride, Linnea danced toward Ben and said, "Way to go, Dad. I guess this means I don't have to worry."

"Anything to keep you out of a French bikini," he teased. "Now, as for your project, do you have all the information you need?"

"Yes, sir," Linnea answered and then she reached for Desiree's hand. "We can still be friends, can't we? So what you and Dad don't agree about Heron Bay? Please, Desiree, I really need your help on my project. You promised, remember?"

Nodding her head, Desiree smiled at Linnea and then at Tip. "Well, the three of us gathered a lot of data that should be put to good use. Maybe there's someone out there who's willing to learn an environmental lesson." She cut her eyes toward Ben and added, "And I think our first audience should be the one and only Bennett Collier, former defender of freedom and current purveyor of propaganda. Are you up for the task, Ben? Brave enough to listen and not interrupt?"

"Common ground, Desiree, common ground; that's what it's all about," he replied. As he watched Linnea and Tip stack maps, graphs, and photos into a cardboard box, he took Desiree aside and whispered, "You still haven't answered my question, Desiree."

"What question, Ben? What are you talking about?" She leaned closer and gazed into his eyes that seemed to swallow her whole.

He nibbled on her ear lobe and said, "Marry me, Desiree. Before or after the hearing, I don't care. Just say you will. Please, please be mine forever." Not waiting for her reply, he removed his Naval Academy ring and slipped it on her finger. He kissed the tip of her nose and said softly, "Think about it, Desiree. You know I love you, and regardless what you say, we belong together."

She twisted his ring until he stilled her hand. She felt her heart yield as his gentleness captured her soul. "Ben, there's Linnea to consider and, of course, Susanna, too," she said, watching Linnea thank Tip and his secretary for their help.

"Susanna's past history and the future is ours if you'll only give us another chance," Ben replied, caressing Desiree with his eyes. "I love you, Desiree. I honestly do."

Desiree placed her hands on Ben's chest and met his glance with love that flowed from her heart into his. "I believe we had this discussion twelve years ago. I trusted you then, but look what happened to us."

"Did you wait for me, Desiree?"

She raised her eyes heavenward and said, "I shouldn't tell you this, but I will. Yes, Ben, I kept my promise to you, but before your head swells, I must tell you the truth. The demands of my career became my passion, my reason for living. After I heard about you and Susanna, I blotted all thoughts of you from my mind and no longer waited for your return. That's why I didn't seek you out."

"If only you had."

"You could've found me if you'd looked," she said softly as a tear streamed down her cheek.

He kissed away her sorrow and asked, "Had I found you, would you have listened?"

She pushed away from his embrace and answered, "Probably not. I was so hurt, Ben. You broke my heart."

"My heart broke, too, Desiree, and I didn't know what to do other than marry Susanna."

"The officer and the gentleman," Desiree said as she kissed his cheek. "You did the right thing. Linnea's a precious child."

Ben smiled and said, "That she is and I love her more than I can say." He reached for Desiree's hand and waited for her response.

"I know, Ben. I understand," Desiree consoled, nodding toward Linnea, who stamped her foot impatiently as she gestured toward a clock on the wall. Laughing, Desiree said, "Someone's waiting for us and not too patiently at that."

"Okay, but tell me, Desiree, where do we go from here?" Ben asked, reluctantly releasing her hand.

"That depends on your skill with dioramas."

"Dio whats?" he asked.

She winked at him and said, "Well then, since you're obviously clueless, I guess I'll just have to show you."

"That's fine with me because I want to see everything you've got," he replied, his eyes fired with shameful lust and heated desire. "Take me, I'm yours."

"Heart and soul?"

"Stem to stern and back again," he answered as he ushered Desiree through Tip's maze of filing cabinets and on out the door. Calling over his shoulder, "Thanks, Commander," he smiled when he heard Tip reply, "Fly high, son."

Linnea walked on ahead, but she dropped back when Desiree said, "Wait for us, Linnea. Your dad seems confused about diorama design, so I think you'd better explain our plan."

Slowing her steps, Linnea glanced back at Ben and then at Desiree, both of whom seemed captivated by the other. As she waited for them to catch up with her, she rested her box filled with materials against a water cooler and mumbled, "Adults! One minute kissing, the next fussing at each other, and now they're holding hands. If they're all lovey like this now, they'll do who knows what if I leave them alone." She shuddered and added, "I guess I'd better keep them busy with my project. It's for their own good, of that I'm sure."

"Here, Linnea, let me carry that for you," Ben offered. "You're about to drop it," he added, watching Linnea struggle with her heavy load.

Her eyes flashed with stubborn determination as she fumed, "I'm not helpless, Dad. I can manage perfectly fine, all by myself; besides, I wouldn't want to interfere with your courting."

Guilt flickered in Desiree's eyes. She quickly loosened her hand from Ben's grasp and took a handful of pamphlets from Linnea's box.

"Thanks, that's better," Linnea said, now smiling as she positioned herself between Ben and Desiree. "Why don't you grab some, Dad? That way you can make your hands useful."

Ben's eyes darted toward Desiree, who blushed at the steamy thoughts that raced like a thoroughbred through her mind. "Yes, Ben, get the maps or the graphs; take something."

He leaned over the top of Linnea's head and whispered in Desiree's ear, "Tonight I will."

Linnea cleared her throat and said, "I heard that, Dad."

"Oh," Ben replied and then he explained, "All I meant was that I'm ready for a diorama, whatever the devil that is. I've probably conquered hundreds of them during my career."

Desiree and Linnea rolled their eyes and smiled smugly at one another which caused Ben to retort, "I saw that, ladies. Are you making fun of me?"

When Linnea answered, "Never, Dad" and Desiree chimed in with, "Whatever gave you such an idea?" he shook his head and let the women lead the way. Watching Linnea match her steps to Desiree's brought a smile to his face and a twinkle to his eyes.

As they reached the front steps, Linnea rushed ahead and said, "Come on, Dad. Get with it or we'll never get this job done.

Desiree said I'll need some art supplies, you know, paints, brushes, and heavy cloth. I don't suppose you brought any of that with you this trip?"

"No, I didn't, but that's what stores are for," he answered.

"To the mall then, to the mall," Linnea sang, charging forward to the parking lot. At Ben's car, still parked in space #59, she plopped her box on the hood and waited by the front passenger side.

Ben and Desiree strolled across the street at a more leisurely pace and acknowledged the lot attendant's friendly wave and warning, "The Senator sure raised cane 'bout losin' his spot, so you'd best get ready to hear it from him. I tried to put in a good word for you, though."

"Thanks," Ben replied as he fished in his pocket for his keys. Joining Linnea by the car, he handed over her maps and graphs and said, "I can't wait to see what you're going to do with this stuff."

"It's all her idea," Linnea replied. "So if it's a disaster, it'll be her fault."

Desiree watched Ben and Linnea load the trunk with the materials she hoped would solve two problems, Linnea's assignment and Ben's blindness to the need for environmental preservation. She felt confident about the success of Linnea's project, but she worried that Ben's mindset presented an uphill battle.

She admired the easy style of parenting Ben had obviously mastered with Linnea and wished he could adopt a similar caring attitude toward the environment. With her scientist's eye, she noticed that when Linnea laughed, so did Ben and when Linnea talked, Ben listened patiently and with intensity. That's when she decided to give his approach a try but with one twist; she'd use his parenting techniques against him and defeat him on his own home front. Thinking, parent-child, lesson taught, lesson learned, I can do this, she believed her plan would work. Then she frowned and chided herself for her simplicity. After all, what did she really know about parenting?

Wondering what type of a parent she would've been, she sighed with regret for the mother-child bond she knew she most likely would never experience. Vicarious parenthood and stolen moments with another woman's child, she thought, that's my fate and my future; how lucky Susanna Delaney is and she probably doesn't even realize her good fortune. Then she considered her own past behavior. Thinking, instead of believing the worst of Ben twelve years ago, I should've contacted him. Maybe we could have saved our love or maybe not; I don't know, but if only we'd talked, things might have turned out differently for us.

"If only, if only, if only," she repeated quietly. Fighting her emotions, she turned her back to the tender scene of Ben with Linnea and studied instead the stained glass dome of the Old Capitol that glistened in the bright Florida sunshine.

Suddenly, her melancholy reverie of lost years and lost chances ended when Linnea shouted, "Hotter than a firecracker! Watch out, Desiree!" Over her shoulder she caught a glimpse of Linnea standing beside the open car.

As Linnea frantically fanned the air with one hand and cooled her face with the other, she fumed, "Fix it, Dad, now. Desiree can't ride in this hot car; she'll melt since she's not used to this heat." She pointed with disdain toward the control panel, frowned, and said, "I'll bet that thermostat reads 500 degrees."

"I'll start the air conditioning," Ben replied. "It'll take just a second to cool the interior, then we'll go, that is, if Desiree isn't afraid she'll cook on the way across town." He eased behind the wheel and fired the engine that roared its high powered response.

"I'm up front," Linnea called as she slid across the leather seat. Motioning for Desiree to come forward, she snuggled next to Ben and patted the seat by the window. Nonchalantly, she announced to Ben, "Desiree can sit here by me."

"I thought you were concerned about body heat," Ben commented.

"I am, Dad. That's why I'm riding here," Linnea replied matter-of-factly.

"So I see," he said as he watched Desiree walk toward the car. When she followed Linnea's command to "Sit here," he apologized, "I'm sorry, Desiree, but Linnea seems to think you and I need a chaperone."

Desiree patted Linnea's hands that she'd folded primly and said, "That's fine, Ben. Maybe she has a point."

"Trust me, I know what I'm doing, so that's that," Linnea said. She reached across Desiree's lap to open the glove compartment and finding a pad and pencil inside, she handed them to Desiree and commanded, "While Dad drives us to the mall, you can make our list. Okay?"

Ben chuckled and replied, "Spoken like Senator Delaney's granddaughter: delegate, delegate, delegate."

"Don't you mean legislate?" Desiree asked.

"That's not Big Jack's style; delegation of responsibility is," Ben answered. He waited for traffic to clear from a side street and edged his car into the right lane. "The Senator's a master at chess and personnel management is his forte."

Linnea crinkled her nose and disagreed, "Momma says Poppaw's not a people mover; he's more of a catalyst for action, an idea man."

"I see," Desiree said although she wondered if Ben's comments about the Senator stemmed from a less than cordial experience with the man. She studied Ben's face and noticed he suddenly seemed tense and much less exuberant than he'd been only moments before. Thinking, there's something Ben's not telling me about the Delaneys, she decided that conversation would have to wait for another time.

Ben turned on the radio and whistled along to the tune playing. When he started singing the lyrics to "Up Where We Belong," he looked to Desiree for approval and smiled when she blushed.

Linnea glared ahead and ordered, "Oh, Dad, please quit. You know you can't sing." She flipped open a case of compact discs she'd stored under the front seat and said, "Let's listen to one of these."

Ben feigned hurt and shrugged his shoulders. "Be my guest, but don't turn up the bass." To Desiree, he explained, "Tallahassee has a noise ordinance. Did you ever hear of such a law?"

"Yes," she answered, "Boulder's had one for decades."

"Oh, that's right," he replied. "How could I forget the city that also passed a zero population growth policy?"

Linnea leaned forward and asked, "What's that mean, Dad?"

Bluntly, he answered, "Antidevelopment."

With a tone of wisdom in her voice, Linnea said, "A city with no new housing? No room for new families, new babies? I wonder how that city feels about sex?"

"Linnea!" Ben replied, a look of horror flashed across his face.

Linnea patted his knee reassuringly and said, "Don't worry, I've already had the sex talk at school, but you know what I think?" Without giving him a chance to answer, she said, "Hanging out with you and Desiree may be the best sex education class I've ever attended. So before you two get too friendly, you might want to remember who's watching."

"My little watchbird," he said, shaking his head.

"Tweet, tweet," Linnea replied, bursting into a fit of giggles. Nudging Desiree with her elbow, she asked, "Do you really make him sweat?"

"What?" Desiree asked.

"I heard him tell Momma you're the only woman who ever made him sweat. I wanted to hear more, but they closed the bedroom door and had a big fight. Isn't that right, Dad?"

Ben stared straight ahead and said, "I didn't know you were listening."

"It's okay because even if I hadn't heard, Momma would've told me. She shares everything with me."

Under his breath Ben mumbled, "Almost everything" as he steered his car into a parking area at the front of the Governor's Square Mall.

"Well, now, let's get busy," Desiree said, hoping to reduce the tension lines that crisscrossed Ben's forehead. "It shouldn't take us very long to pick up a few supplies and then we can get to serious business."

"Better than monkey business," Linnea commented, inching closer to Desiree and out of the glare streaming from Ben's dark eyes that now appeared even darker. She asked Desiree for a handkerchief and explained, "I need one to clean him up. Look at Dad's face; he must be thinking about you because he's sweating, big time. Wait until I tell Momma."

"Linnea,'" Ben warned, frowning deeply.

"Dad," she replied, mimicking his disturbed expression.

"Let's go shopping," Desiree interjected. Hearing her words, she shook her head, not believing that she, the minimalist, had just uttered with enthusiasm words that were not a part of her regular vocabulary. She wondered if three other words such as "I love you" might soon follow.

Peeping from underneath her eyelashes, she watched Ben turn off the ignition and liked what she saw. She prayed for strength to maintain her objectivity and for courage to follow through with her convictions.

As though Ben could read her mind, he reached across Linnea and gently stroked Desiree's forearm. With quiet confidence and honest reassurance in his voice, he said, "You'll rest easier after the hearing and so will I. When we put the board's ruling behind us and move on, everything will be all right. Together, that's the way it'll be."

"Regardless of the decision?" she asked, tightening her heartstrings as she waited for his reply.

"I meant what I said in Tip's office. For you, I'll cancel the whole development."

"Dad! Stop saying that," Linnea said, brusquely pushing at Ben's hand that now covered Desiree's finger adorned with his Academy ring.

Not wanting to star in another scene in a public place, Desiree quickly opened her door and motioned for Linnea to follow closely behind.

Ben let them stride ahead, but he didn't miss the way Linnea once again matched her steps to Desiree's and adopted Desiree's womanly walk that still made his heart beat faster and stronger.

Linnea looked back over her shoulder and catching Ben's eye, she said to Desiree, "Momma's probably worried about us, so one of us had better check in. Maybe Dad will call her while we're in the store; it'd save time, don't you think?"

"That's between you and him" she answered, pointing to a telephone stand by the mall entrance. Knowing that Linnea's suggestion made perfect sense, Desiree attempted to still the twinge of jealously she felt at the thought of Ben on the phone with Susanna. She closed her eyes and willed her mature, reasonable personality to sublimate the hormone-charged spirit that seemed more determined than ever to take up permanent residency in her weakened psyche.

"What's wrong, Desiree? You seem upset," Linnea said, gently touching Desiree on the arm. "Was it something I said?"

Surprised by the concern she heard in Linnea's voice, Desiree stopped curbside and answered, "No, Linnea. I just have a lot on my mind, that's all." She dug in her pocket for a quarter and finding one, she handed it to Linnea and said, "Here you go."

Linnea flipped the coin in the air, and as it fell to the pavement, she said, "Call it, Dad. Heads, I phone, or tails, you talk to Momma."

Ben watched the quarter spin and roll in his pathway. Walking forward and without saying a word, he stopped the coin's motion with his foot and picked it up. Tossing it to Linnea, he said, "Go call your mother and tell her you'll be staying with us tonight. She can reach you at the Killearn Inn."

"But, Dad. What about my clothes for tomorrow?" Linnea asked and with sparks of panic in her eyes, she added, "And what about her? Is she staying with us, too?"

He nodded his head and put his arm around Desiree's waist. Holding her tightly, he said, "That's my plan, and as for your clothes, young lady, the Delaney women have yet to pass Parisian's without buying something, at least that's what my accountant says."

Linnea tightened her fist around Desiree's quarter and fumed, "Momma's not going to like this one little bit and you know why."

"Call her," Ben ordered, silencing Linnea with a look as he nodded toward the phone. "We'll wait for you over there in the Candy Box."

Sullenly, Linnea turned and walked to the pay station. As though she couldn't resist, she said, "I bet I know what you'll buy. Chocolate kisses, lots of them."

Ben laughed and replied, "If I'm lucky, there'll be no charge for the only kisses I want. What do you think, Desiree? What are my chances?"

Linnea spun around and watched in horror as Desiree closed her eyes and accepted Ben's kiss that showed every sign of blossoming into full blown passion if left unchallenged. Linnea stamped her foot and complained, "Why is this happening to me? Taking care of Momma is hard enough, but now I have to worry about him, too. And then there's her and my project! What am I going to do? Does anybody care?" When neither Ben nor Desiree answered, Linnea repeated, "I said I don't know what I'm going to do."

An elderly woman stopped in front of Linnea and stared at Ben and Desiree, who seemed oblivious to their surroundings. "Honey," the woman said, "you might as well save your breath because I don't think those two can hear you."

Lowering her eyes, Linnea replied, "Please excuse them, ma'am; my dad's not himself."

"Tsk, tsk," the woman responded, peering around Linnea for a closer look.

Blushing crimson when other passers-by giggled at the sight, Linnea apologized to one, "I'm sorry; this is all so embarrassing" and to another she swore, "I really don't know them. I just got here myself." Then clenching the quarter in her fist, she marched to the telephone and muttered, "I wonder what Dad would say if he saw me kissing that cute waiter Etienne? Maybe I'll just have to find out."

Now all smiles, she reached for the phone book, looked up the number of Chez Pierre, and placed her call.

"Hi, Etienne? It's me, Linnea. We met today at lunch." She listened for a moment as she watched Ben escort Desiree into the candy store. Beaming with mischief, she said, "If you're not busy this weekend, I'd like for you to attend my Cotillion Ball at the City Country Club." Then she ended the conversation by whispering, "Oh, good. I'll meet you there at seven. I know we'll have fun. By the way, my dad's a chaperone, but don't worry because he won't be a problem. I'll see to that."

She replaced the receiver and skipped toward the Candy Box where Ben and Desiree passed time by sampling fudge swirls and mocha cremes. Joining them at the counter, Linnea propped her elbows on a glass showcase and said to the clerk, "I'd like whatever they're having, but please give me twice as many. I've heard chocolate intensifies a woman's appetite for worldly experiences."

When Ben raised his eyebrows inquisitively, Linnea smiled sweetly and explained, "Double the pleasure, double the fun. Isn't that what you always say, Dad?"

"Something like that," he grumbled as he watched Linnea select a fudge square and moisten her lips in rapturous anticipation. Trying to shut out Linnea's all too real Spice Girls imitation that made the hairs on the back of his neck stand at attention, he asked, "Did you make your call?"

"Sure, Dad, I even made arrangements for Saturday night's Cotillion. You haven't forgotten my coming out party, have you?" she replied, licking her chocolate-stained fingers with reckless abandon. "I'm ready to party all night if the right man asks me."

Desiree wet a napkin in a glass of water and handed the cloth to Linnea along with a woman-to-woman look that clearly meant, Be careful, Linnea, and don't push your luck. Satisfied that Linnea seemed ready to cease torturing Ben, Desiree turned to him and said, "Aren't you glad that Linnea took care of her escort situation for the ball? Now you don't have to worry about her and that waiter dancing cheek to cheek on a moonlit terrace." When he looked puzzled, she added, "That was Susanna's suggestion at lunch, wasn't it?"

"Oh, right," Ben replied, watching Linnea carefully as though he feared someone had snatched away the true Linnea and had left a wild teenager in her place.

As for Linnea, she winced at Desiree's words and threw her arms up in the air in mock surrender as she confessed, "You'll find out soon enough so I might as well tell the truth now. I invited Etienne to meet me Saturday night at the Club. So, that's that. I know Momma will approve, especially since you're going to be with me, too. So, in addition to my project supplies, we'd better get lots of dancing shoes while we're here."

"Wait a second, Linnea. I'm not buying that waiter a pair of shoes," Ben huffed as he tightened his fist.

"Oh, Dad," she sighed, "I didn't mean for Etienne. Desiree's the one who'll need new shoes." She pushed away from the candy counter and pointed to Desiree's worn pumps.

"For me? Why?" Desiree asked. "I should be on my way back to Colorado by this weekend."

"Bet not," Linnea replied with a twinkle in her eye. Then she explained, "Momma probably has some other social function planned for Saturday night, so I really need someone to keep Dad in line at the Cotillion. Please, Desiree, please say you'll stay. It'll just make your time here a few days longer, and besides, after you see all your efforts cave in at Dad's hearing, you'll probably need to regroup awhile before you go home." She reached for Desiree's hand and squeezed it tightly as she whispered, "I need your support, Desiree. It's important."

Unable to resist Linnea's pretty eyes filled with trust and need, Desiree replied, "Okay, but your dad may prefer to select his own companion for the evening, especially if his project loses at the hearing." Turning to Ben, she asked, "So, what about it?"

"Isn't double the pleasure, double the fun what I always say?" he answered, beaming a smile so bright that had all the fudge in the Candy Box melted to syrup, no one in the store would've been surprised. Winking at Linnea, he added, "I think I'll send the society editor at the paper a little notice for her Sunday column. Picture this "Lifestyle" headline: Father-daughter double date with mysterious Frenchman and wetlands wonder."

Together, Linnea, Desiree, and Ben laughed at Ben's joke, but had they known someone devoid of a funny bone lurked in the background taking notes, then maybe their gaiety would've ceased. But oblivious to the eavesdropper's presence, they ordered sweets to go and made their way into the mall, unaware their party might end before it even got started.

# Chapter 10

Desiree knelt beside Linnea, who slept soundly in the middle of Ben's king-sized bed. Such a darling child, Desiree thought, gently covering her with a soft cotton sheet. "Sweet dreams," she whispered as she kissed Linnea's cheek and tiptoed to the French doors that overlooked the back 9 of an exclusive golf course complex.

Hearing, "Welcome home, Desiree," she followed the sound of Ben's voice and joined him on his patio adjacent to the master bedroom. She smiled at the sight of him, a brave warrior at heart, who now lazed like a tired pup on a white wicker sofa made soft by pillows stuffed with thick foam.

"What's wrong?" she asked and then added, "Don't tell me a budding environmental artist wore you out."

Ben reached for Desiree's hand and replied, "Come closer and find out for yourself." He tugged gently at first and then a bit harder, enjoying the playful give-and-take he felt in her touch. "Still holding out, are you?" he said in response to her silent refusal to follow his bidding.

"Maybe so, maybe not," she answered as she leaned toward him and accepted the kisses he trailed from her wrist to her shoulder.

Wanting to make the most of their time together, Ben gathered Desiree in his arms and made room for her beside him on the sofa. There he cradled her tenderly and soothed her spirit with deeper kisses he'd saved only for her.

"I've missed you," he said.

"Oh?" she replied, pausing to savor the touch of his hand as he flicked her curls from the nape of her neck and concentrated his loving attention on one of her most delicate spots. But when she thought she heard Linnea stir inside, she stroked his cheek and reminded him they were not alone. Nodding toward the bedroom, she said, "Linnea has school tomorrow, so she needs her rest. We probably should go into the living room."

Kissing Desiree quiet, Ben whispered, "Hush then, my precious. It seems to me if we don't talk, we won't disturb Linnea's sleep." When he felt Desiree relax in the comfort of his arms, he teased her eyelids with tantalizing kisses and smiled when she moved his hand to the top button of her blouse.

Releasing first one and then another, he lowered his head and caressed her bare skin. In response to his touches that intensified the lower he ranged, Desiree sighed. All thoughts of propriety dashed from her mind as she felt her need for Ben deepen.

Together they toyed with her remaining buttons. As Desiree unfastened them, Ben rewarded her actions with a kiss for each one that gave way and two for those that fell to the floor. And when the last button finally opened, Ben surveyed the glory of Desiree and surrendered himself to the moment he'd dreamed about. Sighing, "Desiree, Desiree, I love you," he pleaded with emotion in his eyes and love in his heart. "Tell me you still love me, that you want me. Please, Desiree, tell me you still care for me."

She listened to the rhythmic beat of Ben's heart and although she felt the words he wanted to hear spring to her throat, she said instead, "I'm sorry, Ben; it's too soon for us to think of love. We should settle some other issues first. That's the wise thing to do, don't you agree?"

Instead of answering her question the civilized way she'd expected, Ben chose a more unorthodox route to convey his thoughts. With one skillful move, he flipped her on top of him and drove her almost to the edge with kisses and touches so superb she thought she would scream with desire and delight.

He nuzzled her throat and stroked the ridge of her shoulders with determined fingers that showed no signs of stopping before they reached the center of her being.

Dizzy with excitement and delirious with need, Desiree held his head in her hands and encouraged him to move his lips lower where he adored her beauteous bounty, covered by midnight blue satin and lace. Hungrily, he nibbled at the dainty front clasp of her bra that separated his demanding tongue from the objects of his desire. When he untied the ribbon closure and rejoiced at his prize, he devoured her with fiery kisses that spiraled Desiree's heart into impassioned ecstasy and Ben's love into bold overdrive.

"Let's lose these," he said, tugging at her blouse and bra that soon found their way to the marble and slate patio floor.

Answering, "Off with this," she freed his shirt from the confines of his trouser waist. Before long, at the foot of the sofa appeared a mound of clothing, the work of a formerly well-dressed couple who'd chosen to disrobe each other one piece at a time in the moonlight that now bathed them in a most becoming and wonderfully iridescent glow.

Desiree felt her innermost sensations come alive with Ben's exploration of every curve and crevice of her body. As for Ben, he gave his love freely when Desiree reacquainted herself with his most exquisite and definitely all-male feature.

The quiet of the night broke for only an instant when the sofa creaked with the swift movement of Ben, who held Desiree like a fragile doll as he rolled over and came half circle with her so that she lay intimately underneath him.

"Oh, Ben," she sighed in pleasure, her spirit aroused by his perfectly placed caresses on her hardened peaks and soft valleys that'd remained untouched for twelve years. More of Desiree became available for Ben's adoration, and he took full advantage of the situation. Enraptured and captivated, he bestowed upon Desiree all the caring and love he'd long harbored for her in his heart and in his soul.

He watched Desiree bloom in answer to his sultry gaze and soul-shaking kisses that both consumed and enticed. Realizing the depth of her desire for him, Ben bowed his head and gave thanks for the safe return of Desiree to his heart and to his home. "I love you, Desiree; I always have," he confessed and waited for her reply.

With eyes bright and lips smiling, she winked, coyly pushed away his hands, and said, "My turn, Ben." She raised up on one elbow and studied his toned physique. Tawny brown from days in the sun, he'd lost neither his looks nor his style. Kissing the tip of his nose, she trailed kisses with her eyelashes from the base of his throat to the top of his thighs, consequently driving him almost to the point of no return.

When he moaned his response to her and caressed her hair, he urged, "There, Desiree, there."

In return, she teased, "Patience, Ben; we've waited this long, so what's the rush?" Then she massaged his firm stomach and the pleasure of his thighs, which caused him to shudder with torrid desire. "Here, Ben?" she asked, kissing him so wildly he feared he might explode.

"That's enough, Desiree, unless you plan for us to finish what we've started," he said huskily as he slowed her divinely agonizing strokes and caresses with a kiss powered by intensity and charged with fire. "You know how much I want you, but you deserve candlelight and roses, satin sheets, and champagne kisses. That's what I want for you, now and always."

"Does this mean we should say good night and sleep on our feelings?" she asked.

"That's your call," he answered as he folded her in his arms and added, "but surely you realize my restraint's failing fast."

"Mine, too," she confessed. She closed her eyes and tried to deal with the reality of their situation. Yes, she still loved Ben, that she couldn't deny, and she believed he honestly loved her, but even so, she also realized their time and place were less than desirable.

Although her mind screamed, "No, Desiree, not now, not here," her heart pounded, "Yes, love Ben; don't wait any longer," which caused her thoughts to counter with, "Physical involvement will most certainly dim your objectivity" and her feelings to respond, "Forget that sorry theory. Studies show lovemaking heightens awareness and sharpens perceptions, so chance it. How can you lose?"

"Well?" Ben asked, unaware of Desiree's internal debate that warred inside her soul. Holding her tightly, he felt her heart race. The stronger the beat, the more he wanted to find his way into her most sacred place. Thinking, say it, Desiree, say it now, I beg you, he bit his lower lip as his personal pain flamed with urgency and need.

Desiree felt all cues in her body signal she was ready to surrender to Ben. She knew deep in her heart she was his to take, to cherish, to love, and he was hers. Their destinies had collided, and even if they made love just this once, the time and place no longer mattered; love did. Listening to her heart, she found herself whispering into his ear, "Now, Ben, now."

"Are you sure?" he asked.

"Yes, yes, yes," she said as she welcomed him home.

He touched her here, she kissed him there, and soon their hearts beat as one, lovers ready to enter paradise and totally unaware of any wolf headed straight for their door.

He nuzzled her dimpled cheek and then parted her lips with his tongue, causing her to arch her body toward him. As he placed kisses along her throat, he rested his hand on her heavenly mound. Gently, he sought the tenderness of her inner thighs and soon explored her center, moist with passion and demanding more. Unable to wait one moment longer, he placed his hands underneath her and positioned her tightly against him. When he felt her writhe in response to his closeness, he entered heaven and slowly began to move.

Desiree answered eagerly and matched his rhythm stroke for stroke. When he increased the tempo and his depth, she tightened and he loved her well, slowly and completely, and brought her to climax before he allowed himself to fall.

For Ben and Desiree, time stood still as they made up for the years they'd lost.

\* \* \* \* \*

When a night owl called and a mockingbird answered, Ben opened his eyes and feasted on an amazing sight. Above the tree line, millions of stars sparkled like diamonds cast upon a canopy of black velvet. He tipped Desiree's head toward the spectacle and said, "I ordered this for you. I hope you're impressed I carry such weight with the Powers above."

"What an ego you have, Ben Collier. A saint you're not; that's all I know."

"Are you calling me a sinner?"

"It could be worse now, couldn't it?" she teased, moistening her lips in anticipation of his next kiss.

Ready to accommodate her every need, Ben moved closer, but unfortunately, fate drew their love fest to a hasty close when the hoot of a lonely owl changed to that of a mad woman totally out of control.

"Stop right now whatever you two are doin' up there," a woman shrieked hysterically as she brought the golf cart she'd commandeered to a screeching halt at the walkway edge. Then she cackled, "Surely you're not misbehavin', but if you are, then for Pete's sake, put on some clothes 'cause I'm comin' on up!"

Muttering a foul oath, Ben watched the intruder stride toward the stairs that led directly to his patio. When he recognized the woman by the yellow peasant blouse, orange capri pants, and high heels she wore, he added some other choice words to his greeting and grabbed the garments closest by his side. Gallantly, he covered Desiree with his shirt, pulled on his pants, and said, "Susanna, pipe down. You don't need to shout. None of us are hard of hearing."

Susanna took a long hard look at Ben and huffed, "I see you've had a workout tonight." Then she spun toward Desiree and hissed, "You're history, sister, so do us all a favor and hit the road." When Desiree didn't scurry away but instead placed her arm around Ben's waist as he fastened his trousers, Susanna fluttered her hands and screamed, "Get on outta here, now! I know what you're up to and I'm gonna tell."

"What are you talking about?" Desiree asked, her blue eyes refreshingly soft and cool in contrast to Susanna's dark glare streaked by red anger and alcohol haze.

"Your plan, cookie, that's what," Susanna replied, stamping her foot impatiently against the steps as she made her way onto the patio. She marched forward and quickly appraised Ben and Desiree's love nest. Patting the sofa's cushions, she sneered and said, "Not exactly goose down, now is it?" Out of the corner of her eye, she watched Desiree's eyes widen and then said, "For a millionaire several times over, Ben's one hardheaded tightwad. Of course, that you may already know, but I've more I can tell you about him, that is, if you have twenty years to listen."

Ben shook his head at Susanna and warned her with his eyes, but she merely snorted at him and picked through the clothing that still littered the floor. "What's this?" she asked, holding Desiree's bra at arm's length.

When Ben tried to snatch it out of Susanna's grasp, she held it up, snickered, and then crowed, "Just what I thought, a 34B. If I'm not mistaken, that was my size when I was 14 and still bloomin'. Too bad you stopped developin', honey, 'cause I know what Ben likes, and sweetie, I'm sorry, but you don't have half of what it takes."

She pranced in front of Ben and Desiree and lowered her blouse beguilingly. As she bent forward and exposed her curvaceous front, she bragged, "Now these are more to his likin'. Take it from me, I know my Ben." When Ben covered his eyes, she whined, "What's wrong, Ben darlin'? Don't tell me you've forgotten what a real woman looks like!" She flipped her hair, formed her permanently lined lips into a sexy pout, and shimmied wildly.

Stunned, Desiree stood back and made room for Susanna's uninhibited antics as Ben cursed and then pleaded, "Not the exotic dance, not now, Susanna, not ever again. Please stop, stop it now. I beg you."

"You haven't forgotten, have you?" she taunted, tossing her hair and gyrating around the patio to a driving tune only she could hear. She stared at Ben and Desiree, who'd lowered their eyes, and challenged them to join her. "Come on, you two Puritans. I'm up for a threesome. I dare you to try some real fun."

"Stop it, now, Susanna!" Ben repeated, blocking the entrance to the bedroom in case Linnea might awaken and walk outside at the sound of the commotion. "What are you? Drunk or crazy?" he fumed. Protectively, he pulled Desiree to his side.

Ben's words and actions seemed to recharge Susanna instead of stalling her bumps and grinds. Still holding Desiree's filmy bra, she swung it over Ben's head, and roping him with it, she shouted to Desiree, "This is how I lassoed this big bull the first time I saw him." Catching the look of horror that dimmed the shine in Desiree's eyes, she added, "Believe me, you and 'Rocky Mountain High' were the last things on Ben's mind that night we met in Panama City."

Desiree had heard and seen enough, so she raised on her tiptoes and moved to retrieve her bra from around Ben's neck. When she lifted it over his head, he ducked just in time to miss Susanna as she lunged forward and grabbed for the bra.

"No, Susanna," he said, wincing at the ripping sound he heard.

"Oh, that's too bad," Susanna said with a feigned sigh of regret as she admired the torn bits of material she now held in her hands. She wadded the remains into a ball and added cattily, "Don't worry, Desiree. Linnea always travels with an extra trainin' bra. I'm sure she won't mind loanin' you her spare."

Desiree glared daggers but held her temper. She didn't want to fuel the confrontation with Susanna that had every sign of turning really ugly if allowed to continue.

"Give up, pussy foot?" Susanna asked, licking her lips.

Under her breath, Desiree said to Ben, "I can't believe you ever loved someone like her."

He started to reply, but instead, he frowned and stared into the distance. Then he answered, "Love was never the issue. Linnea was."

"Don't blame my baby, you love sick jet jock," Susanna retorted. "You'd better watch your p's and q's or else."

"Or else what?" he demanded, a statuesque picture of bold maleness, bare chested and barefooted.

"I'm gonna tell, that's what," Susanna answered as she stuffed the tatters of Desiree's bra into the front of Ben's pants.

Fuming with rage at Susanna's audacity, Ben turned his back on the women and unzipped his fly to remove Desiree's shredded garment. With ice in his voice, he reminded Susanna she should think before she spoke, otherwise, she might live to regret her words.

"I doubt that, darlin'," Susanna replied and eased toward him with her signature pageant winner's walk that declared, "Beauty and poise, I've got it all; love me, sweet thing, 'cause I'm the queen of this ball." As she held Ben's eyes with her self-assured glance, she ran her hands across his chest. Caressing the dark hairs that formed a perfect T from his pecs to his navel, she said with a purr, "Ooh, darlin', let's dance, real close."

Desiree clenched her hands into a fist, but knowing she should keep her fighting spirit under control, she released them and tugged on the hem of Ben's shirt that barely covered her thighs. "Why don't you take your act somewhere else?" she asked Susanna as she stepped in between Susanna and Ben.

"Well, I never," Susanna huffed as she staggered closer to Desiree and reached one hand behind Desiree's back. Lifting the tail end of Desiree's only covering, she peeked at her backside and hooted with glee, "You poor thing, you; where's your caboose?"

"Excuse me?" Desiree replied, mortified and horrified by the unexpected exposure.

Laughing, Susanna said, "Now I know why you never married. Men seek out shapely women; better for plantin' their seeds and bearin' the fruit of their labors of love, so to speak." As she patted her own very round bottom and fluttered her eyelashes at Ben, she concluded, "Your problem, Desiree, is that you lack a man attractor like the one I've got."

"What are you talking about?" Ben asked as he wisely changed places with Desiree.

Susanna coldly eyed Ben and answered, "Anthropology lesson, that's all. Just somethin' I remember from a professor who said males naturally select women who emit fertility signs, you know, curves and cushions, the whole baby factory package." Casting yet another appraising look toward Desiree's bottom and shaking her head, she said, "What she offers wouldn't make the grade for any primitive man on the hunt for a promisin' childbearer." Then she winked at Ben and concluded, "Guess havin' a baby would be a tough order for her to fill, given her body shape and all."

Desiree who'd always prided herself on her rational side now felt driven to the other extreme. But luckily, reason prevailed when instead of verbally striking back, she simply held Susanna's hands and defused the tense encounter by saying, "I think we've had enough excitement for one night. Why don't we slip inside and I'll put on a pot of coffee. Here, Susanna, let me show you the way."

"Is she for real?" Susanna asked Ben, who stood proudly to the side and watched Desiree lead Susanna by the hand toward another patio door.

Smiling, Desiree instructed, "Watch your heels on the astroturf. I wouldn't want you to hurt yourself." She turned only long enough to catch a glimpse of Ben patting his heart and pointing to her as he mouthed, I love you.

Oddly subdued and uncharacteristically quiet, Susanna allowed Desiree to hustle her across the small patch of faux lawn and into the kitchen that smelled of poster paints, chalk, and plaster.

From inside the bedroom, Linnea called out sleepily, "Dad? Where are you?"

"Right here, Linnea, on the patio," he answered as he hid from sight Desiree's clothing that had escaped Susanna's wrath.

Linnea snuggled deeper under the covers and asked between yawns, "Where's Desiree?"

"She's here with me, darlin'," Susanna answered as she frowned at Desiree, who hurriedly wrapped herself in a man-sized apron with "No fear" embroidered across its front.

"Momma!" Linnea said, suddenly very much awake. "Wait until you see my science project. We worked on my diorama half the night."

"How nice," Susanna replied, primping as she studied her full reflection in the mirrored finish of the refrigerator door. She patted her hair in place and whined, "Why didn't you ask me to help? I always got A's on my homework."

Thinking, I bet, Desiree puttered with the coffeemaker and searched the cabinets for dishes and silverware. She turned to Susanna and asked, "Where does Ben keep the cups and saucers?"

"Beats me," she replied. Then she shrugged her shoulders and added, "Kitchens really aren't my thing. They're so, so common."

"Hmm, well then, I guess I'll have to keep looking."

"Whatever," Susanna said as she turned her attention to a large drawing that covered the kitchen table. She looked at it curiously and commented under her breath, "Surely this isn't Linnea's project. The poor child's gone off the deep end if she thinks this mess will impress anybody."

Hearing Susanna's comment, Desiree thought, that's what you think. She peered over Susanna's shoulder and explained, "Linnea's depiction of an estuary system illustrates an environmental danger that may not concern you, but it should."

"Do tell," Susanna replied with a sneer and a contemptuous frown. When Desiree looked poised to launch into a detailed explanation, Susanna cut her off with a curt, "Let Linnea tell me about her work."

Just then Linnea, wearing a University of Colorado nightshirt, entered the kitchen and seeing Susanna's dour expression as she scrutinized the diorama, she frowned and said, "You hate it, don't you?" She backed away from her mother and looked to Desiree for help.

Desiree felt her heart go out to Linnea. She knew how hard Linnea had worked on her project, carefully sketching to scale every element of the estuary system she'd wanted to portray. Desiree smiled when she remembered Linnea's determined refusal of all offers of help as she'd painstakingly drawn, sculpted, and then painted every tree, plant, wildlife, and sea life image in a progression from marsh to bay.

Unable to stand by and let Susanna belittle the beauty and importance of Linnea's efforts, Desiree cleared her throat and said, "I was telling your mother that your diorama illustrates a serious theory about aquatic life." Nodding encouragement to Linnea, she said, "Go ahead, explain to her what happens if an estuary isn't protected." When Linnea hesitated, Desiree pointed to the painted cloth and said, "Show her what all this means in terms of lifeless, polluted waters. Your dad said he enjoyed the lesson, so I'm sure your mother will, too."

"She's not interested," Linnea said, doggedly hanging her head.

"Oh yes, I am," Susanna countered. "But first, I really could use some coffee. Don't you have it ready yet?"

Visibly perturbed by Susanna's level of insensitivity, Desiree sighed and asked Linnea where she might find some cups.

"Dad's a mug man. He keeps our special ones up there," Linnea replied, pointing to a cabinet high above the sink. Then she opened a pantry door beside the refrigerator and pulled out a metal stepstool. "This is for me," she said and dragged the stool toward Desiree.

"Hold on, Linnea," Ben said as he walked into the kitchen. "Let me finish buttoning this shirt. Then I'll get whatever you ladies need."

"Always the hero," Susanna mumbled darkly, still frowning at Linnea's project.

Ben ignored Susanna's comment as he opened the cabinet door, took out two Navy mugs, and handed Linnea one with #1 Daughter stenciled on its back. Saving a matching #1 Dad mug for himself, he reached into another cabinet and selected a neon orange mug for Susanna and a pastel blue one for Desiree.

"Thanks, Dad," Linnea said as a slight smile crept back into her eyes when he poured her a cup of Columbian coffee, which caused Susanna to squeal, "No, Linnea, don't you dare drink that. It'll stunt your growth and stain your teeth."

Linnea rolled her eyes and bragged, "Dad and I drink coffee together all the time. He doesn't have a problem with it, so you shouldn't either."

Susanna leaned against the range, put her hands on her hips, and replied, "I can see for myself the bad habits you've acquired, young lady, and I, for one, don't approve."

"Such as?" Linnea challenged.

Susanna tapped her fingers on the ceramic range top and rattled off a list of infractions. "Sleepin' over without callin' first for permission, stayin' up late, drinkin' coffee. Need I say more?"

Defiance beamed from Linnea's eyes as she replied, "I tried to call, but your line was busy." When she added accusingly, "For hours," Susanna shrugged her shoulders and continued to rant and rave.

"Cavortin' with the enemy; you were seen at the mall, dearie," she spat out as she glared heartlessly in Desiree's direction. Without skipping a beat, she added, "With her, who I might say has no taste whatsoever if that shirt you're wearin' is hers. Bad habits, Linnea. You're pushin' my tolerance with your unacceptable behavior."

"You're one to talk, Susanna," Ben interjected as Desiree watched from the side of the room. She wondered what the people in the suite next door thought about such a spirited 2 a.m. family chat.

Susanna's face flushed with color at Ben's words as she sputtered, "Fine, Ben, if we're gonna talk about my bad habits, then by all means let me illustrate your point. Where do you hide the booze? I want some Rebel Yell in my coffee, now."

Linnea suddenly rushed to Susanna's side and begged, "No, Momma, no, please don't drink anymore tonight." Then she fell to her knees and apologized, "I'm sorry I worried you. It's all my fault. If only I'd worked on my project last weekend, then I wouldn't have needed help from Dad and Desiree."

"Some help you got," Susanna sniffed as Ben stared at the ceiling and Desiree, with sorrow in her eyes, watched Susanna manipulate Linnea and cruelly assign blame and guilt to an innocent child who deserved only praise.

Linnea's face clouded as she pleaded with Susanna, "Please take it out on me, not them and especially not Dad. He doesn't mean to upset you." Lowering her voice to a whisper, she rationalized, "He's been working so hard lately. That's why he's tired and cranky, that's all." Then becoming more like a mother than a daughter, she stroked Susanna's hair and patted her hand.

Susanna wiped imaginary tears from her eyes and sobbed, "If only that evil woman hadn't come here to wreck Heron Bay; if only, if only." Wringing her hands, she looked down, shook her head, and blubbered, "I heard she's forced one of the State Offices to investigate the development. That's why I came over here, to warn your dad, not to make trouble or to break up his slumber party."

"There, there, Momma, don't worry any more," Linnea consoled. "I stayed in the middle of the bed to keep them apart, just in case, and as for Heron Bay, Dad said he's got the hearing under control."

Turning her face so Linnea couldn't see, Susanna smirked at Desiree and said, "Wonderful, then all our troubles will cease and she'll be out of our life." Under her breath, she muttered, "This time forever."

"What was that?" Ben asked gruffly although he'd heard exactly what Susanna had said.

While Ben and Susanna traded accusations and Desiree tried to project herself out of harm's way, Linnea tiptoed to the sink with her mother's coffee mug in hand. There she poured its contents down the drain and filled a large tumbler with water.

She waited for a second or so and then gently nudged Susanna's elbow. "Here, Momma, drink this. It'll make you feel better."

Susanna spun quickly around and seeming to lose her balance, she fell forward and bumped into Linnea. The glass Linnea carried spilled and splattered a stream of water across the kitchen table.

Desiree gasped and Ben closed his eyes at the terrible sight. As Linnea tried to salvage her science project, Susanna stood to the side and snidely remarked, "Oh come on, people, lighten up! What's an estuary without a little bit of water?"

# Chapter 11

"See there, Linnea, all your wailin' and whinin' last night was for nothin'," Susanna chided as she fluffed Linnea's hair into a puffy style that matched her own teased and sprayed bubble do. Admiring her handiwork, she stood back and added, "I can't understand whatever made you think you needed somebody else, and especially that Desiree person to help with your little assignment. We did just fine by ourselves, didn't we now?"

Frowning, Linnea sighed as she struggled with a box filled to the top with pamphlets describing the Seminole Reservation, St. Marks Wilderness Area, and Apalachicola Forest. Her eyes blurred at the sight of all the pretty pictures of the places she'd intended to highlight in her presentation to her science class. Unfortunately, though, she'd been upstaged by Susanna, who'd turned the classroom into the theatre of the absurd by belting out one show tune after another to illustrate environmental concepts and pollution principles.

"I asked you a question, Linnea, so answer me," Susanna huffed. When Linnea looked away, Susanna complained, "As I live and breathe, I don't see why you're still mad at me about that gooey mess we left at your dad's. Any fool can tell our work was A+ quality. That other would've gotten you a C- at best." She smoothed the ruffles of her blouse and drawled, "Well, no matter 'bout that now. Everything worked out just fine anyhow seein' that you had those brochures as backup. Right, darlin'?"

Muttering under her breath, "You wouldn't understand," Linnea stepped out of the way of a group of students on break between classes. Her frown deepened when two boys broke from the crowd and walked toward her. When they dropped to bended knee and delivered a crude imitation of Susanna's earlier rendition of "Old Man River," Linnea covered her ears and blinked back tears.

"See how I impressed your friends with your message 'bout that nasty ol' river basin," Susanna said as the boys snickered behind her back.

"Right, Momma," Linnea answered sarcastically. "I bet my whole class will think of you every time someone talks about preserving the Ochlockonee."

"Oh they will, darlin'," Susanna cooed. "If you don't believe me, just go on and ask one of those good-lookin' young men who're walkin' our way."

Linnea turned and caught a glimpse of one of the boys pointing toward Susanna as he rolled his eyes and hummed the chorus of "If I Could Change the World." "That's enough! Stop it!" Linnea cried, angrily stamping her foot.

Nonplussed, Susanna dismissed the boy's mockery with a wave of her hand and said, "He'd better watch his mouth 'cause here comes your teacher, Ms. Perez. Remember who you are, Linnea Delaney." Radiating her cosmetically bonded and buffed smile, Susanna said under her breath, "Hand me that box of yours. It'll look better to your teacher if she sees me still helpin' you out."

"Okay, but don't throw anything away."

"Sure, baby," Susanna replied, but she added with a slur in her voice, "Don't fret, I know just where to put your fine little project."

Linnea's eyes softened as she said, "Thanks, Momma. I really appreciate your help, and I'm sorry if I caused you more trouble."

As Susanna watched Ms. Perez walk toward them, she sniffed and replied, "It was worth the effort, but I am kinda tired. But don't you worry. I plan to catch up on my beauty rest 'cause I hate havin' circles under my eyes. Maybe a honey facial will help." Susanna started to say more but stopped when Ms. Perez called Linnea's name.

"Come here, Linnea; I want to congratulate you and your mother." Putting her arms around Linnea's shoulders, Ms. Perez smiled and said, "Team Delaney scored 100% this morning. But tell me, Linnea, how did you come up with your environmental awareness outfit? It added such a nice touch to your talk." Smiling at Linnea's recycled jeans, Ecology Now bandanna, and Forever Wild tee-shirt, she added, "I wouldn't be a bit surprised if our headmaster doesn't get calls from the other parents saying we should drop our school uniforms in favor of ecology wear.

You're a trendsetter, Linnea, as well as an A student. I'm very proud of you."

"What do you say, sweetie?" Susanna prompted Linnea, who stared at the tips of her loden green hiking boots laced with leather ties.

"Thank you, Ms. Perez," Linnea replied, seeming to wilt under Susanna's domineering gaze.

"Why, I thank you, Linnea, and especially your mother. It's not often we're visited by a celebrity." Turning toward Susanna, she said, "Your participation in our program was wonderful. The class loved your imitation of a great blue heron in flight and then landing. However did you do that? And in high heels? That was an amazing performance!"

Smiling brightly, Susanna tossed her head regally and gushed, "Oh my, how you flatter me, Ms. Perez. But to tell you the truth, I surprised myself at how much I know about this great state of Florida: the streams, forests, and that other ecology stuff people seem to fuss about all the time now. Why when I was a tiny baby, my daddy, Senator Jack Delaney, you know of him I'm sure, well, he used to read me books about forest friends and little fishes in the sea. I guess it's no wonder that early on I knew I wanted to dedicate my life to protectin' Nature. And that's exactly what I do when I travel to visit with investors and the like, promotin' Ben Collier-designed developments. Ben says he doesn't know what he'd do without my help. Isn't that so, Linnea?"

Linnea winced and studied the pattern in the floor.

"Well, anyway," Susanna continued, "speakin' of help, Linnea and I were just havin' it out, so to speak, about her lapse in memory."

"Oh?" Ms. Perez asked, her dark brown eyes filled with concern.

"Yes, I'm afraid Linnea forgot that I'm the one at home she should turn to when she needs help. Although she oughtta know better by now, she's still been hopin' all mornin' her dad'll show up here with some sort of artwork he and Linnea pieced together last night." Disdainfully, she turned up her nose and added, "Now I'm no art critic, but I've got to say I took one look at the drawin' and I knew in my heart their paint and powder picture just wouldn't do for your class. That's when I stepped in to help.

Maybe now Linnea'll believe there's only one person in this whole world she can count on and that's me." With a look of radiant victory in her eyes, Susanna patted Linnea's box of environmental information and declared, "This learnin' box was my idea, a mother's expression of true love for her child."

Looking bemused, Ms. Perez replied, "The mother-child bond is strong and few deny the power of maternal instinct."

"Well, yes, case in point is right here," Susanna said. She nodded her head and smiled at Linnea.

Ms. Perez stood back and took an appraising look at Linnea, who now protectively held Susanna's hand. Pursing her lips, she said, "Sometimes, though, that role becomes reversed, but I guess you wouldn't know anything about that."

"Actually I do," Susanna sniffed and looked away before she said sadly, "I lost my own mother when I was a teenager. She'd been real sick with a broken heart, so with my daddy off politicin' around the State, it was my job to stay home and nurse her the best I could. I tried to save her, but she died anyway. That's how I learned what it takes to be a good caregiver."

"Oh, I'm sorry. I hadn't heard about your sorrow," Ms. Perez said as she watched Linnea stroke Susanna's arm with touches of reassurance and understanding.

"No problem," Susanna replied. "Bein' on my own, except for Daddy, of course, I grew up knowin' what I wanted and how to get it. I do hope Linnea's picked up some of my strong will and determination. She'll need them in this hard world of ours. That's why I insist she carry my Delaney name. I don't want her to ever forget the source of her strength and fire."

Ms. Perez patted Susanna on the shoulder and said, "You've done a fine job with Linnea. I wish all parents cared as much about their children as you do," to which Susanna replied, "Well, I try but it's not always… "

Suddenly, a bell rang and the corridors came to life with the chatter of students and the sounds of locker doors slamming shut. Ms. Perez smiled apologetically to Susanna, shrugged her shoulders, and said, "Third hour's about to start, so we should go back to class. Ready, Linnea?"

"Yes ma'am, I'll be right there," Linnea answered and then said to Susanna, "I'll see you at the house this afternoon, Momma."

When Ms. Perez was well out of earshot, Susanna pursed her lips, lowered her voice to a whisper, and said, "No, Linnea, that won't work. I have plans for today and tonight; business, of course."

Linnea's face clouded as she replied, "But I thought you said we were going to make dinner tonight."

"Oh, what I meant was that maybe you could help Consuela fix dinner for my guests since I have so much goin' on." Susanna patted the top of Linnea's head and added, "Nothin' fancy, a Key West salad for me will be fine. I want my evenin' gown to fit like a glove this weekend so no extra calories on my plate, please."

"Fine, whatever you say," Linnea conceded as she turned to follow Ms. Perez down the hallway. With her back to Susanna, she wiped away the tears that brimmed from her tired eyes.

"Bye-bye, baby," Susanna called to Linnea, who walked alone down the now empty corridor. To herself, she said, "Whew, I'm glad that's over. Whatever would that child do without a fine mother like me to bail her out of bad situations?"

Susanna strode down the hall and hummed along to the staccato beat her heal taps made as she clicked her way across the freshly waxed linoleum floor. As she passed by a row of trophy cases in the main entrance, she paused to admire her image in the glassfronts.

Spying a trash receptacle by the front door, she studied her surroundings and whispered, "The coast is clear, so bon voyage natural resources." She swung open the trash can's lid, dispatched Linnea's box with a flourish through the wide opening, and smiled at the solid sound the box made when it hit bottom. "In the can, baby, in the can, biodegradable waste, properly disposed," she said with a sneer, a laugh, and a final cautious look over her back.

"Looking good, Miss Delaney," sounded a smoky voice to her left.

Spinning around, Susanna clutched at her throat and cried, "Trey, darlin'! Thank goodness it's you."

"Who'd you expect, Susanna?" he asked. "As soon as I got your message to meet you here, I came on over." Trey tossed his shoulders back, saluted Susanna, and added, "Your wish is always my command. Just like old times."

"Well, we'll see about that," she answered as she admired Trey with doe-like eyes. Then she linked her arm in his and nodded toward the front entrance.

He opened the door for her and feeling her tense when he put his hand at the small of her back, he said, "You seem jumpy, Susanna. What gives?"

"Oh, nothin'. I'm just kinda exhausted from last night," she replied, angling her walk to a glide as she climbed down the steps toward the sidewalk. "I had to help Linnea out of a mess Ben allowed to get out of hand."

"Sounds tiresome," Trey said as he stroked Susanna's flushed cheek.

"I tell you what, Trey, last night was absolutely exhaustin' and this mornin' wasn't much better."

"How so?" he asked as he admired the outline of her full, pouting lips.

"To make a long story short, Ben and that Colorado woman cooked up some ridiculous scheme to deprive me of the opportunity to help Linnea with her schoolwork. So I had to hunt the three of them down at Ben's hideaway where I found him behavin' badly with that awful Desiree."

"Oh, my," Trey consoled, "How terrible for you and for Linnea, too."

"Well, thank goodness Linnea slept in Ben's bed, so no hot bunkin' happened, and I don't think she saw what actually transpired between the two of them."

Trey nodded and asked with a sly wink, "But you did?"

"Oh yes," Susanna answered. "They didn't leave much to my imagination."

"Please don't get mad at me, Susanna," Trey said, stepping slightly to the side, "but don't you think Ben has the right to his own life? After all, he is a single man."

Susanna centered her hands on her waist and retorted, "That still doesn't allow him to forget he's the only father my child has ever known, so he oughtta act like one."

"Speak of the devil," Trey mumbled as he spotted Ben's large black Rolls lurch to a stop at the curb. "Looks like the ace himself has arrived. Linnea should be pleased."

"Maybe so, but too bad for him that he missed my show," Susanna replied. Smiling to herself, she added, "I think I'll give him an encore performance over lunch."

"What about me?" Trey asked, his eyes stricken with disappointment.

"You're my dessert partner, darlin'," she said with a purr. "How about strawberries and cream, poolside, tonight? Just thinkin' about the possibilities makes my mouth water."

"I like the sound of that," Trey said and then he added, "We should have lots of privacy since it looks as though Ben's going to be pretty much preoccupied with his own taste treat."

Susanna glared a hole through Desiree's heart as she watched Ben walk to the passenger side of the car and open the door for Desiree. "Why's she lettin' him do that?" she shrieked when Ben framed Desiree's face with his hands and tilted her head back. "Shame, shame, shame," Susanna wailed. Then she hid her eyes from the sight of Ben parting Desiree's lips for a power-charged kiss so potent with energy ions that Trey reached for his handkerchief to soothe Susanna's furrowed brow.

"The nerve, the unmitigated gall of that piece of recycled fluff!" Susanna fumed. "Just who does she think she is, comin' here and puttin' on a show like this in front of my Linnea and the whole school?"

"A brave woman, I'd say," Trey answered.

"Or a fool," Susanna countered as she strode forward, waving her arms frantically.

"Hold on a minute," Trey called out as he reached for her, but Susanna eluded his clasp, charged to Ben's car, and shouted, "More bad news, Ben. Somethin' terrible's happened. If you'll unhand that woman, I'll tell you what's goin' on with Heron Bay. I guess you don't know the latest."

Ben either didn't hear Susanna or maybe he didn't care as he continued to pamper Desiree with adoring eyes and loving promises.

"Kiss now and cry later, Desiree McAndrews!" Susanna screamed. "You're nuts if you think my Ben'll want you after the hearin' this afternoon."

"What did you say?" Ben asked, shaking his head in disbelief.

"You heard me, fly boy," Susanna replied and then bragged, "I got the session moved up to this afternoon, so Desiree's either gonna fail as a no show or as an idiot who stirred up trouble unnecessarily. You'll see and thank me for it later, that I promise."

"You're impossible," Ben said as he helped Desiree from the car. Reaching into the back seat, he pulled out Linnea's repaired diorama, handed it to Desiree, and said, "Don't pay any attention to her. She's out of control most of the time and what we're witnessing now is no exception."

"You might as well put that ugly thing away," Susanna advised. "I did Linnea's project for her, and she's still acceptin' praises from her teacher and the whole class. It was all so good."

Ben ran his hand through his hair and muttered, "I bet."

Susanna motioned for Trey to join her by Ben's car and said, "Trey and I have some business to conduct before we go downtown, so I'd suggest to save time, let's ride together."

"The four of us in one car?" Trey asked, his eyes wide with surprise.

"My Fleetwood or the Rolls? You pick, Trey darlin'," she replied.

Trey motioned toward Desiree and said, "Maybe Ms. McAndrews should choose."

Susanna winked at Ben and answered, "Oh, I think not. Her judgment's flawed; always was and always will be. But I tell you somethin' she can do. Since Linnea doesn't need that project you're holdin', she'd want it recycled, so I think Ms. McAndrews should be the one to put it in the bin at the top of the stairs." When Ben and Desiree exchanged puzzled looks, Susanna explained, "Go on, dearie, put that mess in the green can with the recyclin' logo on top. Surely you know the sign."

Desiree looked stonily at Susanna and said, "Fine, I'll take Linnea's work on in, but her project deserves display and I'll settle for nothing less."

"Suit yourself," Susanna replied and then added, "but before you go bustin' in Linnea's class, I think you oughtta take a look at what she had me throw away. The can's right there inside the door."

As Desiree made her way up the stairs, she protected Linnea's project against the light breeze that brushed across her face. Mumbling, "That insane woman, my poor Ben, and his sweet, sweet Linnea," she pushed into the foyer and walked toward the trash can anchored beside a trophy case. At first she considered passing on by, but unable to resist the urge to see its contents that seemed so important to Susanna, she pushed open the lid and peeked inside.

"No, oh no," she said, disbelieving her eyes. As confusion and disappointment filled her mind, she stared into the distance and declared louder than she'd intended, "This couldn't have been Linnea's doing."

A school monitor stationed at a desk in the front office looked up from a stack of floor passes and asked, "Do you know Linnea Delaney?"

Desiree glanced in his direction, lowered her eyelashes, and replied, "I thought I did, but maybe I was wrong." With Linnea's diorama nestled firmly under her arm, she backed out the front door only to meet the cool, gloating stare of Susanna.

"Ready for another lesson?" Susanna asked with fury in her eyes. When Desiree didn't answer right away, she goaded, "That is, if you're brave enough to ride in my car, but I figure you're too much of a chicken."

"Old hens never scared me," Desiree replied, her eyes reflecting her inner battle of whether she should maintain her dignity or soil her hands in a down and dirty fight. As she debated her next move, she watched Susanna swagger closer to her.

"You're not callin' me an ol' hen, are you?" Susanna huffed. She tapped her foot angrily and puffed air like a steam engine warming up.

Desiree studied Susanna's expression and weighed her thoughts. Deciding not to give Susanna the fight she seemed determined to stage, Desiree looked down and calmed her spirit.

"Say it, Desiree, say it," Susanna demanded, but when Desiree remained silent, she crowed, "If you won't speak your mind, then I will." She inched toward Desiree until they stood nose to nose, their eyes locked in combat and their chins firmly set.

Sensing Desiree's struggle to control her temper, Ben stepped in front of her and said, "I'll take care of this for you."

"Thanks, Ben, but I have my own way of coping with unpleasant people. Meditation always helps." Desiree closed her eyes and pictured Boulder Canyon, beautifully rugged with clear streams and jumping trout. Feeling peace wash through her, she opened her eyes and smiled at Susanna.

The sight of Desiree, composed and calm, seemed to inflame Susanna. As quick as a cat and with a growl in her voice, she went for Desiree's jugular by declaring low and mean, "At least I produced an egg for the man who feathered my nest." Then preening like a peahen, she tossed her head back and cackled rudely.

Before Desiree had a chance to respond, Susanna snatched at Desiree's hand and led her down the steps to her shiny, white Cadillac parked beside Ben's car. "I guess you won't be ridin' with me, but it's probably just as well," Susanna said. She winked at Desiree and added, "There's more I could tell you, but I think I'd rather wait 'til we're alone."

Ben approached from behind and cast a warning glance at Susanna as he broke her hold on Desiree and said sternly, "That's enough, Susanna."

"So you say," she replied, "but I'm just warmin' up." She sauntered toward the driver's side, and with her eyes cut meanly toward Desiree, she challenged her to respond.

Desiree steeled her will and leveled Susanna's stare with her own determined gaze. When she watched Susanna flinch, look away, and then sputter about bleeding heart Pollyannas, Desiree shook her head sympathetically at the sight of a beautiful woman acting like a spoiled child. Sighing, she ignored Ben's call for her to walk with him to his car and strolled instead to Susanna's car. Smiling to herself, she ran a fingernail dangerously close to Susanna's custom painted initials scripted in gold on the door and said, "I think I'll ride with her."

"Not by yourself. I won't allow it," Ben said. He felt his heart pound a mile a minute at the thought of Desiree alone with Susanna.

Desiree studied Ben's worried expression and smoothing his brow with the light touch of her hand, she said, "Well then, I suggest we ride together." She winked demurely and watched Susanna scowl in dark defeat.

"All right then. Let's go," Ben said, "but I hope you know what you're doing, Desiree." He stood to the side and helped Desiree slip into the back seat that reeked of leather opulence and heavy perfume. When Ben slid in beside Desiree, he patted her knee and directed her attention to the open windows of Linnea's classroom.

There she caught a glimpse of Linnea giving Ben a thumbs up sign as she proudly pointed to the Forever Wild shirt Desiree had surprised her with the night before. Resting against Ben's shoulder, Desiree smiled, her faith now fully restored in the beauty of a precious twelve-year-old and the honor of one good man.

Susanna grimaced and fired her car's engine into action. Turning to Desiree, she bragged, "I've got a Corvette runnin' under my hood. Bet it's better than anything you have." Then she floored the accelerator and the car roared off like a rocket.

For several miles, no one spoke. Neighborhoods blurred and shopping centers floated by one after the other as the foursome made their way toward the city. Ben and Desiree seemed lost in thought, and Trey nervously gnawed on a cigar as though it were a pacifier. Susanna relaxed behind the steering wheel, and having engaged the cruise control, she yawned and settled back for a spin around the beltway.

As they approached the I-10 junction with Cypress, Susanna slowed for a group of road workers, who smiled toothy grins and waved at her as though they sensed royalty was passing by. Pulling into the south exit lane, Susanna broke the silence in the car by saying, "I need to stop by my dressmaker's to pick up the gowns I designed for my appearance schedule at the competitions I'm judgin' this season. I always like to keep extras on hand. Besides, maybe Miss Sara'll have somethin' special in her shop I can change to. It's important for me to look my best at the hearin' today."

Ben checked his watch, frowned, and said, "Better make it a quick stop, Susanna. I want to put this session behind us."

"That's my Ben, always a team player," Susanna said.

Under his breath, Trey muttered, "I don't think Ben's 'us' includes you, Susanna."

"Well, it'd better," she replied, bringing her car to a full stop in front of a row of shops that faced Raintree Road. She ignored the posted "No Parking" signs and said, "These places are so convenient for people like me with special needs."

When Desiree raised forward to object, Ben pulled her back to the seat and said, "Let Susanna get a ticket. Maybe that way she'll learn that rules apply to everyone, including her."

Desiree giggled at the concept as she watched Susanna extricate herself from behind the steering wheel and survey the sidewalk for parking guards who might be close by.

"Guess the cops are snackin' at the donut shop," Susanna said and smiled triumphantly as she shut the car door with a bang. She toddled toward a Nighty A Go Go store and paused to admire the window display of sexy lingerie. Swivelling her hips Madonna-style, she spun around to catch Ben's eye. When he grimaced displeasure, she frowned, turned toward the entrance of the store next door, and walked into the Pins and Needles Stitchery Shoppe.

Ben sighed his relief, leaned forward to tap Trey on the shoulder, and said, "If you don't mind, I'd like to have a private word with Desiree before Susanna gets back. You understand, I'm sure."

"No problem, pal. I've been meaning to check out the Te-Amos in that tobacco store down the block, so I might as well take the time now." As he left the car, he asked, "Is there anything I can get you two while I'm out?"

"Yes, there is something you can do for me," Desiree answered. She pulled a business card from her purse, scribbled some numbers on it, and handed it to Trey. "Please call my office and tell them I'm on my way to the hearing. I want them to know I'll brief everybody as soon as I get there."

"Wait a second, Desiree," Ben interrupted as he pointed to Susanna's cellular phone stored in the front console. "Use Susanna's phone since I'm sure I pay the fees. Go ahead and place your call."

"Maybe I don't want to tip my hand," Desiree replied.

Ben's eyes clouded for a moment, but then he grinned and teased, "Good idea because I'd much rather kiss that sweet hand of yours anyway." When Desiree blushed, Ben said, "See you later, Trey, and take your time, buddy."

"All right then, I'm off," replied Trey. He made a hasty exit from the car that showed signs of rocking into action at any moment.

When Trey was out of sight, Desiree snuggled against Ben and said, "Peace and quiet, finally."

"It's about time. We've had a full morning already," Ben replied. He leaned closer and accidentally brushed against Desiree's wrap skirt that barely covered her knees. "New outfit?" he asked as he rested his hand on the hem of her animal print sarong.

"Umm, yes. Linnea picked it out yesterday when we were shopping," Desiree answered. "What do you think?" she asked. She settled back to savor Ben's touch that sent swirls through her head and sparkles to her eyes.

"Nice cheetah pattern," he said, stroking Desiree's skirt as though he was petting the animal represented in silky twill colored a soft, tawny brown. "Feels good," he whispered as he allowed power, strength, and desire to flow from his fingers straight to Desiree's warm and willing heart.

She closed her eyes and prayed the divine feelings Ben imparted would never cease. Not wanting to break the spell, she relaxed against the increasing pressure of his hand. Thinking, thank you, Linnea, for making me buy this outfit, she smiled at the memory of Linnea and the store clerk, whisking her into a dressing room where she'd gamely stripped to her lingerie in less than it'd taken the savvy sales associate to say, "Honey, this three piece, value-priced outfit is definitely you!"

Breaking into Desiree's thoughts, Ben said, "I love the way you look right now, racy and kind of bad in a good way. But tell me one thing. Do you dress like this for all your hearings?"

"No, I don't, and I most certainly wouldn't have worn this outfit today if I'd known about the scheduling change," Desiree replied. Suddenly, she worried her attire would send the wrong message about her and her work.

"Well then, I'm glad you didn't know about the change of plans because, Desiree, you're a knockout," Ben said as he admired the way her black top fit snugly in all the right places. He lowered his eyes to her tiny waist and touched her belt buckle trimmed in golden brocade. "This was a good choice, too," he said, "but here's what I think is the best feature of the whole outfit."

With the tip of his finger, he flicked open her silky sarong and exposed Desiree's long and luscious bare legs. Gleaming at the sight, he declared, "I'm sending that clerk a bonus for convincing you to buy this skirt. It's a winner and so are you." Then he lowered his head to her knees and tenderly trailed kisses along the top of her thighs.

Quivering in anticipation, Desiree unchained her spirit for a ride on the wild side. Ben advanced, Desiree acquiesced, and soon she no longer regretted shelling out $176 for a Jungle Jane outfit that'd brought Ben literally to his knees.

"Excuse me, excuse me!" sounded a petulant whine from the side of the car. "It's me; I'm back and I need some help with these dresses."

"Not now, Susanna, not ever!" Ben shouted, enraged by her interruption.

Susanna strode forward and ripped open the car door. Her eyes widened, and she quickly retreated two steps back as she put her hand to her mouth in a gesture of mock surprise. Gasping loudly, she stared first at Ben's face contorted by intense pain and then she peered into Desiree's eyes that'd become liquid with lust and hot, hungry fire. Sneering, she said under her breath, "Looks to me like I got here just in time to save my detail man a cleanup job. The nerve of you two, movin' and cooin' like doves in my backseat. Just you wait 'til I get downtown. There's gonna be more than blueprints flyin' sky high. I'll see to that."

Storming to the trunk of her car, she opened the lock and smiled at the cavernous space designed to hold a minivan load of baggage. She pitched inside her newly purchased fashions of silk, sequins, and satin and two Nightie A Go Go shopping bags filled with feathered boas and Spanish lace.

As she slammed the trunk lid shut, she noticed her reflection in the chrome bumper and smiled. Hearing Trey call her name, she swirled her hair into a bubbly chignon and smoothed the skirt of the tailored suit she'd changed to in the dressmaker's fitting room. "I'm ready to go, Trey darlin'. But first, tell me how I look." For his benefit, she twirled around twice and almost tripped on the second spin.

"Whoa, sugar," Trey said, steadying her with his brawny arms. He stepped back and surveyed her appearance from head to toe. "You look superb and like a woman in control."

"Not like some flea-bitten circus cat?" she asked and nodded toward Desiree.

"You're one of a kind, Susanna, a looker with a brain and a will of iron to boot," Trey assured her.

"I think I'll keep you around," she replied with a purr and then she added, "Your snooty wife had better watch her step, or I just may have to bump that ice maiden back to her daddy's big house in Old Mobile."

"Now, Susanna, you know how I feel about you, but Pamela's Alabama timber money is hard to pass on," Trey replied as a look of concern flashed in his eyes.

Susanna pinched his cheeks and said, "That doesn't stop you and me from havin' some fun every now and then. Besides, I don't ordinarily kiss and tell, that is, unless I'm provoked, so you might wanna keep that in mind and stay useful to me. Where've you been, anyway? I thought I could count on you to watch those two."

Conspiratorially, he lowered his voice and said, "Sorry about that, but when I made a call for Desiree, I found out something I think you'll find most interesting."

Susanna's eyes brightened as she gushed, "Oh, goody. Start talkin'."

"Does the name Celeste Kulhaney ring a bell?"

"Do you mean the woman who works at Nature's Way?"

"One and the same, that's her," Trey answered and then added, "Miss Kulhaney seems to share a passion for someone near and still very dear to your own heart. She sounds as though she'd do almost anything to spend some quality time with Ben."

"Well, let's get shakin' 'cause I can feel trouble bakin'!" Susanna chirped. "Things are finally goin' my way."

Trey held Susanna's door for her and smiled at Desiree who asked, "Is everything set at my office?"

"Yes, ma'am," Trey replied with a wink directed toward Susanna as she shut the door and walked around the car.

Susanna restarted the engine and pulled away from the curb. When she spied a parking attendant crossing the street, she flashed her lights and waved a kiss to the man, who frowned until he caught a glimpse of the car's personalized DELANEY license plate. As Susanna glanced in the rearview mirror to catch the guard's waved reply, she snarled when she saw confirmation of Ben's need for Desiree. Furious, she cranked the CD player to drown out Desiree and Ben's murmurs that escalated with every turn of the car.

Suddenly, all sounds emanating from the back seat ceased, but the quiet didn't last long. When Susanna swung wide to avoid a pothole, Desiree's sultry sigh changed to a soft moan.

Trey stared straight ahead and reached for a fresh cigar and his lighter. As for Susanna, she blared the horn and slammed on the brakes.

Glancing across her shoulder, Susanna locked eyes with Ben and angry words spewed forth from her like lava from a volcano. "Read my lips, Ben Collier. I know what you're doin' and you'd better stop this very instant. This is my car, not a playpen for sensitivity trainin'."

Blushing with guilt, Desiree gasped, "Oh my!" and primly repositioned her skirt over her knees.

Susanna watched Ben's eyes flash disappointment. Winking at Trey, she drawled, "So much for Ben's afternoon delight." Then she turned and flashed a grin at Desiree as she angled her car back into the line of traffic headed toward town.

# Chapter 12

A hush fell over the auditorium as the heavy double doors swung open and Ben, flanked by Desiree on the right and by Susanna on the left, walked proudly through, his head held high and his attitude set for success. As they passed the lower section filled with concerned onlookers, Desiree nodded her greetings to dozens of environmentalists she recognized by the eco-posters they waved above their heads.

Her eyes shifted to the center rows on the left side of the room. Seeing the Nature's Way staff positioned at strategic points throughout the audience, she smiled. She hoped her team's background efforts would pay dividends for the environment and marshal support for similar challenges across the country.

"Looks like all of Granolaville turned out this afternoon," Susanna said with a haughty laugh. She smirked smugly at a grey-haired woman dressed in a shift and sandals and commented to Ben, "Isn't that Simone Lancaster, one of the Pink Ladies from Community Hospital? I do believe she's wearin' love beads. Probably brought them with her when she and what's his name moved here from California."

"Hush, Susanna, Simone might hear you," Ben cautioned. Turning to Desiree, he explained, "Sometimes Susanna speaks without thinking first."

"So I've observed," Desiree replied. She looked away as Susanna singled out others in the audience for additional caustic opinions about their dress, their politics, and even their sexual preferences.

Hearing one personal condemnation too many, Desiree asked Ben angrily, "Does she know what she's saying?"

Susanna leaned across Ben and replied, "If the *she* you're talking about is me, then I think you should ask me directly if you really want the truth."

"Fine," Desiree retorted. "Do you speak from facts or from your own twisted perception of reality?"

"Well, I never," Susanna huffed and then she sniffed into a handkerchief she pulled from her purse. To Ben she whined, "You never told me *she* was so mean." When he looked protectively toward Desiree, Susanna stalked forward and added tartly, "Of course, though, the true reality of the situation is that you quit talkin' to me about Desiree years ago, so I guess it's no wonder I didn't know how mean-spirited she is. Is that why you dumped her?"

"Stop right there, Susanna! You're out of line and you damn well know it," Ben replied as he watched the color drain from Desiree's cheeks.

Off to the side in a section designated "Press Passes Only," several reporters turned at the booming sound of Ben's voice. As though an alarm had sounded, notepads rustled open and cameras rolled to catch the action for the five o'clock news.

The audience, too, seemed to sense news breaking as those seated closest to the aisle craned their necks to catch the arrival of the key players. A man who'd been debating with another the merits of a 4 iron over a 3 quickly ended his conversation when Ben, Desiree, and Susanna passed by his row. Jumping to his feet, he called out, "Come on, Ben; get this hearing started. Half of us have tee times we don't want to miss."

A woman seated close by kicked at a putter the man'd stored under his chair and said, "People like you, sir, are part of the problem. How many more acres of wetlands must be sacrificed for golf courses and condos? Pretty soon the entire Gulf Coast will be covered in zoysia grass instead of sea oats, and the only sand above ground will be that filling duffers' traps along a Par 3."

"Seems to me that's a better use of the land than lettin' it breed mosquitoes in boggy ol' swamps," another person shouted.

When several young people wearing Nature's Way ball caps pushed forward, Susanna put her hand to her mouth and said, "Ooh, lawsy, Desiree, it looks like a convention of creek hoppers just came to town." Making a face, she sniped, "They do stick out in a crowd, probably 'cause those campin' types are more at home grubbin' around in the woods than interactin' with polite society." Then she pointed toward a woman with braided, reddish brown hair held back by a Sierra Club ribbon and asked, "Is that one of your people chargin' the aisle?"

Desiree glanced to her left and gasped at the sight of Beverly rushing menacingly toward the golfer, who now brandished his putter above his head like a sword. Clapping her hands to stop the altercation before it escalated into a full scale battle, she said, "Please, everyone, settle down. I beg you, please!"

"I'll handle this," Ben said to Desiree, adding, "Politeness never works too well with crowd control, but hopefully reason will." To the leaders of the group who continued to shove forward, he shouted, "That's enough, folks! We'll be out of here in half an hour or less once we get the meeting started."

Ben turned to his group of supporters and gave them the thumbs up sign as a signal their multi-million dollar Heron Bay project was out of the cancellation danger zone and positioned to move forward through the permitting process.

"I saw that, Ben," Desiree said, putting her hands on her hips.

"What!" he asked.

"Your gesture that says Heron Bay's headed for approval," she replied. "But it's not going to happen, you'll see," she added with a defiant shake of her head.

"That's debatable," he replied with a wink. "One thing's certain, though. Nothing will be decided today unless someone gains control of this crowd. Any ideas?"

Desiree batted her eyelashes and said, "Being a hot shot military man, you of all people should have an answer."

He grinned and replied, "Okay, if you want to see my Caesar dividing Gaul into three parts maneuver, then you'll have it,"

"Perhaps we'd better break the ranks into two camps, instead of three. The math works better than way," Desiree whispered coyly.

"Maybe so," Ben agreed. He motioned for the man with the putter to come forward and said, "Sir, if you don't mind, I'd like to borrow your club for a moment."

"Sure, go ahead, but I would like it back."

Ben nodded his understanding and using the putter as a pointer, he commanded, "Attention! Take your seats wedding style. Left, right."

"What'd he say?" someone in the audience asked.

"Huh? Say what?" another person echoed.

"You heard me," Ben replied, and then he barked his command two levels louder than the first time, "Those in favor of the Heron Bay development move on this side to the left. The rest of you sit across the aisle on the right side. Go on; take your seats. Now!"

When no one moved, Desiree said, "Here, Ben, let me give it a try." She cleared her throat and said in determined, measured tones, "Listen, everyone. If you'll settle down, we can let the hearing begin. Please, let's allow the facts to decide this case, not our emotions. That way all sides will win in the end."

Ignoring Susanna's snide, "You're a nut case if you believe that," Desiree took the putter from Ben's hand and as though she held a magic wand, she calmly separated the two groups with one simple directional wave. She stood her ground and watched as the development supporters settled on the left side of the auditorium and the environmental activists headed to the right. Satisfied with the seating arrangement, Desiree returned the golf club to its owner and accepted applause from both sides for her peacemaking actions.

Ben felt his heart fill with adoration for Desiree's style and courage. Unable to verbalize his feelings at that moment, he instead channeled praise to Desiree and hoped she hadn't closed the pathways of her mind to him. Message sent, he stood tall and waited for a sign that she'd read the love in his heart and the commitment in his soul.

Susanna stared coldly at Desiree whose appearance of concern suddenly changed to one of joy. Sneering, "What's she so happy about?" Susanna turned and acknowledged the waves of some of the Heron Bay investors who seemed placated by Ben's serene bearing of assurance and control. What Susanna and the others didn't realize, though, was that Ben's confidence stemmed from his love for Desiree and not from the Heron Bay proposal that might or might not become a reality.

Seeming buoyed by Ben's aura, Susanna pointed to him and addressed the pro-development side by saying, "Rest easy, big spenders and deep pockets, one and all. Ben senses victory is headed our way. This afternoon we'll celebrate and dance down the highway to Perdido Key. Who wants the first waltz with me?"

A flurry of hands waving in front of her face blocked Susanna's view of the back rows, but she handled that situation by standing on the only empty chair in the front row. She surveyed the takers and teased a few by cooing, "In your dreams, sweetie. Better take a number and wait for the second set." When she spotted Trey in the back of the room, she pointed to him and said, "He asked me first, so I guess Mr. Trey LaBlanc's the man." She turned and watched Ben's expression that now mirrored stone. Pouting, she whispered in his direction, "You're just actin' like you don't care, but I know you really do."

Ben closed his eyes and remained silent.

"Go on and play hard to get if you want," Susanna said and then she added, "I won you before and I will again." Quickly spinning on her heels and with her back turned to Ben, she waved to Trey and called out, "Come up here with me and sign my dance card, suga'."

With an exaggerated wiggle of her hips, she held Trey's attention and that of the entire male audience in the auditorium except for Ben. Blowing kisses to a group of deeply tanned men wearing colorful Polo shirts, she presented a picture of superiority that matched the calculating looks of the attentive bankers seated front and center and wearing finely tailored three-piece suits.

As Susanna fluttered her false eyelashes nonstop in Trey's direction, he swaggered forward, chest puffed out, and eyes bright with mischief. Halfway down the aisle, he caught a glimpse of an attractive young woman with shiny blonde hair seated in the center of the Nature's Way section. When he heard a woman ask, "Did you bring the TVA report, Celeste?" Trey did a double take and seemed to like what he saw.

"Trey, Trey, over here," Susanna barked. "Sit by me at the big table on the stage."

Ben, hearing Susanna's order, tapped her on the shoulder and said, "Sorry, Susanna. The front's reserved for the principal parties, that's all."

"Oh really? Are you sayin' I'm supposed to sit back there with all those common people?" she asked, her eyes large with surprise and dismay.

Ben nodded and turned to watch Desiree move toward the conference table, decorated only by a water carafe, three tumblers bearing the Florida seal, and a stack of notepads. He admired the gentle sway of her hips as she approached the chair designated "Ms. McAndrews, Nature's Way." Unable to take his eyes off of her, he missed Susanna's mocking imitation of Desiree's walk that caused even the stiffest banker's lips to break into a grin.

Hearing laughter, Desiree tensed and turned in the direction of the giggles. Seeing Susanna's antics, she quieted Susanna and the entire pro-development crowd with a look born of grace and intelligence that quickly restored a level of dignity to the proceedings.

"Pooh on her," Susanna fumed when all eyes shifted away from her to Desiree. "And him, too," she added as Ben dashed to Desiree's side to help with her chair.

"Thank you, Ben," Desiree said politely, bending her head toward his to catch his whispered, "I love you, Desiree." Although she felt her heart race at the look of admiration in his eyes, she masked her feelings with coolness and motioned for him to take a chair at the opposite end of the table instead of the one closest to her.

From behind a curtained area at the back of the stage, Tip Carlisle strode forward, escorted by Senator Delaney and another man who wore an expression of moneyed concern. As Tip pulled out his chair and sat down, Big Jack bent toward him and hissed slyly, "Knife through butter, easy she goes." Then he signaled his companion, who approached Ben with a grin and a seedy handshake. In hushed tones, the men spoke briefly and much to Ben's surprise, the man passed him an envelope filled with money and "special op" orders Ben hadn't expected to receive.

Tip, seeming distracted by Desiree's short skirt and shapely legs, jumped when Big Jack jovially slapped him on the back and said, "I'm glad there's a man of your experience heading up our Fish and Wildlife Division. When did you say your appointment's due for renewal?"

Lowering his voice and avoiding Desiree's eyes, Tip answered, "In three months."

"Well, don't worry. I'll talk around on your behalf," Big Jack said as he smiled at Desiree and led his companion to their front row seats beside Susanna and Trey.

"Statehouse politics?" Desiree asked as Tip waited for the noise from the audience to subside. Then her expression darkened when she saw him acknowledge a sign from Big Jack, who sat confidently back in his chair and waited for the show to begin. Opening a file folder, she sighed in disgust and prepared for a long afternoon.

Tip adjusted the microphone wired to the center of the conference table and observed to Ben and Desiree, "Looks like everyone's settled, so let's get going here." After clearing his throat, he proclaimed to the audience, "The Environmental Regulations Board is now in session." Then he surveyed the crowd and said, "I'd like to remind everyone present that today's discussion is an informal hearing. Even so, as the designated moderator, I need to set some ground rules. First, I'd like to hear a description of the project in question. That'd be from you, Ben. Then I'll let the opposition speak. Ms. McAndrews, that's your time to outline your concerns. After that, I'll take comments from the audience, one at a time, please." When no one objected, he smiled broadly and declared, "Showtime, Ben. You're cleared for take off."

Some in the audience applauded and some laughed good-naturedly, but others shook their heads in disapproval when one man muttered sourly, "This hearing's wired; what a joke."

Ben waited for Tip to take his seat to the side of the podium and for the audience to settle into their chairs. Then he stood and facing Desiree, he said, "I'll keep my remarks short." Ignoring a ripple of applause that sounded from the back of the auditorium, he established eye contact with the audience and said, "When completed, Heron Bay will represent the final jewel in a crown project that all of Florida can point to with pride. As those familiar with Collier Development will attest, structurally there are no finer buildings, and aesthetically and environmentally, Heron Bay will complement its natural surroundings. Nothing will be destroyed for monetary gain; in fact, woodlands and wetlands will be protected by the design of the complex."

"Prove it, Mr. Collier," Desiree challenged.

"One speaker at a time, please," Tip reminded Desiree. Edging toward her, he said, "You'll have your chance to speak, Ms. McAndrews, so wait until Ben finishes."

Ben waved off Tip's assistance and said, "That's okay, sir. I welcome the opportunity to address Ms. McAndrews' concerns." He reached into his pocket and took out a folded piece of paper. Reading from the top, he said, "Nature's Way fears needless destruction of the wetlands." When Desiree nodded her head, he answered. "That's not a problem as boardwalks will be built over the wetlands to protect the natural habitat from the intrusion of mankind."

When applause sounded from the left side of the auditorium, Ben raised his hand to silence the crowd and continued, "Another fear stems from population and pollution problems." He looked to Desiree in anticipation of her response, but when she avoided his glance, he sat down and said, "I've also taken care of those issues by assuring that needed improvements will be made to the local Perdido Key infrastructure. In closing, I must emphasize that Heron Bay will be in full compliance with all local zoning ordinances and state building codes."

Tip nodded to Ben and turned to Desiree, who eyed Ben suspiciously as she watched him sit down. "Your turn, Ms. McAndrews," Tip said. "I hope you'll keep your remarks as brief as Ben's."

"Sorry, sir," she replied. "It seems to me that all Mr. Collier presented was a glossed over attempt at covering up the serious nature of his planned carnage of one of the last places of natural beauty."

"How so?" Tip asked.

"Let me count the ways," she said, leaning forward as she placed her hands flat on the table. Then turning on her charm, she stood up, faced the audience, and said, "First, I'd like to thank the officials of Florida who are willing to allow local citizen input about responsible development. Had those in power before been as astute, maybe we wouldn't be concerned today about the wholesale destruction of one of the last remaining unspoiled wetlands areas in Northwest Florida. A look at what's going on in neighboring Orange Beach in South Alabama shows the aftermath of developers reaping the most out of their investments."

She opened a folder and produced the front section of the *Mobile Register*. Holding it above her head, she said, "As you can see, the lead article concerns a developer who had an entire dune structure flattened without a permit or any form of approval and all under the guise of site preparation for a luxury condominium project. As a result of that man's sinister actions, nothing remains on the formerly pristine 300′ beachfront lot to show the extent of the devastation because the protected beach mice and their dune habitat are gone." With sadness in her eyes, she looked toward the ceiling and said, "Plowed under are the glorious sea oats and coastal grasses. In fact, nothing's there now except a stack of pilings and the developer's sign that advertises his 450 unit condo that 'Need Not Be Built'."

Tip shrugged his shoulders and said, "That's certainly a sad turn of events, Ms. McAndrews, but all that happened in Alabama, and we're talking here today about Florida."

"That's just my point, sir. Last week a precious part of Alabama was devastated. If Florida isn't careful, a similar catastrophe will happen here. Granted, Mr. Collier's proposal doesn't concern beachfront property, but it does impact on another fragile part of the environment. If you'll let me continue, I'd like to call on some other people in the audience who are prepared to speak this afternoon."

Tip looked toward Ben and asked, "Okay with you?"

"Sure," he answered. "I stand by my project and give my word that I am not the bad guy in this equation."

Desiree sighed in exasperation and explained, "I didn't say you were, Ben, but I believe if your project isn't stopped, the door may open for other bad guys to drive their bulldozers straight through."

Shaking his head, Ben motioned for Desiree to continue.

"All right, then," she said as she ran her finger down a list of twenty-some names.

In the audience, Susanna fidgeted in her chair and complained to Big Jack, "Don't tell me she's gonna drag all those people up on that stage."

The Senator frowned and stood up. Motioning to Tip, he said, "In the service of time, maybe Ms. McAndrews could summarize whatever the devil it is she's gotten those outsiders to say, then we can turn our attention to more meaningful activities."

When boos and hisses echoed from those seated to the Senator's right, he waved an accusatory finger at the more vocal of the group and said, "Before any of you speak, you oughtta have to show a Florida driver's license or proof of property ownership." The pro-development interests burst into applause at the suggestion and roared their approval as Big Jack bowed from the waist and sat down.

Tip quieted the audience by rapping twice on the microphone. "There, there, everyone, this is an open forum and Ms. McAndrews has the right to call outside consultants, so let her proceed."

Desiree closed her eyes and prayed for strength to resist the urge to retaliate against the deck she sensed was stacked against her. Instead, she resolved to present the best case she could. Returning to her list, she said, "I realize that not being a native Floridian, I run the risk of seeming intrusive. However, I am a steward of the earth, and I feel others are present who've also assumed that mantle of responsibility, so I would greatly appreciate your cooperation as I say what some of you may not want to hear." She turned to Ben, who sat back and beamed a look of adoration toward her.

Blushing, she glanced away and centered her attention on the stack of papers piled high in front of her. "Also, I realize time is a concern, and so for that reason, I will follow the Senator's request and paraphrase the key issues with the understanding that the supportive data compiled by my consultants will be entered into the public record." She paused and looked at Tip for his reaction.

"Sure, sounds logical and downright democratic," he answered. "So go ahead, Ms. McAndrews; tell us what you've found."

Desiree tucked a strand of her hair behind her ear and settled down to business. "From the Sea Lab at Dauphin Island...," she started.

"Excuse me, Mr. Moderator, but isn't Dauphin Island somewhere over there in Alabama?" Susanna interrupted.

Desiree didn't give Tip a chance to reply. Instead, she turned to Susanna and said, "Yes, Miss Delaney, thank you for the geography lesson. However, the point I wish to make relates to biology, so if you'd care to listen, you might learn something I think you should know." Pausing to smile when her supporters called out their encouragement, Desiree explained, "Sea Lab personnel investigated a 100' swath of dark brown gunk that washed up on the beach in front of the Holiday Inn at Gulf Shores. In light of the 50,000 hardhead catfish carcasses found in the Perdido Bay area late last month, researchers feared the massive fishkill was related to the unsightly foam."

"Who cares about hardheads? Can't eat 'em so what's the big deal?" Susanna asked well above a whisper.

Desiree grimaced at Susanna's insensitivity and continued, "Although analysis determined the brown foam was nontoxic plankton, scientific evidence indicates that residential growth in the South Baldwin area and the resultant product of septic tank runoff may have contributed to tremendous number of phytoplankton blooms that caused the brown coloration of the foam." She displayed a set of graphic photos and concluded, "And so, ladies and gentleman, take a look at this disturbing consequence of human population."

Listening carefully, Ben pointed to a drawing of the state-of-the-art water treatment facility he planned for Heron Bay and said, "I don't anticipate a brown foam situation at Heron Bay."

"My point, Ben, is that when more people take over an area, environmental problems develop," Desiree replied as she moved on down her list. "Let's consider wildlife preservation."

Big Jack rolled his eyes at Susanna and asked, "What now?"

Desiree, speaking slowly, said, "I realize that coyotes, *Canis latrans*, are not considered an endangered species, but they have thrived in this area since their introduction sometime in the 1920s by fox-hunters who wanted a new challenge or by people who wished to raise exotic pets. By nature of the coyote social structure, family packs prefer free range areas with lots of brush. If projects such as Heron Bay are allowed, the protective habitat for this living species that didn't ask to be brought here will go the same way as that of the endangered beach mouse."

Susanna hooted at the concept and nudged her father. "Ben's little sweetie sure seems desperate if she thinks people around here care a fig about a howlin' and maraudin' coyote. Maybe I oughtta ask her to trap me one. A couple of chomps and those nasty, yappin' little dogs our neighbors have would be history. What do you think, Daddy?"

Big Jack laughed loudly and turned to announce to those seated close by, "Ms. McAndrews may not realize it, but she's got a handle on nuisance control."

Frowning, Desiree made a small fist and held her breath as she counted to ten. Determined to ignore the running commentary between Susanna and the Senator, she introduced another point. "So far, I've touched on the danger of human overpopulation as related to water quality and wildlife habitat destruction. Now I'd like to mention irreplaceable plant life." She called for Beverly to come forward with a stack of photographs. Holding one so Ben could see, she said, "Let the record show that I'm presenting an overview of a natural wildflower bog located in the heart of the proposed Heron Bay site plan. Look closely and you can see blooming orchids, marsh pinks, pitcher plants, and hundreds of blazing stars."

When several in the audience asked to examine the photos, Desiree handed the pictures over and said, "Imagine our world without this kind of beauty. Thank goodness for groups such as the Friends of the Prairie, who formed in Escambia County to protect the endangered Perdido Pitcher Plant Prairie."

Ben watched Desiree glow as she eloquently explained, "For those of you who may be unfamiliar with the insectivorous pitcher plant, you might be surprised to learn that the elegant 'snake lily' thrived in the late 1700s in the Pensacola and Perdido Bay wet savannah areas. Unfortunately, precious acres of grassy fields that once were covered by pitcher plants have been replaced by thousands of houses and golf courses."

Susanna sneered when someone behind her observed, "Finally, the Nature lady is talking about Florida and I like what she says."

Turning around, Susanna leaned across the back of her chair and said, "Sir, let me tell you somethin'. If people wanna see those weeds she's braggin' on, they have to tromp through wet grass. Now tell me, do you know anybody who'd want to ruin a good pair of shoes just to watch a plant slime down some nasty ol' bugs? Who besides that tree hugger sittin' up there on that stage cares about somethin' as gross as that?"

When Desiree's eyes filled with frustration, she looked toward Ben.

Glaring at Susanna, he pounded his fist on the table and declared, "I, for one, care and I plan to reserve an extensive part of the Heron Bay site for a natural bog. No bulldozers will reach that area; that's a promise."

Senator Delaney sprang to his feet and shouted, "Ben, son, what are you sayin'? Surely you're not committin' some 2,000 acres to a wildlife preserve."

Ben smiled into Desiree's eyes and said, "That's exactly what my plans call for. See, it's sketched in here," he added as he unrolled a drawing. "Linnea came up with the concept of a natural preserve with boardwalks for all to enjoy. I think her idea has merit and I will see that it's implemented. I give you my word." He watched Desiree's eyes soften as she listened to him detail his conservation and recreation goals for Heron Bay.

Susanna sighed in disgust and wailed, "Please stop this hearin' before that woman up there gets Ben to say he'll cancel the offshore drillin' leases we're negotiatin' for Apalachicola. That area's loaded with untapped oil and gas reserves that're worth millions, maybe billions." She covered her face with her hands, and then peeking between her fingers, she said, "Tell me when this is over. I can't wait to get outta here so I can head for the nearest bar. All this cockamamie babblin's killin' my soul."

"There, there," said Big Jack as he consoled Susanna, who quivered like a butterfly. "Tip has this meetin' under control. Hush now, he's about to say somethin', so let's listen." As Susanna rested her head against his shoulder, the Senator watched Ben hand Tip a typed document.

Tip turned his back to the audience as he perused Ben's statement. Biting his lower lip, he took a deep breath and spun around. He looked first at Desiree and then at Ben before he addressed the audience. Slowly, he stood up and said, "I'd hoped we could draw this session to a close today, but I've just received a suggestion that I think might resolve this discussion. For it to work, though, Ms. McAndrews will have to agree to the proposition Mr. Collier has just placed on the table."

An audible sigh erupted from Desiree's supporters that matched the gasp that sounded from the pro-development faction. "Look out, Desiree," Beverly called, to which Trey replied, "I think Ben's the one up there who needs the help, not Desiree."

"Quiet, quiet," Tip ordered, tapping roughly against the microphone. He hastily passed Ben's proposal to Desiree and said, "This is his offer. Do you accept it?"

Desiree read the message and answered, "I do. It's a date."

As smiles twinkled in Ben's eyes, he said, "I'll call the airfield crew and have them ready the Jetcruzer for immediate takeoff."

"What's goin' on?" Susanna asked as Big Jack ran a hand across his forehead and hastily conferred with the man seated beside him. Susanna tugged on her father's arm, but he pushed her hand away. Sniffing back tears, she turned to Trey, but he, too, seemed preoccupied. "What about me?" she asked, pulling at Trey, who feigned a look of Hollywood sophistication as he zeroed his attention on the pretty blonde seated beside Beverly in the Nature's Way section.

Following the direction of Trey's look, Susanna frowned and said, "If that cookie you're eyeballin' is named Celeste, I'd suggest you quit droolin' at her 'cause you just look stupid and you're not makin' a very good impression. It'd be awful if your lollygaggin' messes up my plans for tonight."

Trey unwrapped a Cohiba cigar and licked it lustily. "Don't fret, Susanna. I wouldn't dream of spoiling your little soiree, besides, I feel luck is on my side tonight. The very prospect of Miss Celeste breathing her secrets hot and heavy on the back of my neck makes me sweat."

"Trey LaBlanc! You're disgustin' me!" Susanna exclaimed and stamped her foot on the center of Trey's left shoe.

Trey howled like a wounded pup, and Susanna screeched for all to hear, "Let the public record show that Heron Bay's most attractive and understandin' partner objects to any offer Mr. Ben Collier has tendered without requestin' approval from all partners. Furthermore, because of numerous contractual failin's on the part of the principal party, I have no choice but to withdraw my support of the Heron Bay project and to contemplate a law suit for the damages I've suffered."

"Bravo, Susanna!" Big Jack cheered and then he bragged, "That's my darlin' baby girl, a chip off the ol' block. Way to go, Susanna!" He raised his hands in a victory sign and mugged for the camera crew from Channel 6 that'd sprung to action at the back of the room.

Tip raised his eyebrows at the commotion coming from the Delaney section of the audience. Standing, he rocked back on his heels and announced, "Quiet, everyone! The principal parties have agreed to a site visit of the Collier Development Plantation located on St. George Island and then they will conduct a follow-up survey of Heron Bay at Perdido Key. Ben assures me that since Heron Bay will structurally and environmentally replicate the Plantation, he believes a study of that project and the Perdido Key site will supply Ms. McAndrews and her constituents with the proof they need to allow Heron Bay to move forward. So, this Environmental Regulations Board hearing stands adjourned for today. Thank you for your attendance and participation." Tapping the table with his hand, he declared, "That's all for now. Good afternoon."

Ben and Desiree faced each other. His eyes filled with excitement, Ben reached his hand toward Desiree and said, "Trust me. I know you'll like what you're going to see."

"Maybe," she answered although in her heart she already knew anything Ben presented would most likely strike a responsive chord deep inside her, her feelings for him were so genuine and so true. But knowing she couldn't run the risk of jeopardizing her objectivity, she resolved to tighten her heart-strings and hold to her convictions that'd brought her to Florida in the first place.

Together and as if on cue, Ben and Desiree stood, and after very formally nodding to one another, they walked their separate ways toward the audience. There Desiree faced the amazed looks and pointed questions of her colleagues, while Ben handled icy handshakes and cold stares loaded with strong disapproval and horrified disbelief.

Suddenly, a uniformed guard pushed open the doors and strode down the center aisle. He shoved his way through the throng of people who'd surrounded Ben and handed him a torn envelope with four words written across its back.

Without reading the message, Ben said, "I'll deal with this later." Seeming mildly annoyed by the interruption, he folded the envelope and started to pocket it, but he stopped when the guard said, "It's important, sir, something you need to know."

Frowning, Ben sighed as he unfolded the note and allowed his eyes to race across its cold words. He breathed deeply as the veins of his neck tightened and the lines of his forehead deepened into a scowl.

From out of the corner of her eye, Desiree caught the look of dark distress that beamed from Ben as he searched across the room for her. Sensing his need, she excused herself from her supporters and inched her way toward him. At his side, she touched his arm gently and asked, "What's going on? Tell me." When he didn't answer, she repeated more urgently, "Tell me, Ben, what's wrong? What is it?"

Ben stared blankly ahead and handed Desiree the note, which she quickly scanned. "Oh, no, surely not!" she exclaimed as she reached for Ben. "There's a mistake; this couldn't have happened."

"Oh, but it did and it's my fault," Ben said, clutching at his throat. Then with his voice rich with grief, he added, "I didn't keep my word, and now Linnea's paying the price for my selfishness."

"What do you mean?" Desiree asked, her voice blurred by confusion and concern.

Ben balled his right hand into a fist and replied, "Linnea counted on me to meet her at school, but I didn't show and I didn't bother to send anyone else to pick her up either. Instead, I chose to showboat here for your benefit and for the chance to enhance my own damned property portfolio."

"No, Ben, don't say that. You haven't done anything wrong; you're not responsible," Desiree replied, frantically looking into his guilt-ridden eyes.

Ben, sickened with shame and remorse, reclaimed the note and stepped back from Desiree. In a slow cadence, he read the message aloud, "Rolls totaled. Linnea driving." He paused and then asked, "Tell me, Desiree, who do you honestly believe should've been behind that steering wheel this afternoon?"

Before Desiree could respond, the guard tapped Ben on the shoulder and consoled, "I'm sorry, sir, but I thought you'd want to know."

"Where is she?" Ben asked.

Leaning forward, the guard answered in a whisper, "This way, sir, but I should warn you, she wasn't alone." Then he turned and motioned for Ben to follow him outside.

Desiree watched Ben walk a step behind the guard, who parted the crowd that now stood united as though they could sense they were witnessing a personal tragedy of greater importance than a battle over land use. As Desiree listened to the precise clicks of Ben's heels against the hardwood floor, she wished she could turn back time. Thinking, if only I'd thought, if only, if only, she looked at Susanna, who glared back at her and waltzed menacingly forward.

Determined to right all wrongs, Desiree met Susanna's harsh stare and matched her step for step. "Out of my way!" she called, daring Susanna to attempt to block her exit as she charged after Ben.

At that moment, Desiree knew exactly what she had to do, and she would not let anyone, especially Susanna Delaney, get in her way. Like a protective lioness, Desiree embraced the goal of the true mission she faced. Although she'd dreamed of making the world a better place for future generations, she now heeded the unspoken cry of a tiny world she sensed was sorely in need of repair. Whatever it took, she would work diligently and selflessly to see harmony restored to the life of the man she loved and that of his precious Linnea. With that thought firmly entrenched in her mind, she sought peace in prayer and bravely marched forward, ready and willing to accept the consequences of her actions.

Blinking back tears that stung her eyes, she made a cruel pact with herself and resolved to silence the dreams of her head and the hopes of her heart.

# Chapter 13

Escorted by two members of the Florida courtesy patrol mounted aboard twin, sleek Harley Hawgs, the Collier-Delaney entourage made record time as it sped toward Community Hospital. Ben and Desiree rode in the first car, a Buick LeSabre driven by Tip, whose every attempt at light conversation failed miserably. In contrast, Susanna, following closely behind in her Cadillac, seemed to delight Big Jack, her only passenger, with animated chatter that kept him on the edge of his seat.

Other drivers pulled off to the side of the road at the sound of motorcade sirens and the sight of flashing blue lights. Those who recognized Susanna, the Senator, and Ben beeped their horns and a few waved greetings, which Susanna and her father acknowledged with beaming smiles. Ben, though, sick with sorrow and consumed by guilt, ignored the public accolades and instead looked straight ahead.

Every so often, he nodded his head in response to Tip's comments, but in actuality, he didn't hear one word, so lost had he become in an abyss of remorse as he internalized his struggle between anger and regret. Desiree, seated behind Ben, sensed his anxiety and tried to alleviate the tension she felt emanating from him, but she, too, met defeat as he recoiled from her consoling touches and kind words.

"Let me share your pain," she offered, but Ben wasn't about to allow any of that.

With eyes downcast, he answered, "No, Desiree, this is my burden, not yours. In no way are you responsible for Linnea's accident. I'm the one who put my needs first and disregarded my duty to an innocent child who trusted me. I only hope I can make amends."

"Don't be so hard on yourself," Tip advised. "There's no need." Suddenly, the Buick bolted forward. "Did you feel that?" Tip asked, frowning as he tightened his grip on the steering wheel.

"Maybe the accelerator jammed or you have a clogged fuel line," Desiree commented, but when she felt the car resume its normal speed, she said, "Everything seems working fine now."

Within moments, though, another bump rocked their car forward. Glancing into the rearview mirror, Tip watched Susanna's car lurch forward and nudge his rear bumper a third and a fourth time. Frowning, he said, "Those Delaneys can act the fool bigger than anybody I've ever seen, but whatever on earth do they hope to gain this time? Surely they don't think they can turn this highway into a racetrack like the one in Daytona."

Desiree turned and looked into the passenger compartment of the tailgating Cadillac. For an instant, her eyes locked with Susanna's that flashed hatred. Thinking, I will not play that sad woman's game, Desiree deflected Susanna's look of overt hostility with a compassionate glance of her own as she prayed for a sign of the innate goodness of womankind. Then she faced forward and centered her thoughts on meditative strength. Allowing peace to calm her soul, she visualized Linnea the way she wanted to remember her — eyes alive with excitement and a loving spirit filled with mischief.

Desiree recalled the memory of Linnea the night before as she'd patiently instructed Ben in the fine art of French braiding her hair. Although he'd tried his best, his efforts had produced a wild, unmanageable style that'd so delighted Linnea she'd insisted Desiree capture the moment with her camera. Desiree smiled as she opened her purse and touched the roll of film Linnea had ordered her to have developed "immediately if not sooner" so she could show the pictures to her friends. Then Desiree giggled as she remembered Ben's horrified reaction to Linnea's request for a dragonfly tattoo she'd sworn was all the rage and something she absolutely had to have.

Hearing Desiree's laughter, Ben asked, "What's so funny?"

She leaned forward and answered, "Oh, Ben, I'm just happy because I'm certain Linnea's fine. I can see her and can feel her sweet presence. She's really all right; I know it in my heart."

"I hope you're right," he said as he glared ahead.

"Trust me, Ben. I sense her spirit's alive and her heart's beating strong for you and for her mother. Linnea's going to be fine; you'll see."

"Listen to Desiree," Tip said and then added, "I can't explain why, but I believe she's gifted in ways neither you nor I can understand and I think she knows what she's talking about."

Ben looked from Tip's weathered face to Desiree's angelic eyes and wondered if she actually had the power to see into the human heart. Holding her eyes with his own, he gathered his thoughts and then said, "I'm a man of science, Desiree, and military-trained to deal with factual evidence. So forgive me for doubting you, but I still find it difficult to suspend my disbelief. Are you certain you're not just trying to ease the situation and make me feel better?"

Desiree huffed her reply. "Although images of pleasing you have passed through my mind more frequently than not over the past few days, this is one time when concerns about you have taken a back seat to thoughts only of Linnea. Trust me, Ben; I can see her right now. She's counting the minutes until you arrive. In fact, I think she's becoming a bit impatient."

"Is that so? Tell me more."

Desiree rolled her eyes and said, "What do you think I have back here? A crystal ball?" She folded her hands across her lap and rested against the blue headrest that made her eyes radiant with jeweled beauty and sweet serenity.

For the first time since Ben had learned of Linnea's accident, he, too, relaxed and allowed Desiree's peaceful spirit to soothe the worries from his brow and erase the fears from his heart.

When Desiree watched the tension drain from Ben's shoulders, she prayed for the best outcome to a bad situation. Then she turned and waved to Susanna, who scowled darker than ever as she sank low behind the steering wheel.

Susanna's eyes formed daggers as she muttered, "I wonder what Ms. McAndrews is up to now. She looks as if she's just done somethin' that makes her look good and me bad, and, Daddy, I don't like that one iota."

"Well, darlin', I guess we'll soon find out since we're just about at the hospital entrance. It's on ahead but not far." When Susanna slowed her car and swerved to avoid hitting a speed bump, he said, "I think you oughtta pull up curbside instead of goin' in that public lot Tip's headin' for. Wonder why he's leavin' Ben and Desiree over there?"

Sneering at them, Susanna sputtered, "Well, I don't really care 'cause I'm stoppin' right here, right now. I'd rather dance with a snake than be seen walkin' with that woman. She's so sweet she makes me wanna... "

"There, there, Susanna," Big Jack consoled, "go on and take that place beside the patient entrance." Pointing to a spot bearing the name of a physician he knew, he grinned and said, "I got that boy his slot in medical school, so I think he owes me a favor or two."

She parked where Big Jack indicated and paused to admire her reflection in her vanity mirror. Patting her hair into place, she dabbed some perfume along her throat and said with a purr, "Ooh, I sure hope there's a 'Dr. Feelgood' waitin' inside there with a pocketful of Darvon or somethin' smooth like that. I need some swift medical attention for my splittin' headache. It's a bloomin' wonder I can even stand up, and to think all our problems happened because of that woman who's turned Ben into a fawnin' lap dog. Somehow I've got to get her out of this town before she brings more troubles to my happy home. Daddy, tell me the truth now. Don't you think I'm right to run her off?"

Big Jack watched Susanna glare at Desiree as Ben sprinted toward the emergency room entrance. "Seems like Ben's runnin' from her himself, so maybe it's already a done deal without you havin' to lift one pretty finger."

"I'm not so sure of that," Susanna whined, "but I do like the way she's hangin' back."

Big Jack cast a wary look at Desiree, who waited alone beside a set of automatic double doors, and said thoughtfully, "Interestin' she's not with Ben. Maybe he's figured out she's a complication he doesn't need and has told her as much."

Susanna's eyebrows shot up as she listened intently to Big Jack's conjecture. "Oh, Daddy, I hope you're right. I'd sure love to know what's goin' on between them, but I guess that'll have to wait since I really should find Linnea. I wanna help her get her story straight about the accident."

"Susanna!" Big Jack said as he wagged a finger at her. "Linnea's honest. I think you should keep her that way."

"Hmm," Susanna sniffed, "the sooner she learns to use the wiles and ways of a woman, the better off she'll be. Since I know how it's done, I feel it's my duty, no, it's my responsibility, to share my talents with my daughter and that's precisely what I'm gonna do."

Big Jack laughed and replied, "You do have your own method, no doubtin' that. So if you'll excuse me, I'll wait for you inside, especially since it seems Desiree is waitin' to talk with you. See her? She's standin' over there by the door. If you want, I'll warm her up as I go by."

Susanna responded by fluttering her eyelashes and moistening her lips while she watched Big Jack acknowledge Desiree as he passed through the doors and marched on inside. "Make way for Momma 'cause here I come," she said as she got out of her car and sauntered beside Desiree, who greeted her with a polite nod. Inching closer and without giving Desiree a chance to speak, she warned, "Bad things happen to people who get in places where they don't belong, dearie. Surely your momma taught you that lesson long ago."

"Excuse me?"

"I'm tellin' you that you have no business here; zippo, nada, none, get it? You witchy woman, you, you... "

"What are you saying? Why are you so mean to me? And what is it you're so afraid of?" Desiree asked rapid-fire as she watched Susanna's expression darken and her eyes smoke angrily.

"You heard me, Desiree McAndrews, so go on your merry way this very instant. I'm the woman who's needed inside, not you, so I want you to leave, now." When Desiree stood her ground and offered her hand to Susanna in sympathetic understanding, Susanna grabbed Desiree by the wrist and dragged her toward the street. Like a woman possessed, she flagged a passing cab that screeched to a halt, and using words loaded with profanity and passion, she shrilled to the driver, "Take this backbitin', two-faced trespassin' woman to the next county and bill Ben Collier for her fare."

"Oh, I think not!" Desiree replied as she broke free of Susanna's grasp and quickly opened the cab door for Susanna. Pushing her into the back seat, Desiree closed the door with a bang and spoke sharply to the driver. "Please drop Miss Delaney at the first kindergarten you see. Tell them Senator Delaney sent instructions that his spoiled daughter should be placed into

'Time Out' immediately. He wants her to cool down before she reenters the adult world." As she watched Susanna squirm and express her indignation at the top of her lungs, Desiree whipped out a $20 bill, handed it to the driver, and said, "Her ride's on me so make it last until this money runs out."

Without waiting for Susanna's next move, Desiree dashed into the hospital waiting room. Approaching the Senator with a cheery smile, she suggested he might want to come to the aid of his daughter outside. When he asked for an explanation, she simply replied, "Susanna's receiving a refresher course in one of life's little lessons, something like 'what goes around comes around'. I'm sure you of all people understand that one, sir." Then leaving Big Jack with a look of consternation blazed across his face, she walked triumphantly down the hallway.

Desiree's moment of victory didn't last long, though, as her focus soon switched from the eldest Delaney to the youngest member of his family, who whimpered, "Please don't be mad, please, please" in response to Ben's gruff, "I knew you couldn't be trusted."

Hearing the tone of Ben's voice run the range of mild displeasure to booming discontent and then back again, Desiree wondered what'd caused Ben, the repentant sinner she'd comforted during the ride to the hospital, to evolve into a raging judge and jury who now spewed forth a litany of wild accusations and unbelievable punishments. She listened a bit longer and soon the answer became readily apparent. Ben's wrath wasn't aimed at Linnea. Instead, he'd zeroed in on her driving companion, who seemed to have little to offer in his defense.

Ben, crazed with worry and needing an outlet for his anger, shocked Desiree when he erupted with an inflammatory, "What were you thinking, Etienne? This innocent child is a minor and you're an adult. Do you understand what I'm saying, son?"

"Oui, monsieur, mon faulte, tres mal, tres, tres stupide."

Desiree watched Ben close in on Etienne and feared the worst when Ben gritted his teeth and uttered a streak of purple prose such as she'd never heard. It was only when Linnea shrieked, "Make him stop, Desiree. Please, please!" that Ben backed off, but not for long.

He gauged the distance between himself and Etienne and closed the space to less than an inch. Then as he raised to his full height, he lowered his head to Etienne's and bellowed loud and long, "We have laws in this State and believe you me, I'll have your green card jerked in a heartbeat. Before night falls, I'll see you're put on the first slow boat to Gay Paree. That's a promise, Monsieur Ponytail."

Desiree's heart went out to Etienne, who winced and wilted under Ben's tough prosecution. Then she took a closer look at Linnea and could almost understand Ben's outburst. Etienne appeared unscathed as he bore no visible signs of physical trauma, but Linnea hadn't fared nearly as well. Bruised, bandaged, and sporting a neck brace, she squirmed against a wooden board strapped to the wheelchair she'd been placed in after her emergency examination.

"Back and neck injuries?" Desiree asked a nurse who'd wisely stepped between Ben and Etienne.

"Precautionary procedure, ma'am, doctor's orders," the woman replied as she offered Ben a washcloth to dry his brow that'd beaded with sweat.

A stream of tears fell from Linnea's eyes as she cried to Desiree, "Why doesn't he care how I feel?"

"Oh, but he does," Desiree reassured her.

Ben continued to look daggers at Etienne and remained sullen and silent.

Desiree read his look as one that foreboded eminent and severe bodily harm, so she reached for Ben's arm and tugged gently. "Go on, Ben, tell Linnea what you said on the way over here."

Ben and Desiree exchanged long glances and then he concentrated on Linnea. When he heard her whisper, "Forgive me, Dad. I'm sorry I broke your car," he felt his macho facade crumble.

On bended knee, he reached for her bandaged hands and held her gently. "Linnea, Linnea, whatever am I going to do with you?"

As serious as a judge, she answered, "It's not me I'm worried about; it's Etienne I'm scared for. Please, oh, please, don't kill my boyfriend. I like him so much and none of this was his fault. Besides, he's my date for the Cotillion."

"Boyfriend?" Ben asked, the tips of his ears reddening at the thought. "You can't be serious. What's going on here?"

Linnea's eyes flashed with exasperation as she pleaded with Desiree, "Help me and Etienne, too. Explain things to Dad; you can make him understand." With a final angst-filled gasp, she rationalized, "If he'll listen to anyone, that person's you."

Whether or not Desiree could've successfully interceded on Linnea and Etienne's behalf became a moot point as a sudden "That's not quite true, sweetie" exploded from Susanna, who swept forward on her father's arm as they strolled down the corridor. When they pushed past Desiree and stood in front of Linnea, Susanna stepped away from Big Jack and stopped cold in her tracks. There she dropped her head and wailed pitifully as she swayed from side to side. Then, appearing very much like a tidal wave, she virtually covered the area with a surge of tears at the sight of Linnea, wheelchair-bound and encased in a cocoon of sterile gauze and translucent surgical tape. She teetered on her spike heels toward Ben, rested her head on his shoulder, and cried, "Look at Linnea, Ben. Why, oh why, couldn't this have happened to me and not her?"

As Linnea protested, "Oh, Momma, I'm really okay. The doctor said he just wants to be sure everything's fine," Susanna waved off her words and persisted in snuggling into the hollow between Ben's neck and his shoulder. As if on cue, she turned loose another reservoir of tears that cascaded down her freshly rouged cheeks.

"Oh no, surely not another display of the Delaney crocodile waterworks," Ben sighed with disgust. He turned to Desiree and away from Susanna, who sniffed and sobbed into the silk handkerchief Big Jack quickly pulled from his coat pocket as he rushed to her side.

Frowning darkly at Desiree, Big Jack wrapped his arms around Susanna and said with cold authority, "Never mind him or her, darlin'. Ben'll regain his senses as soon as the Heron Bay decision comes down. That's when he'll execute a royal about-face."

"I pray you're right, Daddy," she replied, her eyes dancing with hope and excitement.

"Yes, my dear, prayer's good, so I think I should say one right now." The Senator waited for a moment and then he folded his hands and intoned in a voice worthy of a grand cathedral,

"Dear Lord, please make Ben's epiphany swift and true, and while you're at it, go ahead and please, oh please, remove the evil forces that've come into our midst."

Taking in Big Jack's every word, Etienne gasped and his swarthy complexion blanched white, his face a reflection of terror and guilt. He shared a quick look with Desiree whose own expression mirrored disbelief.

"Moi?" Etienne asked Linnea. "Is your distinguished grandpapa talking about me?"

"Never you," Linnea piped up in Etienne's defense. "Or Desiree either," she added as she sat as tall in her chair as her confined state would allow her to move.

Ben, in a show of solidarity with Desiree, put his arm around her waist, and after smiling approvingly at Linnea, he declared, "As God is my witness, I can assure everyone here that Desiree McAndrews is anything but evil. If anyone dares to doubt the purity of her heart and the divinity of her actions, then I challenge that person to step forward and say so in front of me."

Susanna rolled her eyes at Ben's words and stalked toward a pharmacy technician who wheeled a medicine cart through a curtained room divider. With a sugary "Hi, handsome, surely you have somethin' in there for a headache," she attracted the attention of the young man, who seemed unable to take his eyes off of her as she unfastened the top buttons of her suit jacket and leaned forward.

She peered into the sea of white cups filled with colorful capsules and pills, and pointing to some little red ones, she said, "Ooh, that's what my doctor prescribes for me all the time. I could really use a couple right about now."

"I'm sorry, ma'am," the technician answered as he stepped protectively in front of his cart. "These meds are for our patients only. Hospital rules, you see."

Susanna put her hands on her hips, sashayed for the man's benefit, and formed her lips into a coy pout. Holding her hand to her forehead and feigning a swoon, she lolled her head back and begged, "Medical alert, medical alert; somebody needs to heal my hurtin' head and breakin' heart." When no one came to her aid, she wailed more pitifully, "What's a helpless woman got to do around here to get a few reds? Strip naked or what?" Not missing a beat, she discarded her suit jacket, kicked off her heels, and toyed with the straps of her filmy camisole. She stopped their slinky progression down her arms only when Linnea gasped and cried, "No, Momma! No, no, don't do it."

Linnea blinked back tears and glanced toward Etienne, who stood as still as a statue. In a panic, she then looked at Ben, who wore a disgusted frown as he apologized to the technician for Susanna's impropriety. Linnea waited until the technician retreated behind a shielded area and then she squeezed her hands into fists and declared, "This is all too much for me. I swear if I ever get home, I'll never leave, and while I'm at it, I think I will stay away from cars, too."

"How about adding men who are too old for you to your 'Off Limits' list?" Ben asked.

Linnea frowned and replied defensively, "Etienne's not some old geek, Dad. He's French and more sophisticated than the boys at school. That's probably why you think he's so mature."

"Wrong, Linnea," Ben disagreed and then he added, "Sophistication isn't the issue here; it's more a matter of right versus wrong."

"The Puritan speaks," Susanna said under her breath as she mocked Ben with her eyes.

Ignoring Susanna, Ben explained by saying, "It's improper for any man to mess with a young child, which brings me to another point." As he edged toward Etienne, he stared directly into his eyes and asked, "Just what were you doing with Linnea in my car this afternoon?"

Looking down, Etienne swallowed twice and jammed his hands deep into the pockets of his designer black jeans that fit him like a glove. Out of the corner of his eye, he watched the Senator seat Susanna on a stool that resembled a throne and then take his place beside her. Hearing her say, "Ben shouldn't be so mean to that young man," Etienne relaxed, but only for a moment because a second later Big Jack lurched past Susanna and positioned himself on Etienne's other side.

"Yes, why were you with my grandbaby?" echoed Big Jack, his eyes scrunched into a penetrating squint as he glared into Etienne's. Rolling his shoulders into a linebacker's stance, he leaned forward and hissed into Etienne's ear, "I suggest, son, you come clean now or you'll have to answer to me, as well as to Linnea's father and he's no man to fool with."

"Sir Aviateur?" Etienne asked.

The Senator reeled back on his heels and said, "Well now, at least you know to address him as 'sir', but I bet what you don't know is that he set records downin' enemy aircraft in dogfights and he took to the skies like a champion every time he got the call. So, if you wanna risk becomin' that man's target, I suggest you think about your answer long and hard 'cause, believe you me, Ben's got the touch and the heart of a warrior."

Gulping once and then a second time, Etienne looked at Linnea and fidgeted with his long hair he'd clasped with a black cord at the back of his neck. He loosened the collar of his white shirt and started to speak, but the words seemed to catch in his throat.

"Well?" Ben asked, "Go ahead, say something. I'm waiting to hear your spin on your afternoon excursion with a minor."

"Dad! Don't!" Linnea squalled, her face contorted with embarrassment.

Etienne stepped forward, and with his hands opened and outstretched in a conciliatory gesture, he explained, "J'regret . . . oui, oui, c'est difficile, Monsieur Collier. Hmm, Monsieur et Mademoiselle Delaney, Mademoiselle Desiree." With all eyes on him, he broke into a cold sweat and swiped at his forehead with a shaky hand.

Desiree stepped forward and said, "Take a deep breath; that may help."

Etienne followed her suggestion, and when his breathing switched from ragged to almost normal, he spoke again, but this time more slowly and in broken English. "I am sincere with my regrets at what happened today. Linnea, I mean Miss Delaney, called in need of help with her car. She said she was alone at school and wanted assistance, and so she asked if I, Etienne, could come help her. Of course, I did, by taxi, livery cab, you know what I mean?"

Etienne paused and inhaled deeply. When he exhaled, Ben leaned toward him and sniffed the air around Etienne's mouth.

"Sir?" Etienne said, stepping back.

"Homemade Breathalyzer test for alcohol," Ben explained. Then he added, "You passed, by the way, so go on now and tell us what happened when you arrived at Linnea's school."

"Merci, I shall," Etienne answered, sporting a smile of tentative relief. "Then, we, Linnea and I, that is, went to the car. It was, how shall I say? Unlocked?" He looked toward Linnea who beamed encouragement back at him. After clearing his throat, he continued, "Yes, the door was open, but Linnea had no key to the engine, that's when she said it was okay because you, Sir Collier, would still want us to drive your fine car if we could get it to go."

"Is that so?" Ben grumbled. He narrowed his eyes at Linnea and frowned so deeply that she blushed and stared at Susanna's shoes and suit jacket that still littered the floor.

"So, I said to Miss Linnea that she should not worry because I would hot wire the car as I am accustomed to do with the tractors at my familial vineyards in Bordeaux. Then with a zip we could go. So, that is what I did, and we went, but not far because… because… "

"My turn, Etienne," Linnea interrupted. She paused dramatically and then confessed with a sad sigh, "I had trouble with the car because I drove it the same way Dad does down that hill… You know, fast and faster still and then straight into the curve halfway down, but I guess I didn't handle the turn exactly right."

"Evidently you had a very bad driving instructor," Susanna commented with a sneer as she narrowed her eyes at Ben, who stood quietly beside Desiree.

"Whatever," Linnea continued. "Anyway, before I could put on the brakes, the car flipped over the guardrail, flew across the ditch, and landed in the thicket of bamboo and pampas that grows beside the big bend."

Linnea's description brought forth a mixture of sounds that reverberated off of the tiled hospital walls and sounded much like an ancient Greek chorus at its most fevered pitch. As horrified sighs passed between Desiree and Ben, the Senator and Etienne gasped in unison. Susanna, though, bested them all as she took center stage and grooved to her own beat that she punctuated with hysterical cries of "Oh, Lord, no!" and "Not Deadman's Curve!"

Linnea raised her eyes heavenward and bit her lower lip as tears flowed from her eyes to her chin. Babbling almost incoherently, she concluded her story by admitting, "I must've misjudged my speed on the middle part of the road. So, see, everything that happened today was all my fault, not Etienne's." She paused, and struggling to regain her composure, she said, "Dad, I'm sorry about your car, and Momma, it wasn't Dad's fault either, so don't blame him. Just nobody be mad at me or at each other, okay? I promise I won't do anything bad again, ever." Then she lowered her chin against her neck brace and closed her eyes prayerfully.

Each person reacted to Linnea's words at different levels of intensity. Etienne puffed his cheeks full with air and quietly exhaled in a gesture of unbridled relief. The Senator, rubbing his chin, walked away from Etienne and poignantly studied a painting of Florence Nightingale that hung at an odd angle on the wall.

Desiree stood off to one side of the group where she exchanged compassionate looks with Linnea and then with Ben who she loved with her eyes as she watched him make his peace with Etienne and then kneel beside Linnea's chair. She admired Ben's ability to restore joy to Linnea's sad eyes and happiness to her troubled heart when he teased her about scoring a perfect landing that he swore was destined for the record book.

"It's good to hear you laugh again," Ben said. "I'm thankful the only thing you broke was my car."

"Have you seen it?" she asked.

"No and I'm not sure I want to after hearing about your flight plan. Next time, though, I think you should let me tag along for the ride, say in about twenty years or so."

"Dad! You can't be serious! That'd make me thirty-two years old," Linnea replied, her eyes wide with dismay. She looked to Desiree, who deferred to Ben with a smile and a wink as he tucked a blanket across Linnea's scraped and skinned knees.

Susanna, seeming frustrated that everyone's attention centered around Ben and Linnea and not her, crowed, "Seems to me we oughtta be celebratin' here instead of cryin' over a piece of twisted metal and chrome." When all eyes turned in her direction, she eased off of her high perch and sauntered toward Etienne.

She smooched the air around his face and said, "That's for you, you darlin' boy; you're a real hero. Thank you for helpin' my baby try to get home. I hope you always stay responsible, not like some men who seem to forget what's really important." Then she nudged Ben with her stockinged foot and ordered, "Help me put on my clothes."

Out of the side of her mouth, she sniped to Desiree, "I know this is a stretch for Ben since he much prefers undressin' me to coverin' me up. It's been that way for years and guess what? There's more." When she watched the color drain from Desiree's cheeks, she flared her nostrils and confided suggestively, "Although he's had lots of practice unsnappin' and unzippin' pretty women from here to Havana, he and I both know there's only one lady he's kept undressed the longest and that's me, yours truly. So, Desiree, I suggest you deal with that bit of unclassified information, that is, if you can."

Desiree turned her back to Susanna and decided she'd rather not participate in Susanna's charade of hollow lies and evil innuendoes. Instead, she watched Ben and listened as Linnea valiantly attempted to convince him he should bypass the penalty phase of her punishment and move directly on to her rehabilitation.

"So I'm grounded?" she asked.

"Only for life," Ben replied.

"But, but the Cotillion. My new dress. Etienne and I..."

"Sorry, Linnea. You're not going anywhere for a while. Don't you think that's fair, Desiree?"

"Who gives a dingedy dong what that hussy thinks?" Susanna bellowed with a snarl like an agitated pitbull. Stormy with rage, she shouted, "Hold on one blasted minute, Ben Collier. I call the shots in my house, and since you've made yourself a transient in our life, I'll have you know that my daughter does not take orders from you and most certainly not from her."

Ben's eyes smoked with red-hot anger as he stepped forward to have his say, but his movement was blocked by the appearance of Linnea's doctor whose demeanor was so intense that Susanna held her breath and became silent, but only for a second.

"It sure seems hot in here. I think somebody oughtta check the A/C," she complained as she fanned her flushed face with both hands.

The doctor brushed her out of his way and barked, "You people are out of control and your insane bickering sickens me! Can't you see this is a hospital and you're in a triage area?" Moving his head like a videographer taping a crowd scene, he waited until quiet was restored and said, "Thank you. That's more like it." Then he turned to Susanna, who eyed him curiously from the top of his head to the soles of his Gucci loafers, and said, "You must be Linnea's mother, Mrs. Delaney."

"Yes, doctor, I am; however, it was my saintly momma who was called Mrs. Delaney. Most people address me by my career name 'Miss Delaney' but you may call me Susanna. Bet you'd like that, now wouldn't you?" she asked as she batted her eyelashes and waltzed toward the man.

Coughing nervously, he stepped back and answered, "Fine, Susanna." Then he faced Ben and asked, "And you, sir, I assume you are Mr. Delaney, Linnea's father."

Ben winked at Linnea and replied, "We have a twelve year history. Isn't that so, Linnea? But my name is Bennett Collier, not Delaney."

The doctor grunted an unintelligible response, checked his watch, and said, "Well, okay then, whatever. Now though, since I need to see another patient, let me run quickly through Linnea's case. She's banged up a tad, but she's young and evidently athletic, so she shouldn't have any major problems with her recovery. I recommend she stay here overnight for observation and then she should rest at home through the weekend. Someone should call my office to schedule an appointment for next week. Any questions?"

Linnea's eyes clouded with disappointment as she spoke up, "Sir, does that mean I can't dance Saturday night at my Cotillion?"

The doctor frowned and replied, "I really don't think that's such a good idea. A pretty girl like you will have plenty of other dances in your future." Not giving Linnea a chance to object, he tapped his watch and said, "So, that's it. An orderly will wheel you to your room."

"Not!" Linnea fumed as the doctor exited behind a curtained barrier.

Susanna made a face and pouted, "That cold fish could use some poachin', but I don't think I wanna bother with a stuffed shirt like him." She fluffed her hair and motioned for Ben to follow her as she said, "I think we should all leave this precious triage to those who understand whatever the dickens that word means. Ready to go home, Linnea?"

Linnea shook her head and answered, "Only if I get to stay with Dad."

"Oh, Linnea, I'm sorry, but I'll have to take a raincheck this time," Ben apologized, his voice strong with regret. "I'm under orders to show Desiree the development at the Plantation. She's on a tight schedule and I have lots of territory to cover with her."

Susanna laughed derisively at his words and retorted, "It seems to me what she has to offer could most likely be covered with a postage stamp."

"Susanna!" Ben warned.

Desiree, now more determined that ever not to participate in the ongoing Collier-Delaney quarrel, picked up a piece of notepaper and wrote down a phone number. She handed the note to Ben and said, "This is where you can reach me after I conclude my business with the Heron Bay proposal."

Ben scanned the number and recognizing the "303" area code as Colorado's, he complained, "But that's not what we agreed to today. You must see the Plantation at St. George Island and then Heron Bay on Perdido Key. That was our bargain, remember?"

"I can handle the visits myself," she replied as she turned to leave.

"No, Desiree," Ben disagreed, racing after her. "We've come too far to stop now. Listen to me for a minute. Please, you can't leave like this, at least not without telling me why."

She stopped at the exit and debated whether she should stay or go. Sighing, she faced Ben and explained, "I'm sorry I intruded into your family relationships. That was never my intent, honest."

Ben took her by the hand and drew her to his chest. Lowering his lips to hers, he kissed her and said, "Surely you can tell you're one part of my life I can't let go. I've missed you so much and I want us to be together." He held her as closely as he dared, considering the time and place, and waited to feel her response to his need.

Desiree's heart raced at their closeness, but she held to her guard and said after several agonizing minutes had passed, "I'm sorry, Ben, but I've thought our situation through and I know it's for the best that I handle the environmental surveys on my own. Besides, Linnea needs you now."

"Desiree, darling, listen to me. I'm sure Linnea will be fine with her mother and in time, she'll understand that you and I needed to work together on this project. I want to show you everything firsthand; it's important to me, to us." He massaged her back and added, "When you're rested, I know you'll agree, so at least say you'll sleep on it tonight and we can make our plans in the morning."

Although Ben's offer tempted her for more than a moment, she shook her head, and looking into Ben's deep, dark eyes, she said, "No, Ben. Regardless how exhausting the past days have been, I've decided to rent a car and drive to the Plantation tonight. Didn't you say it's only about seventy-five miles from here? So please phone ahead and have your house opened. Okay?"

Dejected, Ben dropped his hands from Desiree's waist and answered, "It sounds as though you've already worked out your plans and they don't include me."

She shrugged her shoulders and explained, "Look, Ben. I've been away from Boulder too long already. I've got to wrap up this project quickly."

Ben clicked his tongue against the roof of his mouth and sighed before he said, "It seems to me your Boulder staff has managed fine without you so far."

She winced and answered, "For your information, I've been in direct contact with my office on a daily basis and to keep all assignments on target, I plan to ask Beverly to go there to coordinate our project time lines while I finish up on this end."

"That may take some time," he remarked. "Maybe longer than you think, possibly even a lifetime."

Shaking her head, she continued, "Seriously, Ben, I intend to complete all my work here in a few days so I can leave Florida with a clean slate."

Ben held Desiree's eyes for a long, hard minute and then he followed his heart. Not one to take no for an answer, he gathered Desiree in his arms and carried her through the entrance to an atrium constructed of frosted glass walls that soared to the sky. Protected by the shadows of pampered palm trees and tropical bushes, he placed her on a garden bench and sat beside her.

"Oh, Ben," she said. "You're making this so hard, but I know what we must do."

"So do I, my darling," he replied, kissing her tenderly. Ever so gently, he cradled her against him and whispered divine sweet nothings he'd saved only for her.

"Do you love me, Desiree?" he asked.

"God forgive me, but with all my heart I do," she answered.

And so with a canopy of blue skies and white clouds above them and the scent of passion flowers and sweet gardenias surrounding them, Ben and Desiree allowed their love to flow. Unwilling to let their time together end, Ben said, "Surely you know my feelings for you are true; you are the love of my life, Desiree. I swear it."

She stroked his cheeks and replied, "I believe you, Ben, and for me, that's enough."

"But it's not enough for me," he answered. "Marry me, Desiree, say you will."

Although her heart pounded the beat of love, her mind flashed a message that silenced the burning desire Ben caused to flame throughout her. As a fierce battle raged between her head and her heart, she fought back tears that threatened to rain sorrow and regret for the rest of her life.

Desiree knew her love for Ben was everlasting, but even so, the only choice she could ethically make led her down another road, the one less traveled.

"Well?" he asked. "Will you be my wife?"

She rested her head against his shoulder and spoke the words that crushed two hearts, "No, Ben, I can't marry you. Not now, not ever. I'm sorry, so, so sorry."

Stunned, Ben vehemently protested with his eyes, with his hands, and with his soul, but all to no avail.

Desiree had made up her mind.

Blinded by responsibility, she straightened her clothes, slipped into her shoes, and kissed Ben good-bye. As she stood to leave, she reached for his hand. Into it, she placed his Academy ring and touched his fingers that still burned with his desire to caress her, to love her in every tender place and in every secret way.

Unable to face the hurt she knew she'd find in his eyes, she left him in the atrium, alone with his broken heart and his love for her, the woman he couldn't live without, the woman he didn't want to lose a second time around.

As fast as she could go, Desiree ran toward the exit and wept when she heard Ben call out to her. Walling off her heart from her desire that threatened to send her straight back into his arms, she moved on and didn't allow herself to turn back. That was when her heart shattered as Ben's words amplified in her head and resounded deep in her soul.

"Desiree, Desiree, don't leave me, not now. I beg you. Please, Desiree, please."

# Chapter 14

Trey raised his glass in tribute to Susanna. Bowing his head, he declared, "To the wisest and most determined woman ever born."

"How you flatter me," she replied as she lowered her eyelashes modestly. Peeping at him with childlike innocence, she added, "I swear I wouldn't stand a prayer in this harsh world of lies and deceit without a true ally and confidant like you."

"Now, now Susanna," he answered with a laugh. "I seriously doubt you'd have one bit of trouble holding your own with the devil. Even so, I still like hearing you say you need me around every now and then." He turned away from her and as he stared into his martini, he said almost regretfully, "Of course, if I'm not available, there's always Ben, my buddy, ready and willing to come to your rescue."

Susanna's cheeks flamed and her eyes flashed with intensity. Pacing toward a bay window in the front of her living room, she pursed her lips and sighed, "Yes, Ben, your friend and my..."

"Your what, Susanna? What is he to you, really? Come on now, tell me why after all these years you can't let him go?" As he waited for her reply, he refilled his glass, dropped in an olive, and watched it float in a pool of fine gin and blended vermouth.

Susanna sauntered up to him and held out her glass. "Be a suga' and top off mine, please, darlin'. Maybe that'll put me in the mood to answer your questions." She smiled as she listened to Trey shake a fresh batch of martinis, and then moistening her lips, she crowed, "I bet you're not the only person who wonders about Ben's relationship with me. Thoughts of him lovin' me must drive Desiree McAndrews batty."

"Probably so since she seems to care about him on much more than a purely professional basis," Trey replied as he poured Susanna another drink and watched her down it in one swift gulp. Frowning, he cautioned, "Better pace yourself, sweetheart; you'll last longer that way."

"You're no fun!" she retorted, placing her glass on a table. "At least Ben knows how to entertain me properly."

"Is that so?" Trey asked and then he added, "Does that mean you and he have, how shall I say it? Renewed your nocturnal activities?"

"My goodness, Trey," she answered with a sexy purr in her voice, "you sound almost jealous. Could it be that you have feelin's for me?"

Trey paused and seemed to weigh his words as he placed his nearly empty glass beside Susanna's. Then he looked directly into her eyes and said, "Don't change the subject, Susanna; I asked about you and Ben. I'm not a part of that equation."

"Oh, but maybe you could be," she answered as she raised her eyebrows and smiled brightly. Fluttering her eyelashes, she waited for a moment and then she lowered her voice to a husky tease and asked, "How about it? To me, it seems the perfect answer to this highly unsatisfactory situation I'm facin' right now." Pursing her lips, she explained, "Look at it this way. You and I can have some fun sportin' and courtin' and when Ben sees us together, I'll bet you odds he'll come runnin' back, just beggin' for my affection. But I won't give in to him easily."

"Of course not, that's not your style," Trey said knowingly.

Susanna's eyes twinkled as she swayed her hips and agreed, "You've got that right, suga'. I'll show him Desiree's not the only woman in town who knows the way to his heart. But this time I'm gonna take permanent possession by beatin' her at her own game."

Trey ran a hand through his hair and sighed, "Oh, boy, this should be good."

"Better than good, darlin'. It'll be the absolute best 'cause I'm gonna torture Ben with images of you and me together and when his ego can't handle the thought of losin' me to you, he'll want me back; I just know it." Watching Trey's eyes brighten, she continued, "That's when I'll hold out until I'm sure Desiree's out of the picture. Then and only then will I allow Ben to resume his proper place in my happy home and deep in my lovin' heart. Just think, with Desiree gone and Ben back with me, the coast will be clear for the development of Heron Bay. That's when you, Daddy, and I will start dancin' from one high dollar deal to another, depostin' checks in banks from here to the Bahamas. I can't wait, can you?"

A worried frown marked Trey's brow as he shook his head and said, "You make it sound so simple, but I don't think you've factored in Ben's intelligence. He's not an easy man to fool. He'll see right through you. And me."

Laughing, Susanna tossed back her head and replied, "Don't be so sure of that. Besides, I have my manhandlin' weapon ready to fire."

"Oh? Fill me in on the details. This I've got to hear."

She wagged a finger naughtily at Trey and answered, "Trey, darlin', surely a Southern gentleman like yourself respects the fact that a lady should always have a few secrets that belong only to her." Then walking across the room to a bookcase filled with aviation histories and steamy romances, she reached for a worn volume pushed off to one side, and pulling it from the shelf, she said, "It's all in here, my very own and most intimate *Book of Love* that I've kept from the first day I caught Ben Collier's attention and stole his heart." Slowly, she opened her book and motioned for Trey to come closer.

His eyes widened as he peeked at a page she'd dog-eared and underlined with scarlet ink. "My goodness!" he chortled as he skimmed the passage and then he asked, "Care to demonstrate that maneuver?"

Giggling, she quickly snapped the book closed and taunted, "In your dreams, darlin'. Anyway, I just showed you that part to whet your appetite. There's more and better about Ben and me, but that's information I don't plan to share with anyone, not even you."

He frowned and muttered, "Maybe I've already heard those classified secrets."

Susanna's face clouded as she replied, "I seriously doubt that because if Ben'd told you, you wouldn't be wonderin' now about him and me. Of course, though, I might be persuaded to join you in an impromptu kiss'n tell session, dependin' on the prize."

"You mean if I agree to help you snag Ben in your lair of filled wetlands and property transfers?" he asked as he reached into his pocket. Producing a roll of breath mints, he popped one in his mouth, offered her another, and raising his eyebrows, he winked and said, "Maybe we should seal our deal with a kiss."

"Not if you're insinuatin' I need candy to sweeten the taste of my suga' lips!" she retorted with a pout as she placed her hands on her hips and stepped out of Trey's reach.

"No, no, Susanna," he sputtered, coughing nervously. "That's not at all what I was thinking. I just remember Ben once told me how much you like peppermint swirls."

Laughing, she rolled her eyes and said, "Ben wasn't talkin' about a flavor, silly, but rather a roll he perfected in a T-34 high above Silverhill." She watched Trey's eyes dance, and then crooking a finger at him, she said, "Come here, darlin', and I'll show you one of my own spinnin' moves that I guarantee will drive you wild and into a state of amazin' passionate bliss."

"Oh, yes!" Trey said as he quickly reached for Susanna's face and stroked her cheeks that glowed with excitement. Closing his eyes, he rocked against her and sought her inviting lips, but instead of losing himself to her untamed kiss, he suddenly hesitated and turned away.

"What's wrong?" Susanna asked, her voice haughty with surprise. "Surely you're not backin' out on me now, especially not after I clued you in on my master plan!"'

Shaking his head, Trey studied the pattern in Susanna's Persian carpet and then slowly walked toward the bookcase. When his eyes stopped on a photograph of Ben the day he'd received his Navy "Wings of Gold," he breathed heavily and apologized, "I'm sorry, Susanna, but I don't think the time's right for us to ride on passion's highway to heaven."

Susanna lolled her head back and replied, "Surely you're not sayin' you're gonna pass up the chance to spend a delightfully delirious interlude with me behind closed doors?" Smiling as she watched Trey struggle with his thoughts, she puckered her lips, tapped her foot impatiently, and coaxed, "I'm countin' to ten, so you'd better start movin' if you wanna get groovin'."

Trey reached for his drink, sipped deeply, and swirled the liquid in his mouth before swallowing it whole. Then he placed the glass on a silver tray and returned to the bookshelf where he picked up Ben's photograph and turned it face down. Saying,

"That's better," he swung back around and narrowed his eyes in a dramatic leer aimed toward the center of Susanna's heaving chest.

Bobbing his head lustily, he opened his arms and invited her to come to him. As he watched her prance forward with a look of heated pleasure deep in her eyes, he licked his lips and said, "You're right, Susanna; it's time for us to chase away the past and test some new techniques that just might curl our toes. After all, it is for the benefit of us all."

Susanna wiggled her way into Trey's embrace and led him like a lamb to a white leather sofa that squeaked as they tried first one way and then another to find the optimal comfort zone.

Masterfully, Susanna stroked Trey's cheeks with loving hands and then nuzzled his neck with kisses that blew directly past flirtation and zoomed straight toward dreamland status. Only when she heard him gasp, "Heaven help me, Susanna, but I can't handle this!" did she still her exploration of his most manly pulse point.

"What's your problem now?" she asked, frowning as she propped herself up on one elbow. She stared at the ceiling and then blurted, "I swear I'll scream if you tell me you're worryin' about losin' your wife and her money. Look, it's like this; what we have to gain through Heron Bay makes Pamela's bank roll look as thin as her wimpy hair."

"Oh, Susanna," he moaned. "Call me a fool, call me an idiot, but I'm afraid you and I are about to make a colossal mistake, one we'll live to regret."

"Trey LaBlanc, a man of conscience? Pooh on that notion 'cause we both know you're no Ben Collier, so quit actin' like him. Come on, now, relax and let Nature take her course." She trailed hot kisses down his throat and said reassuringly, "Anyway, it's not like we're doin' somethin' that really means anything. We're just practicin' our parts to divert Ben's attention away from Desiree. So let's declare our rehearsal hall open and get on the boards. If you play the scene my way, I swear you'll end up with a prize I know you really crave."

Trey rolled his eyes and asked, "You mean that?"

"Of course, I do, suga'; let me give you a little preview of what I have in mind," she answered as she silenced him with crazed kisses that carried her message of wanton need and reckless abandon.

They snuggled, cuddled, nipped and tucked, and seemed headed on a direct course toward consummation, but suddenly Susanna pushed Trey aside and declared, "No, no, no!" as she snuffed out the flames of passion at a most inopportune moment. Rocketing out of his arms, she cried, "Forgive me, darlin', but I think you're right. We shouldn't do this. It's as wrong as wrong can be."

Touching Susanna's kiss-swollen kips, Trey grimaced and said, "Susanna Delaney, a woman of conscience? Don't tell me you've developed a case of the guilts!"

She avoided Trey's eyes and nodded her head as she nibbled on her lower lip.

Shaking his head in disbelief, he said, "There, there, Susanna," and then he teased, "Come here, you adorable, high-principled woman." Gently, he folded her in his arms and kissed the tip of her nose.

She heaved a deep sigh and answered, "Maybe later tonight we can steal away for a round of hide and seek. Moonlight always makes me wicked and oh, so wild." She stood and turning her head discreetly, she waited for Trey to regain his composure, as well as all of his clothes she'd peeled from his toned body and tossed across the floor.

Just then, the sound of a car racing up the hillside broke the tension of the moment as Susanna reached for her shoes and said, "I bet Ben's arrived with Linnea, which gives me an idea."

"Uh oh," Trey said as he shook his head and sighed, "What now?"

She motioned for him to follow her to the window where she opened wide her draperies fashioned of heavy silk twill. Squinting at the beam of approaching headlights, she said, "I think we should fake a love scene for Ben that'll tie his heart in a big ol' sailor's knot."

"You're serious about making him jealous, aren't you?"

"Yes, I am," she answered and added, "Surely there's no harm if we just pretend and don't actually do." All sweetness and grace, she tugged at Trey's arm and begged soulfully with doe-like eyes.

He backed away and said, "No more of your games, Susanna. I've had enough for one evening. Anyway, if Linnea's with Ben, she's probably on the edge already and deserves a scene of family unity, not a view of her mother in the arms of her dad's best friend."

"Don't worry about Linnea. She won't mind. Besides that, she's so accustomed to my play-actin' she'd worry about me if I didn't put up a fight for Ben. She knows how much we need him here with us. You understand what I'm sayin', don't you?" Not waiting for Trey's answer, she watched a sports car wind its way up her shell and limestone driveway that twisted between a row of oleanders and coastal grasses.

"Looks like a Fiat or maybe a Miata. Hmm, neither are Ben's style, I wonder...," she said. Then with a deep sigh, she shrugged her shoulders and announced, "Oh well, whatever, we really should practice our clinch so come here, big boy, and give me your best." Her eyes suddenly flashed diamonds as she positioned her back to the window and demanded, "Hurry over here by me, now, Trey, I mean it; I promise I'll make it well worth your while." When she had him within her grasp, she said, "That's more like it. Now hold me real close like this so Ben'll see it's you lovin' me like there's no tomorrow."

Obediently, Trey lowered Susanna's body into a pose of intimacy and appeared ready for a ride of divine pleasure and dizzying delight.

"Yes, yes, oh, oh, yes," Susanna moaned like a woman with love on her mind and lust in her heart. When she heard the car door open and close, she trapped Trey in a tight leg hold and elevated her fevered pitch to an uninhibited mating call by proclaiming loudly, "Trey, Trey LaBlanc! You're one of the true joys of my life and I'm so happy we're havin' this special reunion. Please, oh please, love me like the man you are. Now, darlin', now!"

Trey gazed into Susanna's eyes and whispered with a tone of genuine honesty, "You're such a temptress! For the life of me, Susanna, I swear I'll never understand why Ben turned you loose. He had to've been out of his mind."

Susanna sniffed back tears and raising her voice to a pitiful wail, she cried, "Ben was driven away from me by a dream he should've left behind, one he still seems determined to chase."

"Too bad for him, but so good for me," Trey crooned as he nibbled on Susanna's ear. "Funny how one man's mistake often becomes another's fortune."

"How so?" Susanna asked. Then in a whisper, she prompted, "Say somethin' wonderful about me that'll make Ben regret the error of his misguided ways."

"Oh, Susanna, you're a dream come true. How lucky for me that Ben's fallen victim to his own bad judgment. Now he's all alone, out there somewhere in the night, and I'm here with you, loving you the way you deserve." Holding her tightly, Trey started to kiss her, but when Susanna turned her head toward the window for a clearer display of their passion in action, he abruptly stopped in mid-smooch. "Uh oh," he mumbled as he stared into the evening shadows.

"Uh oh, what?" Susanna asked, her face clouded with a frown.

Looking over the top of Susanna's head, Trey glanced in the direction of the sound of footsteps that danced lightly across the patterned brick walkway he'd helped Ben design for Susanna's front entrance.

"Don't stop now, for goodness sake!" Susanna fumed impatiently. "We're startin' to steam up the windows just right."

"Hush a second and sit up straight," Trey replied.

"Why?"

"Wrong audience, that's why," he raved. "I thought you said Ben had arrived! Oh, this is just great. Thanks a lot, Susanna. Why, if I'd had any idea it was Celeste out there and not Ben, I most certainly wouldn't have played along with you."

Susanna broke from Trey's clasp and slowly closed the draperies. She held his face in her hands and begged forgiveness with her eyes. "Don't fuss at me, darlin'. Everything'll work out just fine, you'll see, and I know when it does, you'll appreciate the stage I've set for the main show."

"Show? Have you lost your mind? You dropped the curtain on my act with Celeste before she even had a chance to test my microphone. You know how much I've wanted to spend some quality time with her. Why'd you set me up like this?"

"That's enough, Trey. I can't be bothered right now with all your questions, so please, please, work with me on this, otherwise… "

"What, Susanna? Go on, say it."

"Otherwise, we stand to lose more than I'm willin' to concede, so I suggest if you're afraid we've offended Celeste with our little charade, then I'll pretend you were only helpin' me rehearse for a production of the Community Playhouse. I'm sure she'll believe anything I say, so quit worryin' and brighten up. That's an order!"

Trey grimaced and gritted his teeth as he waved an accusatory finger at Susanna. "One of these days, Susanna, one of these days."

"That's what I'm countin', Trey, the number of days it'll take to have everybody followin' the way I know is best for them to go. So please don't bother me about my methods. Just make yourself handsome and get ready to charm the pants off of our pretty little guest." She watched his scowl deepen and then said, "Look, Trey, I may've given your love life a real boost, especially if it's true men and women are always attracted to those they can't have."

"Sorry, I'm not following your logic here."

Rolling her eyes, she explained, "It's pretty obvious to me that accordin' to a basic tenet of human psychology, our demonstration of close affection for one another should've increased your desirability factor by at least 30%. That's assumin', of course, that Celeste actually saw us cozied up thigh to thigh. So, then, if she watched, fine, she knows you're hot, but if, on the other hand, she missed our show, where's the harm?"

Not waiting for his answer, Susanna left Trey looking confused and totally out of sorts. Dismissing him with a curt, "Men! The things they bother about!" she smirked and walked toward the foyer. As she closed the doors to the living room behind her, she smiled and danced toward the mirrored entrance. There she primped and preened and allowed the front bell to chime several times. Finally, she curtsied to her own image and opened the front door wide.

As pretty as a picture, she beamed a smile worthy of any newspaper's front page and said, "Celeste, hello. How delighted I am to see you. Please come in; you have a secret admirer waitin' to meet you."

"Oh, thank you, I've been a fan of Mr. Collier's for a long, long time."

Smiling, Susanna ushered Celeste inside and said, "That's lovely, dear, but Ben's not who I'm talkin' about. Until he arrives,

I'm afraid you and I will have to make do with his close friend and mine, Mr. Trey LaBlanc. You may remember him from the hearin' this afternoon."

When Celeste looked uncertain, Susanna added, "He was the distinguished man seated with my party, who, I believe, tried to make your acquaintance earlier."

"The one who offered me a cigar?"

Susanna fanned her neck and answered, "Trey's such a kidder. Loves practical jokes, especially playin' them on Ben."

Before Celeste could respond, Trey threw open the living room doors and dashed between the two women, saying, "Hello there." With a gleam in his eye, he added, "You are one beautiful woman. Forgive me for staring, but I can't seem to make myself stop."

Celeste blushed and looking down, she replied, "Hello, sir. You're very kind." She turned to speak to Susanna, but the words never got out as Trey put his hand on the small of her back and guided her into the living room.

"Please allow me to take you on a tour of Susanna's exquisite home." Looking over his shoulder at Susanna, he asked, "Should I start with the His and Hers Trophy Room?"

Susanna watched Trey exude charm and Celeste reciprocate with rapt attention as they walked toward her prize gallery that held the treasures of the pageants she'd won and the mementos of Ben's Naval career. She smiled as she listened to Trey's voice boom praise of Ben's triumphs as a valiant hero, but when he spoke of Ben's tour with the Blue Angels, she rubbed her hands with glee and silently cheered at the sound of Celeste's ooh's and ah's.

Out of the sight of her guests, she rested against an antique cabinet that held her collection of diamond-studded tiaras. Smiling at her Miss Florida crown, she muttered, "If Trey keeps talkin' like that about Ben, I dare say Celeste will be putty in my hands by the time he arrives. I wonder how far she'll go just to have a chance with him? She may be the very medicine Ben needs for his wounded heart."

Suddenly, she turned when she heard Trey call her name. "Comin'," she answered as she followed the sound of his voice into a dimly lit alcove she'd prepared for cocktail service.

"I'm taking orders," Trey declared, whipping a linen towel over the sleeve of his ultrasuede jacket that matched his smoky eyes. "What's your pleasure, Susanna?"

"Forgive me, but you must start without me," she answered and then explained to Celeste, "I should check on my daughter's room, so if you'll excuse me, I'll send the maid in with some refreshments." Turning regally, she walked into the hallway where she pressed a buzzer hidden in a bouquet of silk flowers.

Within moments, her maid Consuela appeared from a service area tucked between the dining room and the kitchen. "Ma'am?" she asked as she cast an alert eye on a table clock that sounded seven rings.

Susanna narrowed her own look and ordered, "As quick as you can, whip up somethin' exotic for our guests, a dish that goes well with alcohol. I want everyone feelin' relaxed. It's important we not waste time, so go on now, get busy."

"What should I prepare? I'm not sure I know what you want served," Consuela replied with a blank stare.

Huffing, "Why is it I have to make all the decisions around this house?" Susanna put her hands on her hips and grimaced a most unbecoming look. "Just shuck some oysters and serve them the way Ben likes, you know, on the half-shell." As Consuela bowed and backed toward the kitchen, Susanna added, "Don't forget to squirt some libido juice in his Tabasco sauce. I want him burnin' when the love bug flys."

Susanna smiled as she watched Consuela hasten out of sight. Then she redirected her attention toward Trey's conversation with Celeste, who seemed mesmerized by his tales of Ben's glory days aboard NAS Pensacola. Catching Trey's eye, Susanna blew him an approving kiss and exited to her dressing room. There she quickly changed into a glamorous hostess gown that shimmered of jade silk and yellow satin. As she clasped a triple strand of pearls around her wrist, she touched the bracelet tenderly and sang, "Me, me, I, I, my, my, mine."

Her serenade ended abruptly when the sound of a fast car roaring up the driveway drowned out her refrain, but she didn't seem to mind. Instead, she said with an approving purr in her voice, "Now that's got to be Ben drivin' either a Mercedes SEL or maybe a Jaguar XJ12." She spritzed on an overly generous amount of her favorite perfume, paged Consuela through the intercom, and spoke slowly, "Ben and Linnea have just arrived. Greet them at the door, but detain them outside until I'm ready to make my entrance."

Susanna listened for a bit and seeming satisfied that Consuela understood her orders, she sniffed her wrist and said, "Celeste's perfume will fade fast when Ben gets a dose of this love potion I'm wearin', so maybe I'd better stay clear of him until the time's right for me to make my move." With one last puff of hairspray and an extra dab of perfume behind her ears, Susanna readied herself to assume her role as the mistress of her mansion.

Reentering the back parlor, she tapped Trey on the shoulder and whispered in his ear, "Forgive me for breakin' in on your time with Celeste, but Ben's just pulled up the drive so I'd appreciate you takin' her back into the livin' room. I'm sure she'll enjoy the view of the stars from the bay window seat, you know, where I store the love pillows."

"With pleasure," Trey replied, nodding toward the direction Susanna indicated. As he and Celeste strolled toward the closed draperies, Trey motioned for her to watch as he unveiled the sight of an absolutely perfect starlit sky.

"Such a beautiful night," Celeste said, but her eyes took on a special glow when she noticed a shiny Mercedes parked behind her little roadster.

"It is, Celeste," Trey replied. "But tell me, do you know what people say about stars on moonlit nights?"

Celeste smiled curiously and answered, "No, I'm not sure."

Trey grinned and said, "The principle's better demonstrated than spoken, so please, allow me to educate you." Then taking her hand, he closed his eyes, waited ten seconds, and said, "Wish I may, wish I might, thank you stars for making all things right." Then with his eyes still tightly shut, he proclaimed, "My wish has just been granted, so I must now kiss the first beautiful lady with golden hair I see, otherwise, my wishes from this point on will go unanswered." He flashed open his eyes and gasped, "Ah, Celeste, you're blonde, so I have no choice. I must kiss you, now." Without skipping a beat, he leaned toward her and aimed for her lips.

She quickly turned a diplomatic cheek to Trey, but he, seeming to have anticipated her deflection, shook his head to the contrary and suavely repositioned her at a more agreeable angle so he could deliver a full frontal embrace.

On the outside looking in, Ben watched a strand of blonde hair glimmer and he froze as though he'd been cast into stone.

Beside him, Linnea fidgeted and asked, "What's the surprise Consuela said Momma's preparing for me? I want to go inside now and find out what's up."

"No, Linnea, you'd better step back here with me," Ben cautioned and then he added with a nod to the couple inside, "I don't think we should intrude on your mother's party. Let's give her guests some privacy and maybe we can come back later."

Whimpering, Linnea said, "Big deal, I don't care who's here. This is my house, too, so I'm not going anywhere but straight to my room. Today's been just awful and I need some rest."

"What about your mother's surprise?" Ben asked, shifting his position for a closer look at the blonde, who'd stepped into the shadows and almost out of his view.

"Oh, Dad, really now. I'm getting a bit too old to be thrilled by surprises, unless, of course, Momma's stashed away a guy named Etienne!"

Frowning, Ben patted Linnea on her shoulder and commented sternly, "Surely not, but then again, I wouldn't put anything past your mother, especially when her thinking's impaired. I know she's been beside herself worrying about you."

"So, Dad, why are we standing here? If Momma cares about me that much, I think we should go on inside now so she can see for herself I'm really okay."

Ben watched Consuela bustle into the living room and hastily light a tiered candelabra Susanna kept on a table beside the bookcase. When he saw another sparkle of blonde hair glisten in the flare of the candles, he said more to himself than Linnea, "Could Desiree possibly be here? But kissing Trey LaBlanc? Surely not."

Under her breath, Linnea muttered, "I thought you said she'd gone to the Plantation."

"Maybe she decided to meet me here so we could drive there together."

Linnea sighed, shrugged her shoulders, and said, "Well now, I guess if that's the case, then Momma's surprise wasn't really for me, but rather for you. Does that mean I'll spend tonight alone while you play house with Desiree?"

Frowning, Ben looked away and said, "No, Linnea. I'll stay with you until you fall asleep."

"Where will you be when I wake up?" She waited for his reply, but when he turned away for another look at the woman inside, she said, "That's what I thought." Refusing to accept his words to the contrary, she keyed in her personal security number and nudged open the front door.

Ben followed after her but when she made a hasty retreat upstairs, he turned his attention to the pretty blonde, who seemed engrossed in conversation with Trey.

Thinking, Desiree, thank goodness you changed you mind, he rushed into the living room full of anticipation. Suddenly, he stopped cold when he discovered the blonde was not Desiree.

From the back of the room, Susanna laughed triumphantly and clapped her hands in celebration. "Expectin' someone else, I presume?" she teased and then added, "How about havin' one of these little shrimp puffs to ease your disappointment?"

Now a picture of total discontent, Ben waved off Susanna and turned to leave. Only the sound of Trey's voice calling to him stopped Ben from bolting out the front door.

"Come back here, Ben. You've got to at least meet this incredible young woman who actually believes all the good press you plant about yourself in the papers."

"Don't be such a spoil sport," Susanna added with a whine.

Ben paused with his hand on the door and started to leave, but he stopped and turned when Trey added, "This pretty lady works with Desiree over at Nature's Way, so I think it would be politically unwise for you to depart so rudely."

With a shrug of his shoulders, Ben walked toward Celeste and asked, "So, tell me, ma'am, are you here for business or for pleasure?"

"Just to meet you, Mr. Collier," she replied as she looked at him with a cloying mixture of admiration and adoration. Offering him her hand, she fluttered her eyelashes and said, "My name's Celeste Kulhaney and I'm absolutely thrilled to be in the same room with you. I've followed your career and although my boss, Ms. McAndrews, probably wouldn't want me to say this, I think you should fill Heron Bay with sand, red clay, and anything else you find. Personally, I have no problem whatsoever with your plans to build condos and houses all over the swampy place."

"Ah, I see now why Susanna latched on to you," Ben replied as he nodded to Celeste instead of shaking her hand.

Celeste smiled serenely and answered, "Miss Delaney and I share more than a pro-development position. You see, I've had some experience in pageants, too, but not to the extent of your beautiful wife."

Ben frowned and quickly corrected her by saying, "Former wife. We share Linnea and that's the sum total of my relationship with Susanna."

Celeste beamed and said, "Oh? I wasn't exactly sure about your marital status. So, tell me, does that mean you're not presently involved with anyone?"

Without answering, Ben scowled and looked away.

Trey quickly moved to Celeste's side and apologized for Ben's manners by explaining, "He's usually not this surly; I'm sure Linnea's accident has dampened his spirit."

Celeste stood starry-eyed in the presence of Ben and toyed with a strand of her hair. Blushing, she leaned toward Ben and touched his arm as she empathized, "Oh, Mr. Collier, I'm so sorry your little girl got hurt."

He brushed off Celeste's concern with a curt nod, all the while plotting his escape route out of the servant entrance and off on the trail of Desiree, who he surmised had to be almost across the Apalachicola Causeway and well on her way to St. George Island. Wearing the look of a man hopelessly in love, he let his mind wander from the memory of soft Southern breezes whipping across the water to the sweet taste of Desiree's lips. The very thought of Desiree safe in his beach house caused him to shudder in anticipation. He couldn't wait to join her there.

From behind the service entrance, Susanna fumed, "Deal with reality, Ben."

"Excuse me?" he replied, frowning at her interruption.

Pushing forward, Susanna picked up a snapper croquette, and breaking it in half, she licked the crust off of one part and offered Ben a taste. "I told Consuela to make these special for you, so I suggest you have a bite now. It's only polite, you see, to act half-human when you come into our home."

"This is not where I live," he reminded her as he refused the fish cake and everything else she offered. Then turning his back to Susanna and her guests, he stormed into the foyer.

Susanna stamped her foot and chased after him. Blustering with fury, she unleashed a streak of "should'ves and could'ves" that stopped him in his tracks.

"Wishful thinking, Susanna," he countered and then he added, "But you know as well as I that we're never going to live together again, so, please, do us both a favor and get on with your life and leave me to mine."

Feigning a swoon, Susanna clutched a hand to her throat and swore, "You'd better watch your step, Ben Collier, otherwise, I promise you'll fall so hard that you'll never recover." Then she reached for his hand and asked, "Can't you see that you belong here with Linnea and me and not hikin' to who knows where with that woman from Natureland?"

"You're pathetic, Susanna," he retorted and lowering his voice menacingly, he warned, "If you push me too far, I swear I'll open your closet and rattle more than a few bones from your colorful past."

Susanna flushed crimson at his words and falling back against Trey, she declared, "You were never, ever this mean-spirited with me before, but I guess all that changed the day Desiree McAndrews tore into our life."

"Leave Desiree out of this," Ben demanded as he paced his words with his slow movement toward the door.

Laughing maniacally, Susanna sneered, "Interestin' word choice, Ben, since it appears the only leavin' that happened with Desiree is the fact that she left you behind. That's why you're standin' here with us now, instead of countin' stars with her off of some rickety ol' pier." As she watched the blood drain from Ben's face, she motioned for Trey and Celeste to come forward. Seeming satisfied they'd sealed off the front exit from Ben, she sent Consuela in search of Linnea, who now slumped against the banister at the top of the stairs.

"Please, Dad, don't go," Linnea cried softly. "I need you; I really do."

Ben's eyes met Linnea's and that was all it took. At that moment, without question, he knew where he should stay. With a prayer in his heart for Desiree's understanding, he took the stairs two steps at a time to reach Linnea who waited for him, her eyes wide with need and despair.

Holding her in his arms, he comforted her with patient words of reassurance and swore he had absolutely no intention of leaving her. On that promise, he gave his word and he meant it, but still though, in the back of his mind, a nagging thought surfaced about what might happen if he had to choose between Linnea and Desiree.

Then he pictured Desiree, beautiful, intelligent and exciting, kind, good, loving and true. He sensed she shared the ache of his heart as he agonized between duty and desire, the two powerful forces that seemed headed on a collision course for a second time in his life. Although he'd forged a strong parent-child bond with Linnea, now he felt the flames of his love for Desiree rage through him like wild fire, searing his heart and engulfing his soul.

"What's wrong, Dad?" Linnea asked. "You seem so distant."

"No, that's not it," he answered, but in actuality, his thoughts at that moment centered solely around Desiree. In his mind, he pictured her as she strolled along the beach path that led from the emerald waters of the Gulf to his weathered home nestled in a protective forest of coastal pines, sea grasses, and palmettoes. He hoped when she reached the main deck of his house, she would notice first the entwined wildflowers he'd painstakingly carved along the porch railings and then the lovers' knots he'd inscribed with her initials in every panel of the heavy front door. Maybe then she would understand the full extent of his love for her.

Look into my heart, now, Desiree, now, he thought as he closed his eyes and prayed.

# Chapter 15

The walls papered in frosted shades of coral and pearl welcomed Desiree into the living area of Ben's beach house he called the Wind Sailor. She smiled at the name choice, a testament to Ben's respect for the sky and the sea. Turning to take in her surroundings, she paused, her face a reflection of curiosity and pleasure. Every aspect of the Wind Sailor, from the crystal ceiling fans to the parquet flooring, both surprised and delighted her.

She ran her fingertips along a picture frame made from ribbons of silk decorated with tiny shells and fragile sand dollars. She admired the mix of textures and colors and marveled at the selection of materials and design. She'd assumed Ben's beach haven would offer guests an insider's view of his Naval career complete with military photographs, fighter jet models, and tilting carriers at sea, not fine beach pieces, the likes not found in any Destinesque gallery of polyresin gulls and pre-fabricated fish.

She looked around the room, but her attention was drawn to a table solely adorned by a faded chap book of poetry. "Oh, Ben," she sighed, as she picked up the book and held its tattered pages to her heart. She closed her eyes as the memory of a lost summer of passion and broken promises flooded her soul with feelings she still found difficult to handle.

"What happened to us?" she asked as she opened the book to a poem Ben'd written for her to celebrate the day they'd first met in Boulder beside Varsity Lake. Her eyes misted as she read the sweet words he'd struggled to express in the sonnet form she'd taught him months later as they'd climbed Flagstaff Mountain in search of the perfect spot for afternoon delight.

Her eyes raced across the fourteen lines that drove home Ben's theme of courtly fidelity laced with torrid desire for her, the love of his life, then and forever. At least, that was the poetic promise he'd delivered years earlier, but this was now.

"Maybe I should...," Desiree said, but her thoughts remained unexpressed as bells sounded all around, causing her to spin first toward the telephone and then to the foyer where someone with a determined hand pressed the doorbell with a sense of urgency that overruled the demanding call of the phone.

If only she'd answered the telephone instead of the door...

\* \* \* \* \*

"Pick up, Desiree, please, sweetheart. We must talk. Tonight's the night," Ben crooned into his cellular phone as he headed his car toward Springhill Road and the Tallahassee airport. A man on a mission, he plotted his course of action for a special duty assignment that promised a payload of pleasure for the key participants. In his mind's eye, he toyed with his ways and Desiree's means, all of which demanded hands on, heart stopping, over the top action. "Two turning, two burning, my love," he said, as he pushed the redial button and waited to hear Desiree answer his call.

"What's going on? Where is she?" he puzzled, worrying that she might've run into some difficulty during her drive to St. George Island. Reasoning she'd been upset when they'd parted at the hospital, he chastised himself for not insisting that he accompany her. "A fool, a damn fool!" he shouted so loudly that a driver who'd stopped his car beside Ben's at a traffic light rolled up his windows and peeled off a strip of rubber as he roared out of the sight of Ben, who seemed ready to displace his hostility at the slightest provocation.

Ben glared at the red tail lights that streaked away in front of him. "Idiot!" he said with disgust as he redialed the Wind Sailor telephone number. While he counted the rings that'd taken on an ominous, hollow hum, he checked the clock on the dashboard and shook his head. Thinking, something's not right, she should be there by now, he pulled his car to the side of the road, placed a call to another number, and waited.

On the fourth ring, Ben listened as a man said, "Security, front gate," to which Ben replied, "Hello, this is Ben Collier. Has my guest, Ms. McAndrews, checked in?"

"Oh, Mr. Collier, sir, hello. Uh, yes, yes sir, I logged her in over an hour ago, and just like you wanted, I gave her the keys and directions to your house."

Ben frowned and debated his next words. He didn't want to cause false alarm but still he was concerned something had gone wrong with his plan he'd believed was fail-safe. After a few moments, he asked, "What about a map? Did you warn her about the turns along Leisure Lane? And did you tell her to watch for the Bayberry sign?"

"Well, yes, Mr. Collier, I did all of that. In fact, I marked your house on a Plantation map and made sure she had your address on Blueberry Road."

"I see." Ben closed his eyes and shook his head as he added, "I don't feel right about this. She should've answered my phone calls."

"Is your number in service, sir? A gale blew through last week and some lines went down."

"Hmm," Ben replied and then added, "That might explain the problem, but tell me, did she seem preoccupied or out of sorts when you talked with her?"

"No, not really, but she, uh, she..."

"She what?"

"Well, she seemed surprised, maybe even disappointed, about your house."

"What about it?" Ben huffed, full of disbelief that Desiree would ever disapprove of any aspect of the Wind Sailor. Frowning at that thought, he waited for an explanation.

"Just the location, sir. In fact, she actually challenged my notes on the map and insisted your house had to be directly on the Gulf."

Ben smiled, pleased that one of Desiree's expectations about him had proven false. "Is that so?"

"Yes, that's what she said, but I told her when you built Phase I and could've claimed any spot in the development, you chose one in the last tier off the beach."

Picturing the trees that framed his rugged lot, he wondered what Desiree thought of the serenading cricket frogs that'd taken up residence in his personal pine forest. He smiled at the image of her listening to the natural chorus of night sounds.

"Sir? Are you still there?" the guard asked.

As his mind embellished the picture of Desiree sipping coffee from one of his Fly Navy mugs while she rested in the rope hammock he'd strung across the front deck, he felt a sense of relief wash over him. Something deep inside told him she was safe in his house, out of harm's way, and far from the Delaney domain of bald-faced lies and evil deceit.

"Mr. Collier, sir? Hello? Mr. Collier?"

"Oh, sorry, I was just thinking about my guest and some tapes I want her to hear tonight. They're in the house and since I can't seem to reach her, I'd appreciate you letting her know where they are. Can you help me out?"

"Sure, glad to. Should I drive over there now or go later when my relief shows up?"

"Whichever works for you. Just tell her she'll find the key to the seaman's chest on top of the nightstand in the master bedroom."

"Sounds like a treasure hunt," the guard said with a chuckle.

"Something like that," Ben replied, his eyes twinkling at the thought of a pirate escapade with Desiree as the prize. "Anyway," he explained, "she'll find some directions taped to the key, but don't tell her that. I want her to enjoy the surprise of discovery." He raised his eyes heavenward and prayed Desiree's playful, adventurous nature would kick into overdrive at the first hint of a challenge. He'd thrown down the gauntlet and now he couldn't wait for her to pick it up and run with it, hopefully right into his open arms.

Little did Ben know, though, at that very moment, embracing him was the furthest thought in Desiree's mind. Instead, she stood toe to toe and eye to eye with a man accustomed to having his way, no questions asked, no answers given. That was power with a capital "P" and the mark of one who'd mastered the game of "I win, You Lose" long ago.

\* \* \* \* \*

"Senator Delaney! Why are you here?" Desiree asked, her eyes wide with surprise and concern. "Has something happened to Ben?" she added, her voice tense and troubled.

"Not if I can help it. That's why I rushed across two counties to try to put the lid on the pot before bad business boils over and drowns us all in a pool of wasted investments and poor decisions. You and I need to come to an understandin'. Trust me, I think we can work out a deal, a mutually beneficial one."

Obviously relieved that her fears for Ben's safety were unfounded, Desiree sighed, but then she paused and leaned against the open door. She touched the engraved panels and spoke softly, yet firmly, "Sir, I'm not sure I understand what you're talking about, but if you're here on grounds other than professional, then I must ask you to leave."

"Ooh my, Ms. Desiree, I'm beginnin' to see the side of you Ben finds so appealin'. In fact, you seem to me the kind of woman a man like myself might like to get to know better," he said with a lusty leer directed toward the front of Desiree's blouse that'd become loosened in the night breeze. "In fact," he added, "since no one's around, this seems as good a time as any for us to become better acquainted. I promise I won't disappoint you. But first, you need to let me come inside for a little heart to heart chat."

"What?"

Winking suggestively, he pointed to the top of his head and said, "Don't let these silver hairs fool you. I haven't finished livin' by any stretch of the imagination."

"Sir!" she exclaimed, stepping away from the door.

"Believe me, Desiree, there's nothin' wrong with combinin' business with pleasure, at least that's been my experience." He stood tall and smiled hungrily at Desiree. From behind his back, he produced a magnum of champagne and strode forward, saying, "So, Desiree, how about it? Ready to negotiate over a glass or two of bubbly?"

Disgusted and disturbed, Desiree anchored her hands on her hips and seethed, "Senator Delaney, you're about to step out of line." Glaring into his eyes, she blocked his path and added, "Before you say or do something you'll regret, you should leave, now."

Tossing his head back and laughing cruelly, he answered, "Susanna warned me about your pious act, but Desiree, honey child, I'm not buyin' your princess purity routine, especially not after hearin' the wild tales Ben's told about you."

Desiree gasped and held her hands to her heart, stunned by the Senator's harsh words. Then defiantly she shook her head and said, "Forgive me, sir, for calling you a liar, but that's what you are. Although my relationship with Ben is absolutely none of your concern, I know he would never spread rumors about any woman, not me and not even your precious daughter. As for her… "

"There, there, now. Watch what you say about Susanna; after all, she is the mother of Ben's child."

Desiree closed her eyes and turned away.

Inching his way into the foyer, Big Jack closed the door and reached for Desiree. As he placed his hand on her shoulder, he consoled, "Reality hurts, but it's the wake up call we all sometimes need to receive. Helps put things into proper perspective. Believe me, I know what I'm talkin' about from personal experience. Just give me a few minutes of your time and I'll explain what really turns the wheels of commerce and industry. How about it, little lady?"

The more Desiree listened to Big Jack, the more infuriated she became with his chauvinistic attitude. Determined to send him on his way, she said politely but authoritatively, "Sir, I'm neither interested in socializing nor striking a bargain with you, so you should go, otherwise… "

Bristling, Big Jack marched into the kitchen and put the champagne in the refrigerator. Then he spun around to face Desiree, who pointed to the open front door.

"Look here, Desiree, if you'll just loosen up and listen, I bet we can hammer out a jim dandy deal that'll work for everybody. And if you're worried about Ben or somebody else findin' out, then don't 'cause tonight can be our little secret. Nobody but us has to know."

Desiree stamped her foot angrily and walked into the kitchen. There, she swung open the refrigerator door, grabbed the champagne bottle, and shoved it into Big Jack's hands. With ice in her voice, she said, "Don't forget this and please close the door on your way out."

"Whoa now, missy. This rejection you're handin' out to me could hurt my self image, that is, if I let it. But I'm not gonna do that 'cause I like you, Desiree, I really do, and I meant what I said that we could make a powerful political team, you and me. I've got the pull and you've got the pretty pout, of that I'm sure, otherwise, you couldn't have gotten as far into the burroughs of bureaucracy as you have."

Desiree frowned daggers at Big Jack and retorted, "Hold it right there, Senator. I don't mind telling you that I'm both offended and appalled by your categorization of me as a weak female who resorts to mindless tactics."

"Oh no, Desiree, you're misunderstandin' what I'm sayin'. Let me explain somethin' to you that I learned when I entered government service. Effective people use whatever means they have to get the results they want. That's why I'm filled with admiration for your methods, as well as your you know what." He dropped his eyelids and licked his lips.

Livid with rage, Desiree rolled her eyes and warned, "If only your constituents could see and hear you now."

Big Jack ran his hands through his thinning hair and commented, "You're one tough cookie, Desiree. Tell me what it is I've got to do to make you like me."

She shook her head and said, "Don't you get it, sir? Personality preferences are not important; the environmental impact of a proposed development is. Simply put, you and I are on two different sides of a very important issue that requires thorough scrutiny and not the type of good ol' boy networking you propose. Therefore, you and I have nothing further to discuss, so please leave because I have no intention whatsoever of wasting any more time with you."

Big Jack yawned and said, "But I'm tired, Desiree. My flight over here in my ol' Sierra was rough 'cause of all the crosswinds and then after I finally got the dang thing landed, I couldn't get the man at the gatehouse on the phone 'cause it kept ringin' busy, so I had no choice but to jump start the car Ben keeps at the hangar." When he watched Desiree's expression soften, he added cagily, "Even so, I still made it to your door with an offer of peace and a good time, but will you listen? Oh no, not you. You wanna match wits with me and that's why I feel kinda weak and weary. Why, Desiree, you've just about worn me out; it's been awhile, you know."

"Awhile since what?"

He wandered into the living room and fell back into the sofa. When Desiree followed him, he caught her hand and pulled her down beside him. Pawing at her arm, he confessed, "For all my big talk, the truth is that it's been a long, long time since I've kept the company of such an intelligent woman, who, by the way I should add, could write her own ticket to financial security if she'd only climb off of her high horse and listen to the proposal of one who's really pure of heart and a helluva nice guy who's called Big Jack for a woman-teasin' reason." Beaming an arrogant smile, he reached for Desiree's hand and looked into her eyes.

"Whatever are you saying, sir?" Desiree asked, breaking free from his grasp.

With a deep sigh, Big Jack narrowed his eyes and answered, "You're a smart woman, Desiree. I don't think you need a roadmap."

"Oh, but I do," she replied, reaching quickly for the map the man at the security gate had given her. Pitching it into Big Jack's hands, she said, "See, Ben must have had this marked for me so I wouldn't lose my way."

Big Jack sneered at the large heart drawn around the location of the Wind Sailor and cackled, "Off the deep end, Ben is. The poor boy obviously needs an eject button now more than ever."

Desiree walked toward the door and motioned for Big Jack to follow her. When he showed no signs of leaving, she coaxed, "Look, I don't have either the time or the energy to waste on your ramblings about Ben, about yourself, or about any deals you've cooked up. So do us both a favor and go home now, otherwise, I will file a report with the Florida Ethics Commission."

Big Jack's complexion flared crimson as he made a paper airplane out of the Plantation map and sailed it across the room. When it fell to the floor, he said, "Crash and burn, Desiree. That's what you've set into motion with your dalliance with Ben Collier. Mark my words, little lady, when his world falls apart, you'll have only yourself to blame, but it doesn't have to be that way. All you've got to do is listen thirty minutes and then make up your mind what's right."

Desiree studied Big Jack's face and watched him set his jawline tight as he waited for her reply. She considered flinging the door open as dramatically as her slight stature would allow, but then she reconsidered and walked away from the foyer and back into the center of the living area. There she moved a plush ottoman far out of Big Jack's reach and sat down. Cocking her eyes as if she dared him to challenge her one more time, she ordered, "Say what's on your mind, Senator, but let me warn you, the clock's running and I have no intention of extending the time limit. So talk, but you'd better keep your comments repeatable and your hands to yourself."

"Very well," Big Jack replied as he pulled a rough drawing from his coat pocket. Handing it to Desiree, he lowered his voice to a whisper and explained, "Although this survey's been reduced, it depicts the scope of Ben's dream. You can see the geographic area is immense and when developed, it will benefit the entire Gulf Coast." Lurching to his feet, he explained, "Jobs will be created, swamp land will be improved, and families will have their choice of fine homes, condos, or coastal cabanas that'll rival those of Miami's Golden Strand."

Not batting an eyelash, Desiree listened to Big Jack as he seemed to gather steam the longer he talked. She watched him pace from the living room to the kitchen and back again, all the while outlining his case in an almost priestlike tone of reverence and respect.

"Now, there's no denyin'," he continued, "at the first mention of Heron Bay, some critics raised the infrastructure flag and others cried environmental erosion, but I know if Ben's turned loose, he'll see that ample support will be in place for all the residential and retail complexes that'll put our little piece of Florabama heaven on the worldwide map of wonders of the universe. But for this to happen, Desiree, Ben needs my help and yours, especially yours."

"Surely you understand," Desiree interjected, "that I'm here to assess this particular development's impact on the environment. Only after I've completed my investigative work will I be able to comment on Heron Bay. So, my help, as you put it, is not an entity I can hand to Ben, regardless how much I might want to support his efforts."

"I see," Big Jack snorted and then he reached for an envelope he carried inside the breast pocket of his jacket. Without looking at its fattened contents, he pitched it in Desiree's lap and said, "Maybe this persuader some investors asked me to deliver to you will change your mind."

Cautiously, she ripped open the seal and then she caught her breath. "A deed to an Orange Beach condominium and a check for $400,000? Both made out to me?" She shook her head as if she wanted to make the moment disappear. Then she cast aside both documents and watched the papers float to the floor.

"Pick them up, Desiree," Big Jack commanded. "You're bein' given a piece of the pie, but first you've got to accept the plate it's on." He kneeled on the floor and signaled for Desiree to come forward.

Her eyes flashing contempt and anger, she walked toward him and said, "Senator, sir. You can take the deed and the check as well as your 'Big Jack' Delaney and stuff them all in your envelope of corruption and shame. You sicken me and I want you out of this house, now."

Big Jack covered his ears and spun around quickly. Then grabbing at his chest, he cried out in dire pain, "My nitroglycerine, Desiree, please, find it for me. It's in my wallet. Please, please, I need my medicine; help me, please, I beg you." Wincing in agony, he closed his eyes and collapsed into a ball of medical misery.

Desiree rushed to his side and cradling his pitiful body in her arms, she soothed him with comforting words and kind actions. Like an angel of mercy, she hovered over him and finding the tablets he needed, she helped him through his distress.

"Are you sorry now, Desiree?" he asked, his voice shaky.

"Sorry about what?" she replied, her eyes filled with genuine concern for the man's health.

Smiling a lopsided grin, Big Jack answered, "Sorry that your good lovin' almost killed me."

"Sir!" she cried, dropping her hold on the man and consequently allowing his head to hit the floor.

"One more time, Desiree, oh please let me die with a smile on my face," he moaned as he groped her knees and reached higher.

Desiree deflected his hands and raced to the telephone, screaming, "You conniving rat. You're not physically sick at all, are you?"

To which, Big Jack answered, "Sick? Yes, I am, darlin', and I'm ready to announce to the world I'm sick in love with a Colorado critter who's wilder than a Florida panther." He watched Desiree reach for the telephone receiver and wagged a finger at her as he said, "Better not call 911 'cause if you do, our little meetin' here will become front page news."

Ignoring his threat, Desiree lifted the receiver and started to place her call, but just as she did, she turned to the window, suddenly distracted by a flashing yellow light mounted on the roof of a golf cart. To herself, she muttered, "What next?" and debated whether she should help Big Jack up from the floor or leave him there, crumpled, wrinkled, and a sorry sight to see.

Although she considered allowing him to fend for himself, her conscience demanded otherwise, so she dropped to his side and offered him her helping hands.

He accepted her assistance with a leer that sickened Desiree to her toes. "Good thinkin', missy," he said as he stood up and leaned over to brush the creases from his pants. "I knew you'd come around and see things my way, the only way," he added, swatting her backside in a manner less than polite.

Desiree stilled his hand and cut her eyes toward him. Not giving him a chance to speak, she ended their meeting with words she hoped would make him wilt and skulk away off into the night. "That's what you think, Senator Delaney. Your bribes and your threats carry zero influence with me. For everything you said and did this evening, I promise you will pay and pay dearly."

Big Jack, no longer appearing either wrinkled or hungry for love, turned his most polished, camera-ready face to Desiree and answered, "You are a pretty woman and I appreciate your spirit, your fire, but darlin', tonight boils down to a case of my word against yours. Remember, too, that you're the outsider who came to town to stir up trouble for two fine citizens, Ben and Susanna, my pride and joy. So tell me, what else could I, a lovin' father, do but stand up for my child and try to remove the annoyin' stone that blocks her path and that of her financial provider? I don't know anyone on this planet who could ever find a speck of fault in my actions. I'm simply a man who decided to protect his flesh and blood."

Looking away, Desiree framed her reply but decided now was neither the time nor the place for her to respond. She knew the heat of the moment carried enough danger vibrations to rock the entire island and that had never been her intent. Although Big Jack's behavior disgusted every fiber of her being, she turned the other cheek and let his final parting shot sink in.

"I rest my case, Desiree. Will I see you in court?"

She listened to approaching footsteps on the creaky deck stairs and prayed for deliverance from an unbearable situation that'd left her bedeviled and bewildered. Thinking, what now? she turned her back to the Senator and hoped her next caller had any last name other than Delaney!

# Chapter 16

"Hmm, this looks interesting," Desiree whispered. She studied the cassette tape she held in her hands and debated if she should play it immediately or save it for later when her mind was more at ease. Still shaken by Senator Delaney's visit and the total impropriety of all he'd suggested, she wanted nothing more than to ablate the unpleasant memory from her thoughts. "Such a foolish old man," she said with a sad shake of her head and then added, "At least I won't hear his evil voice on this tape."

"You say something, ma'am?" the gatehouse guard called out from the kitchen.

"Nothing important," she replied as she slipped the tape into her skirt pocket and quietly closed the top drawer of the oak chest. "I was just thinking out loud, a nervous habit, I guess."

"Well, ma'am, you should rest easier now that I've set the safety locks on the windows and tested the phone line. Everything checks out." He waved Desiree into the kitchen area where he showed her the master control for the security system and then he reset the alarm.

Desiree smiled her gratitude for the man's efforts and thanked him for escorting Big Jack to his car.

"No problem, Ms. McAndrews," he replied. Flashing a toothy grin, he laughed and added, "That Senator Delaney's some kind of a fellow, life of the party so I've heard, but he's smart, too, sly as a fox and as wise as an owl."

Frowning, Desiree looked away and thought to herself, that's what you think, mister. She shuddered in disgust.

"Did I say something wrong?"

Desiree studied the guard's expression of concern and decided there was little point in exposing the Senator for the weasel he was since she planned to have no further dealings with him.

"Ma'am? Did you hear me?"

"Yes, I did. I'm just a bit on edge is all. Tonight's been one of surprises."

The guard's eyes flashed as he said, "And you still have Mr. Collier's tapes to hear. Did you find them?"

She patted her skirt pocket and answered, "I have one here with me. Are there more?"

"Yes, ma'am, I believe Mr. Collier said tapes, so I guess you'd better look in that chest again. He seemed to want you to listen to them tonight. There oughtta be a player somewhere around here, probably o'er there." He pointed to a closed armoire in the living room and said, "Bet that's where Mr. Collier keeps his stereo and TV. Want me to look for you?"

Desiree shook her head and replied, "No, sir, that's fine. I'll search around later." She offered the guard her hand and said, "You've already spent more time with me than you should have, but I do appreciate your help."

"Glad to be of assistance. Any friend of Mr. Collier's is a friend of mine." He shook hands with Desiree and then leaned forward, his eyes filled with a look of caution. "Someone's always at the gatehouse, so if you need anything, just call. The Plantation was designed as a safe place so don't worry. We're here to protect the owners and their guests."

Although she considered reminding him that the Senator had slipped through the Plantation's security process undetected and unchallenged, she let the issue drop and preferred instead to hope Big Jack was airborne and headed out of her life, forever.

"Well, ma'am, guess I'll leave you now. Enjoy your stay."

Desiree walked to the door and said, "Thank you again for everything. You've been more than kind."

"Hey, ma'am, working with a pretty lady like you is a pleasure," he answered, blushing as he looked away.

Laughing lightly, Desiree waved good-bye as the guard made his way down the steps. Pausing at the bottom, he called out, "Don't forget to turn that deadbolt and sleep tight, but remember the tapes. I promised Mr. Collier, you see."

"I understand," Desiree answered as she closed the door, locked it, and turned off the outside deck lights. Leaning against the door frame, she reached into her pocket and took out the tape. She couldn't imagine what was so important she must listen to it now and not later.

"I wonder, if he... , hmm, surely not," she said, allowing her imagination to run wild. A message for my ears only; this could be interesting, she thought. Succumbing to curiosity, she dashed into the bedroom for another search of Ben's antique chest, just in case she might find another tape.

With anticipation in her mind and excitement in her heart, she knelt on the floor and opened the bottom drawer. Ever so cautiously, she looked inside at a stack of letters methodically arranged by their postmark date. A lump formed in her throat as she read the neatly penned address on the top envelope: LT BENNETT COLLIER, NAS PENSACOLA 32508 and the return address, Boulder, Colorado.

Her hands trembled as she reached for the cache of letters she'd sent Ben years before. Unable to read her words of love and dreams, she held the yellowed envelopes close and said, "Ben saved them all, every last one. But why?"

Carefully, she returned the letters to the drawer and peeked underneath a stack of issues of the *Gosport*. There her hand touched a large manila envelope stuffed with contents she wondered if she should see. Thinking, I have absolutely no business snooping through Ben's private papers, she closed the drawer and shut her eyes as though that would put a quick end to her desire to read whatever it was he'd saved.

She turned away from the chest and walked to Ben's oak bed where she sat down to think about her life twelve years ago. "I'm not here for this," she chided herself as she reached for a chenille throw the color of warm cappuccino. She toyed with its long fingers of fringe that felt like velvet to her touch. Comforted by the warmth and softness of the cloth, she held it to her face and breathed in Ben's raw vanilla scent, all man and all heart.

She tried to banish her thoughts of Ben that were built on the dreams they'd shared and the promises they'd made. "Let it go, Desiree; don't revisit the past, you can't," ordered the sensible voice in her head, to which the soft whisper in her heart countered, "It's okay to love, Ben, Desiree. He's never stopped caring for you anymore than you ever stopped loving him."

"Ben, Ben," she called out, almost as though she expected him to answer. She listened to silence fill his bedroom and wondered if he'd ever tried to will her spirit to come to him, to love him.

"You're dreaming, Desiree. Wake up and get over him," her mind's voice shouted so loudly that she covered her ears to make the words stop.

Weeping into his comforter, she stretched out on his bed and felt her body involuntarily gravitate toward the right side of the mattress and into a rounded crevice that signaled the place where Ben slept.

"Feels right, doesn't it? Just as though a day hasn't passed," spoke her heart in soothing tones of seduction and pleasure.

Desiree shivered as she felt every fiber of her being respond in passionate waves that danced from her head to her toes. She reached her arms to the base of the headboard and held on. Unable to fight the feelings that delighted her, the memory of Ben's love comforted her.

Sitting up suddenly, she felt invigorated, alive, and full of curiosity. With her spirit as vibrant as a meteor, she confronted the reality of her situation. Regardless how hard she might try to blot out her past with Ben, she couldn't. Those feelings were far too precious to toss aside. She knew she had no choice other than to accept the wonder of their memories and move forward.

The past would no longer torment her anymore than the present would compromise her values and her responsibilities. As for the future, time would tell. For now, though, she believed she'd set the convictions of her conscience firmly in place, so she left the comfort of Ben's bed and charged toward his chest of memories.

This time, though, instead of kneeling meekly on the floor, she pulled up a foot stool and made herself at home. Thinking, this may take awhile, she rubbed her hands together and opened the top drawer, ready to confront the past in order to deal with the future. She wondered if her search of the mementos of their love would lay the past to rest or rekindle the flame of love. Would she find a treasure trove of wonderful memories from the happiest time of her life? Or would she find something else?

Rifling through a sheaf of papers, photographs, and matchbooks, she laughed at some of them and cried at the sight of others, but her resolve remained firm as she revisited the places and the feelings of first love. As she turned through all the letters, pictures, and poems, she felt the power of her emotions and the strength of Ben's love and respect for her.

"Oh my," she sighed when she found a tangle of faded pink ribbons. A faint smile danced across her lips as her heart warmed with the knowledge that Ben had saved them. She pictured his face and remembered when he'd stroked her hair and slowly untied the ribbons to set her curls free. Holding on to that tender memory, she twisted the ribbons into a loose braid and gently put them aside.

With her thoughts centered on the sentimentality of young love, she felt her heartbeat quicken, a warning sign to her that she needed to keep her emotions in check. Quickly, she closed the top drawer and turned her back on the chest and its contents. As she moved to leave the bedroom, she said softly, "I'm sorry, Ben. I thought I could do this, but I can't. Revisiting the past has no future, at least not for us. It's over and that's that."

About to close the door, she stopped and turned for one last look at Ben's bedroom. Her eyes focused on the middle chest drawer that seemed to dare her to take a peek. Shaking off her desire to flee and thus protect her heart, she shifted her glance from the chest to the bed. Suddenly her vision blurred, but then it cleared. She wasn't a coward and she could handle whatever she might find.

With her eyes wide open and her heart now pounding a slow and steady beat, she tossed her head high and faced the chest with determination and resolve. Its middle drawer became her next destination.

She tugged at the worn handles and the warped wood stuck, shut solid and as tight as a drum. "This isn't good," she muttered as she thought for a moment and then said, "Soap. That's what'll solve this little problem."

She reopened the top drawer and dug underneath a packet of letters Ben had tied with one of her pink ribbons. "Perfect!" she exclaimed as she found exactly what she needed. Holding two tiny souvenir bars of soap imprinted with the logo of the Aspen Lodge, she smiled as she remembered where she and Ben had spent many wonderful ski weekends. "Amazing, Ben, we were definitely unplugged then!" she said, blushing at the sizzling memory of her uninhibited actions and his.

Sighing contentedly while she alternated between daydreaming and soaping the top rim of the stubborn drawer, she

*Angel Flight*

blew at the residue flakes and then tested her work with a couple of firm tugs. Finally, the drawer groaned as it gave way.

"Well, well," she said, "what's this?" She looked at a garment bag neatly folded in thirds and placed underneath a worn US Navy blanket. Delicately, she peeled back the covers and unzipped the bag. Her eyes first caught a glimpse of blue and yellow and then the number 3, gold wings, and Ben's name, all embroidered in yellow thread. "Ben's Blue Angel flight suit, oh my goodness, oh my goodness," she repeated while she stroked the breastpocket of his special uniform.

Her eyes moistened when she recalled the aviators' tradition of saving their flight suits for their sons. Her throat tightened as the memory of Ben's words pierced her heart, "We'll put this away for our firstborn, who I predict will arrive within one year of our marriage. Is it a date, Desiree?"

Determined not to lose control, she blinked away her tears and tried to think of anything other than the child she and Ben had dreamed of when they'd been so sure of their love.

Thinking, I shouldn't expose this treasure to the salt air; it'll fade the colors or worse, she struggled as she made her heart confront reality. Their baby boy had been a wish and that was all, a blessing they would never receive.

Before she returned Ben's uniform to its storage place, she kissed his name and placed his blanket inside the bag for extra protection over the flight suit. As she fastened the closure, she wondered why he would ever keep something as priceless as his uniform in an area prone to natural disasters.

Deciding she'd send him a pamphlet about hurricane devastation and the inherent loss of irreplaceable possessions, she turned her attention to a flat envelope tucked at the base of the drawer. "Probably an award," she said as she held the envelope to the light and read through the opaque paper. She caught her breath as she made out bold letters that declared the name of a hospital in South Alabama.

"Surely this isn't what I think it is," she whispered. "A birth certificate? What's it doing here with Ben's uniform?"

Without opening the envelope, she stood up and paced around Ben's bed. Back and forth she walked, debating with each step whether or not to take a look.

"I shouldn't; I really shouldn't open this," she said, but a tiny voice inside her head contradicted that notion by saying, "Go on, you know you want to see, and besides, didn't Ben tell that security guard to have you go through his chest?"

When Desiree still hesitated, the voice became a bit louder as it insisted, "Look, Desiree, this envelope is just one more piece of Ben's life he obviously wants you to know about. He'd be disappointed if you didn't care enough to see what he's placed here for you to find."

She breathed deeply and pitching the envelope on the bed, she sat down beside it and let temptation and her own curiosity move her fingers to the seal. "Oh, what's the harm? Ben and I have no future, so why not?" she rationalized.

Ever so carefully, she removed the document from the envelope and took in the details, one at a time. Reading aloud, she uttered the words barely above a whisper, "Certificate of Birth, South Baldwin County Hospital, Foley, Alabama." As her eyes raced over the names of the newborn's parents, she cried, "Oh, oh, oh! It's true about Linnea!" Tears threatened to flow, but she stifled them and gently replaced the certificate in its envelope. With a heavy sigh, she said, "Ben shouldn't keep this here. Susanna would have an absolute fit if she knew." Slowly, she took a deep breath and then puzzled, "But maybe it was all her idea in the first place."

Desiree held her head in her hands and rocked back on the bed. Unable to still her emotions, she allowed her tears to flow. When she regained her composure, she dropped to her knees and with her hands folded, she closed her eyes and prayed, "Dear God, please watch over Ben and those he loves. He's a good man, honest and true, but even so, he still needs your help. Please take care of him when I'm gone and help him understand what I must do."

Humbled by the proof she held in her hands, she returned to the seaman's chest where she placed Linnea's birth certificate in its hiding place and closed the drawer firmly.

She pulled up the stool, sat down, and waited for her emotions to subside. Deciding the time for secrets had passed, she opened the bottom drawer and took out the stuffed envelope she'd left undisturbed before. When she reached inside, she felt another cassette tape, but this one was attached to a note Ben had written on Collier Development stationary. She read his brief message and clutching the cassette to her heart, she said, "Okay, Ben, I found Linnea's birth certificate you wanted me to see, so tell me, what is it you think I should hear?"

Ever so slowly, she walked into the living room and toward the armoire that stood sentry-like in the center of a long paneled wall. Framed on either side by nautical paintings and aerial photographs of mountain ranges, the cabinet seemed to hasten Desiree to its complete array of high tech equipment that would soon answer for her the riddle of Ben's recorded messages.

Selecting the first cassette she'd found, she placed it in the tape deck and pushed "Play." Within moments, she heard Ben's strong, deep voice tease, "We've a journey to take, my darling. So head for the flight deck and get ready to climb aboard."

A smile twinkled in Desiree's eyes as she reclined in Ben's easy chair and listened to his self-titled "Musical Mystery Tour" he'd mixed for her ears only. His Top Gun choices of "Danger Zone" and "Mighty Wings" didn't surprise her one bit, but it was his selection of songs of innocence and lost love that wrapped her in a cocoon of comfort. "Bluer Than Blue" and "Up Where We Belong" set the mood, but Ben turned up the heat with "Unchained Melody" and "When Love Finds You."

Full of appreciation for his clever musical message, Desiree blushed as she felt her heart warm and her thighs soften. Closing her eyes in anticipation of what might follow, she listened intently as the tape stopped, whirred, and then switched to the other side.

Side 2 led off with "A Lighter Shade of Pale" and then the tender pleading of "Have A Little Faith In Me," which caused Desiree to confess, "I do believe in you, Ben." Toying with her thoughts, she waited for the next song and wondered if Ben had any idea of the feelings he'd aroused in her head and in her heart.

Beaming with delight, she listened as the sounds of "That Somebody Was You" presented a soothing blend of clarinet and voice. But her smile changed to a frown when Ben presented her with a story of wounded love in "Don't Go Breakin' My Heart." She raised her eyes to the ceiling and in a voice as soft as a summer breeze, she said, "As God is my witness, the only heart that's breaking is mine because I have no right to claim the love that already belongs to another woman, even if that woman is only twelve years old."

As if in answer to her words, Ben's voice echoed in supreme surround-sound, "My heart is in your hands, Desiree. That's where it has always been and where it will stay, now and forever."

Startled, she stared at Ben's stereo as though she expected him to walk out from behind one of the speakers. How she wanted to hear those words from his lips and not from some prerecorded audio tape. When he didn't appear, she closed her eyes and let her imagination fill in the void. She pictured him sauntering toward her, closer and closer. She could sense his presence and he was masterful. Shuddering in anticipation, she beckoned for him to lower his tall, lean frame to where she sat. With eyes closed and her lips parted, she savored the taste of his kiss as he drew her into a deep and most moving embrace.

Bowing her head, she held on to that thought as Ben's tape once again came to life. Seated on the edge of his chair, she leaned forward in rapt attention as Ben instructed, "Listen to the words of the last two songs. They'll tell you where I am right now in my quest for you, my true love." Obediently, Desiree followed each note and every lyric of "Waiting For My Lucky Day" and the soulful "Un-break My Heart."

As the final notes sounded, she looked toward the door, certain she detected the sound of Ben's footsteps on the wooden deck stairs. She jumped to her feet and ran to the door, but when only silence met her, she realized she'd been mistaken. Ben wasn't there.

Hearing a heavy sigh and unaware the sad sound was hers, she brushed a salty tear from her cheek and sought solace in Ben's chair. Just then, his voice boomed from the speakers. With determination and desperation, he said, "The second tape, Desiree. Play it now. You won't be sorry, darling. I promise you that and more."

Thinking back to the poem "The Road Not Taken," she mapped out the two paths she could follow. Her first thought was to fly away home where no surprises awaited her, where her life followed a secure routine that rarely changed. Then she considered her other option, one that promised passion flowers and fiery dunes. She wondered if she dared believe Ben's words that she would have no regrets. That's when caution broke into her thoughts and warned her that Ben's intentions, regardless how pure, were most likely temporary. After all, he already had a full life and she really wasn't a part of it.

An image of stone, she listened as her intellect dictated, "Sorry, Desiree. This time you must hide your heart and walk far away from Ben's dream that you know can never come true."

Closing her eyes, she allowed reason to battle emotion inside her head. Before long, reason won out and Desiree found herself making plans to return to Colorado as soon as possible. Reluctantly but dutifully, she placed Ben's second tape, unplayed, on his coffee table and turned to leave. Suddenly though, the sound of ducks off in the distance directed her attention outside.

"On the seashore? How can that be?" she asked, her eyes bright. "This I must see!" she exclaimed as she opened the door and listened to the frenzied quacks that called her away from her personal dilemma and right back into the reason for her trip to Florida, environmental preservation of the wetlands and the waterfowl who inhabited the swamps, bogs, and estuaries.

Brought alive by the challenge Ben's land proposal presented, she decided she must handle any situation he presented. No longer fearing for her heart, she picked up Ben's second cassette, popped it in the tape deck, and waited for it to play. "Let's see what this is all about," she said as she leaned against the armoire door and defiantly folded her arms across her middle.

Her militant stance changed in a heartbeat, though, when she heard the opening strains of "Stairway to Heaven," the song she and Ben had danced to the night he first told her of his love for her. Unable to resist the melody that surrounded her world with beauty and desire, she allowed her softer side to concoct images of white, sandy beaches and stars dancing across moonlit waters that glistened with diamonds.

Tempted by these scenes, she recognized their strength as they honed away at her intellect, a situation made doubly difficult by Ben's last words that came through loud and clear via his stereo. "If you still love me as much as I adore you, meet me on the highest dune one hour before sunrise."

"Ben, Ben," she sighed as old feelings resurfaced, passion-charged and as deep as the ocean. "What now?" she asked. Would she and Ben hear the cry of morning gulls? Would they watch the sun climb into the heavens? Wondering what the future held, she readied herself for the beginning of another incredible day.

# Chapter 17

With the moon and the stars as her guiding light, Desiree followed a path of carefully placed seashells that wove a twisted trail through tall grasses and over the tops of rolling dunes. Buoyed by the beauty of the natural setting, she felt her steps lighten as she made her way toward the open beach.

Suddenly she stopped. Her eyes widened, her pulse raced, and her heart swelled with emotion as she surveyed the picture perfect, fairy-tale setting that awaited her arrival on the silken sands of the Gulf Beaches.

Dozens of torches flared brightly and the seductive fragrance of wild hibiscus filled the soft sea air. A satiny beach cabana the color of stardust billowed in the breeze and sultry jazz tunes played in full stereophonic sound.

"Oh, Ben, my darling Ben," Desiree whispered. "What have you done this time?"

Drawn forward by the magic of the moment, she caught a glimpse of a tall man's shadow in the moonlight, but then she did a double take as the one shadow mushroomed into three or was it four? Slowing to take a closer look before she made her descent to the beach, she inched toward the edge of the dune line. Gasping, "Oh, my goodness," she watched as the scene below her came to life in living color.

In the center stood Ben, resplendent in white trousers and a casual beige shirt that had fallen open at the front. Bronzed and barechested, he appeared godlike and very much like a man on a divine mission of passionate pursuit. Around him bustled a team of waiters wearing Finni's Bar & Grille aprons. Ben nodded his approval as the men produced woven baskets overflowing with tropical delicacies and crystal carafes filled with crimson wine.

Desiree tossed her curls in amusement at the thought of Ben planning a menu mix of honeyed mangoes, melons, and red wine. She almost laughed out loud at the concept, but her mirth turned to surprise when one of the waiters unfurled a beach blanket and then tossed it on top of what looked to Desiree like a king-sized mattress.

Emitting a throaty "Oh, oh, oh!" she stopped in her tracks and listened to the sound of Ben's deeply sincere voice. Straining to hear his words, she felt her heart soften as he ordered, "No, guys, no. Not there. Face the bed to the East. Desiree loves sunrises and this is one I don't want her to miss."

The men snapped to attention and quickly repositioned the mattress. Seeming satisfied, Ben entered the cabana and called out, "Thanks, everybody. In appreciation, tell the crew at Finni's that tonight the first two rounds of drinks are on me."

As a rousing "Thank you, sir!" echoed into the winds that'd shifted away from Desiree's vantage point, she watched the waiters pack up their bags, boxes, and coolers and head toward a paneled delivery truck parked along a beach access road.

Desiree glanced all around and hearing no other voices, she took a deep breath and kicked off her shoes. Barefooted and beautiful, she responded to the call of the sea and danced her way down the rest of the path, only stopping to gather a few shells that were less than perfect. But she didn't mind their battered and broken condition for to her they represented strength and endurance. The shells had survived and so would Ben. But would she?

Ben turned at the sound of Desiree's approach. Unlike Desiree, he took neither a deep breath nor his time in making her welcome to the beach pavilion he'd spent the night preparing for her.

Running toward her, he smiled his winning, lopsided grin, and with his eyes full of hope, he met her halfway. He held out his arms and beckoned her forward, but when she shied out of his clasp, he took two steps back and said, "Don't turn from me, Desiree. Not this time. Not now."

"Ben," she answered, "I'm flattered you've gone to all this trouble. I really appreciate it, but this beach blanket party scene isn't me."

"Too artificial? Is that it?"

Not wanting to hurt his feelings, Desiree replied, "Don't get me wrong but… "

"No more 'buts' or excuses, Desiree. I just want to give you a small token of everything wonderful you deserve. A touch of paradise for you and you alone."

Curious, she cocked an eyebrow inquisitively and whispered, "I'm not sure I understand."

"Give me a chance to demonstrate, that is, if you dare," he challenged.

Desiree knew she risked her heart, but the determined and almost desperate look in Ben's eyes gave her no choice but to acquiesce. She held out her hands and allowed him to take her into his arms. Although she tried to remain dispassionate, she couldn't pull off the charade.

One deep kiss led to another and before long, Ben and Desiree left reality far behind as they walked hand in hand away from Ben's "Paradise" and toward the tallest dune thickly covered by beach flowers and soft grasses.

When Desiree glanced over her shoulder at Ben's cabana, the bright torches, and his beach bed, she felt almost tempted to redirect their steps that way, but then a tiny voice in her head cautioned, "Beware the delights of Paradise unless you're ready to handle the consequences that may arise."

To which her heart answered, "Time's fleeting and so are the chances lovers have."

She blushed and held Ben's hand a bit tighter.

"Can it be that Ms. Desiree McAndrews is having second thoughts?" Ben asked, his eyes sparkling with devilish desire.

"And if I were?"

"Hmm," he mused, and then carefully weighing his words, he said, "Then I would hope you would allow me to do this." Not waiting for her reply, he gently lowered her to the silky, soft sand and found his place beside her. Breathing heavily, he held her face in his hands and looked into her eyes. Without saying one word, he asked the question Desiree had longed to hear.

She answered him with a kiss that rocked his soul and changed his world.

Almost as if on cue, a heavenly puff of clouds passed over the moon, giving the lover's the privacy they desired.

Oblivious to time and place, they teased, tantalized, and tasted. Love flared and passion raged with an intensity so brilliant that the clouds parted and the sun rose. At least those were the images that pulsed through Ben's psyche as he rejoiced in the divine sweetness of his beloved Desiree.

Entwined as one, Ben and Desiree savored the love they'd rediscovered, a love Ben swore would stand the test of time and would thrive even through environmental controversy and personal upheaval. He acknowledged the risks of their relationship, but he wasn't about to walk away. Bestowing kisses and caresses, Ben promised his love for Desiree would never end.

Desiree, though, hearing Ben's sweet words and honest promises, felt her heart cry with pain and sadness. She hid her face from Ben, wanting to protect him from the sight of her mournful tears she couldn't suppress.

Yes, she loved him. Yes, she always would. Even so, she knew their time together was drawing to a close, a special time she would always cherish, but a time she had to let go.

\* \* \* \* \*

"I know you're out there somewhere, Ben Collier. So ready or not, here I come."

Drowsy from the warmth of Desiree's love, Ben stirred and wondered who on earth had ventured out on his private beach at daybreak.

"You servin' up grits and eggs in that fancy party tent of yours or do I have to fly back home for an Egg McMuffin?"

Ben recognized the voice that sounded from behind a secondary dune located about fifty yards from where he nestled beside Desiree. With a groan, he touched her shoulder and whispered, "Wake up, sweetheart. Bogey on the rear flank."

Desiree moved slightly and then snuggled into the safety of Ben's chest. Having decided to make the most of her last few hours with Ben, she had absolutely no intention whatsoever of leaving the comfort of his most intimate embrace. Too bad for Desiree, though, that someone else had another agenda that didn't include personal R & R for Ben and Desiree.

"Where are you hidin', Ben Collier? It's just little ol' me comin' to call on the father of my child."

Seething "Susanna," Desiree brushed her hand across her kiss-swollen lips and raised up on one elbow. She peered over

Ben's shoulder and shook her head at the sight of Susanna dressed in high heels and an outrageously loud Hawaiian print sarong that left little to the imagination.

Susanna spotted the love nest and charged forward. When she snagged her heels in a thatch of beach vines, she cursed and kicked off her shoes. Tossing them out of her way, she shouted, "There's more where these came from. Isn't that so, Ben?"

Ben and Desiree shared a look loaded with dismay as they quickly reached for their clothes. While Ben fumbled with his pants and Desiree struggled with her skirt, they laughed at their predicament, but their humor didn't last long. Just then, a gust of swirling wind blasted across the dunes.

"Oh no!" Desiree cried as she watched her skirt and blouse become airborne and sail high over Ben's head and out of her reach.

Susanna roared at Desiree's obvious discomfort and continued her march toward the couple. Feigning modesty, she shielded her eyes and cackled rudely, "Why are you blushin', blondie? And as for you, Ben, I don't see what you're botherin' about. It's not as though I'm not well acquainted with what you have to offer." Her laughter intensified maniacally as she stood almost on top of the lovers whose protective cover was literally gone with the wind.

"Back off, Susanna!" Ben commanded sternly.

"Well, I never," she huffed. "My daddy'll have your hide, Ben Collier, if I tell him how awful you talk to me."

Ben snorted his reply. "Big Jack Delaney poses no threat to me."

Susanna dug her feet into the sand and leveled her gaze at Ben before retorting, "You might want to rethink that statement since Daddy has been so good to you over the years. He is, after all, one of the great men of Florida or have you forgotten that?"

At the mention of the Senator's name, Desiree shivered and looked away.

Ignoring Desiree, Susanna continued, "Daddy's a saint, always ready to help. When I told him I needed a quick trip over here, he didn't even fuss, but I could tell somethin' was wrong. He must've had a rough night but no matter. He put me first. That's a lesson you might want to learn, Ben. For Linnea's sake."

Ben lowered his eyes and colored slightly.

Seeming pleased at Ben's reaction, Susanna babbled on. "Anyway, I think I'll follow Daddy's other rule of kindness to man and beast. So, consider yourself off the hook this time 'cause I know you're just showboatin' for her, that's all." She pointed a finger at Desiree and sneered.

Desiree locked eyes with Susanna and said sweetly, "Good morning to you, too, Susanna." Holding a bouquet of sea oats to her exposed front, she tried to muster a dignified smile.

Susanna bellowed a sigh of disgust and turned her back to Desiree and Ben. Then she swaggered to the dune where Desiree's blouse had landed in a clump of beach brush. "Am I a good woman or what?" she bragged as she picked up Desiree's clothing with a flourish. With her back still turned to the couple, she flung the garments toward them and said to Desiree, "If I were you, I think I'd keep those things covered. Now if you'd like to have the name of my cosmetic surgeon in Venezuela, you might end up with somethin' worth showin'."

"Are you finished, Susanna?" Ben asked as he helped Desiree dress. Then he added, "You've had your fun, so I think it's time for you to end your little show."

"Well, la dee da," she said derisively. She leaned forward and whispered into Ben's ear. "Don't worry, darlin'. When you get finished with her, I'll welcome you home to an entertainment extravaganza you won't soon forget, you big hunky jet jock."

Ben looked daggers at Susanna and answered, "Not a chance."

"Oh, pooh, Ben," she whined. "Whatever happened to your sense of adventure? Maybe I should tell your little cookie some stories about us. Surely then, she'd see why it's time for her to vamoose outta my sight and outta your mind."

Desiree quickly covered her ears with two seashells she found nearby and said, "That's it! I've seen and heard more than enough. Susanna's right about one thing. It is indeed time for me to go back to Colorado. I'll file my final report from Boulder and let the regulating agencies handle Heron Bay as they see fit."

Ben reached for Desiree's hands and pleaded with her to stay. When he caught a glimmer of hopelessness in her eyes, he added, "The only person who's leaving is Susanna. And that's a promise I'll deliver any way I can. I just wish I knew why she showed up here in the first place. I'm sure she doesn't plan to stay. I'll see to that myself."

"Big whoop!" Susanna said with a haughty laugh, and then she shifted her tone to one of cold seriousness as she added, "Daddy flew me here this mornin' so I could get some of my things out of the beach house. I have a date tonight and I need my pearl jewelry I left here the last time Linnea and I spent the night with you. Now that was one fine pajama party." Susanna's eyes twinkled when Desiree winced at Susanna's words.

Although Ben wanted to soften the sting of the steamy images Susanna continued to flaunt shamelessly, he figured explanations and excuses would take precious moments away from his time with Desiree, so he decided to focus on Susanna's announcement of a social life that didn't involve him. "Tell me about your date, Susanna. What are your plans?" he asked, his face signaling relief that she would soon be on her way.

Rolling her eyes and hips, Susanna answered, "This night'll be a perfect blend of business and pleasure for a beauty queen, that's me, you see, and my new beau." A bundle of animation, she explained she'd been called to Escambia County to judge the Miss Sunshine of the South pageant.

Susanna struck a pose that screamed, I'm the glamour person here, and then said, "Miss Pride of Alabama couldn't make it 'cause her momma took sick, so that's when the pageant director called me to fill in. Of course, I said I would, although I would've much preferred havin' more time to prepare myself suitably for this important assignment."

As Susanna chattered on about makeup and evening gowns, Desiree wondered if the woman ever took the time to actually listen to what she was saying. She looked toward Ben, who seemed lost in his own thoughts.

"So," Susanna concluded, "I have to be at the Pensacola Junior College auditorium by noon. That's why we need to talk about Linnea."

Ben listened responsibly as Susanna said, "The preliminary talent competition begins at 1 so I can keep Linnea with me for that part, but then I've got to do somethin' with her tonight after the judgin's completed and the queen's crowned."

"Ah ha, that's it. You need a babysitter while you're out partying with some strange man. I'm right, aren't I?"

Susanna tensed and then fired back a heated rationalization. "Look here, Ben. I'm not about to pass up an evenin' with an important gentleman from Mobile who agreed to judge the finals the moment he heard I'd accepted the pageant director's invitation to emcee their show. So now, tell me, Ben Collier, what do you think of that?"

Ben attempted to hide his joy as he said, "By all means, judge on, Susanna. I'm glad you'll be in your element and with a new admirer to boot. But I'd still like to know who's going to take care of Linnea while you're, how shall I phrase it, occupied?"

Susanna pouted and frowned. Then she answered, "Oh, I get it. It's okay for you to play love slave with Desiree, but if I need some quality time for courtin', then that's a different story. Why don't you just say you don't have time to take care of that darlin' child you helped me bring into this world? Shame, shame on you."

Twinges of torn emotions flew through Desiree as she thought about the birth certificate she'd found in Ben's bedroom. Unable to remain silent, she put her hands on her hips and said, "Let me resolve this problem by removing myself from the situation. I'm out of here. So good-bye and good luck."

"No, Desiree, wait," Ben said hurriedly. "We can work something out. Let's go to the cabana and sit down and talk this out like civilized adults."

Susanna tossed her head back and said with a harsh laugh, "The only heathen I see on this island is her, so maybe we oughtta leave Desiree behind to play with the beach mice. After all, she is the environmentalist."

Ben's face reddened and his eyes darkened as he walked menacingly toward Susanna and ordered, "Stop it, Susanna! I'm tired of your mindless comments about someone as pure, good, and kind as Desiree."

"Oh, please, Ben. Surely you're not that blind as to her true character," Susanna countered as she lowered her voice to a deep growl.

Incensed, Ben put his arms around Desiree and said, "Desiree's a lady in the finest sense, the woman you will never be."

"Keep it up, Ben, and I'll... "

"You'll what, Susanna? Run to Daddy?"

Desiree, having tired of the bickering, stepped between Ben and Susanna. She looked first at Ben and then glared through Susanna. After several minutes of uncomfortable silence, she cleared her throat and simply said, "I'm hungry. What's for breakfast?"

"Anything you want, darling," Ben answered as he took her hand and walked with her toward the cabana.

Susanna tagged along behind, but she chose not to remain silent. "I hope this won't take long 'cause I don't have much time to waste. Daddy and Linnea are waitin' for me at the airstrip and the Plantation guard's holdin' his car for me at the beach house. I'm a busy woman with a full schedule and I don't like to keep my fans waitin'."

Ben smiled at Desiree and feeling the tension leave her hand, he said so only she could hear, "I'll charter a plane for Susanna myself if that's what it takes to get her away from us."

"Did you hear me, Ben?" Susanna asked impatiently. "I said my date's Mr. Taylor Hamilton, a corporate big shot Daddy wants me to meet. I've heard he's an admirer of mine who calls me Cupcake. I can only imagine how he applies his frostin'. Oh golly, I can hardly wait to find out."

"On your first date?" Ben asked.

"You sound jealous. I can tell," she replied. Turning to Desiree, Susanna warned, "Ben can fill your ears with love lies from day to night, but there's one truth I know for sure. He and I will always be connected in the most personal way. That's a fact there's no denyin'."

Desiree smiled serenely and said, "Is that so?" Looking at Ben, she winked and whispered, "It's okay. I know the truth."

# Chapter 18

Ben stood beside Desiree and waited for her reaction to what he considered his finest achievement, the St. George Plantation. Believing he'd brought together the most environmentally sound elements of architecture, land use, and natural resources, he anticipated nothing less than a glowing review. Little did he know his hopes for Desiree's approval were destined for a tailspin even he couldn't prevent.

Oblivious to Ben's charismatic way with words and his stage presence that ordinarily transformed doubters into believers, Desiree jotted a few notes on a legal pad and flipped her folder closed. Nonchalantly, she said, "Well now, that's that. I've seen enough. It's time to go."

Ben executed an about-face and cried foul by saying, "Hold on a second, Ms. By-the-Book McAndrews. We're not finished with our site survey. Look at this list of places you haven't seen yet." He opened his leather folder and produced several documents filled with names of property locations, geomorphic data, and water sample results.

Desiree glanced at Ben's information and nodding toward the section labeled Estuary and its accompanying aerial photos, she said, "Nice work, Ben, but sorry, no sale."

"What?" Ben asked, incredulous as he shook his head in denial. He studied Desiree's expression and wondered how eyes so beautiful could send forth such a look of rigid rejection.

Desiree sized up the situation and adopted a tone of seriousness that matched perfectly the risk/benefit outcome of an encounter session between an environmentalist and a developer. Without blinking, she said, "I'm sorry, Ben, but my mind's made up. Just because your data and site plans support an ecological approach to the development of this wonderful place, you've yet to show me any proof that your Heron Bay project will actually replicate what you've built here."

"I guess trust in the developer doesn't count?" he asked as he casually dropped his arm around her waist.

She relaxed against him and rested her head on his shoulder before answering coolly, "Don't you think I'm the wrong person to ask about trusting you."

A study in chagrin and sorrow, Ben lifted Desiree's hand to his lips, kissed her fingertips, and admitted with a sigh, "I deserve that. I know I should've explained about Linnea years ago. I'm sorry, so very sorry, Desiree."

Desiree felt her heart warm at Ben's sincerity, but she couldn't allow her emotional response to Ben to color her professional judgement. With a look of determination written across her face, she said, "Let's save this discussion about trust for later. Is that a deal?" She nestled her head into the curve of his neck and waited for his reply.

He tightened his lips into a slight frown, furrowed his brow, and answered Desiree in a way she hadn't quite anticipated. "Come with me and I'll demonstrate for you a lesson in trust."

Not one to run from a challenge, Desiree kissed away Ben's frown and teased, "So you think you're ready to play Mr. Trustmaster?"

"That's right, my precious skeptic, but keep in mind one game rule I have. Simply put, I play to win." He nibbled the nape of her neck, and when he heard Desiree's purrs of pleasure, he beamed his million dollar smile and asked, "Care to evaluate my warm-up exercise?"

Laughing, Desiree tossed back her head and allowed Ben better access to her most sensitive love points. With a tantalizing wink, she said, "I'm not sure you've shown me quite enough."

Ben took the bait, hook, line and sinker, and said, 'Desiree, my wonderful Desiree. I love you so much."

"Umm, perfect there, don't' stop," she whispered as she dropped her folder and her inhibitions.

Ben trailed dangerously delicious kisses from her chin to the base of her throat and then he shifted his attention lower. "There are so many ways I want to love you. That's all I've thought about for the past twelve years," he confessed.

Savoring the sensations of Ben's ultimate nearness and his complete adoration, Desiree closed her eyes and drifted to the sacred place reserved exclusively for lovers.

Ben seized the moment and tunneled his vision on one goal. The truth. It was time for him to tell all, regardless the ramifications.

He led Desiree to a meditation bench he'd installed at the junction of the Plantation estuary with Apalachicola Bay. "Sit with me for a while. We must talk. About the past and about me."

Desiree took in the surroundings and rejoiced in Ben's environmentally bountiful decisions, but even so, she still questioned the wisdom of his request to delve into the personal matters of his heart. She wondered if she was ready to hear all he seemed determined to reveal.

Seeming to sense her concern, he held her hands and hoped her softness would respond to the callouses of his life that he carried on his hands. Maybe then she would understand the pain and guilt that raged deep in his soul.

One look at Ben was all it took for Desiree to silence the warnings of her mind. Although she sensed hearing the truth might hurt, she couldn't resist his soulful eyes. She had no choice but to sit down and listen to his version of the "if onlys and what might have beens." Perhaps believing some distance between them might help ease the message he was about to deliver, she took her place at the opposite end of the bench and waited for Ben to speak.

"No, Desiree, don't sit there. You're too far away," Ben said, quickly lifting her to his lap. He gathered her into his arms and placed a line of amazing kisses in all the right places. Happiness filled his heart. Holding Desiree closer than close lifted his spirit higher than high. When a sassy redfish searching for a bug jolted Ben back to reality, he laughed and said, "I prefer the taste treat named Desiree. So, Mr. Fish, swim on. This morsel's mine, all mine."

Giggling like a teenager in the throes of backseat love, Desiree eased off of Ben's lap and snuggled beside him. Hearing Ben clear his throat, she knew his moment of revelation was at hand and she decided she'd better prepare herself for a rude awakening into the harsh realities of life. She closed her eyes and assumed a modified lotus position. Ready to receive peace and joy into her being, she centered her thoughts and opened her mind to the benevolent forces she found in Nature.

Ben, too, closed his eyes, but not in meditation. Rather, he turned to the conventional heavens for divine guidance of the most spiritual kind. Bowing his head, he prayed aloud:

Dear God,
    Please help me and listen to the burdens of my heart. I fell for Desiree the moment I saw her sitting beside Varsity Lake. You know that's the truth. And you also know I meant to marry her that next summer after my *Crusader* fleet assignment. That's exactly what I promised Desiree and that's what I thought would happen. I honestly did. But then everything changed.
    God, I haven't talked to you for a long time, but I guess now's as good a time as any. Let me tell you I'm sorry I cursed you for allowing the accident at sea to occur. Even so, you must know that losing my best friend Frenchy took its toll on the entire squadron and especially on me because that guy epitomized courage and he was one of the best fighter pilots the Navy ever trained.
    Tell me, God, was it wrong of me to give Lt. Jacque de Ville's child a father she could call Dad?

Desiree shivered when she felt Ben quiver from the darkest depths of his soul. Wanting to comfort him, she dropped from her meditative stance and knelt in front of him. She placed her healing hands on his knees and gently massaged the tenseness from his body. When Ben's eyes clouded with emotion, she reassured him as best she could. "Will you let me share your pain?" she asked.

"How can I expect that of you?" he replied as he looked toward the spectacular blue sky decorated with a few white clouds. "I kept a promise, but I also broke one and as a result, I hurt you. Please forgive me, Desiree."

Stroking his cheek, Desiree sighed, "Oh, Ben. I understand. I really do."

"I, I…," he stammered. "I failed you, the most decent woman I've ever known."

Desiree hugged Ben's legs and studied his reflection in the shaded waters of the estuary. He looked tired, distressed, and despondent. "You're too hard on yourself, Ben."

As though he'd thrown open the floodgates of his life's missteps and miscues, he laid out a litany of his regrets and his transgressions that he'd gunnysacked for years. Lowering his head into his hands, he said, "So now you know what happened on that cruise. I only hope that maybe you can understand the reasons for my actions."

Tiny tears streamed down Desiree's cheeks as she said, "My kind and good Ben. You were my hero more than a decade ago and you still are today. You kept your word to a friend and Linnea ended up with the best dad she could've ever hoped to have. Without a doubt, you are a true officer and a gentleman."

Ben kissed away Desiree's tears and held her in a tender embrace. After several minutes of reflective soul searching, he stroked Desiree's hair and said, "I can't stand the thought of losing you a second time, but if that's the decision you make, I'll understand. Just know that I truly regret not telling you all of this when it happened."

Desiree became very still as she sorted through the emotions that blazed a trail from her sensible head to the center of her compassionate heart. Brushing away a stray tear, she asked, "Does Linnea know?"

Ben lowered his head and answered matter-of-factly, "No. At least I think she doesn't."

"How about the Senator?"

"Not a clue," Ben replied and then he explained, "Senator Delaney traveled extensively through Europe on a trade mission during the last months of Susanna's pregnancy. As far as he's concerned, I'm Linnea's father."

Feeling emotionally drained but not wanting to end their discussion, Desiree asked, "Do you and Susanna plan to tell Linnea the truth?"

Ben lovingly caressed Desiree's damp cheeks and then said, "Susanna plans to carry that information with her to the grave."

Desiree looked down and frowning, she said, "I see, but what about you, Ben? Do you agree with her?"

He closed his eyes and sighed the angst of a troubled man. Just then a blue heron called to its mate camouflaged in a thicket of reeds and ivy. Recognizing the sounds of passionate pleading, Ben turned and opened his eyes to a sight that cheered his saddened heart. Two snowy egrets flew side by side to a hollow stump at the edge of a bed of watery grasses and trumpet lilies.

"Well, Ben?" Desiree prodded. "Are you going to keep the secret?"

Ben shrugged his shoulders and directed Desiree's attention toward the majestic birds, who became airborne at the sound of her voice. As Ben and Desiree watched the pair pitch and roll, Ben said, "If I were an artist, I would paint a picture of those birds in the wingtip position and I'd call the painting *Angel Flight*."

"Hmm," Desiree said thoughtfully, remembering that was the original code name she'd assigned to the Heron Bay project. Smiling sheepishly, she said, "I think you're avoiding my question and I believe I know why." She tried to gauge Ben's feelings from the expression on his face, but he masked his emotions as he looked toward the skies he'd torn up first as a fine fleet officer and then as a daring Blue Angel pilot.

Seeming to draw strength from the idyllic setting and the closeness of Desiree, he said, "Linnea needs to hear the whole story. She deserves to know the truth about her father who died a hero's death trying to save a fellow aviator. Frenchy was the champion of our squadron and a good man who counted on me to take care of his innocent, unborn child."

Tears sprang anew to Desiree's eyes as she embraced Ben and together they allowed their feelings to flow. Seated on the weathered cypress bench Ben had built with Desiree in mind, they rejoiced as their spirits bonded into a strong union of love, support, and eternal devotion for one another.

As the sun rose higher, Desiree bit her lower lip and debated whether she should ask Ben one final and very important question. Deciding she needed to know the answer, she asked, "If we had only this day together and no tomorrows in our future, would you still tell Linnea the truth?"

Ben captured Desiree's eyes with his own and said, "As God is my witness, I will be totally honest with Linnea. This time I swear I will make the right decision."

"Ben, Ben," Desiree cried. "Can't you see that you did the honorable and the right thing twelve years ago?" She placed feathery kisses along his chin and added, "I'm proud of you and I love you for the decent and good man you've always been."

Overcome by the power of Desiree's words, Ben reached for her left hand and asked softly, "Will you marry me, Desiree? Will you please become my wife?"

Desiree looked away from Ben and toward the snowy egrets who'd taken up residence beneath a stand of weeping willows and river birches. Smiling at the nesting birds and then at Ben, she whispered her reply, "We'll see, Ben. We'll see."

## Chapter 19

"Umm, so good," Desiree said as she relished Ben's kisses that transported her to another world.

His eyes darkened as they held hers in a long and intimate glance that caused her soul to tremble. When she looked away, he reached for her hand and asked, "What's your decision, Desiree? Tell me now before we take off. I must know."

Desiree's heart raced at a frenetically wild pace. The moment of truth was at hand and words failed her. Although she had so much she wanted to tell Ben, she felt her throat tighten with emotion, rendering her speechless.

Sensing her dilemma, Ben said, "It's all right. I'm sorry I've rushed you. My basic impatience with standing by to stand by, I guess." His voice and his eyes filled with concern for Desiree as he attempted to defuse the tension of the moment by saying, "I just hope whoever said all good things come to those who wait knew what he was talking about." He reached into his pocket for his Academy ring, slipped it on Desiree's ring finger, and said, "Wear this for me until I can exchange it for a diamond."

Desiree started to speak, but a call from the control tower drew Ben's attention back to the cockpit and to the instrument panel filled with high tech dials and fancy readouts. A picture of concentration, Ben completed the pre-flight check and reviewed his flight plan.

He had some very special places in mind for Desiree's eyes only and he couldn't wait to deliver her to them. He smiled at the thought and thanked his lucky stars for having another chance to win the hand and the heart of his beautiful passenger. At least that was his hope, as well as his dream.

Turning to Desiree, he whispered, "Wait until I show you the Alabama Gulf Coast. It's called Pleasure Island for reasons known only to a select few."

Desiree felt her cheeks color. In a moment of shameless bliss, all caution and reserve dashed from her psyche. Delirious with thoughts of mile high madness coupled with seaside lust, she gave her seat belt a final tug and prepared for the ride of her life.

Her heart filled with love and her soul blossomed with admiration for Ben as she watched him assume command of his sleek Jetcruzer. She wondered how she could possibly turn away from him. She knew that even if she lived to be 100, she'd never again meet a man like Ben, wonderful, kind, and true. Then the memory of his kisses flooded her mind and deepened the crimson glow of her cheeks. Only Ben could deliver kisses so passionate that they curled her toes, her eyelashes, and everywhere else in between. Oh my, oh my, she thought, and then she said, "Let's talk about us later. For now, I think we should keep our business and personal relationships separate."

"It's your call but don't rule out the possibility of us forming a dynamite corporation. It could happen, you know, that is, if you'd let Nature take her course," he replied. His eyes bright with joy, he winked boldly and said, "Up we go."

Within seconds, Ben and Desiree became a part of the sky high above Apalachicola Bay. The waters below teamed with dozens of tiny white boats and beefy oystermen, who expertly wielded their metal tongs as they harvested the shallow reefs.

"Tremendous upper body strength," Ben commented as he nodded toward the men whose sinewy bodies glistened in the sun.

Desiree cast a sideways look at Ben and smiled her approval of his own masterful physique. Yes, she liked all she saw. That was an indisputable fact she couldn't disregard.

"Something amusing?" he asked, all the while conjuring up a variety of delectable interludes for two. As he gained altitude in his plane and attitude in his ambitions, Ben skillfully maneuvered a breathtaking path across picturesque coastal towns and hidden beaches. Along the way, he regaled Desiree with stories of crabbing adventures at Port St. Joe and sailing excursions into the Gulf from Mexico Beach.

"Is that when you decided to join the Navy?" she asked, loving the pictures he painted of himself as a young, carefree boy more concerned about surfboards and sailfish than rip tides and reason.

"I'm not sure," he answered. "Early on, though, I felt a kinship with the water and the sky. Both are filled with an indescribable force of energy that makes a man feel alive."

"Are you saying that only men are privy to that sort of relationship with the forces of Mother Nature?" she challenged.

Ben ran his hand through his hair and laughed his reply. "Forgive me if I've made a politically incorrect observation, but I do believe I'm one person who might qualify as an expert in the field."

"A regular big shot, are you?" she teased.

"Come now, Desiree. You've got to admit I have more experience in this area than most people. After all, six month cruises and heavy seas were my life for most of my Naval career."

Taking his bait, she conceded his point by asking, "How many carrier landings did you make and how many hearts did you break along the way?"

"The record speaks the truth about my arrested landings. As for your other question, you already know the answer."

Desiree beamed an understanding smile at Ben, who countered with a look as focused as a sidewinder missile on the hunt for the ultimate heat source. Yes sir, he wanted to claim Desiree as his own, but first he had to get her attention.

"What are you doing?" she asked as she suddenly felt the earth spin underneath her.

With a laugh of brazen glee, Ben answered, "I thought you might enjoy a demonstration of pitch, roll, yaw, and torque."

"But not all at once, Ben!" she screamed as he reassured her, "Don't worry, Desiree. Timing is the grist of luck and I have everything under control. So sit back and let me set your dial for excitement."

Desiree clutched the armrest of her leather seat and held on for dear life. Spinning, turning, rolling, and climbing higher than she'd ever imagined possible, Ben put his plane through its paces and Desiree into a state of wonderment and supreme delight.

"It's, it's... ," she stammered.

"Exhilarating I believe is the word," Ben said as he banked the plane's descent through the light clouds that stretched over Panama City Beach and on toward Seaside and Destin.

Desiree covered her heart with her hand and tried to regain control of her biorhythms that ebbed and flowed in a pattern that matched the swirling waters of the Gulf below. Soon though, her focus shifted to a sense of intense discomfort as waves of nausea kicked into overdrive.

Attuned to the unmistakable signs of motion sickness, Ben handed her a small bag and said, "Don't be embarrassed, sweetheart. It happens all the time during 'fam' flights."

"What are you talking about?" she asked, mopping her face with a tissue.

Ben grinned as he explained the rigors of initial flight training and familiarization flights in Turbo Mentors he fondly called tormentors. "Most student pilots recover fast and so will you the more often you fly with me."

She rolled her eyes at the thought and tried to project herself out of her present situation. Concentrating with all her might, she managed to quell the spinning sensation that churned deep inside her. Finally in full recovery, she said, "Awesome roll, Ben" and then she added with a smile, "Bet you can't do a double."

Roaring with laughter at the challenge, Ben said, "Watch me" and proceeded to pierce the sky with maneuvers Desiree thought had to have been concocted by a maniac.

"Well now," Ben said. "Would you like to take the stick?"

She glanced at him incredulously and then burst into laughter. "Just you wait, Ben Collier. One of these days I'm going to take you to Eldorado Canyon for some rock climbing and then I bet I'll witness your bravado crumble as you dangle upside down off the edge of an unforgiving cliff."

"It's a date," he replied lustily, his mind consumed by the image of Desiree wearing ropes and little else as she climbed directly above his head. "Oh yes, Desiree, oh yes. Make it soon and make it quick because I have some holds in mind I'd like to test."

"Ben!" she exclaimed. "Whatever am I going to do with you?"

"How about marry me?" he asked, his eyes gleaming as he took in Desiree's beauty and breathed in her sweet charm. He knew his mission and set his goal. Whatever it took, Desiree would soon be his.

Thus began Ben and Desiree's whirlwind lovefest by the sea. As they winged their way across Choctawhatchee Bay, Desiree peered out the window at a row of weathered fishing piers tucked along the water's edge. But when Ben offered to circle in for a closer look, she politely declined by saying, "No thanks. I've had enough aerobatics for one morning."

A twinkle flickered in Ben's eyes as he whistled and said, "Just wait until tonight's show."

Desiree shuddered in mock horror and then she winked coyly before asking, "I wonder who will get the star billing? You? Or maybe me?"

With that thought locked in Ben's mind, he eased his plane into a gentle but rapid descent and touched down on a private airstrip west of Niceville.

"Thank you, Ben," Desiree said, her eyes all smiles for Ben's aerodynamic skills and his exuberant nature.

"Thanks for what?" he asked, leaning toward Desiree to accept the kiss she placed on his cheek.

She nibbled at the base of his ear and answered, "Thank you for not showing me how the nosedive got its name."

He laughed and kissed her hair that sparkled like spun gold. As she settled into the curve of his arm, he reached over to release first his seat belt and then hers. With deftly placed hands, he soon captured Desiree's most vulnerable spot and masterfully took her over the top before she realized what was happening.

Breathless, she regained her composure and stilled the pounding of her heart as she studied the outline of Ben's face. Unable to resist touching him, she stroked his brow and followed her light touches with sweet kisses along his hairline.

When he moaned softy, she moved her attention lower. Trailing kisses first here and then there, she made Ben's every dream come true.

"Oh Desiree, my precious Desiree. I've missed you so much," he sighed as he folded her in his arms. "I don't think I'll ever let you go. Maybe we should stay in this Jetcruzer until the end of time. Would you like that?"

Although Ben's suggestion promised around the clock pleasure, she knew reality would soon set in and their loving would have to take a backseat to the demands of responsible adulthood. With a sigh heavy with regret, she shook her head and said, "How wonderful it would be to fly around the world with you, but you know as well as I that the commitments we've made to others must come first."

"Spoil sport," he teased, seeking her lips for one last kiss before he radioed for ground transportation to his home in Grande Lagoon.

"I'll show you who's a spoil sport," she said with a giggle as she ruffled his hair that felt silky soft to her touch. "So much for your perfect hair," she laughed.

"What about my image?" he asked, shaking his head in amusement at Desiree's every flirtatious act that had the potential to set off rockets in his pockets.

Just then, a silver Lincoln Continental rounded the corner of a metal hangar and came to a squealing stop a few yards from the narrow runway. Out jumped a young man wearing a waiter's jacket and a smile from one ear to the other.

Ben's eyebrows formed a deep frown as he raised his hands to his head and bellowed, "Not Etienne! Please, dear God, tell me it isn't so."

Desiree consoled Ben with words and actions, but even she wasn't strong enough to keep Ben from deplaning in a manner that resembled a panther ready to pounce on a jackrabbit. She had absolutely no recourse but to sit back and watch the carnage unfold before her eyes.

As for Ben, he took control of the situation in one swift move as he wrapped Etienne in a hammer lock and roared, "What have you done with Linnea?"

Eitenne, eyes wild with fear, replied, "You are one fine, tres beau papa to worry, but sir, your Linnea is fine. She's quite okay and happy with her mama at the pageant in Pensacola."

"But, but," Ben sputtered, "but why are you here?"

Etienne broke free and took two steps back. Safely out of Ben's reach, he breathed raggedly and answered rapid-fire, "Linnea checked your flight plan and saw you planned to leave your plane here for a fly-in. She said you'd need a car if you wanted to show Ms. Desiree the sights of Fort Walton Beach and all around, wherever it is you want to go. That is, of course, what she said she wanted you to do before you meet her tonight in town. So, is it okay I came all this way out here to save you?"

"Save me?" Ben barked, his eyebrows still knotted in keen displeasure.

"Yes sir, save you and ride you and Ms. Desiree all around. I drive good, you see. Miss Delaney say so for sure."

Ben paced back and forth as though he was conducting an inspection up and down the line. Glaring daggers, he hissed, "Susanna. I should have guessed."

"Oui, oui, monsieur. You are A#1 correct. It was indeed Miss Delaney who also said I should come help Linnea's papa." Etienne relaxed his stance and extended his hand in friendship.

Deeply disturbed by the turn of events, Ben shrugged his shoulders and clasped Etienne's hand. Although he at first considered a bit of bone crushing might be in order, one look at Desiree's angelic face convinced him otherwise. He motioned for her to join them on the tarmac and waited for her to deplane.

A gentle breeze flared her skirt, causing Ben to sigh his approval at the sight of her shapely legs.

Etienne, who watched Ben's every move, sighed also at the view of femininity in motion. "Nice, classy lady, Ms. Desiree, she is indeed," he said. "It will be my great pleasure to drive her around." When Ben scowled at his words, Etienne quickly added, "I mean, of course, with you by her side, Monsieur Cannon."

Hearing his aviator's call sign uttered by Etienne whose expression mirrored innocence more than disrespect, Ben paused. He wondered where Etienne had heard his nickname. Taking a closer look at the young man, he noticed that Etienne had also changed his appearance. Gone was his ponytail. Instead, he now sported a fresh military cut, causing Ben to wonder what or who had precipitated Etienne's transformation from trendy European into an all-American Joe.

"Like I said, sir, you have lots of pretty women, tres chic, for sure, especially Ms. Desiree. And for her I will drive the best way I can."

Looking Etienne straight in the eyes, Ben said, "Yes, Ms. McAndrews is a stunner. I'm sure she'll appreciate your driving ability as long as you keep the car out of the ditch. Need I remind you what happened to my Rolls?"

Etienne shook his head from side to side and then shamefully studied the tops of his polished black waiter's shoes.

"I think Etienne's suffered enough for the accident," Desiree said, taking her time as she walked toward Ben. Handing him her flight bag, she turned to Etienne and said, "But I am curious about one thing, Etienne."

"Oh?" he replied, looking alarmed.

Ben sensed Desiree's tenacious manner was about to surface. Smiling to himself, he stepped out of her way and allowed her a straight shot at Etienne.

Putting her hands on her hips, she stood toe to toe with Etienne and asked point-blank, "Why are you here and not at the restaurant in Tallahassee?"

When Etienne shuffled his feet and colored slightly, Ben nodded to Desiree and said, "She prefers answers first, pleasantries later. It's part of her investigational style, a spin-off of her profession."

Etienne relaxed and sighed before saying, "Oui, I understand. Merci."

Desiree looked less than bemused by Ben's explanation as she repeated her questions of who, what, when, why, where and how.

Under the gun of Desiree's interrogation, Etienne sang like a canary. "It is this way, Ms. Desiree. Last night Linnea called me at Chez Pierre and said that her mama and grandpapa were taking her to Pensacola, so she and I would not be able to dance at her Cotillion Ball. She cried and she cried. It was all so sad for me, Etienne, to hear.

"I, of course, being tres French, understand the way of women, so I said I would move mountains and swim oceans to be with her. That was when Linnea's most beautiful and kind mama, Miss Delaney, came to help."

He took a deep breath and continued, "I heard her say that Linnea should wipe away all her sad tears and rejoice instead because her grandpapa, the wise Senator Delaney, had room in his new Maule Orion aircraft for me to come to the pageant with the trois of them. That way Linnea and I could dance together at the Beauty Queen's Ball and, how is it you say? Tango the light fantastic? That sounded like a good plan, so that is how I got to this place where we stand now. Is it okay, the story of Etienne? How good is it that I am here to help you? Fine, I think."

"I see," Ben and Desiree spoke in unison as they shared a conspiratorial glance of mutual understanding.

Under his breath, Ben mumbled, "Susanna's up to her usual tricks. Why am I not surprised?"

Desiree nodded and returned her attention to Etienne. "So then, you were waiting in the Senator's plane with the Senator and Linnea while Miss Delaney visited with Mr. Collier and me this morning on the beach. Is that correct?"

"Oh yes," Etienne answered and then with a broad smile he added, "She thanked me a million times for coming along because she said Linnea's papa needed my help."

"How so?" Ben asked as his eyes sparked at such a notion.

"It was something about your age and lasting power, I think, sir. Plus Miss Delaney said it was not proper for you and Ms. Desiree to cavort across the Gulf Coast like barefoot lovers in the sand. She said it might cause you to drop dead. Did she mean from a heat stroke, you think?"

Angrily, Ben stared at Etienne and replied hotly, "The nerve of that woman. She knows no bounds."

Desiree reached for Ben's hands and whispered, "Forget her, Ben. You and I have more important concerns we must consider and Susanna Delaney's spiteful agenda is not one of them."

Etienne put his hand to his heart and swore, "As a good man and a Frenchman with a current green card, I promise I did not come here to cause trouble. Au contraire, monsieur. I came here to serve you as you need for me to do. I will drive real good now, and for you I will select the finest of wines for your beach blanket games, if that is what you wish for me to do. And, Monsieur Cannon, should you need to rest, I will offer my hand to Ms. Desiree as her escort, but she should know something about me first."

Etienne paused to catch his breath and leaned toward Ben's ear. Lowering his voice to a hushed whisper, he said, "Ms. Desiree should not think of me in any way that is inappropriate for, you see, I am in, what are the words? A committed relationship I think is how it is put. To your daughter, sir, I am committed as my heart is already taken."

Beads of sweat danced across Ben's forehead. Fuming so only Desiree could hear, he said, "These damned Frenchmen are going to be the death of me yet. Why me, Lord?"

Desiree put her arm around Ben's waist and consoled, "Maybe it's because you're such a fine man with a heart of gold."

"Ah, so nice. Viva la France! Love conquers all!" Etienne said as he politely turned away from Ben and Desiree while they kissed. After a discreet amount of time had passed, he spun back around and announced, "We should depart now. So if you please, follow this way." Not waiting for a reply, he headed for the silver sedan and gallantly flung open the front seat door on the passenger side.

Ben shrugged his shoulders and said, "We might as well go along with Etienne's plans, but don't worry, I have one of my own."

"Okay," Desiree replied, frowning as she checked her watch. A look of concern flashed in her eyes.

"What is it?" Ben asked, leading her toward the car.

She slid into the front seat and studied the car's accessories. "Oh no," she cried. "There's no phone and I really need to talk with Jeff in Boulder. I've got to get someone to pick up the rental car I left at the Plantation, otherwise... "

"To the rescue, Ms. Desiree, pour vous!" Etienne bubbled. "See, I save you right now with this cell phone the Senator said I should carry at all times in case I should find the need to call for reinforcements." He handed Desiree a Toshiba 850 and pointed to its power button.

She smiled her gratitude and placed her call, leaving Ben and Etienne to a highly animated discussion as to who was going to drive.

Ben won by declaring, "Move, son. I'll drive. Somehow I can't forget what happened to my car with you and Linnea in charge."

Sulking like a scolded puppy, Etienne climbed into the backseat where he flipped through worn copies of *The Pelican* and *The Spotlight*. It was only when Ben asked him who'd supplied the Lincoln that he spoke. "Pageant car, sir. Courtesy of Navy Boulevard Wheels and Deals. The car dealer, now he's one nice man. He has a good smile and firm handshake. I met him, you see."

"Does he know you took his car out of the city?" Ben asked, not wanting his name to appear on a stolen car arrest warrant.

"Oui, monsieur. Miss Delaney explained to him as to how you needed me to come help you. So he say it is A-OK and he gave me the keys."

As Ben listened to Desiree's last instructions to her Boulder staff before she rang off, he glanced over at Etienne and said, "I think we should return this car to the place where it's really needed."

Disappointment spread across Etienne's face as he replied, "No beach party for Etienne just like no Cotillion Ball with mon petite Linnea. I came here to help, to be a good man like you, Monsieur Cannon, and this is what happens."

Desiree placed the phone in its carrying case and turned to Etienne. Putting her hand on his knee, she said, "We appreciate your kind help and just to show you how much, Ben and I will be pleased to share our day with you. Have you ever seen Fort Walton Beach?" When Etienne shook his head, she added, "Well then, neither have I. So Ben, please start our tour of your favorite places."

"Considerate women and helpful Frenchmen," Ben mumbled through clenched teeth. "What a combination."

Desiree laughed, Etienne beamed joy, and Ben assumed command of Wheels and Deals' luxury sedan as the party of three headed for the Miracle Strip and then to Pensacola via Scenic Highway 98. During the drive, their conversation ranged from the devastation Hurricane Opal caused at Navarre to the condo developments proposed for Pensacola Beach.

"Where's it all going to end?" Desiree asked as they zoomed past unspoiled beaches populated by sunseekers and beachcombers of every age. "Slow down, Ben. I want you to notice that family under the striped umbrella. Over there, next to the water." She pointed out a couple with two babies who frolicked in the sand and surf.

"Sheer joy, isn't it?" Ben asked.

"That's my point, Ben," Desiree replied, looking into his eyes. "Where will families go once condos cover the coastal area and the beach no longer belongs to the people?"

Before Ben could reply, Etienne leaned forward and spoke solemnly, "Ooh, that would be definite bad news for any man concerned about his grandchildren having a seaside to go to where families relax, fish, sun, and have parties at the shore. How will they ever know about the sea if they can't get to it? Such a sad and most mal thought. Don't you think so, Monsieur Cannon?"

Studying first the determination in Desiree's eyes and then the sadness in Etienne's, Ben nodded and floored the gas pedal. He sincerely hoped the option he offered with Heron Bay would provide an alternative to the battle of preservation versus development.

# Chapter 20

The natural beauty of the Gulf Islands Seashore melded with the historic presence of downtown Pensacola. Intrigued by Ben's description of the sights and sounds of the Seville Square district, Desiree and Etienne searched for signs of architectural restoration at every corner they passed. Soon their efforts paid dividends as they approached row upon row of shops, museums, and galleries that welcomed them to a town known for its cultural heritage and youthful excitement.

"Fiesta of Five Flags? What's that about?" Desiree asked, nodding toward a bright poster tacked to a kiosk on Government Street.

"Oh," Ben answered, "it's an event held every July. That's when Seville Square takes on a carnival atmosphere that rivals Mobile's Mardi Gras. The streets and sidewalks fill with parades, art shows, vendors, and musicians. They even re-enact Don de Luna's landing here in the 1500s. During the fiesta, you name it and you'll see it, whatever your heart desires."

Watching Desiree peep up at him from underneath the fringe of her long eyelashes, he added, "It's true, Desiree. You only have to open your eyes and see how easy it is to let your deepest wish come true."

"Oh, oh, oh," Etienne interrupted. "Look over there at all the flags." He pointed to the banners of Spain, France, England, the Confederate States, and the United States. Saluting the French flag, he declared, "So proud I am that my ancestral flag waves with that of Linnea's. Maybe that's a sign that I will become lucky tonight and my dream will come true, just as you say can happen in this sunny Florida town."

Ben coughed nervously and replied, "I was speaking to Desiree and not to you, Etienne."

Etienne seemed not to care as he spied an empty parking space in front of a block of specialty shops painted in shades of rose and blue. "If you please, monsieur, be so kind as to stop here for only a brief moment. I have important business to conduct on this most excellent avenue."

Ben and Desiree shared a questioning look since they'd planned to complete their tour of the Heron Bay site before picking up Linnea across town. Glancing at his watch, Ben frowned and said, "We really should move on. I want to show Desiree Sherman Field."

Becoming suddenly agitated, Etienne twisted and turned in his seat and wrung his hands in despair. "Please, monsieur, I beg you to stop for just one moment. I'll fly like a bird, you'll see."

Ben uttered a sigh of resignation and relented by saying, "All right, Etienne. But make it quick."

"Merci, monsieur," Etienne said with relief in his voice as he opened the car door and bounded out almost before Ben could pull to a complete stop. He reached into his pocket and produced a handful of nickels and dimes. Giving all his change to Ben, he said, "For the meter, monsieur, should the red flag pop up." Then he dashed off, leaving Ben and Desiree to wonder which store had caught his eye.

They didn't have long to wait for the answer. Etienne made a beeline for a storefront made notable by its bountiful supply of precious gemstones, fine silver, and solid gold.

"Uh oh," Ben growled at the sight of Etienne swinging open the front door of Diamonte's Dazzling Diamonds. "I don't like the look of this. Not one bit."

Desiree smiled at Ben's concerns and reassured him that Etienne's salary probably precluded him from making a major purchase of the type Ben feared the most.

"Think so, really?" Ben asked, shaking his head dubiously. Then he frowned and added, "I'm the one who should be in that store. Not Monsieur Frenchman. How about it, Desiree? Dare to take a look?"

She smiled into Ben's eyes and answered, "The only thing you and I need to examine is Heron Bay. Remember?"

"How could I possibly forget? Even so, what's the harm of a slight detour?"

"Now, Ben," Desiree cautioned. "We have a deal and made a promise we should keep. Business first."

"And then?" he asked, holding her hand to his lips and bathing her soul with total adoration.

"You make this so hard," she replied, feeling her resolve crumble.

Laughing, Ben shifted his position away from Desiree and said, "You're one to talk, my love." Thoughts of passion raced through his mind, causing him to search out a place that offered seclusion and scenery. "Come with me, Desiree. Let's walk through the Plaza while we wait for Etienne. I think we have enough time for a quick history lesson and maybe something more."

Desiree's heart skipped forty beats when she felt the heat of Ben's touch as he stroked her forearm and loved her with his eyes. Within seconds, she followed the call of her heart and allowed Ben to assist her from the car. Silencing the warning signal that resounded in her head, she took his hand and strolled with him down a path that wound through flowerbeds and across a lush carpet of sea-green grass.

"Over there looks as good a spot as any," Ben said. He guided Desiree to the center of Park Square and glanced around in all directions. Having determined they were indeed alone, he wrapped her in his arms and stole a kiss.

"What's that for?" she asked.

In mid-caress, Ben stopped and answered, "Just following tradition, that's all." Then he explained, "Since I don't believe you're a scholar of Florida history, I doubt you know what I'm about to tell you."

"This should be good," she said as she rested her head against his shoulder.

All seriousness, Ben cleared his throat and began his lecture by explaining, "We're standing on sacred ground and possibly even on the exact spot of a very important land deal that I'll lay you odds was sealed with a kiss."

"Is that so?" Desiree asked, holding on to her senses while Ben demonstrated a kiss she knew was not of the continental variety described in any history book she'd ever studied.

"Yes, it's a fact that Andrew Jackson stood in this very park and completed the transfer of Florida from Spanish hands to those of the good ol' USA."

"Andrew Jackson? Are you sure?"

Ben kissed her silent and said, "Such a doubter you are, Ms. McAndrews. You give me no choice but to increase the length of our lessons to convince you."

"What lessons do you have in mind?" she asked.

Leaning closer, he whispered something about feathers and foam that caused Desiree's cheeks to flush and her knees to shake.

"That and more is in your future, my darling. Of course, I can also include a few hands-on sessions in land use and environmental harmony, that is, if you're interested in some special after-hours instruction."

"Depends on who's the teacher," she countered as she blew him a kiss and danced out of his arms.

Running to catch her, Ben thanked his good fortune for the joy of her spirit and the playful passion of her soul. His love for Desiree was complete and he swore he'd never let her go.

"This way, Ben," she called from underneath the canopy of an ancient live oak, its branches draped with thick moss. Closing her eyes, she wished time could stand still. Ben had reawakened feelings in her that warmed her heart and shook the sensibility of her world.

Ben watched Desiree smile and hoped he was the reason for her happiness. "Penny for your thoughts?"

Before answering, she looked into his eyes and reached for his hand.

"Please tell me you're about to make me the happiest man on the Gulf Coast."

She breathed deeply and prayed for courage. Then her words tumbled out. "There will never be another man in my life, Ben. Unless, of course… " She blushed and centered her thoughts.

"Unless?" He wrapped his arms around her waist and held on as though there were no tomorrows. "Surely you see by now we were meant for one another."

Ever so delicately, she turned her back to him and placed his hands on the center of her waist. Covering his hands with hers, she said, "Regardless of the directions of our paths, you will always have a place in my heart. That's a fact I promise will never change."

Ben turned ashen and looked away. Knowing he couldn't allow Desiree to continue the delivery of her message that he sensed had good-bye as its refrain, he searched his mind for ways to distract her before she said the words that couldn't be recalled once spoken. "Wait. Say no more. You need more time to think about the whole picture. Maybe after you've seen Heron Bay, you'll have a better understanding of the life I want to give you, to give us."

"The two issues are not related," she whispered.

"Oh, but they are," he replied. He framed her face with his hands and pleaded with his eyes. Minutes passed as he connected with Desiree in a manner so perfect that passers-by skirted around the couple to give them private use of the special space they'd created in the middle of Park Square.

A flower vendor rolled his cart to a spot on the corner. When he called, "Passion flowers, best rates for lovers," he motioned for Ben to come forward.

"Did you arrange for that man to miraculously appear?" Desiree asked, having settled the erratic pounding of her heart to a more reasonable rate.

"Divine intervention I think is more like it," he replied as he made a mental note to pay the preacher a triple bonus on Sunday. "Wait here a second," he added. "I need to see how much that man knows about horticulture."

Feeling her eyes blur with emotion, Desiree watched Ben walk toward the flower cart. Her thoughts were many as she decided she would give Ben his day and maybe even another night. Then she would sever their ties and let him go. For now, though, she planned to barrel roll with Ben into the sun and make memories she hoped would last a lifetime.

She watched Ben conduct a meticulous inspection of the vendor's baskets filled with flowers of every color and type. Laughing at the picture he presented, she wished for a camera to capture his method of sampling the aroma of the delicate flowers he cradled in his all-male hands. She wondered which bouquet he would bring her. Roses? Wild orchids? She smiled at the thought, but her look of pleasure turned to dismay when Ben returned empty-handed.

She tried to cover her disappointment with a smile but Ben saw through her masquerade. He kissed the tip of her nose and said, "Don't worry, kitten, I plan to fill your life with flowers and a whole lot more. You'll never regret your decision."

Thinking, I wonder, she asked, "Is that so?"

"We'll talk tonight over dinner, but first I have a proposition for you." He winked and placed a tri-folded envelope in her hands. "Go ahead. Open it."

"What have you done this time?" she asked, her voice trembling as she studied his face for a clue.

Unable to resist, Ben said, "Forgive my need for speed, but here, give me that thing. I'll open it for you."

"I think not," she retorted as she fended off his attempt to reclaim the envelope. With one swift motion, she broke the envelope's seal and took out a note written on the back of a Collier Development business card. Reading aloud, she said, "Tonight. 20:30. The restaurant at Perdido Pass. Dress and transportation provided. Counting the hours. Your true companion."

"Is it a date?" he asked as he watched her hold his invitation to her heart.

A row of tears streaked down her cheeks. She loved Ben with every fiber of her body, yet she knew love sometimes wasn't enough. Besides, she'd made up her mind. Tonight would signal the beginning of the end and there was no turning back from the path she'd chosen, a one-way road lined with a ribbon of love everlasting but paved with honor and reason.

# Chapter 21

"Need not be built; need not be built. Is that what you're thinking?" Ben asked as he led Desiree to the restaurant's observation deck overlooking Ole River and Ono Island.

Desiree stepped toward the ledge and facing the marina, she answered thoughtfully, "The site you've selected is the problem, Ben. Not the design and most certainly not all the amenities you've planned for Heron Bay. A gated entry, piers, swimming pools, and hot tubs on every deck. My goodness gracious."

Ben stood beside Desiree and held his breath. He hoped the construction model he'd requested for her scrutiny would arrive on schedule. He wanted her to see his vision sculpted to perfection in painted papier-mâché.

As he listened to Desiree praise his intent to build a community linked by raised boardwalks over protected wetlands, he admired her mediation skills. Thinking it was little wonder her name had surfaced at the top of the President's list for a key conservation appointment, he sighed. Under no circumstances could he handle the possibility of Desiree calling Washington home, thousands of miles away from him.

Oblivious to Ben's concerns, Desiree said, "All I can tell you at this point is that Perdido Key represents one of the last areas of natural beauty within a fifty mile radius." She paused to watch Ben's reaction to her words and then she added, "You've seen enough developments, architectural wonders and disasters alike, to recognize the dangers of opening the door to rampant building. Who's to say what the next development down the road may be. A fifteen story condo? A tract of beach mansions built on concrete pilings?"

"I see," Ben said. "You've surveyed the site and have made up your mind. You're going to submit a negative report, aren't you?" He linked his arm through hers and nodded toward the main dining room. "Before we go in, please consider the last piece of evidence I want you to see. It's a scale model of the property I feel truly depicts the spirit of Heron Bay."

She rested against him and asked, "What's the point, Ben? You've already shown me the site plans, engineering reports, and environmental permits that must have cost you your soul."

Laughing, he cupped Desiree's chin in his hands and looked into her eyes as he said, "I would sell my soul for only one thing and you know what that is."

She raised her eyebrows and shook her head before saying, "The go ahead for a project that's guaranteed to generate a bizillion bucks for you and your other investors? That's it, I'm sure."

"You're not even close, my darling. All I want is you. Say you'll marry me." He cradled her in his arms and embraced her tenderly. Looking at his Academy ring on her finger, he said, "Let's call Mr. Diamonte and order his finest wedding bands. We've lost enough time as it is and I don't want another minute to pass without having you by my side, forever."

Desiree frowned and looked away, unable to face Ben. How could she tell him all that she felt in her heart? How could she say good-bye and walk away? Lost in her thoughts, she didn't notice the door to the terrace swing open.

"Dad, Dad. Are you and Desiree coming inside or what?" Linnea asked impatiently. "A messenger just left a stack of shoeboxes and a rack full of clothes in the hallway. He said you'd ordered everything special from the Riviera Center." She motioned for Desiree to come closer and said, "I think Dad likes me in baby colors. There are four or five dresses my size, all silks and satins in different pastels. He's got to let me grow up sometime. Don't you think so?"

"Sometime he will," Desiree answered. "Just you wait and see."

"Whatever," Linnea replied and then bubbled, "Wait 'til you see the dress he ordered for you. It's the color of Bambi and trimmed in faux fur. It's beautiful."

"Fur!" Desiree exclaimed with an exasperated sign. When Ben shrugged his shoulders and flashed his best boyish grin, Desiree forgave him with a wink and a most kind, "You never cease to amaze me."

"Good," he replied with a brilliant smile that matched the sparkling stars scattered across the perfect Alabama sky. "Shall we, ladies?" he asked as he escorted Desiree and Linnea through the Red Parrot Room and into a foyer outside the dining area that'd been transformed into a ballroom for a most glamorous affair.

"Monsieur Cannon, you are a true bon papa and a man I would like to call Dad," Etienne greeted Ben, who immediately tightened his hold on Linnea's hand. Etienne delivered a crisp salute and added, "You even thought of me, your bon ami, Etienne. Excellent choice of tuxedos. Pierre Cardin, the finest tailor of all time. Merci, merci!"

Ben shook his head, amused by Etienne's enthusiasm. "I hope one of these will fit you. I guessed your size the best I could."

"Don't worry, kind monsieur. I can mix and match if I must since you bought many for us to keep."

"Rented, Etienne. These all go back to A Grand Affair in the morning. That's your job. Okay?"

Etienne inched closer to Linnea and answered, "Oui, oui, monsieur. A pleasure it is for me and Linnea to spend together this wonderful night and then become messengers in the morning daylight. My dream has indeed come true but not in a sunny Florida town. Hurray for Linnea's Cotillion Ball you give her here tonight in the heart of Dixieland, USA."

"Well now," Ben said, surprised by Etienne and Linnea's profuse display of appreciation that included much handshaking and polite kissing. "We should probably change for the evening and let the party begin."

"So many choices to make," Etienne muttered as he and Linnea selected a blue cummerbund that closely matched the color of the dress she'd decided to wear.

"Your studs, son," Ben reminded Etienne and handed him a packet of sterling and pearl cuff links and a black bow tie.

"Maybe the lovely Linnea can help me put these on," Etienne said, his eyes filled with wishfulness.

"Not a chance, son. Follow me to the head," Ben answered as he put his arm around Etienne's shoulder and marched toward the men's room.

Desiree and Linnea turned their attention to the collection of shoeboxes. Sorting through Prada velvet wedges and Gucci slides, Desiree held up a pair of dainty shoes and said, "These will be perfect with your gown. Try them on to be sure they fit."

Linnea kicked off her sandals and stepped into a pair of low-heeled satin pumps. Catching her reflection in a side mirror, she made a face and complained, "I wish these were higher." She looked wistfully at the heels Desiree had chosen for herself and said, "Etienne's so much taller than I am, just like Dad is next to you. Don't you think I need some extra inches, too? Better for dancing, you see." Then she blushed and toyed with a loose strand of her hair.

"Don't forget I was a teenager once myself," Desiree said as she helped Linnea check the color match of her dress and shoes. "So I know exactly what you're thinking, young lady. Please tell me you and your mother have had The Talk."

"About what?" Linnea asked, her eyes wide with curiosity.

Desiree glanced at the floor and answered, "About responsibility for your actions, protection and passion." A look of concern clouded Desiree's eyes. Shaking her head as if to dismiss a thought that nagged at her conscience, she added quickly, "Consequences and complications. Do you know what I'm talking about?"

Linnea fluffed her hair defiantly and answered, "Sure, everything I need to know I learned from you and Dad. You've been great teachers." Keeping her eyes on Desiree's face, she giggled as she watched Desiree's cheeks burn with guilt and shame.

Desiree turned away from Linnea and reached for a shopping bag filled with silky lingerie. She cleared her throat and took an offensive position by saying, "Well then, since you say you've mastered all the basics, I assume you're ready for a little quiz on the finer points of human behavior. To test your knowledge, I'll ask you a few questions while we dress for your ball. For starters, do you have any idea how special your dad is to plan this evening for you?"

"Of course I do," Linnea answered and then she added, "but the big question is—do you?"

"He's something else," Desiree replied softly as she watched Ben leave the men's room and walk toward her. Dressed to the nines in a white dinner jacket, black pants, tuxedo shirt, and bow tie and cummerbund fashioned from the same material as Desiree's ballgown, he stole Desiree's breath. Thinking, GQ models move over, she doubted a more handsome man had ever existed.

"You're not dressed yet," Ben complained, motioning toward Desiree's gown that still hung on the rack beside all the dresses Linnea had rejected as being too babyish. "If you don't like my selection, you can always go native," he teased, delighting in Desiree's most becoming blush and Linnea's pained wails of "Oh, Dad! Not here!"

Desiree wagged her finger at Ben and warned, "You'd better watch what you say, Mr. Collier. We're not alone, you see." She winked at Linnea, who quickly lost all interest in Ben and Desiree when Etienne appeared on the scene, suave and sophisticated and the answer to an ingenue's prayer.

Etienne bowed gallantly from the waist and took Linnea's hand. Kissing her fingertips, he asked, "May I have the first dance, mademoiselle?"

Linnea cast a worried look in Ben's direction and replied, "Thank you for asking me, Etienne, but Dad always dances with me first. That's one of his house rules." Then under her breath, she whispered, "At least that's how things used to be, but I'm not so sure of that now." Her eyes sought Desiree's.

No one spoke and the silence became uncomfortable. Desiree finally broke the quiet when she nodded toward the ladies' suite at the end of the hallway and said, "Come with me, Linnea. Let's change into our dresses. You don't want to keep your dad waiting on the dance floor, now do you?"

While Etienne and Ben paced up and down the corridor, Desiree and Linnea adjourned to the powder room. After what seemed like hours to Ben, the door finally opened and Desiree and Linnea made their grand entrance. Ben whistled his approval and shared a high-five with Etienne, who then raced to Linnea's side.

Falling to one knee, Etienne proclaimed his undying affection for Linnea, who twirled around gracefully for his benefit. She blew him a kiss and motioned for him to follow her. She started to say something to Ben, but seeing his attention was focused solely on Desiree, she and Etienne made a quick escape from parental supervision.

Unable to take his eyes off of Desiree, Ben knew he'd never seen a more beautiful woman. Her every look, her every move appealed to his senses and to his imagination. Thinking, thank you, God, for letting me share this time with Desiree, he could feel her in his arms. He loved her completely and wanted all the world to know. Whatever it took, he was determined Desiree would soon become his wife.

"You're smiling, Ben," Desiree said as she placed a gloved hand on his arm. "It's Linnea, isn't it? She's a wonderful young woman you can be proud of."

"I am," he replied, resting his hand at the small of Desiree's back. "But I'm also quite proud of you for the stand you've taken as an advocate for the terns, plovers, and other nesting birds at Perdido Key."

"What?" she asked, wondering if she'd heard Ben correctly. "Do you know what you're saying?"

"And what I'm doing," he replied, cradling her in his arms.

"Which is?" she asked.

"Have you forgotten what you told me at the house this afternoon?"

"Let your conscience be your guide. Was that it?"

"Yes," he answered and then declared matter-of-factly, "I'm taking your advice, Desiree. I've made my final decision. Heron Bay will not be built."

Stunned, Desiree stepped away from Ben and studied him from head to toe. Then she leaned forward and placed her hand on his forehead to check for fever.

Laughing, Ben covered her hand with his and said, "I'm delirious, all right, deliriously in love with you. You're one dangerous lady."

"Who me?" Desiree asked, playfully pointing toward herself and shaking her head in mock denial.

"Yes, you, my darling Desiree." He kissed her and then said, "It's a good thing I made my fortune before you so convincingly reminded me that I have a responsibility to protect sensitive areas and wildlife habitats."

"Oh, Ben!" Desiree exclaimed. "You're serious, aren't you? I'm absolutely thrilled! You really understand the issues and the inherent dangers. Thank you for listening. You've made me so happy."

He removed one of her gloves and raising her hand to his lips, he placed kisses from her wrist to her bare shoulders. As he listened to her moans of passionate pleasure, he intensified the love factor by ninety knots and soon found himself guiding Desiree toward a private ante-room furnished only with a satin couch and a glorious view of the Gulf.

"Responsibility, Ben," she gently reminded him. "Tonight belongs to Linnea. Remember?"

Frowning, Ben nodded his head and said, "Three hours of tonight is all Linnea gets. Then she and Etienne will return to Susanna's care and you, my lovely princess, will find yourself transported to a palace by the sea. There I will become your love slave, ready to fulfill your every fantasy."

"My fantasy?" she said with a laugh. "It sounds more to me like it's yours."

"How about ours?" he whispered as he bathed the nape of her neck with promise-filled kisses.

Before she could answer Ben, Desiree felt a small hand touch her elbow. Looking down, she faced Linnea whose eyes shimmered with excitement.

"Two bands are here and they're setting up now. It's time for my ball. Please, please. Let's go inside now. Please, hurry."

"Yes, we're coming," Desiree said as she turned to Ben who stood attentively by her side.

"Wait here a second," Ben instructed. "I have a solo reconnaissance duty to perform before the party starts." When Linnea frowned at him, he reassured her he wouldn't take long. Quickly, he scoped out the dining area and determining everything was set as he'd specified, he threw open the doors to the ballroom and motioned for the others to come inside.

Desiree beamed her approval, Linnea squealed her delight, and Etienne bobbed his head as he reached into his pocket for a small jewelry box.

"Is it okay, monsieur, that I give this purchased token to your belle daughter?"

Ben started to reach for the box to check out its contents, but Desiree deflected his hand and said, "Linnea's night should be an evening she'll always remember for its perfection. Don't spoil the fun for her and for him."

Etienne smiled his appreciation to Desiree and tenderly kissed Linnea on her left cheek and then on her right. "Pour vous, Linnea. To make our first time the best."

Ben's blood pressure spiked at Etienne's words, but a calming look from Desiree helped Ben maintain control as he held his emotions in check and counted to twenty.

Linnea rushed to open Etienne's gift. Taking one look, she exclaimed, "It's beautiful! The prettiest necklace I've ever seen. Please help me put it on, Etienne."

Desiree squeezed Ben's hand as she watched him exhale a deep sigh. Linnea was growing up and Desiree could tell Ben wasn't ready to let her go.

"Maybe I should help him out," Ben suggested, nodding toward Etienne, who fumbled with the gold clasp he'd gotten tangled in Linnea's hair.

Desiree shook her head and said, "I think Etienne's resolved the problem. Besides, look how cute they are. They really make an adorable couple."

"She's too young and he's too clever," Ben replied sternly and folded his arms across his chest.

Seeming unaware of Ben's opinion, Etienne reached for Linnea's hand and said, "Wear my tres French fleur-de-lis everyday of your life. If so, I will know you must think of me. Do that often and I will become as happy a man as your bon papa."

Etienne's jubilant spirit became contagious as Ben lightened up and Desiree and Linnea turned on the charm of coquettes as they handed the men their dance cards. With grand authority, Ben directed the Jammin' Bama Band from Shirley and Wayne's to begin the music that resounded from Innerarity Point to West Beach. Within moments, Linnea's Cotillion Ball swung into the slide zone of slow dancing and tango-twisting.

"This is wonderful," Desiree said as she and Ben walked to a table set for two. They watched Linnea and Etienne groove to the tunes of the High Tide Rockers Ben had lured from the Pink Pony Pub for a cameo appearance at Linnea's ball. Enjoying the aroma of thousands of exotic flowers that decorated the ballroom, Desiree rested her head against Ben's and asked, "Did you order all these arrangements from the vendor in the park?"

"Yes, I did, and while you and Etienne picked up our lunch order at Trader Jon's, I called the owner here and persuaded him to rent out his restaurant to us for the evening."

"Ah, the power of money."

"The power of love is more accurate." He stroked her hair and added, "Some things are meant to be and others happen with a little help from above."

"All right, Ben. I'll concede that point, but you'll never convince me that all the food in this room appeared out of thin air."

He chuckled at Desiree's method of extracting key information and said, "Since you persist in saying you must leave tomorrow for Boulder, a city not known for its shrimp, I decided to bribe you with seafood from some of my favorite restaurants. So tell me, my love, how do you rate this feast from Coconut Willies, the Oar House, and the 'Roundback Oyster Bar & Grill?"

"Simply the best," she answered. "But when did you arrange this?"

Grinning sheepishly, he said, "Remember when I left you and Etienne at the Skyhawk exhibit at the Museum and said I needed to call my friend, the editor of the *Gosport*?"

"Yes, I remember."

"Well, I didn't call Art," he confessed. "Instead I phoned an entertainment consultant and she pretty much took my plans from there."

"Hmm, interesting," Desiree replied. "What about the evening gowns and tuxedos?"

Ben colored slightly and admitted he'd faked a trip to the men's room at the Flora Bama Lounge while Desiree and Etienne watched a volleyball match on the beach.

"Made another call, right?" she asked, adoring him with her eyes.

"Is a man allowed no secrets?" he teased as he picked up a white napkin and waved it in front of Desiree.

She snatched it out of his hand and said, "Any man who could orchestrate an evening like this could rule the world single-handedly."

"The single business is over for me," he said, "and all because of a blue-eyed blonde who's the light of my life."

"Oh, Ben," Desiree sighed. "The things you say to me."

"From the bottom of my heart, darling. And that's God's truth, I swear it."

"I've never been happier," Desiree said.

"Nor have I," Ben agreed.

"Me, too," Linnea said, dancing out of Etienne's arms and onto Ben's lap.

"It's four happy party people dancing in a dining hall," Etienne chimed in as he pulled up a chair beside Desiree and reached for a tray filled with shrimp and crab cakes. "A picture of joy we make, that is for sure," he added with a tip of his hand to Ben, who'd given Linnea the best Cotillion a girl could ever want.

Unknown to the celebrants, though, two party-crashers with bad attitudes were headed in their direction. A red Cadillac raced over the Alabama Point Bridge at a speed that challenged all laws of highway safety. The car swerved and careened dangerously close to a guard rail before lurching to a stop at the base of the hill.

"I know they're in that fancy restaurant upstairs. I can smell Ben's cologne from here," Susanna said, her face contorted into a petulant pout.

"Is that so, angel eyes?" her companion asked as he moved his beefy right hand from the steering wheel and massaged her knee through her beaded ballgown the color of silvery pink ice.

"Tell me, Taylor, have you made the acquaintance of my former husband, Bennett Collier? I would think he would've searched out a man like you considerin' the interest in land deals you share."

"Nah, lamb chop. I've only heard about Mr. Collier through your father. Now he's one fine man. Where was the Senator tonight? I missed seein' him at the beauty contest."

Susanna snuggled closer to Taylor and said, "Daddy's probably still watchin' for UFO's in Gulf Breeze, but don't worry, he'll catch up with us in the mornin' in Mobile. Thank goodness for his airplane with extra room, that is, in case you wanna come home with me." She placed her hand on Taylor's thigh and patted him wickedly.

"Whoa there, baby doll. You're makin' ol' Taylor think maybe we oughtta put this car back on the highway and head for a cheap motel." He puffed out his cheeks and inched Susanna's hand higher. "See what I mean, pussy foot? If you don't watch your love touches, you'll have me backstrokin' my way to heaven and back before this evenin's even started."

Susanna tossed back her head, and when her tiara came unpinned from the top of her hair extension, she wailed, "Now see what you've gone and done to me, you bad boy. How can I ever make myself presentable without a stylist to fix my curls?" She posed for a better view of herself in the rearview mirror and cried, "I'm a sight and a bundle of nerves over my precious daughter bein' around the likes of that evil woman from out of state and you're not helpin' matters one bit."

Taylor lurched across Susanna and flipped open the glove compartment. Taking out a metal flask, he said, "A shot of this Wild Turkey is just what you need, cream puff. Doctor's orders, so I say it's okay to have a nip or two before we go in."

"I didn't know you were a physician, too," she said with a purr and a calculating leer.

I'm not the M.D. kind. Hell, I'm better than some ol' sawbones 'cause I'm a love doctor, the man who's got the touch and the medicine to heal a cupcake as tasty as you." He uncapped the top of his flask and said, "Ladies first."

Susanna took a deep swallow and then another. "Zippety doo-da!" she yelped as she fanned her cheeks and then her lips. "Talk about fire in the oven!"

Taylor roared his pleasure with Susanna's uninhibited response. "Where have you been all my life, candy kiss? You're my kind o' woman. I think you and I have a future."

"Is that so?" Susanna replied, her eyes ringing up dollar signs as she studied the size of Taylor's horseshoe-shaped diamond ring that sparkled in the moonlight.

"I think my date sees somethin' she wants. Is this man right or what?" he asked. He slipped off his ring and dropped it down the front of Susanna's low-cut gown.

"Whatever on this earth do you think you're doin', Mr. Hamilton?" She pushed against his hands that roamed across her chest and then groped lower.

"Just checkin' the dimensions of my treasure trove," he answered with a sneer and a lecherous laugh. "I'm sure you don't mind my personal interest in examinin' your goods, beauty belle."

Susanna quickly shifted his ring to a spot of tightest security and retorted, "That's what you think, Taylor Hamilton. When I need a physical, I'll let you know, but until then, I'll thank you to keep your hands to yourself or you may end up an amputee. Understand?"

Snorting derisively, Taylor crowed, "So little Miss Muffet thinks she can tell Taylor Hamilton the rules of the matin' game."

Without batting one mascara-ladened eyelash, Susanna grabbed for Taylor's throat and tightened the knot in his bow tie. Squeezing with all her might, she relented only when his eyes bugged out and he yelped, "All right, suga' lumps. I give."

Taylor slapped his knee and bellowed like a bullfrog, "Damn, you're one fine woman, puddin' pie. I'll cool my heels for now, but I'm tellin' you straight; I'm not about to take orders from any woman, not even from one as beautifully buxom as you, love locks. So rest easy for a while but know ol' Taylor's like a hungry bear with a nose for raw honey. I smell it and I go for it headfirst, takin' my pleasure one gulp at a time. So now that I've said my piece, darlin' dove, tell me if you're gonna sign on as the queen bee of my personal honey hive."

Susanna drained Taylor's flask and answered, "Only if you'll become my worker bee and help me get ever'thing my heart desires."

"Somethin' might be arranged, devil doll. So come here and give ol' Taylor a wet, wet kiss and we'll negotiate the rest." He rolled his eyes and moved in to seal the deal.

## Chapter 22

"Where are you taking me?" Desiree asked as Ben turned their borrowed Lincoln west on Highway 180, leaving the neon lights of Gulf Shores far behind.

"To Paradise," he answered. "I think you'll approve of my lodging choice," he added with a secretive smile. He watched Desiree's eyes sparkle. He couldn't wait to carry her across the threshold of a home he hoped she'd find irresistible. "Maybe if you like it enough, you'll let me buy it for you. I heard it's on the market."

Desiree sighed. She had no intention of switching her residency and she couldn't ask Ben to change his. After watching Linnea's reaction to the shenanigans of Susanna and Taylor, she worried Linnea's life was headed for a definite black and very bleak period. If Taylor, the most obnoxious and totally disgusting man she'd ever met, moved into the Delaney household, Desiree felt certain Linnea would need Ben on a full-time basis to give her stability as well as security.

Filled with concern for Linnea, she put her hand on Ben's knee and said, "It's not that I don't want to stay. It's simply that I can't."

"I don't understand, Desiree. Our differences over Heron Bay are history, so I see no problems ahead of us."

Desiree prayed for strength to explain her decision. She didn't need a revelation from above to guide her actions. Her road was clearly marked. Boulder, Colorado, due west.

"No comment?" Ben asked, a frown creasing his brow. "Well then, maybe it's time I tried another tactic."

Desiree's eyes widened when Ben flipped on the right turn signal and cruised into a parking lot in front of the Fort Morgan Volunteer Fire Department, Stationhouse #1. He shut off the engine and turned up the heat. Holding her closely, he whispered sweet nothings into her ears, but then he lowered the boom with a declaration of independence.

Aghast and taken totally by surprise, Desiree sputtered, "What? Surely you don't mean that."

"Oh, but I do," he replied. "I'm not going to marry you, at least not in the near future. That's plain enough to see. So, Desiree, my sensuous siren, settle back for a night to remember. No cares, no worries, no decisions, and not even as much as one proposal. Let's test the pleasure principle and make some new memories. Are you ready?"

"But Ben, I thought... "

"No, no, Desiree. Let me talk this time." He put a finger to her lips and said, "I adore every cell of your divine body and I appreciate your sharp mind and your loving heart. That's why I'm not worried about our relationship."

Incredulous, she looked at him curiously and huffed, "You're not?"

He shook his head and explained, "My love, I have a theory about us."

"Oh? Really?"

"Yes, really," he answered and then explained, "Love eternal will not be denied. Mark my words. You and I will spend the rest of our lives together. I'm just not certain when you will make the leap from my dreams to my life."

Desiree ran her hands through her hair and tried to make sense of it all. Rendered speechless, she studied the shadows of the tall pine trees that lined the narrow road. Suddenly, her eyes filled with tears she couldn't control.

Ben folded her into his arms and kissed away her sorrow. Before long he felt her relax as her sobs ceased.

"If you're okay, I think we should go on and pick up the key to the house so we can chart a new, unrestricted course," he suggested, a man of confidence and anticipation. After he started the car, he handed her a copy of *Southern Living* and said, "Turn to the travel pages. That's where rental agencies are listed. You look while I drive."

Skimming through the Gulf Shores section, she noted the number of properties available in every price range and of every type and style imaginable. "Which office am I looking for? Ginny

Grace, Meyer's, Fort Morgan Sales and Rentals or Reed Real Estate?"

"The one closest to the Fort," he answered and then added, "That's what the agent I called said." He glanced at Desiree and offered to help her search the listings, but when one of the treacherous S-curves of the darkened road loomed menacingly ahead, he said, "These curves are a bearcat so it's up to you to find the address. I'd better keep my eyes forward."

Suddenly feeling queasy, Desiree closed the magazine and rested her hand on her stomach. She shut her eyes tight as Ben banked the car around a particularly sharp turn. "Ooh, easy there," she said softly.

Concern flashed in Ben's eyes. "The road seems to even out up ahead, but if you want me to pull over, I will. What's your pleasure?"

"No, don't stop; let's go on. I'll be okay."

"Move closer to me," he said, reaching out to her. "That way you can lean into me if we hit another rough spot."

She snuggled next to Ben and relished the moment. Feeling the strength of his body and knowing the wonder of his soul, she rested her head against his shoulder. Within moments, she felt her worries disappear with the light fog that rose in puffs above the Bay.

Pleased to see some color return to Desiree's cheeks, he called out each landmark they passed and promised the next time they came this way, they'd take time to explore the nooks and crannies hidden along the Fort Morgan Road.

"It seems so isolated, so... "

"Primitive?" he asked, raising an eyebrow.

"Oh no, I don't mean that. I think I could love this place, but it does seem as though we left all signs of civilization ten miles back when we turned off of Highway 59."

"It might surprise you to know that plenty of modern conveniences are here. You just have to know where to find them, but I've heard the choices are out there," he said and then explained, "We can gas up back there at Mo's but for a really big boom, Ewing's is the place to go for fireworks. If we need groceries, we're supposed to shop The Pines and Plaza West, and for carryout food, the locals give Penny's Pizza a call."

"What if I want a souvenir to take home?" Desiree asked, enjoying Ben's recital of the information he'd gathered about Fort Morgan.

"That's an easy one. At the Flag Shop, the owners sell windsocks, flags, and more. Walking through that showroom is well worth a visit I've been told."

"What an interesting mix of stores," Desiree said.

Ben nodded and said, "This is what I call living. No fast food restaurants out here. In fact, I don't think there's anything ordinary on this peninsula that's seen a lot of history, as well as some dandy hurricanes."

Desiree admired the scenery as best she could and wished for daylight to come. She wanted to see everything and experience the ambiance of Fort Morgan, a beautiful place she hadn't known existed. "Let's stop here for a minute," she said, unable to resist a spectacular view across Pilot Town. Her eyes mellowed with a sentimental glow as she imagined the personalities of the seafaring men who'd learned their trade at Navy Cove.

"Right here, you say?" Ben asked as he pulled the car to the right and came to a smooth stop. "Is it so you can have your way with me?"

She laughed and tousled his hair. Nibbling on his ear lobe, she whispered, "How about the other way around?"

"You surprise me, Ms. McAndrews. Had I known the salt air would bring out the heavenly hussy in you I would've brought you here lots sooner."

"I'll heavenly hussy you!" she retorted, to which he replied, "Anytime, my darling. Every way and everyday."

Desiree opened the car door and skipped toward the water's edge. Ben soon caught up with her and lifted her high in his arms. Together they enjoyed the serenity of the setting, ideal for lovers of nature and lovers of life. Moving to the flow of the gentle water, they became one spirit united by a sacred bond forged upon hallowed ground.

Ben kissed Desiree's eyelids closed and said, "If this warm-up is any indication of what's to follow, I suggest we find a less public place."

Drowsily, Desiree murmured, "Good plan, but where?"

"This way," he answered and as he gave her his best come hither look, he said, "Let's find our house and wake up the neighbors."

\* \* \* \* \*

Carried aloft in Ben's arms, Desiree counted the steps as they climbed a flight of stairs that led to the entrance of a large white stucco beach home with a red tiled roof. Surrounded by swaying palm trees and pink oleanders that reached for the sky, the house seemed to anchor the entire neighborhood of beautiful houses and quaint beach cottages.

"Happy?" Ben asked.

"Oh yes," she replied as she listened to the call of the Gulf. The mesmerizing sound of the waves crashing to the shore intrigued and excited her.

"Don't worry. We'll play in the surf later, but right now I have another form of exercise in mind." With great flair, he threw open the front door and much like an anxious bridegroom, he carried Desiree across the threshold and into the home designed for playful pleasure.

"It's beautiful!" she said as she jumped from Ben's arms and ran to a set of glass doors that opened to the Gulf.

"Allow me," Ben offered, helping her with the blinds.

"Oh my, this is incredible. A dream come true," she said, her eyes filled with admiration for the furnishings and seaside decor.

Pleased, Ben watched Desiree tour from room to room as she explored the wonders of the house that included skylights, fountains, and fireplaces upstairs and down.

"Total elegance, an architectural beauty. I love this place," she declared from the loft that presented a panoramic view of the beach and the Gulf.

Ben checked out the master suite and rubbed his hands together in anticipation of what might follow. Thinking, *the stage has been set,* he smiled at the brass bed. He turned down its silky coverlet and plumped up the pillows.

"Sleepy?" Desiree asked, peeking around the corner of the bedroom door.

He yawned and crooked his finger for her to come closer.

Laughing, she put her hands on her hips and said, "Not yet, Ben Collier." Then she danced across the hardwood floor and darted outside to the deck. Noticing someone had installed landscape lighting along a boardwalk that led to the beach, she activated the switch and illuminated the dunes.

"Beautiful!" she cried, clapping her hands.

Ben walked toward her and teased, "Shame on you, Ms. McAndrews. I'm surprised that you of all people would commit such a flagrant environmental violation."

"Me?"

"Yep," he answered, turning off the boardwalk lights. "You see, it's nesting time for the sea turtles when they swim to shore and lay their eggs in the sand."

"I know that," she said, resting her hand on the light switch.

"But did you know that artificial lights along the beach draw turtles off their natural course? And that's not a good thing to happen to a sea turtle in a nesting mood."

"Oh," Desiree said, quickly dropping her hand from the switch. "Thank you for telling me. That's an important bit of information I should've known." Then she laughed and added, "You continue to surprise me, Ben. You've become such an environmentalist and almost overnight."

Winking devilishly, he said, "A man's never too old to learn, especially when he has an exciting teacher like you carrying the grade book."

"Whatever are you saying, Ben Collier?"

"That I think I could use a review session," he answered, penetrating her heart with a look that sent heat waves through her. Needing, wanting, and loving him, she knew the moments they shared tonight would have to last a lifetime.

She turned for a last look at the moonlit beach. Touched by the power of the seascape and the depth of Ben's love, she felt her eyes pool with tears.

"Don't cry, Desiree, not now," he said, turning his face from her so she would not see his own sadness. The thought of losing her tore at his soul, but he realized he would soon have to let her go.

He wrapped his arms around her waist and drew her closer. "I have lots planned for us before I put you on the plane to Denver, so maybe we should rest before your flight. Tell me, though, what do you think about life on the Gulf Coast? I'm curious to know your observations."

She snuggled into the curve of Ben's arm and gathered her thoughts before answering. "I like the freedom of Fort Morgan."

"Better than St. George Island?"

"I wouldn't necessarily say one place is better than the other," she answered. "It's just that these property owners seem to be such individualists. This is definitely not a cookie cutter development." When she caught Ben's pained frown, she hastily added, "Not that your Plantation at St. George Island is."

"Is that so? Tell me more." He nuzzled her neck and breathed in her womanly scent.

"Look at the placement of these houses," she continued as Ben delivered kisses, both tender and divine. "People here must truly respect each other's love for the beach. No views are blocked so everyone can enjoy sunrises and sunsets and all the hours in between. How special it must be to have such thoughtful neighbors all around."

Ben admired Desiree's intuitive understanding. To him, she was perfection at all levels. A woman of character, she also was a woman of desire. Touching her intimately, he relished the intensity of her response to him.

"Ready to go inside?" he asked. "Nap time, maybe?"

She looked toward a screened room on the other side of the deck and shook her head. "Anybody can sleep in a house, but how often does one have a chance to spend the night on a sleeping porch with its own private beach?"

"You are a South Alabama sea sprite," he said. "Mine and mine alone," he added as he carried her to a hammock and snuggled beside her.

"And what do sea sprites do?" she asked, her pupils dilated with a blinding mixture of love and lust.

"A little of this and a lot of that," he answered as he demonstrated balance and timing with unparalleled success.

Renewed love blossomed and bloomed as Ben and Desiree fired the night with passion so meteoric that some neighbors reported seeing star showers all the way from Surfside Shores to the lighthouse at the Fort.

* * * * *

Waking at daybreak, Desiree blinked her eyes at the brightness of the sun's first rays. Beside her Ben slept, his arms still wrapped around her. She kissed him awake and thanked him for giving her the most wonderful night of her life. "I love you, Ben," she whispered.

"I'll always love you," he replied, sadness once again darkening his features.

She rested her hand on his heart and said, "Please save a space for me inside there."

"That's where you've always been."

Feeling her heart break, she held his hand to her lips and said, "Let's say our good-byes here and not at the airport. It's better that way."

Reluctantly, he let Desiree go as she reached for her clothes and handed him his. "You're sure about this?" he asked.

She studied the sky and allowed her tears to flow unchecked. "You've given me more than you'll ever know," she whispered. Dressing slowly, she smiled at Ben, the love of her life.

Ben searched the depths of Desiree's eyes and when she looked away, he cursed under his breath and jerked on his pants.

Not looking back, Desiree returned to the house and walked into the kitchen, a miracle of modern design and technology. She flipped through a cookbook and decided she'd whip up a quick breakfast of eggs and croissants. But when she opened the breadbox and the refrigerator, she called out to Ben, "Uh oh, this is a sad sight I think you should see. Come on in and take a look. We forgot to stop for food."

"An empty galley's no problem," he replied as he straddled a kitchen stool. Reaching for a stack of restaurant reviews stacked neatly on a counter, he pointed to a clipping from the *Mobile Register's Bay Weekend* supplement and said, "This paper's 'Well-Fed Reporter' claims the Morgan Pass Restaurant down the road is the place to go for breakfast. Read what he says here about the ladies known for their coffee and grits."

"How much time do we have?" Desiree asked.

Ben checked his watch and said lustily, "If we share a shower, we can probably have breakfast and catch the first ferry to

Dauphin Island." Winking, he added, "I want you to tell all your friends back in Boulder that I courted you by air, land, and sea but all to no avail. You heartbreaker, you." He ran his fingers through her hair and gave her a kiss she wouldn't soon forget.

With reluctance she pulled away from his embrace and saying she'd sponge bathe at the airport, she ran to the car. She knew if she spent another moment with Ben in that seductive house that reeked of romance, there'd be no way she could let her conscience be her guide in matters concerning her and Ben.

He followed behind, his steps slow and his heart heavy. Given no other choice, he secured the house and helped Desiree with her briefcase and flight bag. In silence, they began the journey neither one wanted to make.

\* \* \* \* \*

The ferry ride across the Bay offered plenty of diversions for Ben and Desiree as they divided their time between sightseeing and visiting with other passengers. As they departed from the Fort Morgan landing, they listened to a crewman tell the story of the Battle of Mobile Bay and the sinking of the *Tecumseh*, a Yankee ironclad.

The ferry's path across the shipping channel thrilled Desiree as she watched cargo ships from foreign lands enter the Bay for a stop in the Port City of Mobile. Wanting a better look, she convinced Ben they should climb the narrow steps to the observation deck beside the pilot's station. She raced ahead but in the process, she lost her footing on one of the slippery rungs and tumbled back toward Ben.

"Nice catch, sir," said a man wearing a Michigan tee-shirt.

"I bet you don't practice catch and release with that little keeper," added another man, who tipped his General Motors cap as he winked at Desiree.

Blushing, Desiree slipped out of Ben's arms and headed portside where she caught her first glimpse of Fort Gaines and picturesque Dauphin Island. "I really love it here," she said, reaching for Ben's hand.

He put his arm around her shoulder and said, "We can turn back now and retrace our steps. That's an option, you know."

She lowered her eyelashes and replied, "We've got to go on. My flight won't wait and you promised Linnea you'd meet her at the airport. I'm sure she's waiting for you now. How long is the drive to Mobile from here?"

"About forty-five minutes or so," he answered as he led her back to the car and started its engine. Driving off the ferry ramp, he enjoyed Desiree's spontaneous dissertation about the horrific presence of the gas rigs she swore trashed the beauty of the Gulf and the Bay.

His eyes twinkled with pride as he said, "The gas and oil companies had better watch their step if a lady from Nature's Way decides to get on their case. Maybe I should warn them eminent danger in the form of Desiree McAndrews and Company is headed their way."

Desiree smiled. She loved him so.

\* \* \* \* \*

"It's about time he showed up," Susanna whined. She watched Ben and Desiree enter the main terminal of Bates Field and frowned. "Well now, isn't that sweet?" she said with a sneer as she leaned forward for a better view of Ben kissing Desiree. "I'll be so glad when that troublemakin' woman leaves town. Maybe then my life can get back to normal."

"Is that what you really want, lady bug? Or do you wanna climb to the top of the money tree with a man who knows the ways and has the means?" Taylor puffed on a fat cigar and blew smoke rings that floated high above Susanna's head.

Big Jack reeled back on his heels and crowed, "Looks like a match made in heaven is about to add millions to the Delaney portfolio. Bless your soul, Taylor Hamilton. Welcome to the family."

Etienne sized up the situation and wailed, "Poor Linnea. Once happy but now so sad."

Tears filled Linnea's eyes as she watched her world tumble like a house of cards. "Good-bye, Dad. Good-bye, Momma. Welcome to hell, Linnea," she muttered under her breath.

Unaware of the moods of the welcoming party that awaited their arrival at the gate area, Ben and Desiree road the escalator to the top floor and faced the music head-on. Desiree immediately recognized the look of distress etched in capital letters across Linnea's sad face.

Excusing herself from Ben, she motioned for Linnea to follow her. Inside the powder room, she leaned against a cold formica counter and said, "Before I leave, I want you to have something special. This is for you." She removed Ben's Academy ring from her finger and dropped it into Linnea's hand. Kissing her on the cheek, she said, "Take care of your dad. He's a wonderful man who loves you more than words can tell."

"But what about you?" Linnea asked, her eyes heavy with genuine concern.

"Say a prayer for me every now and then and know I'm keeping you and your dad in mine."

Before Linnea could respond, Ben tapped lightly on the door and said, "They just called your flight, Desiree."

She hugged Linnea one last time and then opened the door. Nodding politely to Susanna, Taylor, Etienne, and the Senator, she kissed Ben and stroked his hair. Then turning and not daring to look back, she slowly made her way down the corridor and up the steps to the Delta jet that would carry her home. As she took her seat by a window, a voice in her heart demanded she look outside.

There on the tarmac stood Ben, heartbroken but not alone. In one hand, he held Linnea's. With his free hand, he patted his heart and pointed to Desiree.

"I love you, Ben. I love you," Desiree whispered as she bowed her head and wept.

# *Epilogue*

Six Years Later. Boulder, Colorado

Blond curls flying and deep blue eyes sparkling, six-year-old Cannon McAndrews chased ahead of his mother. "This way, hurry up!" he called over his shoulder. Shifting the weight of his miniature North Face backpack, he raced to a cairn that marked the steep trail toward Blue Lake in the Indian Peaks Wilderness Area a few miles west of Boulder.

Desiree increased the length of her stride and quickly passed Cannon, who promptly bolted past her, laughing all the way.

In his small fist he held a bouquet of mountain primrose and marsh marigolds, precious wildflowers Desiree had warned him to leave alone for the enjoyment of others who hiked the trail from Mitchell Lake to Blue.

"One more cairn, Cannon," Desiree called. "Blue Lake is just ahead of the last pile of rocks at the top of the ridge. Be careful, hero. Take your time. We have a few hours before the storm clouds roll in."

Cannon ignored Desiree's caution and forged ahead, a model of determination and daring.

"Like father, like son," Desiree said as a smile twinkled in her eyes.

Cannon claimed a flat rock on the edge of the lake as his own. Kicking off his Timberline hiking boots and scratchy wool socks, he stretched out on the ledge, wiggled his toes, and declared, "Ah, that's better." He used his backpack as a pillow and struck a resting pose. When Desiree approached from the left, he squeezed his eyes shut and said, "Guess what I am, Mommy."

"A sleeping toad?" she asked.

"No way," he huffed. "I'm a marmot. You oughtta know that."

"A monkey is more like it," Desiree teased as she sat beside Cannon and accepted the flowers he'd pilfered from the trail.

"Monkey's hungry. Feed me now," Cannon replied, rubbing his tummy and rolling his eyes.

Desiree leaned over and kissed the top of Cannon's head. With a smile in her voice, she unzipped her daypack and said, "I think you would eat twenty times a day if I let you."

"Then I'd grow as big as a bear," Cannon replied, holding out his hand for the blueberry and raisin power cookie he'd stashed in his mother's pack earlier that morning.

Desiree watched the sun glisten through Cannon's hair. When she saw a devilish look brighten his eyes, she thought of his father and a pang of guilt raced through her. Thinking maybe she should have told him and then deciding it was probably better for everyone that she hadn't, she concentrated on the food she and Cannon were about to share.

Together they enjoyed their snack of granola bars, trail mix, and crystal clear water from Eldorado Springs. Then Desiree delighted in Cannon's perseverance as he demonstrated his finest fly fishing techniques as he cast his line time and time again in pursuit of an elusive cutthroat trout that swam below in the icy water.

"Look way up there," Cannon said, spotting two jets that trailed ribbons of white smoke as they soared in tight formation high above Mount Toll.

"I bet they're Air Force Thunderbirds practicing a pass and roll," Desiree observed. Her mind flashed a picture of Ben, handsome and masterful in the cockpit. Sighing, she closed her eyes and listened to the powerful force of the engines that shook the mountains.

Cannon tugged on the sleeve of Desiree's parka and said, "I bet they're not Thunderbirds. Those are Blue Angels from the US Navy up there in that plane."

Startled by Cannon's words and wondering if he had read her mind, Desiree asked, "What makes you so sure of that?"

Cannon put his hands on his hips and answered, "They just are 'cause they know that's what I'm gonna be when I get out of school. So they're showing me their tricks I'm gonna learn how to do." He smiled a lopsided grin that brought tears to Desiree's eyes.

"If you fly for the Navy, you'll have to train at NAS Pensacola and that means I'll be very lonely here all by myself with you far away from home," she said sadly.

Cannon took off the green Frogman bandanna he wore around his neck cowboy-style and used it to wipe away Desiree's tears. Patting her hand, he said, "Don't worry, Mommy. You can come with me. I think we might like the beaches they have in Florida."

"Alabama has a pretty one, too," Desiree said, remembering the romantic night she'd spent with Ben on the Gulf Coast.

"Well, lookie there," Cannon sang as a fish struck at his Adams fly. "I'm gonna catch that fish and fry him up in a pan," he shouted with glee.

"Oh no you're not, buster," Desiree replied. "Catch and release. That's the name of the game."

Laughing, Desiree and Cannon fished and talked, but oh, how their conversation would have changed had they known the Boulder Airporter had just made a special delivery to their door on Regis Drive.

\* \* \* \* \*

"Is this the place, Dad? Are you sure?" Linnea asked as she rang the bell.

Ben looked at the mailbox hanging precariously on the brick wall and said, "Only Desiree would have a holder made of twigs and leaves to catch her mail. This is her house. It hasn't changed a bit in the past eighteen years, same flower boxes, same cracked steps. This is where she lives. I can feel her near."

He smiled as he peered through a window beside the front door and saw the slate floor they'd skidded across on a snowy day when they'd been in such a hurry to build a fire that they'd neglected to remove the ice from their boots before racing inside to their love den.

"Evidently Desiree's not alone," Linnea commented, fluffing her long dark hair that cascaded around her shoulders like a cape. "Check out the Batman bike somebody crashed into the bushes over there."

A light of realization dawned in Ben's deep blue eyes as he made a quick calculation. Now he understood what Desiree had meant about the gift she said he'd given her. "A child, a child!" he yelled so loudly that Linnea checked the street for annoyed neighbors.

Hushing him, she said, "I think Boulder has a noise ordinance, Dad." Then she studied his face and asked, "Don't you think it's possible Desiree married someone else?"

Ben shook his head and replied, "Not a chance. The boy's mine. I mean he's ours, mine and Desiree's. Oh dear God, please let it be true." He put his arm around Linnea and kissed the top of her head.

"I hope you're right," she said and then added, "I've gotten pretty sick and tired of listening to you moan and groan about losing the love of your life."

"That bad, huh?" he asked. "Have I been that obvious?"

"At times you've been a royal pain you know where," Linnea answered. "But still though, you've been a great dad all along, patient and understanding when other dads might not have been."

Ben looked at Linnea quizzically and waited for an explanation.

"When I changed my name from Linnea Delaney-Collier to Linnea de Ville, you understood. Thanks, Dad," she said as she stood on her tiptoes and gave him a daughterly kiss.

Suddenly, the sound of a Volvo sputtering up the street caused Ben's heart to perform a Cuban eight. "It's Desiree's old car. I don't believe she's kept it running all these years."

As the car approached the driveway, he narrowed his focus and caught a glimpse of Desiree, as beautiful as ever and sitting proud behind the steering wheel. In the back seat, though, a boy playing with a fishing net and a creel commanded Ben's attention.

Desiree carefully pulled up her steep driveway. Stopping inches from Ben who'd stepped in front of her car, she screamed, "Ben, Ben! Dear God, please tell me it's true."

Ben tore open her door and lifted her from the car. Tears streamed down their cheeks as they held each other as though they'd never let go.

"I love you, Desiree. I love you so much," Ben shouted for all of Table Mesa to hear.

More quietly, Desiree said, "And I love you, Ben. I always have and I always will."

Cannon climbed over the driver's seat and wailed, "Hey there, everybody. How about me?" He pouted for a moment as he eyed Ben curiously before asking, "Who are you, Mr. Man, and why are you kissing my mommy?"

Linnea helped Cannon from the car and knelt beside him on the driveway. "Come here, little guy," she said, "I have something special for you." She dropped Ben's Naval Academy ring into Cannon's tiny hand and said, "This belongs to you. Your dad would like you to have it, I'm sure." When Cannon looked confused, she explained, "That man standing over there with your mom is your dad and his name is Bennett Collier."

Cannon peered over Linnea's shoulder and squinted his eyes at Ben. Grinning, he said, "He doesn't look like a son of a bitch to me."

Mortified, Desiree pulled away from Ben and shouted, "Cannon! Where did you learn such words?"

"From everybody at Nature's Way," he answered innocently and then pointing an accusatory finger at Ben, he said, "You oughtta do the right thing and marry us. That's what people always say whenever Mommy mentions your name."

Ben roared with laughter and said, "Son, that's exactly what I've been trying to do for years. But tell me, what's your full name?"

Reeling back on his heels, he stood tall and saluted Ben as he answered, "I'm Cannon McAndrews, sir, but you may call me Batman." Not waiting for a response, he ran to the bushes, jumped on his bike, and careened wildly down the driveway.

"A need for speed. My boy's got it," Ben said as he gathered Desiree in his arms. Kissing her passionately, he whispered, "This time I'm not letting you go."

To which Desiree replied, "We'll see, Ben. We'll see."

Linnea laughed and said, "Forget it, Desiree. Dad's already called the Boulderado and reserved the mezzanine for the wedding of the year. That's why we're here. He said he didn't care what he had to do; you and he are getting married. No if's, and's, or but's about it. By the way, I have some other great news. When I told Etienne about the wedding, he said he'll fly in from Paris for the ceremony and will bring cases of the finest wines from his vineyards. Maybe we should go ahead and make it a family affair and have a double wedding. What do you think, Dad?"

Ben groaned and rolled his eyes as Desiree hugged Linnea and said, "I don't think your dad's quite ready for that, but I have a suggestion. Why don't you come live with us? We'll turn this old house of mine into a happy home for us all. How about it?"

Linnea beamed her acceptance and said, "Welcome to heaven, Linnea."

Ben felt his heart swell with pride for Desiree. Always putting the needs of others before her own, she was a woman like no other he'd ever known. Turning to her, he held her hands in his and vowed, "I promise you my love and my life, forever."

They kissed deeply and might have remained locked for days in their state of rapturous love and committed passion, but Cannon broke the spell. Charging forward, he tugged on Ben's arm.

"What is it, tiger?" Ben asked as he stooped low to hold his boy for the first time.

"Will you teach me how to fly?" Cannon asked, making a buzzing airplane sound that brought a smile to Ben's face.

Ben cradled his son in his arms and replied, "Up where we belong, Cannon Collier. That's where I'm taking you and your mom, forever."

# *Addendum*

### Who's Where Now

**Desiree McAndrews-Collier.** Homemaker, consultant for Nature's Way, Sierra Club activist, den mother for Cub Scout Pack 007, Boulder, Colorado.

**Bennett Collier.** President and CEO of Angel Flight Gulfstream Air Service, volunteer pilot for Medevac United Express, and an environmental partner with the Night Hawk Corporation, Boulder, Colorado.

**Cannon Collier.** Little League pitcher, Cub Scout, and the reigning terror of Bear Creek Elementary, Boulder, Colorado.

**Linnea de Ville.** Freshman at CU-Boulder, aerospace engineering major with a minor in French, selected for a NASA internship at Huntsville, Alabama. Destined to become an astronaut.

**Taylor and Susanna Hamilton.** Residents of Fairhope, Alabama, where Susanna offers elocution lessons to the debutantes of the Eastern Shore of Mobile Bay and Taylor paves the beaches of South Alabama with asphalt, condos, and souvenir shops.

**Big Jack Delaney.** Condo king of Orange Beach, Alabama, and a permanent fixture at Papa Rocco's and the Happy Hookers Lounge, Fort Morgan, Alabama.

**Etienne.** Manager of his family's vineyards in Bordeaux, France.

**Trey LaBlanc.** Exporter of papermill products for his wife's company and importer of fine tobaccos and cognac. Also owner of Club Cigar, best known for its exotic dancers from Havana.

**Celeste Kulhaney.** Manager of Nature's Way, Florida, by day and hostess at Rusty's every other night.

**Jeff and Beverly.** Resigned their jobs at Nature's Way in order to explore an alternative lifestyle in Ward, Colorado. Last postcard sent from the Inca Trail.

**Deb and Elinor.** Left the Nature's Way office in Florida in order to accept a special assignment in Cancun involving tequila sunrises and Power Point instruction.

**Tip Carlisle**. Fishing guide in the Florida Keys and *Navy Times* contributing writer.

And lastly, **Heron Bay** at Perdido Key, Florida. Deeded by **Ben Collier** to Nature's Way and Forever Wild in honor of his beloved wife, **Desiree McAndrews-Collier**, a woman of character and conviction, who dedicated her life to making the world a better place.